The Making of
Incarnation

ALSO BY TOM McCARTHY

Remainder
Men in Space
C
Satin Island

The Making of Incarnation

Tom McCarthy

JONATHAN CAPE
LONDON

1 3 5 7 9 10 8 6 4 2

Jonathan Cape, an imprint of Vintage,
20 Vauxhall Bridge Road,
London SW1V 2SA

Jonathan Cape is part of the Penguin Random House group of companies
whose addresses can be found at global.penguinrandomhouse.com.

Penguin
Random House
UK

First published by Jonathan Cape in 2021

penguin.co.uk/vintage

A CIP catalogue record for this book is available from the British Library

ISBN 9781787333291 (Hardback)
ISBN 9781787333307 (Trade paperback)

The quotation on p108 is from the song 'Gary, Indiana',
with lyrics by Meredith Willson

Typeset in 12/15.25 pt Dante MT
by Integra Software Services Pvt. Ltd, Pondicherry

Printed and bound in Great Britain by Clays Ltd, Elcograf S.p.A.

The authorised representative in the EEA is Penguin Random House Ireland,
Morrison Chambers, 32 Nassau Street, Dublin D02 YH68

Penguin Random House is committed to a sustainable future for
our business, our readers and our planet. This book is made from
Forest Stewardship Council® certified paper.

For Isadora and Alexis Lemon McCarthy

Incarnation is our grace. It alone creates colour, touch, distance, and music, the lithe resilience of the flesh and the desire that will not halt ...

Denis de Rougemont

Contents

Book Three

Prolegomenon

On the Dynamic Properties of Waves in Periodic Systems

From the S-Bahn, through shuttling latticework of tree branch and bridge truss, you glimpse it just below Tiergarten as you travel east-to-west, or west-to-east: a five-storey blue hulk. The building levitates unnaturally above the ground, jacked up on two giant, tubular pink ducts that protrude and curl downward from its sides then join together at its base, as though it were a crab reared up in fear, or anger, or some kind of mating ritual. What is it? It's the *Versuchsanstalt für Wasserbau und Schiffbau*, Research Institute for Hydraulic Engineering and Shipbuilding, outpost that Technische Universität Berlin has maintained, through a royal lease that's somehow weathered wars, land-value hikes and all the rest, on this small, elongated island around which the Landwehr Canal bifurcates into sluiced sections before merging back into a single flow out of whose grain all knots, spirals and other traces of past interruption or obstruction have been smoothed.

Or, scanned at a res higher than most S-Bahn riders have at their disposal: it's a complex of buildings, slotted into one another. The eye-catching, crustacean one's the *Umlauf- und Kavitationstank UT2*, its looping claw a conduit capable of pumping 3,300 tonnes of water round and round at nine metres per second – perfect for wake field and cavitation research, forced motion and propulsion tests and like manner of fluid-dynamic enquiry. There, amidst the roar of a two-megawatt ship diesel engine and vibrations of the vast pump's switch blades that shake wall and floor's sheet panels, dramas of rarefaction and compression, cyclic stress and supercavitation play themselves out on demand, putting model hulls, rudders and propellers through their paces, coaxing from these inception numbers and erosion-progress rates. Below this towering monster, strewn about its feet like strips of food or half-spawned offspring, lie a series of long, flat hangars. It's in one of these, the one housing the *Seegangsbecken*, the Seakeeping Basin or wave generator – intermittently replenished, like the UT2, by the same liquid mass diverted from and, eventually, released back into the Landwehr and thence onwards to the Spree – that today's action is taking place.

Here, Neptune's wrath is about to be unleashed on a platform supply vessel, an anchor handling tug and two oil rigs. Resident technician Arda Gökçek, Dipl.-Ing., VWS's Keeper of the Sea, stands at the basin's absorption end, moving his thumb and fingers round a MacBook's glide-pad, scaling metrics, modifying ratios, adjusting up or down wave height and stroke length, characteristic and gravitational velocities. When the profile on his screen, the rhythm of its curves and intervals, aligns with that of today's target values, Gökçek's hand breaks contact with the laptop, hovers an inch or two above its keyboard while his eyes cross-check the graphic contours one last time, then falls decisively back down on the space bar. More than a hundred metres away, at the basin's far end, the wave-generation mechanism groans; drive arms, pulleys and linkage arms, drive pegs, flange bearings and connecting rods stir, clasp and thrust, shunting a slanted flap repeatedly against the water's bulk. And then it comes, down the long, narrow stretch, peak doubling the ceiling's intermittent strip lights one after the other, raising each inverted, spectral light-line up towards its source before the trough swallows the reflection once more in its darkened vortex: the first wave. It's followed by another, and another, and another, soaking the green tiles along the basin's sides, redrawing the same high-water mark over and over with complete precision.

Do the boats and platforms sense them coming? Of course not; all propagation vectors of the medium they sit in have been plotted here, phase boundaries and resonant frequencies rendered transparent; there's no wiggle room for ambiguity, and even less for fantasy – yet Gökçek still, each time he watches replica cities, dams or cruise ships, harbour walls or wind farms in the propagation section in the last, contracting moments just before the first wave hits, fancies that he senses, in the models' very composition, the clinging together of their atoms, an increased level of concentrated stasis; a *tensing* almost, as though they were bracing themselves; as though, somehow, they *knew* . . .

Now the waves are among them, tossing and convulsing them, sending them veering – laterally and vertically, longitudinally, trans-versally and every which way in-between – down paths that seem quite random but in fact are not at all, that's the whole point: cameras at the basin's sides are tracking and translating every heave and surge and sway, identifying, within the furious tangle of the lines, some kind of pattern to be viewed both retro- and prospectively, its fuzz transmuted into clean parameters that, once modelled, can be not only scaled back up for the benefit of future offshore installation planners but also, traversing their own vec-tors of circulation and displacement, transferred and extrapolated and fed into who-knows-what. Over the next sixteen months, today's worked-through data will be brought to bear on fields as variant as infrasonics and seismocardiography, the study of germ convection around airline cabins and the spread of rumour over social networks. Things are connected to other things, which are connected to other things. Yesterday, one hundred and three Asian miners died in a methane explosion; a small South American state underwent a coup; a large pod of whales beached itself off Western Europe's coastline. The pages of Gökçek's newspaper, lying open on a stool beside a half-drunk coffee cup, rustle as he climbs a nearby stepladder, borne upwards in his slipstream. From on high, the technician watches the boats lurching and bobbing drunkenly amidst the swells and currents, hurtling past the bat-tered reefs of the oil platforms' legs and anchors. The elevation calms him; he's above the struggle, uninvolved. Visions of the Bosporus drift across his mind's back reaches, morphing through various formations – less a place glimpsed from car windows and mosque terraces on holidays, extended family visits, than a vague ancestral memory, an idea …

The wave-generation mechanism groans; the flap shunts on to the same rhythm. The pillow-block journal bearings holding the driveshaft in place need lubricating: Gökçek can tell that from the note of irritation in its tone. On the smooth stretches of the basin's water, before the models break its surface, there's an outer coat of oil and dirt, a no man's land littered by corpses of the insects lured there by the mirrored swathes of airspace and bright rafters, the false promise of companionship. The anchor-handling tug, its prow of hardened paraffin, has got itself wedged in one of the oil rigs' leg struts. Computer modelling won't show you everything. Sometimes you have to actually *do* it, make a little world, get down amidst dumb objects and their messiness. From the basin's exterior, where it rests on J-hooks beside coils of hosing, wiring, torn canvas and string, Gökçek lifts a pike pole and leans in over the edge, trying to prise the vessel free. His right foot, raised behind him for stability, nudges the stool; coffee slops out, blotting the news pages. On a worktable beside the stool are an isopropanol spray can, a CD-ROM, a roll of toilet paper, an ice-lolly stick, a crumpled plastic glove of the type used for washing up, weights, floats, a fire extinguisher, an off-cut block of wood, a fold-out ruler, a hand-held torch, a tote bag, an external hard drive, a red marker pen, a plastic cup with small screws in it, a blue case of cross-point screwdrivers, a grease tin and a scrunched-up piece of tissue paper stained with a red substance. Further back, against the wall, models superfluous to today's scenario are stacked: a submarine, an ICE train, fifteen wind turbines, a life-sized emperor penguin and the city of Mumbai. In front of them stands a new prop, delivered to the Institute an hour ago from London in an outsize box, the unpacking of which has strewn about the floor styrofoam plugs and wedges that, being moulded to fit tightly round the model while it was in transit, now inversely (and disjointedly) repeat the outline of their precious cargo, also styrofoam: a spaceship with distributed, partitioned fuselage- and wing-configuration and a kind of half-detached, golf-ball-like annexe teed up just above its highest section. Gökçek's pike pole, finding its sweet spot on the tug's hull, prods it loose. The tug capsizes momentarily, spins on its side through a full clockwise circle and a third of an anticlockwise one, then, righting itself, glides round the leg struts to find open water. The flap shunts; the wave-generation mechanism groans. Gökçek returns the pike pole to its J-hooks and moves off in search of engine oil.

Alone among the props, the emperor penguin is not only replicated at a scale of one-to-one, but also (since the effect of turbidity on shallow-substratum colour was a subject of enquiry in the session in which it recently starred) painted black, yellow and white in the appropriate places. It's been cast in 'porpoising' mode: wings folded into torso, head held up in alignment with the body's central axis, feet wedged together and pointed down vertically to form a rudder. The meticulous streamlining has been undone, though, by its positioning: to stop its out-of-water bulk rolling across the floor, its neck has been rested across the roof of a train carriage, which (since the carriage has been cast at 1:22.5) not only makes the bird seem monstrous, gargantuan, but also angles it unnaturally, un-aerodynamically upward. Made to focus on the building's ceiling, its painted eyes seek out the skylight. Beyond this, the outside air is brisk, flushed by light breeze. Higher, much further up, two intersecting vapour trails have carved a cross against the blue – a vote cast on a ballot slip, the signature of an illiterate, an X marking the spot: *Here*.

Book One

1. Markie's Crime (Replay)

In the third of four school buses edging their way up Camberwell New Road sits Markie Phocan. The buses process in formation, a cortège. Taxis, vans, double-deckers, dustbin lorries and the odd rag-and-bone cart alternately hem them in and, turning, parking or reversing, create pockets for them to slip, if not through, at least into, claiming a few yards before they run up against hard fabric of immobile bumpers and exhaust pipes. Winter sunlight falls across the scene; if they'd been new, or clean, it would have made the buses glint, but since they're neither, it just coats them in a dust and diesel aura. Across the side of one someone has finger-scrawled the word *Fuck*; beneath this, somebody (the same person perhaps) has written *Thatcher*; but this name has since been scored through, substituted by *GLC Commies* – which, in turn, has been struck out and replaced with *You*.

Markie's sitting in the fourth row, by the window (driver side). Next to him, Nainesh Patel is thumbing through a set of football cards, picking out swaps. On the aisle's far side Polly Gould's tipping her head back, tapping space dust onto an extended tongue. Trevor Scotter leans in from behind her and, sliding his hand horizontally across the plumb-line between packet and mouth, interrupts the flow for long enough to grab some of the powder in his upturned palm. Polly spins round, but by the time she's facing him her outrage has already lost momentum. What's she going to do? They're not allowed sweets. Trevor throws his palm up to his own mouth, gloating at her. Then, swinging his eyes sideways, he brings both his and Polly's gaze to rest on Vicky Staple's head, above whose curly hair he rubs his hands, releasing a fine sugar and E-number fallout. He and Polly laugh.

'She got pink dandruff ...'

Vicky, staring at the seat in front of her from behind thick NHS glasses, says nothing. Paper planes and spitwads soar through the loud air. In the door-side front seat Miss Sedge sits impassive, shoulders sagging. No one's getting injured. They're crawling round the Oval now. Markie can see, over the wall, the scoreboard and the top rows of the upper stands; then, further round the ground's perimeter, rising above it, the gas holders. The tallest one is about two thirds full today, its green dome's convex meniscus giving over to a skeleton of interlocking diamonds. Vauxhall Gardens' hot-air balloon floats, tethered, to the gas holders' north, ropes on its underside converging on a flimsy-looking basket. Lowering his back and craning his head as the bus traces Harleyford Street's curve, Markie tracks the balloon across the windscreen until it slides from view beyond the upper border. The aluminium of the vehicle's carapace behind which it disappears is thin and translucent; the sun, head-on to them now, shines through it to illuminate the letters SCHOOL BUS stamped across it, broadcasting them to passengers in reversed form: *SUB LOOHCS*. Below this the same letters, smaller and similarly reversed, though this time through reflection of the front shell of the bus hugging their tail, run across the driver's rear-view mirror: *SUB LOOHCS*. To Markie, these are real words, drawn from a hybrid language whose vocabulary and grammar he can just about intuit; doubled, they present a header and subtitle, repeating a single cryptic instruction: *sub loohcs – look below ...*

Now the last two buses have got stranded in the middle of the Vauxhall Cross box junction, blue-and-white insects caught in a yellow web, old chassis shuddering while cars honk and weave around them. The driver of Markie's, unconcerned, leans on his outsize wheel and picks his teeth, ignoring other motorists' shouts and V-signs. As Nainesh murmurs 'Heighway ... Shilton ... Coppell ...', the lights release them. Markie wonders if the two events, the intoning of footballers' names and the release of buses, are connected; whether Nainesh has just *caused* the captive spell to break. To a last, long horn-blast, whose tone falls off as they pull away, they speed on to Vauxhall Bridge. Beside it, on the south side, a giant lot sits cleared, sticks and surveyors' string dotted and threaded flimsily about it. Nainesh looks up from his spread and, pointing at the empty space, announces: 'Going to be a secret headquarters for spies.'

'How do you know?' asks Trevor.

'My dad told me.'

'If it's secret, then how does he know?'

'He knows,' mutters Nainesh, burying himself back in the cards.

Polly tilts her head back and taps out another load. In the seat in front of her Bea Folco, headband knotted at right temple, stares out of her window. There's no rear-view mirror, nor any other reflective surface, showing Bea to him and vice versa, but Markie senses nonetheless a symmetry – both of them turned or folded outwards from the bridge's cambered spine, he facing east, she west – somehow connecting them. On his side, on the water, tugs from Lambeth River Fire Station are testing their canons. The water jets start at their bases bold and firm, then jag towards their apex, morph into a set of liquid hooks from which hangs a mist-curtain inlaid with small rainbows. Is this salute for them? For Lyndhurst Primary's four-bus procession? Markie, even at ten, understands that it's not, that the world goes on doing what it does when he's tucked away in classrooms; that this snatched peek at its weekday workings is a special and uncommon thing – almost illicit, as though he were spying on it: embedded in forbidden territory, reconnoitring the buildings and the traffic, the embankments and dilapidated barges, towers and cranes and church spires, Parliament downriver, though the haze; dispatching back (to whom?) some ultra-classified report, compiled in mirror-alphabet, or just in thoughts ...

Polly, without warning, throws up. She pukes first on to the floor between her legs, then, turning in disgust from what she's brought up, out into the aisle. It triggers screams and raucous laughter, sudden drawing up of legs to chests, a simultaneous evacuation of all bodies from the event's epicentre and, pushing back against this from the seats on its periphery, a wave of curious encroachment. Miss Sedge has stridden over – a little too briskly, almost landing knee-length leather boots in vomit that is pink and lurid and still, as per the manufacturer's design, cracking and popping as the upthrown enzymatic juices release from melting flakes the pressurised carbon dioxide trapped inside them.

'She was eating Pop Rocks, Miss,' says Vicky.

Miss Sedge plants her feet on the vomit-lake's shores, leans over and winches Polly from her seat. As she's led to the front, the girl turns back and shouts at her informer:

'Four-eyed cunt!'

For the rest of the ride, the lake shape-changes with the bus's movement, spawning pools and channels, oxbows, forks and branches. Trevor, playing the joker, hooks his arm between two seat-backs and hangs right above it; when the bus, clearing the bridge, turns sharp right into Millbank, he loses his balance and starts to slip – or is this still part of the act? No one gets to find out: Miss Sedge strides over again and plucks him away too, slaps his face one-two with both sides of her free hand, then bundles him into the front row beside her and Polly. As he turns round to take a curtain call, leering back glow-cheeked at his classmates, his smirking eye catches Markie's; Markie looks away. The vomit's smell's coming on strong now; children start lifting scarves and collars to their noses. Markie wedges his gloves, conjoined by outward rolling of the cuffs into a ball, between his face and the window, seeking in their softness and sweet counter-smell a passkey to release him from this cabin, magic him outside to merge with cleansing spray, with light's extracted spectrum ...

They've arrived now. Into the parking bay the buses pull, two on each side of the *Mr Whippy* van that's blocking out the central stretch. In Markie's there's a rush towards the door, which remains closed while Miss Sedge shouts instructions for outside assembly. When it finally accordions back, children tumble on to the pavement and suck air into their lungs like surfacing free divers. High above them, from atop the Tate's stone portico, armed with flag and trident and flanked by her lion and unicorn, Britannia stares down like a disapproving headmistress. Orders go ignored as busloads mingle, bringing one another up to date: Cudjo Sani, on the lead bus, threw up too; on the second one a fight's left Jason Banner with a bleeding scratch across his cheek … Some children slink away into the garden; others hop up and down the building's steps. It's on these steps that teachers re-corral them into class-groups: four inclining columns that are led up past the Tate's vertical ones – only to crumble, bottlenecked by the revolving door. Beyond this, the marble atrium's an echo chamber, multiplying cries and whistles to unbearable cacophony; all four class teachers shout in an attempt to bring the noise under control, which only makes it louder. One of the Tate's guards, whose burly figure and demeanour mark him as an ex-serviceman, steps in, unleashing a deep bass that quietens the children less from obedience than from curiosity: his voice seems to rise from the whorled depths of the staircase down which the floor's two-tone mosaic disappears. Their attention won, he orders them to leave their coats in the cloakroom's group area, then oversees this order's execution, mess-inspection memories flickering across his eyes as arms wriggle out of anorak- and duffel-sleeves.

Markie hangs his coat up on a hook, but keeps the gloves. Holding them up to his face again, watching Bea drop her parka to the floor and step out of it (the zip's stuck), he starts experiencing a sense of overlay – the same effect as when Miss Sedge, back in the classroom, slides one sheet of acetate above another on her overhead projector to create across the wall an image not found on the individual sheets themselves. For a few moments, he's half here in the Tate's vestry, and half in the changing rooms at Peckham Baths – in *both* locations without really being in either. It's not just the mass transit and disrobing, nor that the same type of metal coat-hook lines both spaces' walls. No, this composite effect is pegged on something more particular: an afternoon, a little more than two weeks ago; Markie paired, as today, with Nainesh, two to a cubicle, peeling off socks and trousers – and realising, from the voices sailing past the flimsy metal panel separating their stall from its neighbour, that Bea and Emma Dalton were changing right next to them.

The understanding hit the two boys simultaneously; both suddenly fell quiet, eyes moving up and down the flaked partition, which rose far too high to allow over-peeping – but (eyes signalled one another) *its base* ... Its base gave off at shin-height, leaving a low, narrow void-strip. Nainesh, smiling, slowly crouched down to the floor, beckoning Markie: *Here, come* ... They had to press their cheeks right to the quartz-and-granite slab to reach the vantage point: from there, the hidden space swung into view around the panel-base's hinge; and, as though looking upwards while passing through some portico as lofty as the Tate's, they saw two sets of bare legs towering above them like the trunks of redwood trees, parallels playing perspective tricks by narrowing *and* widening out into thighs before converging, at what should have been infinity but was in truth a mere two feet away, into unfoliaged waist-canopies, joins forming folds that bracketed more folds, all flesh-lines moving in strange synchronicity as Bea and Emma, oblivious to the perverse gazes being directed at them from below, marched up and down on the spot, singing the aria they'd been learning for the upcoming school concert:

> Toreador on guard now, Toreador! Toreador!
> Mind well that when in danger thou shalt be,
> Fond eyes gaze and adore,
> And true love waits for thee, Toreador,
> And true love waits for thee!

The angle prevented Markie from seeing Bea's face; Emma's either – but Bea was closest to him, and it's Bea around whom the visual conundrum has accreted in the fifteen-day interim: how to reconcile the two views, the two angles, the two vistas – trunk and visage – two parts of a whole whose *whole*ness he would love to somehow hold to him, clasp and sink into; but ...

They're being handed over to one of the Tate's school-group guides. A slight woman in her twenties, she starts telling the children all about Joan Miró.

'Miró,' she trills in a voice full of what Markie instantly recognises as not enthusiasm itself but rather an intent to enthuse, 'learnt to paint when he was about your age. He loved the shapes and colours of his native Barcelona, which were bright and curvy and just full of life. He loved these shapes and colours so much,' she continues, 'that he's carried them inside him ever since. Although he's an old man now, and one of the world's most famous living artists, he still paints with the imagination and the vision of a child – which is why we're always *particularly* happy when children like you come and look at what he's done. Now, I'm going to pass round these ...'

Worksheets are distributed. There are shapes to spot and tick off; symbols (sun, moon, woman) ditto; then questions about how the paintings make the children feel; a box to fill with their own bright and curvy drawings; and so forth. Trevor rolls his into a hardened tube and swats Jo Fife over the head with it; Vicky starts worrying at the edges of hers, tattering them. They're instructed not to touch the artworks, nor to stand too near. Then they're led, past two more sets of columns, through the polished mausoleum of the building's inner hall to the side galleries. Once in, they fan out through the rooms, zigzagging from wall to wall as they I-spy; clustering in twos and threes to compare notes and rates of progress; squeezing on to benches or planting themselves cross-legged on the floor to copy titles. Markie ambles his way past hangman figures, scribbled stars and charmingly imperfect circles, undulating harlequins, hanging pendula of heads and limbs, past kites and suns (he ticks that one off) and a snakes-and-ladders game that's left the board to take over a house – up, down, diagonal, the whole space – with cats and fish and jack-in-the-boxes joining in, while the game's die, which has mutated into a cuboid chrysalis, hatches a dragonfly or hornet or who knows what other manner of misshapen insect. He holds his glove-ball to his face each time he pauses in front of a painting, and breathes in its compacted softness while he contemplates the image. The glove-ball is misshapen too; not, strictly speaking, a ball – at least not a sphere – but elongated and with finger-tentacles, also turned felt-side outwards, protruding from its base, a fragile home-made teddy squid or octopus ...

It's in the third or fourth room that he pauses for the longest. The schoolchild-spread has thinned right out by now; Markie finds himself alone in front of a big picture. The picture shows a kind of skittle-person standing on a beach, throwing a stone at a bird made up of a few basic shapes. The person has a single, massive foot on which he seems to rock; the bird, a punk shock of red hair, a rooster's comb. The person's face is featureless save for a single egg-yolk-yellow eye in which a red-flecked, black-dot pupil sits; the bird's head, similarly, is formed of nothing more than a blue circle with black dots for eye and nose. It also has a tail of crescent moon. Between the figures, bird and person, the stone is a kind of moon, too: pockmarked, half shaded and half bathed in pale-grey light. The person's throwing it at the bird by means of a thin black beam that serves him for an arm, pivoted around a black-dot navel in his skittle-belly: as he rocks back on his swollen foot, the beam seems to rotate or to be catapulted down to fling the stone towards the bird. There's even a dotted line showing the former's trajectory towards the latter, like a cutting dash marked on a dress maker's pattern sheet. The strange thing, even in this strange set-up, is that not only is the stone hurtling towards the bird; the bird, too, seems to be flying *deliberately* towards the stone, its head straining to meet it in mid-flight. Around this drama the beach stretches, empty and yellow as the thrower's egg-yolk eye. Beyond the beach, the sea is black, devoid of boats, swimmers or even waves and swells, patches of light and shade or anything that might communicate the qualities of water. It's not really trying to represent a sea at all – just oil, black and opaque, applied unmixed and undiluted from a paint tube, spread in a horizontal strip across the middle of the canvas. Above it, and above the beach, above the boy and bird and stone, a scumble-mass of dark-green clouds erupts and billows angrily, unfurling from their hems and underhangs more darkness.

Why does Markie stand in front of this one for so long? It's rich in I-spy targets (two moons), but he doesn't tick them off. There's something beyond odd about it, something not right, something – even by the game-rules of this painted world in which he's interloping – *wrong*. It has to do with the bird flying towards the stone rather than from it. With its flaring red coxcomb, its taut semicircle stick-wing, it seems to be springing from some brake or heather off the painting's bottom edge, to rise exultantly towards the stone; to be *willing* the collision. The whole space seems to be willing it. There's an inevitability about it; all the scene's routes and ranges, all its ambits, gradients and courses seem to have been plotted – lines and angles, dots and seams. It's not just that that's wrong, though: there's something else, too … On the beach, the barren and indifferent beach, its jutting shoreline where yellow meets black, two thorn- or fin-shaped sandy points are (just like the dot-eye of the thrower) daubed with red – that is, with blood. Which must mean that the bird's stoning, the event which the painting is showing, has *already* taken place – although it hasn't: this is lead-up, instant-just-before … *That*'s what's wrong – so wrong that Markie feels the need to plant his feet more firmly on the floorboards, to affirm some kind of stable ground or grounding. It could be, he tries to tell himself – it could be that the skittle-person stoned another bird before the curtain on this scene was raised; that he's a serial bird-killer, knocking off one bird after another, *thunk thunk thunk*, all day long; or perhaps part of a bird-hunting party whose other members we can't see … But Markie knows, even as he trots out the explanations inside his head, that they won't hold up: in this painting's universe there's only one bird, and only one person – nothing else. They *are* its universe, locked together in celestial terror, the yellow, lidless and black-centred sun in the thrower's face the only source of light, condemned to gaze unblinkingly, to shine in red-flecked perpetuity on its own crime …

'Oi! Phocan!'

Trevor has materialised in the room. Has he just slipped in, or has he been here for a while? He, too, seems to have taken in the painting, and to have been taken in by it as well, but in a different way. He's sliding his eyes between it and Markie, back and forth, and beaming a malevolent, complicit smile. The two aren't friends, but Trevor's face, like Nainesh's back in the cubicle, seems to presume some kind of mutual understanding, to signal recognition of a co-conspirator. He's standing a few feet away to Markie's left – or, actually, crouching, head and shoulders lowered almost to waist-level and one foot extended backwards: set, spring-loaded, ready to jump upwards and across. His eyes point at the bird, then at the stone, then at the glove-ball Markie's holding in his right hand.

Markie knows exactly what Trevor wants; the clarity of the communication's almost psychic. It's not from mischievousness or a desire to break rules that he now straightens his right arm; it's the positions, distances, relations … He's *obeying* rules, scored in the tablet of the canvas. He draws in his stomach, feels his navel turn into a vortex of dark energy, and, stretching his right arm back behind his head, rocks on his suddenly enormous-seeming heel, first back, then – fast, forcefully – forwards, bringing the arm pivoting around its point, the hand swinging down in a dot-arc whose geometric regularity he doesn't need a paintbrush to discern; it's written in the air, in the flight of the glove-ball that the hand releases, hurtling now through the gallery's empty space to meet Trevor's head – which, his legs having propelled his body into momentary flight, is gliding eagerly towards it …

Thunk. The collision's softer, feltier than bird's and stone's. Nor does Trevor die: he falls back to the floor, feet landing out of sync with one another, torso thudding to a halt above them in a graceless, unaesthetic manner. His fists pump in celebration of some imaginary headed goal – but it's not about him any more: his part's completed; Trevor's body and entire existence can now fall away like spent booster tanks. What it's about now is the glove-ball, which has undergone both course-change and sudden acceleration: contact with Trevor's head has catapulted it back out again – not towards Markie, but across a new, third plane; the one that, in a painting, exists only in illusory or perspectival form, but, in a room, a real room like this gallery, is there, voluminous and light and dusty and traversable. Simply put: the thing is flying through the air towards the picture. For a stretch that lasts a fraction of a second but which Markie, returning to afterwards, will be able to enter and rerun from many, widely spread-out points, he watches, frozen in position (right arm and shoulder lowered in the casting's follow-through) and at the same time plunging forwards with the missile, straight into the clouds, their angry, black-hemmed green ...

Then, with another *thunk* – a clear one that reverberates around the gallery – the glove-ball hits the canvas. It strikes high up and centrally, above and to the right of the picture's own missile, near the arm-beam's apex. Does it actually remain there for a moment, or is this just retinal delay? For what seems like several seconds Markie sees it clinging to the painted surface. Figure, bird, stone, beach and sky and sea all shudder, unsettled by their world's off-centring. Then slowly, almost languidly, the glove-ball peels itself loose and, spent too, drops to the floor. Then nothing: total stasis – in the work, the room, in everywhere and everything. It's like a kind of vacuum. Markie's ears go funny; in the space between them, there's that loud absence of sound that brings with it a sense of vertigo, of cranial expanse beyond all manageable scale. Then, from all around, from every object and each surface – bird and figure, frame and wall, from lights and doorways, benches, exit signs and air, swooping and billowing and bearing down, zeroing in, accusatory and righteous, on him and him alone (Trevor has long since slunk away) – comes the alarm.

The next few things all happen very fast. Adults appear about him in a rush, their limbs and faces merging: Miss Sedge's leather boots are in there somewhere; so are guards' caps and jackets, and clusters of furious mouths working their jaws at him, words lost beneath the electronic wail, and hands grabbing his arms. Markie makes no attempt to evade these. He hasn't moved at all since the alarm went off. There are kids pressing in too: scurrying over to witness the capture, drink in the scene's red-handedness, grab a front seat to the dumbshow kangaroo court in session right before them, watch some ritual of punishment or sacrifice play itself out. They're to be disappointed, though. Markie is bundled from the gallery by a guard who parts the sea of gawkers with an imperious arm-wave; led through a side door marked *Staff Only;* then a fire door, and then down a corridor with concrete, untiled flooring; across a musty locker room in which casual shirts and trousers hang; and, finally, up some rather flimsy metal stairs into a chamber where two more guards – one white, one black – are sitting before a console.

Once here, the warder releases his grip on Markie's arm – and the boy starts to shake. The seated guards watch him for a few seconds; then the white one, turning from him with an air of cold disinterest, asks:

'Where's his mother?'

'He came here with his school,' the warder answers.

'Teacher, then.'

The warder leaves. The white guard turns back to the console, a banked set of TV screens with a control panel beneath them. The black one is still watching Markie. This one's older, with a thickset frame and wavy-electric hair that's greying around the temples. After a while he mumbles:

'Maybe he want some water.'

The white guard glances fleetingly at Markie, then at his colleague, who looks back at him expressionless but firm. They stay this way for three or four seconds; then the white guard clicks his tongue in irritation, rises from his chair and leaves the chamber.

The remaining guard shifts his gaze back leisurely on to the boy. It's an overbearing gaze – but calming, too: after a while Markie realises that the shaking has stopped.

'You want to see the replay?'

The man's voice is deep and slow: the same West Indian bass that Markie's heard on Brixton market stalls and jerk stands, from Rastas in knitted hats grouped around cab-office doors and cafe counters. The alarm's wail that has pursued him all the way to this chamber from the gallery falls quiet.

'You want to see, or not?'

Markie's not sure what the man means. He stands there stupidly, just looking back at him.

'Come.'

He's beckoning him over. Markie comes. The adult guides him to a spot beside his chair from which he, too, can watch the screens. There are nine of these, stacked in three rows of three: regular black-and-white TV sets, like you'd see in the window of an electronics shop – only these ones, rather than parading an array of makes and models to appraising customers, present a wall of identical, repeating units: pared-down, grey-cased monitors whose two black knobs are unadorned by channel markings. They seem, at first, to all be displaying the same scene: a silent room, shown from an overhead, slightly aslant angle. But this is an illusion, brought on by the uniformity of scale and setting: Markie starts to notice that some of the rooms have benches in them, some not; that some have doorway-openings at the screen's left, others at the right, or top, or not at all; that some have one or two people in them, others none, or many. The people move strangely: at normal speed, but with a motion that's somehow imprecise and fluid at the same time, as though they were immersed in water, and the rooms were aquaria. Ever since he passed the restricted staff and fire doors, Markie's had a sense of being backstage, amidst the scaffolding and props not just of the museum but, somehow, of the entire experience he was supposed to undergo here today. This vision now – multiple, partitioned into cubicles whose occupants can't see each other but into each of which he, like an unobserved Britannia, can peer down, or up, or both at the same time – compounds this feeling. It's as though he were looking at another world – another world that is still recognisably *this* one. There are children milling around three of the screens; there, on one of them, is Polly; on another he picks out Nainesh, Vicky … there's Miss Sedge … and there's Trevor, standing alone, trying to busy himself in his worksheet while glancing up from time to time towards the camera, wondering if it has found him out …

The guard switches a button on his console; one of the screens goes blank, then jumps back into life as lines flicker and jag across it. The man's creating this effect by pressing a lever, a small joystick; when his thumb eases off the stick, the jagging stops – and Markie sees a small boy, whom the rolled-up gloves in his right hand as he stands before a figure, bird and landscape drained of colour identify as no one but himself.

'But how … ?' he starts to ask.

The guard pauses the joystick and raises an eyebrow to elicit the question's completion.

'I mean …' Markie tries again, 'I'm here.'

The guard smiles for the first time now.

'I said we'd watch the *replay*,' he tells Markie. 'Look.'

His thumb nudges the joystick to its right. The boy on the requisitioned screen does nothing. He continues to do nothing for some time. The guard nudges the stick further rightwards, scrambling the screen into jagging lines once more; then releases it as a change in the lines' texture betrays the presence of a second figure, entering to the boy's left.

'Here's where it hot up,' the guard murmurs.

Unscrambled once more, same-but-different Markie's arm comes back and forwards, and the glove-ball travels towards same-but-different Trevor's rising head and on into the canvas, all with the dislocated liquid motion everything on these monitors has. The guard is slowly nodding. When he turns once more to face him Markie sees approval written in his features.

'Nice action,' he tells Markie. He pronounces it *ak-shun*. 'Now we go slow' – ditto – 'motion.'

There's more nudging, and more jagging, then the boy stands in the gallery impassive once again. This time his arm comes back in incremental shifts whose constituent units, morphing from one position to the next, seem to arrive in place before each new position's image has established itself – then, no sooner than it has, slink off towards their next position, with the result that the arm, at any given moment, appears to occupy at least two phases of its transit simultaneously.

'Charlie Griffith in his prime,' the guard says fondly. 'Open shoulders, planted feet, head down ...'

Markie's not sure what he means. On another screen another guard, perhaps the one who brought him to this chamber, is talking to Miss Sedge, then gliding discontinuously off with her out of the picture. His guard here is replaying the throw again, pausing it just after the release, as though to contrast Markie's action with that of the figure in the painting that still hangs there as a backdrop. Markie's gaze, though, is drawn away from this by the scene shown on the screen at the stack's bottom-left corner. Against the wooden floorboards of an otherwise deserted gallery, a single person stands: a girl. Her face is turned away, but the headband tells him that it's Bea. Not just the headband: as she breaks now into a walk, away from the camera to her screen's, and the whole screen-bank's, outer border, something about her motion transmits, even through the fish-tank time-lapse of this circuit, clearly to Markie – so clearly that it seems to him almost deliberate, a call ... The monitors are silent, though. The chamber's silent. The West Indian guard has drifted into memories of inswingers in Bridgetown. Miss Sedge and the white guard are gone too, lost in some corridor, some stretch of in-betweenness. It's all happening, and not, in greyscale, here and somewhere else, draining away.

2. Distance Creased

The first thing disgorged by File C16 of the Institute for Industrial Psychology's archive once its binding ribbon has been loosened – the first object to slide from the card folder and lie face-up on Monica Dean's allotted table here in LSE's bright library – is a photograph of women working among tall plants. They're reaching, holding shears up, cutting fruit, which, bending, they deposit in large baskets. The plants (hops or giant runner beans) are tied to poles and laid out in neat rows, beyond which other poles, still taller, hold a net in place around the whole enclosure, sculpting its mesh-pattern into sags and apexes, like ones you get in circus tents or radio cages. On the photo's reverse side there's a handwritten caption: *Agricultural labourers, England, 1882.*

The file's next photograph shows women feeding cotton into machines that scutch, willow and gather it on spools which, arranged in a ring, themselves feed a larger, central twist-spool. In the next picture – same year, 1889 – this twist-spool, or one like it, has in turn become a spinning chorus girl alongside scores of others: circled layers of spools stacked in a tower that looms above the solitary woman tending to the doubling winder, threading its central bobbin, making sure each fibrous tendril's tautened to the correct stretch and temper. For a second, this operator (faceless, since her back is to the camera, hence to Dean) takes on the look of a performer, mastering a harp or piano. This impression quickly passes, though. Her posture has nothing commanding about it: bowed head, outstretched arm and crooked back seem held by the cords, not the other way round – governed by them, like the limbs and torso of an old marionette.

Each file has the same type of ribbon round it, pink. They make them look like gifts, like chocolate boxes, perfume cases – or the briefs that Dean's used to preparing for D&G's barristers. If there's a ritual element to legal procedure, there's one also to these holdings' presentation to her: how the wooden elevator bears them up from hidden stacks; the slow glide of the archivist from the dispensing station through the waist-high turnstile separating restricted and (by prior appointment) public zones; the way Dean has to don white gloves to handle them ... Then image after image of these century-and-a-half-old people planted in rows, on floors, in trestles. Most of them, buried in their tasks, seem unaware they're being recorded; occasionally, one will look back at the camera in a manner that seems neither defiant nor inquisitive, but just resigned: one more piece of equipment ...

Here's a line of women on high stools beside a workbench, peering through stand-clamped magnifying lenses at cogs and gears they've picked at random from a belt that trundles by in front of them. It's more recent: 1925, a caption, typed this time, informs her ... *By increasing stool-distance from bench to 18 inches, shadow on working point eliminated. Strain reduced by 5% through consequent adjustment in arm-angle* ... There are more like this in the next file: women at benches, tables, spindles; belts and cables all around them – horizontal, vertical, aslant; wire, rollers, wheels and hooks. There are men, too, stranding, vulcanising, cooking, pressurising, insulating, braiding; reeling lengths of cable on huge turntables that, like the cotton feeders' spools, feed onwards, up to huger wheels; working with iron, rubber, lead. They're making bridge-parts, painting cookers ... *25% of painting time saved by introduction of flat for round brush having wider spread* ... They're fitting diodes into speakers and assembling batteries; assembling hoovers, fridges, tractors; moulding golf balls, aeroplane tyres, rubber gloves they quality-control by slipping on to cast-iron testing-hands that run in a saluting guard-of-honour line above the conveyor (also rubber); truing bicycle wheels by turning them in automated stands whose mechanisms are driven by belts wrapped around more bicycle wheels ...

Here's a strange one: female workers at a hairbrush factory, perched beside buffers. They're taking almost-completed brushes from wheel-mounted bins that sit just to the left of each of them and holding these up to their buffers (set into the workspace's back wall at the same, regular interval as the workers: twenty women, twenty buffers) – which, Dean deduces from both the blurred texture of the buffers' surface and the scene's implied mechanics, must be spinning: the women are distress-texturing the reverse-side of each hairbrush's head, thereby preparing it to double as a clothes brush. Attached to the photo is a sheet of text that's typed, but not directly: there's no dent or imprint in the paper, and the lettering, faint and purple, suggests an early form of photostat-ting – incorrectly executed, since the text's column has been sliced right down the middle, its left-hand portion censored or redacted:

> ed the buffer to sit comfortably at
> s were adjustable in height and distance
> creased by 12%

Dean holds the sheet up, draws photo and caption closer to her, then extends her arm again. It makes no difference: the women keep their backs turned, and continue plying their buffers. Their own hair is covered by cloth hats, from beneath which the odd wisp snakes out to curl across a cheek. Phantom images, sediment left in Dean's mind by childhood bookshelves full of harems, handmaid-ens and vestals, hover about the picture, transforming these drab factory girls into ladies-in-waiting tending to an empress, combing and re-combing untwined tresses, chaste and decorous through afternoons in the royal bedchamber, an enclave closed off from the world of men, of time, soft music drifting in from neighbour-ing rooms, from halls and ballrooms, foyers, cabinets, saloons . . .

She's been holding this buffer photo for a while now. Why? Not sure. What does it tell her? Nothing. On, then: she has work to do. She has instructions.

3. The Ten Commandments for Depicting Space Travel in Movies

Or, just: *The Ten Commandments* – the rest is self-evident, from the context. The title's new; the format is more punchy. It runs, as it stands, like this:

1. Physics – condensed, applied, particular, molecular, atomic, photonic, planetary, plasma, nuclear, nano-, astro-, geo- and etcetero- – this shall be thy Lord and God. Physics has built your spaceship; it has raised it from the bondage of the earth and is propelling it to wheresoever you boldly are going. It is a jealous god: make graven images to other ones – particularly to the god of aesthetics, whose idol is the harlot of sensual perception – and it will visit the iniquity of the fathers upon the children, unto the third and fourth generation, yea even to the end of thy franchise's line.

2. Thou shalt not show thy astronauts perambulating over alien planets as though they were strolling through Central Park. Just look at Arnie (slide 1) wandering about the Martian landscape here: even a body as solid and muscular as his would weigh about a third of what it does on Earth. Ever wondered why Armstrong and Aldrin bounce around on those Moon-landing films? (If some smartass quips *Because they're faked* then I shall commandeer his body and dispatch it to the Marshall Space Flight Center's Antimatter Lab for instant condensation and annihilation!) On Jupiter, the scales tilt in

the other direction: there, you'd weigh in at almost three times your terrestrial load. Each time you raised your thigh and knee to take a forward step, it'd be like (slide 2) training on a leg press pegged to max.

3. Thou shalt not let thy FX boys create giant, billowing explosions every time a starship fighter or space station is destroyed. That they're being overpaid to cook up stuff that looks cool isn't an excuse for contravening basic laws of possibility. For an explosion, or any form of combustion, you need oxygen – and there is no oxygen in space. Look at these (slide 3) flames in *Starship Troopers*: they're even licking upwards (flag on that too; there's no 'up' or 'down' in outer space) round the vessels' hulls. And when the vessels deflagrate completely, we get huge booms – which, by dint of the aforementioned lack of oxygen or similar medium through which sound-waves might travel, is equally impossible. Kubrick, by contrast, gets it more or less right in *2001: A Space Odyssey*: when Bowman (slide 4) blows *Discovery One*'s hatch to re-enter the ship, there's an *im*plosion, playing out in a vacuum, and in silence ...

Ben Briar turns his face to the plane's window. Outside, through the triple membrane, he can see the transatlantic predawn stretched round the earth's curvature, a triple membrane too: haze, cloud, permafrost landmass. They must be somewhere above Newfoundland or Greenland. Troposphere and Arctic gauze, whisky on ice, his PowerPoint presentation. In *Interstellar*, on the scientist Mann's ammonia-rich planet, frozen clouds furnish an upper ground that can be walked on – which is bullshit too: ice couldn't hang suspended like that. He should add this; maybe in Commandment Number 9, the gravity one ...

4. Honour the laws of speed and distance. A radio signal from Earth would take twenty minutes to arrive at Mars, our next-door-neighbour planet. If you're being a little

more adventurous, and sending missions to the far end of the galaxy, you can extend that period to months, or even years. Instantaneous telecommunication, back-and-forth *deploy-the-heat-shield/how's-the-wife/are-the-fish-biting* repartee between Mission Control and Canis Major, is a major no-no. If an astronaut picks up a message while careening through Andromeda or Triangulum, it's a safe bet that its sender died more than a century ago.

And on that note:

5. Thou shalt not have thy hero travel back in time. As Einstein showed us, time can warp and stretch, but neither he nor any other scientist with an ounce of credibility has ever claimed it can run backwards. The only property capable of moving across dimensions is (q.v. Commandment Number 9) gravity. Even if time travel *were* possible (and once again: it's not), to effect it would require more that the sum total of all energy existing in the universe. Having journeyed to the past, you couldn't do anything when you got there, and there wouldn't even be a 'there' to get to and do nothing at. The fantasy that you can go back to a 1930s high-school prom, screw your own grandmother, stop World War Two from taking place and change the outcome of the 1953 World Series is precisely that: a fantasy ...

Is the grandmother bit too risqué? It isn't Disney he'll be dealing with in London. Degree Zero are hip's *ne plus ultra*; or as hip as you can be with a turnover north of fifty mil a year. And judging from the specs, this project itself must be budgeted at roughly double that. It's a grand space opera in the *Star Wars* mould, with princesses, kidnappers, pirates, smugglers; imperial federations gathering tribute from surrounding vassal-planets, rates for which are renegotiated every solar cycle at galactic councils in the recesses of whose auditoria, corridors and ambassadorial docking bays secret alliances are proffered, struck, betrayed ... Briar's got

31

the treatment right here, wedged beneath his whisky glass. It's written by one Norman Berul, and it's crawling with cardinal errors. Take this scene, in which the lover of a dowry-bearing, peace-cementing bride-to-be signals his paramour (said betrothed – though not to him) by means of lasers flickering in the sky above her royal chamber, projected from his ship lying just outside the stratosphere of her intended's (who is also his adoptive uncle's) planet ... Setting aside the fact that, if the pining bride can see it, so (presumably) can the cuckolded king and all his courtiers, servants, general subjects, right down to the space drunk pissing in the alleyway outside the planetary dive bar – even overlooking that fact, the scene is a non-starter, since ... Briar sets the printout, water-marked by the glass-base's condensation, down again and moves Commandment Number 7 up one place:

6. Know this: lasers cannot be seen in space. The laser-pointers stoners whip out when they're tripping at Dead concerts –

change Dead reference; these kids weren't even born

– at techno clubs are visible because the air in auditoria and warehouses is saturated with dust particles. Same in your bedroom: it's because you never vacuum that you can amuse yourself by making your cat (slide 5) overbalance as he clutches at the red or green line he can see but not touch. You bastard. But in space – no dust, no cats, no line. That room's been vacuumed: it's *all* vacuum. Weapons-grade beams might blow holes through your spaceship's hull, but you won't see them. Even if you were a Jedi warrior, you wouldn't see a laser beam, let alone be granted the reaction time to parry it with your own sabre. Light travels at the speed of ... yes, light. A reflex that kicks in before the thing to which it is a reflex has been registered by the reflective agent isn't a reflex but a temporal conundrum that (q.v. Commandment Number 5) is an abomination in the eyes of Physics.

7. These things matter. One hundred and fifty years ago President (slide 6) Lincoln helped charter the National Academy of Sciences. Why? Because he grasped that an understanding of science by the populace was of prime importance to modernity and progress, to the republic, to democracy itself. The other road, the path of ignorance and superstition, leads straight back to Salem. And maybe, just maybe, Lincoln also intuited the role that speculation, entertainment, the imagination would play in the new republic's future. After all, didn't its creation both demand and entail one giant imaginative leap? Physics, for all its evidence-based leanings, is a creative journey too, a plunge into the far-flungest –

farthest-flung

– farthest-flung reaches of imagination. We fold space inside out in an attempt to picture how the universe is shaped. We tease parallel worlds from the peepholes of boxes that have cats inside (we're bastards too). We smash particles together at insane speeds just for the thrill of seeing what will happen. And all these activities cost (slide 7) money, and (slide 8) more money, and (slide 9) more money. We scientists burn our way through so much money as to make your own extravaganzas' price tags look like collection-box spare change. Where does our money come from? Government. And what shapes Government's budgetary policy? Public opinion. If Joe Public ain't excited by the prospect of discovering the Higgs boson and unlocking multiverses, Congress don't send us the tax dollars to discover and unlock them.

8. That's where you guys come in: you are our interface. Through you, we seed the public with a love of science. And we're your interface as well: to credibility, to disbelief-suspension, to all that Aristotle-101 shit. If the set-up in your flick doesn't look *plausible*, your viewers aren't transported,

or enchanted, or even willing to part with their own cash to see your movie in the first place. Which is bad – for you, for us, for everyone. We're your safeguard against that eventuality, just as you're ours against our own supply-chain cut-off. It's symbiotic: hummingbird and bee balm, gut and good bacteria, pilot fish and shark. Which, to bring things back round to our own point in the multiverse, our current fragile patch of space-time, is why you've invited me here to your lovely and impressive studios – and why I, as Two Cultures Consultancy's Senior Partner, have accepted said invitation. Which brings us . . .

Briar lifts his glass again, takes a sip, then eases back into his seat, lumbar-support pads rising to meet contours of his spine and ribs. NASA never used to fly him first class. Fifty-eight, he's a boy in a toyshop in this setting – has to suppress an urge to press each button, plug some lead or other into every socket, find skin surfaces on which to smear each of his courtesy toiletry-pouch unctions. He part-lowers his laptop's lid and activates his pod's free-standing entertainment console. Comedy. *The Big Bang Theory*: why not? Here's the Aspergic Sheldon in his living room, debating with his neuroscientist girlfriend Amy rules pertaining to dilemmas thrown up by some hypothetical Dungeons and Dragons game-turn. Amy is, as always, cold and logical. Sheldon, by contrast, plays it camp and passionate: he's genuinely hurt that she can't see the in-play permutation his way, paces agitatedly about the set, holding back tears. Behind him, there's a whiteboard, covered with the algebraic shorthand Sheldon and his pals are always scrawling. Briar hits *pause* on his armrest-set and, squinting, peers at the image closely, scrutinising the notation.

It's a Feynman diagram, with straight, arrow-bearing black lines and wiggly, plain blue ones modelling the procession of fermions and photons through an interaction sequence. Someone's done their homework: all the vertexes have one arrow line travelling in to meet the sine line and another travelling out again, slanted at forty-five degrees. Positrons are labelled $e+$, electrons $e-$, photons with a gamma, γ. Briar thrusts out his lower lip and nods approvingly, tilting his drink at the screen as he raises glass to mouth once more. Just as the liquid hits his tongue, though, the satisfaction it's about to consecrate is rudely snatched away, evaporated from his very palate, by the sight of ... What's this? At the whiteboard's bottom right we've got a kaon, composed of both up and strange antiquarks (u, $\bar{s}$: fine), breaking down into three pions ($\pi+$, $\pi+$ and $\pi-$: fine too), with two intermediate steps that involve a W boson (blue $W+$: good) and a gluon (green g: all good) – but the gluon, whose procession should be indicated by a spiral, is instead being represented by a zigzag that in turn spawns branches to which arrows have been added willy-nilly, like so many sprouting leaves ... which, as any Caltech nerd would know, is totally ridiculous. It makes a mockery of the diagram, the characters, the scene, the show's whole universe. To go that far, do all the research, then ...

Briar swallows, but it's tasteless. He raises his laptop's lid again:

9. Black holes. Don't get me started on black holes ...

– but finds that he can't concentrate. He throws the remnants of his whisky, watery by now, ice caps all CO_2ed, down his throat's hatch and pings for service, orders up a new one. Zigzags. When the stewardess has left he flips his laptop lid shut, stows the thing away and scrolls on through his in-flight entertainment system's menu, settling eventually on the cartoon channel.

4. Corydon and Galatea

Dr Mark Phocan, M.Sc., C.Eng., shunning the quads and cupolas and college lawns that pull the disembarking trainloads eastwards, drives past Oxford station, dips under the tracks and heads away from the town centre towards Botley. A minute or two later, somewhere past the hump of Osney Bridge but before Binsey Lane bus stop, he crosses the unmarked boundary beyond which the city's aura, like a Wi-Fi signal, stops transmitting: from here onwards, church halls and day schools are no longer photogenic; restaurants are unable to charge heritage supplements; lamp-posts, paving stones and bollards lie abandoned to their unaugmented there-ness. When the drab parades of newsagents, launderettes and betting shops in their turn taper off, to be replaced by megastores set back behind vast lots, generic signage – Currys, Jewson, Pets at Home – more vibrant than the saplings planted around each concession's border, Phocan's mood shifts, as it does each time he makes this journey, to the kind of neutral that's brought on by the awareness that he could be anywhere at all in Britain; anywhere, at least, that's nowhere.

Beyond this, it's park-and-ride and ring-road territory – plus, not for Phocan, who's been trundling down this route for several years now, but invariably for first-time visitors since the side road hasn't been uploaded into TomTom, Garmin or CoPilot, a confused spin round the McDonald's drive-thru or three-pointer in the Enterprise returns zone before retracing in the opposite direction, west-to-east, the stretch just prior to the large intersection of A420 and B4044, cab driver asking if they're sure they've got the right address, *ain't nothing else around here*; then, just as the phone's coming out, emails are being popped open, thumb-tapped signature-address spawning a blue pin that seems to hover, what the fuck, above their very car – *that's* when they generally spot the turn-off, unnamed and un-signposted, for Finns Business Park. It's an estate un-parklike as they come, consisting of a main drive from which offshoots lead either to dead ends or, looping, back round to the drive, flanked or plugged in either case by plain industrial units. Phocan's pulling up and parking beside one of these units now: a low-lying semi-prefab, ground floor brick, upper corrugated iron, entirety dwarfed by an electricity pylon whose wires run above (but not quite along the same axis as) its long rectangular roof. On the main door, beneath a logo that depicts a sheep and stick, words legible only to those who, like him, have already approached them announce the unit's occupant as Pantarey Motion Systems, Private Limited Company no. 4037859, Est. 1982.

The sheep, yes ... A story goes with that. It seems Pantarey's founder, Anthony (Tony) Garnett, suffered from insomnia. Since adolescence he'd been fed the old canard about sheep-counting, which piece of trite folk-wisdom he'd summarily dismissed as nonsense – until, during a trip to Western Australia on which he was (as you'd expect) beset with jet-lag, he found himself replaying across the inside of his eyelids well into the small hours images of sheep that he'd observed moving through gates, into and out of dip-troughs and so forth about his cousin's farm the previous day. These images weren't really painterly, or even cinematic: they were more – let's say – *schematic*, their schematism in its turn presenting a conceptual quandary. What most stood out for him was the way the movements, the displacements – the real ones from which these night-time shadow-plays were drawn – were at once beyond a certain point quite unpredictable *and* governed by a general drive or aim: that of Cousin Dermot to manoeuvre the animals from Point A to Point B. Garnett pictured dots in space – the location of such-and-such animal at a given moment, the corresponding location of such-and-such another one at the same instant, then another (animal/instant/both) – conjoined by lines: of transit, detour, switchback; lines themselves dictated by the general flow of the collective, or collected, mass and by the less mechanical yet no less operative strings of need, fear, rivalry and yearning linking one sheep to another, to their power-of-life-or-death-commanding master and his dogs – a set of shifting hook-ups that, while chaotic and perhaps so endlessly self-modulating as to fall within the category Random, paradoxically displayed, when taken at the level of the whole, the spectacle of order and control in action, of harmony unfolding across the gradient field of a muddy and fly-saturated pasture. There must be, Garnett told himself as the first wisps of daylight crept in round the curtains, some way of *comprehending*, or at least of capturing, not simply at the level of the field's totality, but also at the scale of its constituent parts and moments, its haptic and recursive structure, the temporo-spatial information hiding, like so many Ithacans, beneath the wool and bleats and nervous little leaps, of somehow *rendering* this information, setting it to work. For Western Australian farmers? Perhaps not – but Garnett sensed immediately that the implications of his dawn ruminations had far wider scope. For the next week, the sheep, the real ones, much to simple Dermot's chagrin, were fitted with reflectors, magnets, paint-drippers, track-scoring styluses and all manner of passage-indicating prostheses. Garnett's insomnia remained unresolved (it got worse) – but Pantarey grew from these preoccupations, these antipodean gambols. Whence the logo.

Phocan, like all his colleagues, has served up this foundation myth repeatedly to the clients he leads through, or pauses beside, this door. Is it entirely true? Who cares? The man's a father to the company, a shepherd to his flock. The stick was depicted, for Pantarey's first three decades, as a staff or crook (though Garnett toyed with the idea of showing it with keys and stoppers, like a flute). On the logo's redesign in 2012, it turned into a non-specific object, evocative of data wands, airport-security sticks and the like;

the sheep itself grew semi-abstract, half a cloud. 2012 was also the year that Pantarey's IT Officer Yusuf Hossain implemented, company-wide, the security protocol (for scanning foreign drives, writers and the like for viruses and malware) known as Sheep Dipping – unconnected (that software's ownership lay elsewhere) to the firm's origins; but for Garnett the coincidence served as a confirmation, token that some kind of wheel, in running through its generational revolutions, had carved his personal iconography into the columns of the industry's own temple, laid down his intellectual sediment in its very bedrock.

Past the door, in lieu of a lobby or reception, there's a cube-shaped space inside which sits, atop a wooden plinth, a glass display case that, in turn, contains another cuboid frame, a rudimentary box that's been built around yet one more box: a Pentax camera – Garnett's, circa 1978. This last, innermost object always, even to Phocan, born long enough ago to vaguely recall parents' necks being strung with such albatrosses, never mind to the dig-nat majority who traipse past it, appears as eerie and outlandish as would (say) a similarly encased hand-cranked chocolate grinder, copper steam-iron or Canopic jar. Behind the first layer of transparent glass, the camera's lens, opaque and Cyclopic, passively malevolent, holds both Phocan's figure and the small blocks of Finns, sky and general daylight that have wandered through the door with him into the entrance chamber captive on its surface, flattened in gnomonic whirl. VGA leads that seem as thick (proportionally at least) as early transatlantic cables emerge from the innermost box, snake their way through purpose-drilled holes in the extra wooden casing, then coil and gather against the display's outer border, fraying into skin-shedding cross-sections. When Garnett first designed the thing – and that is what this is, no model but the very one, his prototype motion translator – these led to an IBM processor larger than this whole room, the display of which component on the plinth would, naturally, present a certain obstacle of scale. Instead of trying to surmount or circumvent this, the space's designers have opted to affix to the wall above the cabinet, in vinyl lettering, a passage first in Greek:

λέγει που Ἡράκλειτος ὅτι πάντα χωρεῖ καὶ οὐδὲν μένει . . . δὶς ἐς τὸν αὐτὸν ποταμὸν οὐκ ἂν ἐμβαίης (Πλάτων)

then, below, in English:

Heraclitus says: Everything flows and nothing remains still . . . You cannot step into the same stream twice (Plato)

Garnett himself provided the translation. His first discipline, before Engineering, was Classics: he studied it right here in Oxford – up the road, back past the station, sherry and spires and 1890 issues of *American Journal of Philology* that you had to blow the dust off before reading in a library that (as he has often told his incredulous staff) you could actually *smoke* in, Corydon proclaiming his doomed love for Galatea in dactylic hexameters, Magdalen's own deer-park pastoral ... A world not Phocan's: he's straight kinetics, Bristol to Imperial to Pantarey. Streams may be one-use-only, but the staircase leading on beyond the entrance chamber he's ascended many times, passed again and again the photographs that flank it, framed pictures of sensor-fitted athletes, soldiers, actors; of drones, robots and virtual assembly lines, all culminating in an upper landing-level picture that shows nothing more than strings of data, jiggling luminescent on a screen. Past this, behind another door, a corridor zags sharply, first one way then another, through the upper floor, like a right-angled maze; and, maze-like too, it seems to defy spatial logic, spawning rooms that extend further than they should be able to before bumping against the passageway's next parallel or perpendicular avenue – offices, workshops, server-repositories ... Phocan, navigating the dark space with ease, glimpses in one of these rooms a collection of dummy heads and torsos in various stages of completion and/or demolition – sight which, though familiar, always makes him cast his eyes about in search of a frustrated Q who'll cluck impatiently *Now pay attention, 007 . . .*

It's not Q or his spectre he'll be meeting today, though: it's M – the man himself, sheep-contemplator, motion- and ancient poetry-translator, temple-inscriber, bedrock-impregnator and, more prosaically, employer. In the most well appointed of the labyrinth's chambers he finds Garnett at his desk, perusing diagrams of satellite dishes from which phalanxes of numbers (all Arabic) and letters (some Latin, others Kanji) radiate.

'Mark.'

The *Markie* disappeared some three decades ago, about the same time as his glove-ball. Still, there's something strangely infantile about being addressed in this way, first-name, by this older man. The informality's not bidirectional:

'Mr Garnett. You wanted to see me.'

Garnett motions for him to sit down.

'Have our lovebirds arrived yet?' he asks.

'I don't know,' Phocan answers. 'I just got here myself.'

'You drove from London?'

'Yes. I could have given them a lift; or picked them up from the station – although I don't know what they look like.' He tries to picture the awaited guests sharing a taxi, performing the habitual lost divagations – which prompts him to ask: 'Are they a couple? Have they even *met* before?'

'Not sure,' says Garnett. 'All I know is they're students. At it all the time, couple or not.' He chuckles to himself, then asks: 'How's Lucy shaping up?'

The question takes Phocan aback. Lucy's the intern, the apprentice. It's not Garnett's enquiring after her that's disconcerting; it's the segue. Before he answers, he scrutinises the worn face across the desk, probing its eyes for some flicker of innuendo, or . . . There's nothing. If there's a proxy wish written there, it's one less carnal than concerned, in a *paterfamilias* way, with the moulding of charges, shaping of futures.

'Fine,' he eventually responds. 'She's curious.'

'What's curious about her?'

'No, I mean she shows an intellectual curiosity.'

'That bodes well,' Garnett says. 'She went to Tokyo with you?'

'Yes,' Phocan nods. 'The JAXA work's advancing nicely.'

'So I see.' Garnett taps the satellite-filled pages on the desk in front of him. 'Talking of outer space: how's the Degree Zero project panning out?'

'Good too,' Phocan reports. 'I'm visiting them next week. *Incarnation.*' He speaks this last word in false deep-tone, as though voicing a trailer. 'It's actually three or four projects: there's the modelling of objects; there's the plotting of various movements – in one scene, movements perhaps not unlike our target ones today ...'

'Perhaps not.' Garnett now taps his nose. 'Always good to keep an eye open for lateral applications ...'

'And then,' Phocan goes on, 'there's a disaggregation scene: a spaceship, super complex. They've got the water-tank people at VWS working with initial gross models. But I thought that we might also try to sound out NW, the wind-tunnel crowd, when I go there next month with the Austrians, the ...'

'That's exciting,' Garnett cuts in.

'What is?'

'The wind tunnel. First time we'll have trialled PIV. It could be a stepping stone to going fully markerless in high-precision situations.'

'Let's hope so,' Phocan says. 'I was at BAE again just a few days ago, and tried to discuss using markerless on unmanned aerials with your friend Pilkington, but couldn't get much from him – certainly no commitment to expanding contract terms. He doesn't talk much.'

'He's a complex figure. Lots of skeletons.' Garnett's face turns contemplative, slightly melancholy even. 'But in any case,' he picks up, brightening again, 'we're way out in front. Nobody's close to us on pose-estimation and deep learning-based tracking ...'

'There's still lots of noise inside our data,' Phocan cautions. 'Even Physis 6. With markerless, mean absolute error goes right up to thirty millimetres – way too much.'

'And with markered?'

'Less than ten – mainly due to skin artefact. When we do skinless, with cadavers, error drops to almost zero; though cadaveric evaluation has its own limitations, in terms of movement ...'

'Kasper thinks ...' Garnett begins, but this time Phocan interrupts:

'Kasper's put all his eggs in the T-pattern basket. The problem with that is ...'

'I know, I know,' Garnett holds up a stilling hand. 'I've heard you out on this, just as I've heard out Kasper on the pitfalls of your faith in quintic and spline fillers. You two,' he chuckles again, 'are my Jacob and my Esau, tussling over inheritance – which makes me like Isaac, old and blind ...'

'I wouldn't call you blind,' Phocan dutifully reassures him.

'We all are.' Garnett brushes the offering away. 'That's what makes our whole schtick possible. We're shooting photons through the darkness, hoping for some bounce-back, for some ping of ...'

The sentence tapers off. He seems distracted, as though listening to something only he can hear.

'Of what?' prompts Phocan.

'... of something,' Garnett answers vaguely. 'Certainty, enlightenment ... I don't know ...'

Now Phocan can hear it too: the sound of the building's front door opening again, of voices in the entrance chamber, new arrivals being regaled with anecdotes of restlessness and sheep. That Garnett, despite the diminished aural powers that go with age, should have picked it up before him must be down to an attunement, to some sensory affinity with the very passages and walls, the bricks and girders of this complex that he's built from his own head, spun out of half-sleep. Rising now, his boss announces:

'That's our amorous pair.'

The two of them step out, process past rooms in which more dummies are dotted about. The heads are black and featureless, the torsos, too, their 'skin' being formed of tightly knitted cloth to which are affixed silver nipples – not, in the cause of realism, on the pectoral area, but everywhere, prolifically, bubbling like plague boils out of arm, buttock, midriff, thigh. More nipples lie around: in plastic drawers, on workbenches, strewn all across the floor. They've been both hand- and purpose-made by guests of Her Majesty lodged on the other side of town, HMP Bullingdon – markers, new 'pearl' ones, perfectly spherical (the old type, mummified in reflector tape, presented folds and rifts that broke light up into divergent planes – good enough for first-pass overviews but about as helpful as a broken lens or randomising feature when it comes to more exacting capture). Some dummies are mounted on bases, upright; others lie prostrate where they've fallen, like Pompeians; in one corner of a workshop a whole mound of them is piled up in a crate, victims awaiting resurrection by some situation, some scenario, however temporary, of approximated life ...

They'll have to wait, though: the humans have their own scenario to bring to life today. Phocan follows Garnett on towards the capture studio. This comes after two more turns, beyond another set of doors: the building's central and most cavernous space, known simply as The Cell. Velveteen, rubber-floored, rectangular, The Cell is draped at intervals with black cloth – sometimes stapled in large redacting squares to its white walls, sometimes hanging down from hooks, like arrases or theatre curtains. Theatre-like as well are the long aluminium rails that run along the border of the wall and ceiling like an offset and unornamental cornicing – and run perpendicularly to this too, brace-affixed to each of the room's transoms, while a central length of the same railing, held in place by longer pendular bracing, cuts along the ceiling's middle, intersecting with each of the cross-rails so that the overall rail-structure forms an enclosed and enclosing frame, a kind of involuted exoskeleton. Hanging in turn from this, their wires coiled round their beam-trellis in creeper-like profusion, are a set of light-emitting cameras: Pantarey's own HDI220s, upgraded this year to incorporate FGPA and DSP, 120 fps with 16-megapixel sensors and four LED-rings with 850-nanometre spacing – in short, the latest word in sensing-recording tech.

Phocan glances at the numbers on the cameras, printed large and white on the black surface of each: 1, 2, 3, on up to 12, as laid out in the specs that he and Kasper Sennet handed the technicians three days ago. Sennet's already here in The Cell, talking to Biomach's emissary. The cameras are positioned round the aerial boundary of a square that has been formed within the larger rectangle down on the floor, its edges demarcated by white tape. To one side of this square, they've set up several chairs and two desks. On the latter, spread out in a phalanx, are five monitors, on each of which the surface area of the taped square that they abut is shown – not in a photographic manner, but rather as a topographic layout. The depiction varies from screen to screen. One represents the nipple-studded objects lying within the square; another the same objects and arrangement twelve times, from twelve different angles; a third homes right in on a single marker, both enlarging it and placing it in cross-hairs at whose intersection point its pixels shimmer, like a desert sun or target in a sniper's long-range viewfinder. A fourth portrays the sight-lines issuing from each of the feed-cameras, and their points of intersection – multiple, converging in the air above the floor into ever tighter clusters round the bed and bedside table and flowers. Despite their differences, one feature all screens have in common is their division of the floor-square into regular white sub-squares that overlay its plain black rubber surface with a grid. The fifth screen simply shows this grid, aslant and foreshortened, from above – from right above: not only, that is, from above the grid but from above the overhanging cameras as well, such that the cameras themselves are rendered as numbered square-cone shapes hovering in a ring about the scene: twelve Olympians gazing down bright-eyed, *glaucopis*, on the stage.

Was a bed mentioned? There's indeed one here: the largest of the floor's three objects. Though represented on the screens as no more than a rectangular parallelepiped, it is, in its material reality, a genuine queen double: memory-foam mattress, white Egyptian cotton sheet (200 thread count), two Siberian goose-down pillows – subject of debate, these, when they configured the space: Sennet argued that they'd break the sight-lines; Phocan countered by affirming their necessity to some of the requisite, you know, *manoeuvres*. Next to this, the bedside table, plain, white, unadorned save for – third and final object (objects really) – a vase bearing flowers. Yes, flowers: a bunch of freesias. Why not? Romance lives, even in the grid. Besides which, they don't want the scene to be too arid or (despite its end) too clinical, lest other flowers droop or fail to spread and blossom. What they need is a warm, intimate setting – or a set, laid out here before the *theori* both human and *ex machina*, awaiting only actors for its drama to begin.

And here they are, being led in now by curious Lucy Diamond: a woman and a man, mid-twenties. Their arrival has provoked much interest here at HQ – no mean feat, since they've had lots of famous people through these doors over the years: top football players, pop stars ... Nothing quite like this, though. Neither face is recognisable, and their names, were they known to the general staff, would garner no reaction – but somehow, not long after Garnett had picked up their presence, everybody else had too, the knowledge travelling from floor to floor. A professional demeanour's been maintained by all whom the two visitors passed in the corridors or workshops; faces set to neutral-friendly, welcoming nods nodded; but there's still a *frisson* that can't be suppressed, hanging about the air. Are they good-looking? Sure – but not strikingly so. The woman has brown hair, wavy and shoulder-length; the man's is black and short, matching the stubble on his face. He's wearing jeans, jumper and jacket; she has culottes, trainers, a loose-hanging shirt ... They're both Caucasian; she has slightly darker skin than him. Students, Garnett said: Phocan wonders what type. He and Eldridge, the Imperial gang, never looked that insouciant. Maybe art students. *Are* they a couple? If they've just met for the first time – on the train, or at the station, on the platform, in the taxi as they whipped their phones out, popped their blue pins – then it would have made for quite an interesting conversation …

Once Diamond, same age as the pair (perhaps the reason, it strikes Phocan now, for Garnett's thought-progression in his office a few moments ago) has deposited them in The Cell, it's Sennet who takes them in hand. He explains how motion capture works, shows them the nipples, trying to be as deadpan as he can as he pronounces the word, *nipples*, but he can't today and breaks into a smile, which thankfully both visitors return. He then introduces them to Jayani Perera, Hip Specialist at Biomach, this session's client. Perera, in turn, explains today's field of enquiry – namely, the stress that's placed, by the positions commonly (or indeed uncommonly) encountered during heterosexual intercourse, on femur, ball and acetabulum (how much, precisely, by each varying position, where, and for which partner), the concomitant risks of impingement, or even dislocation, in sexually active (and why shouldn't they be?) beneficiaries of total arthroplasty. As she talks, she first sculpts hip-joints in the air, running her palms round globed caput femoris, ringed zona orbicularis and the outlines of ischia and ilia, sliding her fingers up and down greater, lesser and third trochanters, all spectral. After a while, her hands default to her body, pointing at her own hips as she pushes them forwards and withdraws them in a manner as innocuous and unsuggestive as the context allows, which is not very. But at some point these hands start travelling – first to the man, whose loins she draws slowly forward through their thrusting range, then to the woman, whose waist she leads through its inverse and corresponding motion.

The pair allow their bodies to be guided by Perera: a seal's been broken, border crossed; from here on in, they're part of the equipment. Phocan and Diamond are now able, without any awkwardness, to convey them to their respective changing areas, formed by the hanging from the rails of more velvet sections.

Phocan takes the man, Diamond the woman. Having invited his charge to strip, Phocan starts sticking markers to his skin: around the waist, across the thigh, the buttocks, in a column up the back-bone to T-junction at the shoulders and perform a switchback down each arm; then a few outliers – on calves and ankles, cheeks and forehead – to help mark overall bodily outline.

'Won't some of these come off when we … you know, with the movement?' the man asks.

'Don't worry,' Phocan tells him. 'We've got plenty on you. We can afford to lose a few.' It is a problem, though – one he's dis-cussed with Sennet, failing to find much of a solution other than this overcompensation, this profusion that makes of this poor student's flesh a nipple-cushion as densely studded as the dummy-torsos. 'But if you notice one has come off,' he adds, 'leave it on the bed; don't stick it back on. It would have a slightly new posi-tion on you, which would feed us bad coordinates.'

'Will you be here?' the man asks. 'In the room, I mean?'

'Normally we would,' Phocan answers. 'But in this instance you'll be left alone. The sensors will be on, the disks recording. But it's not a film: they're just transcribing movement. Nobody will see your faces; nobody will *see* you at all. And it's not record-ing sound …'

He pauses; in the silence muted gasps, imagined sighs of pleas-ure flitter about their ears. Phocan looks the man up and down, checking the distribution. The legs are thin and hairy, turning smooth and waxy at the hips. He pictures the woman's thighs wrapped around these, which prompts him to remove from each the highest marker. Of the two he's just unpicked, he retains one but – final touch – sticks the other to the man's lower forehead, like a bindi on a Hindu bridegroom: Vedic third eye, intuition … He hands him a bathrobe – a kimono, still virginally plastic-wrapped, compliments of Tokyo's Chofu Creston in which he and Diamond stayed two weeks ago while there installing the space agency's HDI220s – which the man unfolds, shakes out and slips about him, holding in the sides the better to admire

48

embroidered storks and fountains. Phocan parts again the velvet curtain and they leave the cubicle – at the same time, it turns out, as Diamond and her charge emerge from theirs. The young woman sports a matching complimentary kimono, Diamond's; on catching sight of one another thus attired, man and woman simultaneously pinch a fold between their thumb and forefinger, holding the pattern and soft fabric up to view, a plumage-display, stork to stork, fountain to fountain, smiling. For a few seconds, the seven of them – man, woman, Diamond, Sennet, Phocan, Garnett and Perera – stand in meditative Shinto silence. It's Diamond who breaks it:

'I hope I've done the marker-distribution right,' she says to Phocan. 'I concentrated on frontal and antero-posterior axes.'

'Sounds good to me,' he tells her. Speaking, he's conscious of the silent Garnett's gaze on him. It's an approving one. He, in his turn, gazes at the couple, at these stand-ins called upon to underwrite a thousand marriages, a thousand renewed couplings. Diamond's had the same idea as him: the woman's forehead has a bindi-nipple on it too. For a fraction of a second, Phocan senses one more act of standing-in or substitution at work here; the presence, veiled, redacted, of a coupling unconsummated, of a bride uncaptured – too young, a child almost – exiting the frame. Sennet's briefing the students further:

'Once you take your bathrobes off,' he says, 'the cameras will detect the markers, and, through these, your exact positions. As long,' he adds, pointing at the floor's tape-demarcated central area, 'as you stay within the borders of this square – that is, inside the white lines. Of course, you've got the bed, but ...'

Perera picks the thread up: 'As discussed,' she tells them, 'we want to ascertain the stress occasioned by a wide range of positions.' Her diction, coupled with the Sri Lankan accent in which they're delivered, makes Phocan wonder whether these words are reproduced verbatim from her research brief or whether she always speaks with such lilting formality. 'To that end,' she carries on, 'we ask you to engage with one another in as many variable configurations as you are able. You can move about the bed, the bed's edge, floor or table …'

All eyes follow her prompts, jumping from each area to the next, before coming to rest atop the bedside table. Freesias? Sennet, clicking away at the screens' settings, running them through their own configurations, pauses to add:

'Obviously there's no duvet or top-sheet, since they'd block the reflectors and defeat the object. We've set room temperature to 23, so hopefully you'll feel quite comfortable. But if you need us, or need anything, just ring.' He points to a buzzer next to the doors.

'Nobody's following us live?' the woman asks in a variation on the question that the man posed to Phocan. 'From another room, I mean …'

'No,' Sennet answers. 'Only the sensors. You have total privacy.'

The woman nods slowly. Is she disappointed? Is she just taking in the information? Or is she trying to reconcile the two terms in her head? *Privacy, sensors:* odd coupling, bedfellowed together in a conjugation as strangely contrived as this whole set-up. The only term that really seems to find its fit, to have a place here, is *total* …

'Any more questions?' Phocan asks.

Woman and man shake heads.

'Well,' Phocan beams a broad smile at them, 'we'll leave you to your own …'

His voice trails off. He turns to Garnett, inviting his boss to sum things up before the session proper starts. But Garnett raises his hand once more, delegating commentary to his charges. It's Sennet, stepping back slowly from his monitors, who completes the sentence:

'Devices.'

5. Client A

An hour or so into the Old Street meeting, Dean finds herself experiencing an acute sense of déjà vu. It's not the vague type, trace levels of some half-remembered episode contaminating the admixture of the present, jarring it, for a brief moment, into a blurred double-vision of itself ... No, this is sharp, precise and instantly identifiable: what's inserted itself between this conference suite's long board table, leather swivel chairs, occupants thereof (on the one hand) and (on the other) her *apprehension* of these surfaces and personae is a photograph, a picture from a bundle she was served up on the second day of last week's stint in the LSE library.

The photo, taken some time in the 1950s, showed a managerial scenario: seven executive types – five men, two women – seated at three long tables set up in a U-shape round a hanging screen. On to the screen a film was being projected: it (in turn) showed a male worker, or perhaps experimental subject, sorting objects into a series of compartments, while beside him an imposing clock kept time. In their office, or laboratory, or cinema, the manager/scientist film-viewers seemed to be assessing the man's skill at this task, and hence (Dean surmised) his aptitude for such-and-such a post. She passed over the image at the time, angling for larger catches – didn't make a note of it or snap it with her phone; but now ... now it seems to hang about the room's corporate air, both spectral and enlarged, a frame and backdrop for today's whole gathering.

The set-up: a 'symposium'. Dorley and Grieves, law firm in which she, as junior associate, serves, is offering, for a consideration of one thousand pounds and change an hour, its services to Peacock, a consultancy. Despite this contractual relation and – to Dean – confusingly, Peacock are not D&G's client in this interaction; rather, they're acting as intermediary between the IP-specialists and their *actual* client, whom both parties, in all correspondence, documents and (now) verbal dialogue alike have followed the convention of referring to as *Client A*. Blind council: when a party's feeling shy, if you perform due diligence, check they're not gangsters, terrorists, what have you, it's all kosher, from a legal point of view at least. More than mere intermediaries, Peacock are *staging* the symposium, in the full dramaturgical sense. They laid down the rules of engagement some weeks ago: D&G's team have been instructed to present 'encomia' into which they, the Peacocks, are permitted, frequently and at will, to interject, interrogating their theses, premises, presuppositions and so on; the D&Gs, thus challenged, will elaborate, expand, extrapolate – and out of all this back-and-forth, like fragile truth wafting about the Agora at the end of a Socratic dialogue, to be breathed in and feasted on by all, will arise some peerless understanding of the current state of patent and copyright law; or at least of the parts of it falling within today's (disorientatingly vague) remit-parameters – namely, those of 'gesture'. It's being filmed, the whole exchange, recorded for eventual viewing by other consultants back at Peacock and, presumably, this Client A themselves, who'll trawl its contents for strategy prompts or market-recognition tools or whatever else it is they're after. Whence Dean's apprehension of this other, older scene, this object-sorting skit: in both scenarios, the players are simultaneously acting and not acting, doing what they're doing both because they're doing it for real *and* as a show, put on for post-hoc viewing by an audience that's lurking out of sight, beyond the frame ...

There are, needless to say, big differences too – not least the props: in this state-of-the-art conferencing room, it's on not a canvas pull-down but a 65-inch back-lit LED that the embedded scene is appearing. A video-clip, it shows a dancer in great bat-like silken wings twirling her arms, causing a web of floating ribbons to gyrate around her.

'Loie Fuller,' Dean's colleague Julius Leman, mid-encomium, is telling Peacock's delegation. 'Creator of the "Serpentine Dance" she's demonstrating here. She managed to patent the chemical compounds she used in her colour gels; and the salts that gave her cloths and stage sets their strange luminescence; but she never managed to patent the dance itself.'

'Why not?' Robert Elsaesser, Peacock's point-man, asks.

'The US Copyright Office,' explains Julius, 'denied her suit – in 1892, against an imitator, Minnie Bemis – on the grounds that her, Fuller's, performance, irrespective of its groundbreaking unique-ness, had no overarching structure, wasn't "about" anything ...'

In the short pause while notes are jotted down, the dancer continues to twirl and gyrate. The gif, a digitised transfer from celluloid, has jumps and flecks, birthmarks of the old medium; like the spinning silks, it loops back on itself, over and over.

'1892 ...' Elsaesser's teammate Roderick picks up the baton. 'Seems like a long way to track back.'

'Copyright's a long game, my friend,' Clive Dorley, QC, mur-murs across the table at him.

'Naturally,' Roderick concedes. 'But maybe we could focus more on where the legislation's going, not on where it's come from.'

A collective under-the breath chortle, indulgent and patronising at once, issues from D&G ranks. The Peacocks, looking slightly hurt, retreat into the kind of silence that demands an explanation.

'Law,' Dorley provides one, 'works on precedent.'

'It's Janus-faced.' Juliet McKraken, Senior Partner, backs him up. 'Looking backward to discern the future ...'

Roderick's objection overridden, Julius ploughs ahead by jump-ing back three centuries.

'This lady,' he announces as the screen gives over to a pale figure swathed in ermine and red velvet – static this time, jpeg of an oil painting – 'is Queen Anne. Her 1710 decree, modestly titled "The Statute of Anne", is technically to do with publishing, in that it endorses an author's rights over and above those of the printer who puts out their book. But what it *really* does is set out a whole raft of statements and provisions tying landed property to immaterial thought, paternity to "personality", private work to public interest ...'

Dean, listening, fidgets with her own speaking notes, which seem trivial and unworked-through by comparison. She draws an arrow in their margin with her pencil for no other reason than to make the others think she's annotating, fine-tuning some insight ...

'... via the legal deposit scheme.' Julius is still in flow. 'Very of its time. Part and parcel of the era of enlightenment and revolution. Seven decades later, the framers of the US Constitution more or less copy and paste the statute: Article 1, Section 8 – the "Copyright Clause" – applies at first to books and maps and charts; then printed music gets tagged on in 1831; then dramatic works in 1856 ... photographs 1865 ... movies 1912 ... sound recordings 1972 (this one surprises people: you'd have thought sound would have come much sooner). Then – and here, perhaps, is what most concerns us – in 1976 a new Copyright Act extends protectable status to choreographic works and pantomimes.'

'And that's the latest upgrade?' asks Elsaesser. 'That's where we're at now?'

The D&G crew once more let loose a volley of indulgent-patronising chortles. Dorley quips: 'If things were that simple we'd all be out of work.'

A pause, while Peacock's delegation wait for the missing information to be supplied. Julius lets it run on for a few seconds, for effect, before taking up again:

'This is what happens: after that last Act is passed, you start getting instances of litigation that, in turn, set precedent. So in 1977, the producers of a Broadway musical successfully sue a Hollywood studio when a dance is reproduced without permission in a film. But over the following years, several other suits fall flat. People find that when they try to copyright individual moves or "steps", it doesn't work.'

'Why not?' Elsaesser asks.

'A step,' Julius answers, 'is an isolated unit, not a sequence. Think back to Queen Anne's authors: they could copyright a book, but not a word. So a composer, now, can copyright a symphony, but not a note; a painter a painting, but not a brushstroke. It's the same with movement. The devil's in the detail, though: thousands of hours of court-time have been spent arguing about the exact point at which a unit *turns* into a sequence. It's still up for grabs. And then, it gets more complex, on two fronts.'

He takes a sip of water. He's got the floor, and wants to hold it for a while.

'Firstly,' he resumes, wiping his lips, 'there'd already been successful acts of registering and litigation *prior* to 1976, the year choreographic copyright takes hold. Hanya Holm, a German émigré, managed to register her choreography for *Kiss Me Kate* in 1952. But that was thanks to having documented it in Labanotation – Rudolf Laban's system for codifying dance moves, for recording them in scores: it was covered by the older law protecting written manuscripts. By the same token Johnny Hudgins, an African American, won compensation three decades earlier for blackface tributes to him performed here in London, on the grounds that they were drawn from a "dramatic composition". That was an outlier, though.'

'How so?' asks Elsaesser.

'This,' Julius informs him, 'was back in the 1920s – an important period, given the rise in stock of African-diaspora culture: Harlem Renaissance and all that ... It brought two separate world views into conflict. The folks sharing moves in uptown New York ballrooms hadn't inherited the same proprietorial notions as their European-descended counterparts. They'd *come* from chattel, after all, not held it. So they turn up at the Savoy and the Apollo on Saturday nights, tap and swing around together, unpacking and tweaking one another's steps, and – *hey presto!* – the Lindy and the Charleston are born. But no one owns them. Then a downtown Broadway maestro gets inquisitive, or brave, and ventures north of 120th Street; and his eyes jump from their sockets; and before you know it all the sequences have been incorporated in some musical – whose producers copyright it. This pattern will continue in the entertainment world for decades: think of rock 'n' roll, or hip-hop. Crudely put: white people nicking stuff from black people pretty much describes the history of popular music.'

A reflective, or perhaps embarrassed, silence follows. There are no black people in this room. Elsaesser moves things on by asking:

'What's the second front?'

'The second front,' says Julius, 'hinges round a single word: *derivative.*'

'*Derivative*,' repeats Elsaesser.

'*Derivative*,' confirms Julius. 'Copyright grants to its owner a bundle of entitlements: to display, perform, distribute and reproduce a work, and to create' – he raises his fingers in inverted commas – '"works derivative of the original". What does "derivative" mean?'

He pauses again. Was that a question? The Peacocks look at one another awkwardly before Elsaesser, spreading his palms, hands the unsolved riddle back to D&G.

'Everything's derivative of something else,' says Julius. 'Nothing comes from nowhere. Copyright disputes, in the choreographic field, have traditionally been argued on a genealogical basis, rather like paternity suits: if Work A can be demonstrated to have been the "father" or "grandfather" of Works B, C or D ...'

On the long table, water glasses stand untouched, bubbles in them fewer, slower, smaller than before – third-generation stragglers, great-grandchildren of some lost spring. From ermine and velvet, Queen Anne looks on palely. It takes a few seconds for Elsaesser to frame the obvious question:

'And how is that demonstrated?'

'By having the best lawyers.' Dorley's older, wiser voice floats up from his chair's recesses.

There's a round of laughter, which, since Dorley doesn't join it, soon dies out. He wasn't joking.

'Show them the K-pop case,' McKraken instructs Julius.

Obediently, Julius calls up a file that's lying minimised on his docking station. On the LED, Anne crumples out of view, a genie returned to her flask, to be replaced by a troupe of contemporary, floppy-haired Asian boys advancing in syncopated steps across a lunar landscape, chasing an elusive alien girl. These in turn are sucked away to docked oblivion as Julius pops another file and the scene changes – or, in fact, doesn't: here, in grainier texture, is a striped and blanche-faced *mimique* performing, in similarly extraterrestrial environs, more or less identical movements.

'D&G took on this case ourselves, three years ago, and won,' Julius overdubs. 'We acted for the estate of Jean-Louis Barrault, the French mime artist this band were ripping off. That they're doing this is obvious. Self-evident. But in *law*, that's nothing; it has no significance. What allowed Barrault's descendants to prevail, despite the migration in medium, vaudeville to video-streaming, and the quite considerable time-lag, over fifty years ... What swung it for them was the fact that Barrault, prior to his death, had – unusually – bought back all rights to his own work from the various producers who'd contracted him over the course of his career. If not, proprietorship would have been corporate rather than individual – and, to further muddy the waters, dispersed; it would be a matter of tracking down whichever outfits had acquired or inherited the holdings of whatever other outfits held them prior to that.'

During the last few moments, the Peacock gang have, in some kind of Pavlovian reaction to the content of his spiel, been sitting up straighter, straining forwards, eyes lit up with new levels of attentiveness. Are they actually breathing faster? It seems so to Dean, although it could just be the overheated ventilators on their laptops, or an uptick in the suite's AC ...

'This,' says Elsaesser, voice charged with more directed purpose, 'is intriguing – in point of view of where Client A's interests lie.'

'Can you be more precise?' McKraken asks.

Elsaesser, weighing his words, answers:

'In corporate, rather than individual, ownership ...'

'... of movement, yes,' says McKraken. 'So we've understood – which is why we've asked Julius to paint the spectrum for you ...'

'A task he's doing admirably,' Roderick jumps in again here. 'But I wonder: why are we hovering around dance and music? I mean ... entertainment's certainly part of the picture; but it's not the *focal* point. Client A, as we've outlined, is more interested in these questions as they pertain to what we used to call "the industrial arena".'

Dean, sensing that she's going to be called on soon, tenses up.

'The law,' Dorley's benevolently chiding voice weighs in once more, 'works not just by precedent, but by analogy as well.' The Peacocks look confused, so he continues: 'Choreography may seem like a niche subject; but it's the paradigm for all fields in which flesh and bones, bodies in motion, meet with the legal codifications that both support and constrain them; as such, choreographic legislation should be seen as the umbrella for *all* argument involving movement. Which, if I understand correctly, is precisely Client A's concern.'

The Peacock team, quieted once more, sit back. Dean scrutinises them. Besides Elsaesser and Roderick, there are two others: a young woman about her age and a man in his mid-thirties who's been taking notes continuously; plus the three camera people, two male and one female, filming the proceedings – one front-on, one from each side. They're all got up in smart-casual attire: slim chinos, open shirts or jumpers topped by blazers for the men, jackets over patterned dress or jeans for the women. She's checked Peacock's website: they have lavish premises in Hammersmith – brainstorming studios, hospitality suites, summiting pods ... D&G's own offices in Goodge Street have two large rooms set aside for just this type of pow-wow. Why have they been Ubered out here, to this new-build Old Street flexi-hub with spaces hireable by month, or day, or hour? Despite the first-name informality, the free-flow format, the light, glassy airiness bathed in aroma of fair trade, she senses that this meeting has been crafted, from top down, not only to ensure that things are rigidly hermetic, but, beyond that,

58

to confer upon itself, its own occurrence, a degree of anonymity, or – is it too much to think this? – of *deniability* . . .

McKraken says: 'The principal difference between the worlds of dance and the more commercial applications that form Client A's zone of enquiry is that, in the latter realm, it's usually *technology* that's patented; not human movements.'

'Well, yes. Let's . . .' Roderick flips through his notes and, finding what he wants, strikes out on a fresh tack with newfound confidence: 'Let's take the scenario – the everyday one – whereby a person swipes a smartphone or a tablet. Right?'

McKraken nod-shrugs acquiescence.

'Could we not,' Roderick asks, 'see that person *themselves* as the tool that opens up the file or application? The sweep of the hand or fingers, their particular configuration, could be thought of – in principle at least . . .'

'As proprietorial?' McKraken asks.

'Why not? The action's been devised by the device's engineers, designers, programmers . . . In effect, it's the true "content" of their work: the soft- and hardware are just trappings – props, or prompts. So although *you* perform the action, it's *their* creation – the designers'; just as a given dance sequence is its choreographer's. And yet, as we all know, a hand-motion or a gesture – even ones instantly identifiable as associated with a certain product or personality – isn't afforded the same, or any, level of protection. Not yet . . .'

'It's a non-starter,' Dorley cuts him off. 'That line of thinking has reared its head from time to time over the last few years, and promptly had its bottom smacked and got sent to bed early. Heavy-metal singers trying to register their devil-horn signs, stuff like that . . . Those cases always fall at the first hurdle: frivolous, dismissed.'

'Those ones, yes,' Elsaesser concurs. 'But at the more sophisticated – the more *technological* – end of the spectrum . . .'

'Gesture-based interaction in HCI systems,' Roderick starts reeling off a list he's been holding back, powder-dry, until now.

'Hand-topology and skeletal-data descriptors, encoded via Fisher kernels and multi-level temporal pyramids ... Linear SVM classifiers applied to feature-vectors, computed over presegmented gestures to pluck recognition moments from continuous streams ... We're thinking of the type of work that companies like Bewegung and Kinect and Pantarey are doing.'

'We've advised Pantarey,' McKraken interjects.

'We know you have,' replies Elsaesser.

The dynamic's shifting – Dean can sense that. Now it's the D&G team who find themselves quieted by the Peacocks' knowledge of the field, wrong-footed by their having kept it under wraps until this point, as though playing dumb had been a strategy to draw out their interrogees. She recalls vaguely the Pantarey contract, for which she prepared some of the secondary paperwork: it involved pre-emptive registration of a gizmo, some kind of high-speed, light-projecting camera. Are Client A a company like that? It seems unlikely: the length and expense to which they've gone in orchestrating this whole formalised exchange would place them further up whatever chain D&G find themselves part of here – a larger operator, tweaking cords from a far higher stratum, an atmosphere more rarefied ...

It's Elsaesser who lets the silence run on this time, then decides when and how to end it.

'In all kinds of fields,' he says, 'gaming to manufacturing to warfare, gestural operation's taking over from the joystick model that in turn replaced the hands-on one. What Client A is interested in interrogating – interested in *speculating* on, let's say – is how this, over time, might impact our legal understanding of specific hum-tech interfaces. Not the *gestures*, but the *interfaces*; the configurations.'

'If we move,' Roderick again, 'beyond the old dichotomy of man/machine, of operator/tool, and begin to view the whole thing instead as a ... as a kind of *constellation* ... held in formation by a force-of-gravity specific to its own context: a specific task, a particular design-moment, a uniquely-codified relation ...'

He lets the thought hang in the air, held in formation by the force of its own logic. On the 65-inch, Barrault's still alien-chasing on the moon, eyes round and bulging from the combined effects of atmosphere, lust and intoxication. McKraken, trying to wrest control of the proceedings back to D&G, turns towards Dean and says:

'This might be a good moment ...'

This is it. Julius is vacating his chair, yielding both floor and laptop to her. The slides are in there, uploaded already; still, there's a false start while she toggles between thumbnails, reddening ... Then it's up on the widescreen: the first of the ancient photographs she's copied, cropped, enlarged – though not enough, she's sure, to make them anything other than small, flimsy offerings at this high table ...

It shows a woman sitting next to a vast vat of chocolate. The woman herself, her form, is imprecise: her shoulders and arms have doubled, tripled, run into a blur of motion-shimmy, while her face has been erased almost completely, leaving discernable just the outline of a nose and sunken eye socket. Beside the vat, there's a tray; on the tray sit thirteen little coils of chocolate – a baker's dozen, bite-size dollops neatly laid out in two rows. Unlike the blurred human figure, objects – vat, tray, dollops – have remained in perfect focus; you can even see the craters and escarpments in the huge, half-set mass of unscooped chocolate, the declivities and trenches carved into its mudflat as it's quarried. Running between vat and tray – slicing between them in both directions, just at the point at which the woman's arm blurs most – is a streak of light so sharp that it looks solid: a continuous line, a track swerving and jagging as it races back round to rejoin itself and form a circuit.

'A Cadbury's worker,' Dean tells the assembled company. 'From the Gilbreth collection. This one,' she continues, clicking to the next slide, 'is a spanner driller.'

'What collection?' asks Elsaesser. 'What is this exactly?'

On the screen, a ghost-figure, the wispy remnant of an over-alled man, hangs between a crate of spanners and a fixed drill head. While the worker's no more than a pall, both machine and spanner-crate have kept their form; hurtling electrically between these last two, where the ghost's transparent fuzz of arm ends in a smoke-puff hand, there is – once more – a light track: multiple tracks this time, pursuing roughly but not exactly the same course, each one as bold and vibrant as a neon tube.

'Gilbreth,' says Dean. 'Lillian Gilbreth. She worked first with her husband Frank and then alone, from the teens right through to the nineteen sixties, rationalising workplaces: shop floors, assembly lines, eventually whole industries. Back in their day, the Gilbreths were minor celebrities; there was even a film made about them, their family life. Now they've lapsed into obscurity, but …'

'What are those light tracks?' Roderick asks.

'They're called cyclegraphs,' Dean tells him. 'She – Gilbreth – developed the technique of attaching a light-ring to the finger of a seamstress or machinist, and allowing this, through long-exposure photographs, to trace the shape their hand made as they went about their task.'

'Why's this one broken?' asks Elsaesser as, in the next picture, an ectoplasmic haze of laundry woman floats above two stacks (one crumpled and one tidily arranged) of handkerchiefs. This time, the tracks of light running, just off the midriff of her dwindling body, to and fro between the sharply defined linen piles are formed of Morse-like dots and dashes.

'Gilbreth,' explains Dean, 'has used an interrupter here to have the light blink on and off – quickly, ten times per second. That way, the long exposure will reveal not just the path the woman's hand makes, but also how long it takes to make it. That's the point, the object of the exercise. Manual labour is repetitive; a hand-kerchief folder, or lathe operator, or what have you, will perform the same action again and again, thousands of times a day. With her cyclegraphs, Gilbreth could demonstrate that each "doing", every iteration of the action, involves the worker's hand travelling (for example) three feet and two inches, and takes 4.1 seconds. More importantly, it allowed her to work out that, if the worker's employers were to lower the workbench by an inch and a half, and move it a little closer to, or further away from, the machine, or tools, or product, then they could bring that action's cycle down to two feet and eleven inches, and 3.6 seconds. Multiply that saving by however many thousand for each worker's day; then by three hundred for their year; and then that figure by the company's roster ...'

'But ...' Roderick's not convinced. 'A photograph is flat. How can it measure *distance*? You'd need depth.'

Dean has the answer to this quibble at her fingertips, one of which brings up the next slide.

'Stereoscope,' she comments – unnecessarily: the picture is a diptych, showing an index card-stamper's action (an arced light track, like the outline of a trout or salmon leaping up a stream) from two sides, front and profile. 'But,' she presses on, 'Gilbreth went further: once you have what she called a "stereocyclegraph", then you can make a three-dimensional model of the action. Look ...'

Now there are four boxes on the screen: cut-away boxes, black, whose three sides (always the floor and two right-angled walls) are wallpapered with white graph squares. Mounted inside each box is a careening light track; this time, though, these tracks appear solid not just through a trick of shutter-time, but because this is what they are – genuinely solid, shaped from moulded frames of metal fixed in place with little hooks which, if you squint, you can just see. In one of the four tracks, the bright metal circuit has dark stripes painted at half-inch intervals around it to recreate the interrupted blink-effect seen in the last-but-one image.

'By producing physical iterations,' Dean says, 'Gilbreth could help workers learn the best way to perform their action – by running their hands along the moulds cast from their most efficient colleagues, for example ... She could also tweak the casts, the wireframes, themselves, to improve the modelled action further – often in collaboration with the workers, with an eye to their own comfort. It's no good having a more efficient hand-path if it makes the woman's back give out after three years. More enlightened companies like Cadbury's, a Quaker family business, understood this. Plus, if the woman's back lasts ten years rather than three, then she's more profitable, too: you don't need to keep training up replacements.'

She clicks through two more photos of assorted wireframes in their boxes. Their shapes morph through a large range: some are suggestive of a roller-coaster track, others of cowboy hats with rims and peaks, others of trunked or long-necked creatures – elephants, giraffes – or antennaed insects, or snakes uncoiling, frozen in mid strike ... At the base of every picture there's a string of numbers and letters, squiggles that look like miniature sketches of the outline beneath which they're scrawled.

'How big are these boxes?' asks Elsaesser.

'Like shoeboxes, I guess,' she answers. 'The action's modelled at scale, one-to-one.'

'And how many of them are there?'

'I don't know. She kept on producing them for decades. But lots of them were discarded after they'd served their purposes. From what I could make out from the records I saw, it looks like the Smithsonian have gathered up a few. MIT, too. But the main Gilbreth Archive's held at Purdue, where she ...'

'With who?'

'The University of Purdue, Indiana. They helped facilitate her research, after 1940 at least ...'

Dean's finger hovers on the mousepad, itching to click on to the next picture. But there's no next picture; that's her lot. She's played her hand, got nothing else. She reddens again, unsure of what to do with the display, control of which she's now relinquishing; then decides to revert to Julius's last slide, the gif of the moonstruck Barrault. No one in the room says anything; the Peacock people don't even seem to be taking notes. Dean senses that her presentation's been a flop; she's about to excuse herself, to slink off to the toilet, when Roderick asks:

'Would you say ... ?' He pauses, then reformulates the question: 'Would you see these models as a kind of "first citation"?'

'Legally?' she asks.

Roderick nods.

'I suppose that would have to be argued, like the K-pop case – although it's not the same. I mean ...'

'Maybe,' Elsaesser adds, 'they could be viewed as an alternative form of Labanotation – sculptural rather than written. They *record* a sequence.'

'Yes,' says Dean. 'But ...'

She finds herself too flustered to pay much attention to the rest of her faltering answer, which in any case is drowned out by other conversations striking up around the room, a mishmash of exchanges, crescendoing, separating out and coming back together.

'... that with music,' Julius is saying, 'it's more codified: since the Dubset Agreement, streaming's become standardised, IP-wise. You've got your MixSCAN algos scanning traffic, distributing royalties and so on ... But *movement*, of the type Client A's interested in ... We're still in Wild West times in terms of any generalised ...'

'... when legislation's going to come,' Elsaesser's reasoning. 'It has to: might be two, five or ten years downstream, but ...'

'The notion,' Dorley's still in pooh-poohing mode, 'that one could apply the same criteria universally to movement as to music-downloads is quite fanciful. How would you ... ?'

'Sure: but the *constellation*,' Roderick trots out his buzzwords again, 'the *moment*, the designed *relation* ... Now, with motion-capture heading markerless, and viewing capability pretty much everywhere – why can't the algos scan that too, in all types of ...'

'... in on the ground floor,' Elsaesser's impressing upon McKraken. 'Future patenting, or maybe retrospective acquisition ...'

For the remaining minutes of the meeting, Dean finds herself picturing, once more, the spools she saw a week ago: the circled layers, stacked like orders or committees, each layer overseeing the one below, reporting to the one above, but unable to see the one above that, or the next ... The image stays with her on the ride back to Goodge Street, and all afternoon – and resurrects itself the following week, when Dorley summons her into his office.

'It seems,' he tells her, 'that your little wireframes struck a chord.'

'With whom?' she asks.

'With Peacock,' he says. 'Client A. Whomever. They want more.'

'More what?'

'More,' Dorley repeats. 'I'd like you to explore that avenue a little further. I thought you could take up where you left off.'

'Explore ...' she starts, then falters. 'What exactly should I do?'

'I think,' says Dorley, 'you should get yourself a plane ticket to Indiana.'

6. Stagings

They sit in rows, all facing the same way. Light – fluid, synthetic, over-spilling from the screen in front of each – coagulates in spectacle-lens glass before draining away over skin that, no matter what ethnicity box (optional) its owner might have ticked on Degree Zero's application form, in this room is recast in grey. All of them wear headphones, thick and padded as the walls of sanatoria. Some have sandwich packages open in front of them, others rice-noodle concoctions composted in plastic tubs; every desk sports, standing sentinel beside its glide-pad, a lone porta-bottle with an inbuilt perma-straw extruding from its lid. In many ways, it's a generic office scene – with one divergence.

It took Phocan a while to put his finger on it last time he came here to Berners Street as well; but passing through this outer room packed full of low-grade modellers, concentrated airlock between public-facing, poster- and award-draped lobby and the Art Dept's inner sanctum, just before reaching the keypad-operated door to whose code sequence this room's denizens aren't privy, he recalls Eldridge mentioning it to him on that other visit too, at the same exact spot he's twigging on right now: none of them have phones. Not charging on the desk, nor peeping from pockets, nor even sprouting cables from the recesses of shirts and jackets: they're *verboten*. Slip one out, or even have its ring crow from your handbag to betray you, and you're gone – no grace, no first-time pass, just your P45. These guys don't even have an internet connection: beyond DZ's intranet, or more precisely narrow avenues of this (the CAD, Maya and Autodesk files to which they've been given individual clearance), their isolation is complete. It's non-stop lockdown in here, one that's met not with the racket of tin mugs rattling on bars and catcalls ricocheting down corridors, but instead with quiet mouse-clicks, *insert components, line, repeat line, circle, pan, zoom, centre, undo, save*, as edges are laid down and rotated, surfaces rolled out, objects created, their mosaic patches willing themselves into definition, landscapes unwrapped – and, simultaneously, rewrapped, cooped within strict geometric confines, parameters and ratios recalculated with every mutation, several times a second: a collective, restless and resigned sketching, in variously transposed or extrapolated versions, of cell walls.

'They've all done vocational degrees,' Eldridge tells him this time, barely bothering to lower his voice as his tapping fingers tease open the inner door. 'For them, coordinate space began in 1982, with *Tron* – a decade before they were born. Try talking to them about soil mechanics, dead loads or cadastral surveys, and they'll go completely blank. This stuff,' he thumb-jerks back dismissively, 'is all they know.'

Memories, shared, follow him and Phocan as they step over the threshold: Imperial College's banked lecture halls, Fluids 21, Bernoulli and Boundary Layer equations, Hyde Park railing-hopping, drunk 2 a.m. dips in the Serpentine, a roast chicken carcass left out on the table of their digs' kitchen for so long that a new carapace grew right across its quadripartite rib-vaults ... They remain unvoiced, though, Eldridge contenting himself with quipping:

'Fuckin' kids.'

They laugh – but there's a double edge, an unease, to their laughter. Is the coders' youth the actual gag? Or is it the fact that this group's baby-facedness allows these two men in their prime to cast themselves as old that furnishes the punchline? They *are* old: in this world, forty's ancient; not having a command of Blender, Topsolid or Tekler wired into your neural system places you in not simply a previous generation but, beyond that, an entire evolutionary category that new mutations have consigned to oblivion.

Isn't *that* the real joke? Phocan's ilk thinking they're midwifing the future into being, when all the time they're navigating their own obsolescence? Eldridge, despite the bohemian tendencies he harboured even fifteen years ago, now realised or at least half-realised in 'creative-industry' employment, has always had a sharpness Phocan felt he himself lacked: call it self-awareness, insight ... Perhaps his irony today's a roar against extinction – fading now, dying off too as they enter the inner room.

This space, although no larger than the outer, equally devoid of natural light, seems instantly more airy, spacious and just generally patrician, a field marshal's CIC. To its walls are pin-tacked scores of photographs and diagrams of spaceships and space stations, both real and fictitious: docking bays and sleeping quarters, exercise pods, gyrodynes and probes. Beneath these, lying on the floor, hand-drawn sketches sample and remix the elements and features of their vertically arrayed source images: a solar panel here, an observation window there, the axels of a centrifuge set one way, rubbed out, relaid along another axis ... On a large table in the centre of the room, just where a papier-mâché landscape of the battle terrain would be if this really were a military HQ, there sits a scale (1:72) model of the Kern Federal Starship *Sidereal*. It's incomplete – partly because still under construction, partly because Herzberg, *Incarnation*'s art director, is using the old cut-away effect, the better to facilitate understanding and corroboration between all involved parties: graphic designer, construction coordinator, set dresser, screenwriter, prop builder, costume designer, VFX supervisor, CG director (Eldridge), cinematographer, first, second and third assistant directors and, end of the line, apex of this particular food chain, director (Lukas Dressel). Right now, a core triumvirate of the above (first, second and fourth listed) are conferring round the carved and whittled styrofoam ship, soliciting, or fending off, a set of interjections from their Special Technical Adviser Ben Briar.

'Which bit's the CC?' Briar's asking.

'CC?' repeats Herzberg.

'Crew compartment. Where they live.'

'We kind of thought they'd live all over,' Herzberg tells him. 'The stokers, Tszvetan's crew, his homies, his lieutenant smugglers, can be quartered below deck, under these giant propellant tanks. The Princess gets the guest suite, which is adjunct to the *Sidereal*'s main body. We've made it that way to accentuate her purdahed status. Tszvetan himself we'll see mostly pottering about the navigation deck. That's where we need shoe leather from you.'

'Shoe leather?' now it's Briar's turn to be stumped.

'Stuff to do while he's speaking his lines. Buttons to press, levers to pull ... that kind of thing.'

'There haven't been "levers" on spaceships since the 1967 Soyuz,' Briar coldly informs him.

'Well, whatever,' Herzberg counters. 'Touchpads, vocal interfaces ...'

'Tszvetan's a pilot,' Berul, *Incarnation*'s screenwriter, pipes up here. 'A navigator, captain, helmsman. He steers his way. It's important to frame him like this: at the bridge, in command of his direction, of his fate – until the thanadrine episode, at least, when he'll veer wildly off course ...'

Federal Starship Commander Tszvetan is what, in the industry, they like to call an *archetype*. His bloodlines run far back: through Han Solo to Rick Blaine to Drake, Raleigh and such licensed privateers. Throw a little pinch of Pete 'Maverick' Mitchell and Huck Finn into the mix and you've more or less got Tszvetan's character pool: rebellious, independent and, by virtue of these traits, through choice rather than duty, fiercely loyal. His rich back-story, worked up through weeks of research conducted first in parallel and then amalgamated in a Dorset hotel to which the whole scriptwriting team had, like a jury, been sequestered, involves loss of parents, kidnapping, being set adrift in a small space-pirogue that washed up or rather (pace *Superman*) crash-landed on a 'random' planet, Kern, upon whose populace the strapping if barely bridled colt, reaching maturity, made such a strong impression (winning the Tagel Races three years in a row, notching up endless kills of enemy pilots during the Third Saraõnic War, etc., etc.) that Kern's ruler, Louis Q, conferred upon him the effective status of a nephew – ironically, since unbeknown to both, they are *in fact* related, by occluded blood. As ranking federal officer and decorated ace, and royal ward to boot, Tszvetan has been granted quite a bit of leeway to conduct his own free galaxy-wide enterprise – enterprise that, in a star system as wild as this one, borders at times on rampant criminality; although it's also vital, given the tangledness of inter-federal treaties and alliances, to be attuned to the nuance of any given situation, each chance deep-space encounter, and to tailor one's behaviour accordingly. Nor should this buccaneering interfere too much with his official duties – which, of course, it doesn't: wise Louis Q understands, like the Felipes and Elisabeths of yore, that these activities go hand in hand, each acting as a spur and tonic to the other.

At *Incarnation*'s outset, we find Tszvetan guiding the *Sidereal* into Doon Leer, giant harbour of the planet Argeral, erstwhile foe of his adoptive Kern but now, post-Landis Détente, its trading partner and uneasy 'ally'. Due to various subplots put in solely for the sake of complicating things – i.e. of signalling complexity – the *Sidereal* has been posing, through its three-moon-cycle voyage over from Kern, as a scientific mission sent out to observe various celestial transits; but, once clocked and hailed by Doon Leer Port Authority, it casts aside this cover, announcing itself as a vessel full of smuggler-traders – which is true, but not the whole truth. In reality, Tszvetan has been sent as Louis Q's own proxy, under orders to advance the latter's suit of tendering to Argeral's Crown Princess Tild an offer of betrothal.

'You're losing me,' says Phocan as Eldridge recaps the plot for him. 'Tendering proxy what suits?'

'He's delivering a question-popper – a marry-me-baby: Louis Q wants the heiress-apparent as a trophy bride who'll cement the *pax romana* between his kingdom and hers, Kern and Argeral. *That's* why Tzsvetan's pitching up now in Doon Leer ...'

It's over at a second table, in the corner of this room, by an elite detail of Eldridge's own lieutenants, his most trusted modellers, that Doon Leer is being designed. These modellers, too, are stealing freely from the pictures pinned up to the wall; but they're transcribing straight to screen without the intermediary of paper. Their overriding brief is simple: Go Big. Dressel wants the film's depiction of Argeral's port to be iconic; to not only serve as source, reference and gauge-stick for all future sci-fi *auteurs*, but to loom in the imagination of a whole civilian generation too, haunting their dreams and colouring their experience of a hundred real-world spatial interfaces – their era's *Strangelove* War Room. Argeral's the big boy in the B-Roth star system: the actual seat of military power (although, like several other former vassal planets, Kern, due in no small part to Tszvetan's prior heroics, has managed to inflict local defeats on the imperial fleet, thus carving out small pockets of resistance) and the *de facto* economic hub. Everything passes through Argeral; no matter from what dark provincial back reach of what sub-planetary shithole they've been mined, traded or plundered, through the zones of which provisional or regional authorities they've passed in contraband form, it's upon arrival here that material, goods, services, etc., become converted into credit – in *Incarnation*'s lingo (the writers have compiled a phrasebook), 'charged'. And Doon Leer, being the administrative, military and fiscal portal through which each and every vessel, soul and item entering or leaving Argeral must be processed, is the feature of the planet that first greets voyagers as they press their eyes to viewfinders and windows: glowing, throbbing, tractor-beaming their small ship, whatever orders they might relay to its puny motors, down towards it. Dressel wants this whole economico-galactico event field, this politico-spatial set-up, translated into establishing-shot tableau, into a wide-lens ballet of tugs, giant cargo freighters, tiny pilot drones gliding up and down beams cast out by port traffic-control towers, avenues and corridors of light and movement all converging on this greatest of all harbours; to render perspectivally the city's power and majesty, vectorially the fascination its approach occasions: all lines lead to Doon Leer.

Accordingly, the Art Dept boys and girls have pilfered their way through Canaletto, Cole and Turner, not to mention Berkey, Paul and Hoesli: a gondola-sprinkled grand canal here, a network of citadels and lookout posts joined by ribbed generators there, funnel-clouds swirling at their edges, all projected in one-point. For their main template, they've lifted the bare bones of the vista that greets Dorothy and her friends as they skip down the yellow brick road to the Emerald City: Doon Leer, in the preliminary sketches, rises crystalline from grey-zone conurbations that proliferate about it, from the outlying agro- and industrial sectors feeding into and off it, buffer zones between its glory and the unkempt wood and desert lands that stretch for miles around Argeral's surface before giving over, past the planet's rim, to the abyss of outer space. The city's composed (at this distance, at least) of squares, or rather rhomboids, stacked atop each other like innumerable slanted bricks – slanted, and electrified too, since they glow. All of which gives the metropolis the look of somewhere in a perpetual state of assembly, a throbbing compact of great crystalline slabs, an expanding vert and azure chessboard.

This is easy for the modellers to render, since squares and rhomboids are their building blocks too. What's not so simple is the port's multitude of aerial ingress and egress routes: make them too straight and the whole vision will look rigid and anachronistic; too wavering and the core vanishing-point optics will get lost.

'We were picturing,' Eldridge is telling Phocan now, 'the way bees come and go from hives. There'll be infinite variations in the routes, but overall, since they all eventually pass through the same tiny hole ...'

'It's funny you should think of bees,' says Phocan. 'Just last week we were working with the Institute of Zoology, tracking exactly that. I got stung twice.' He folds his left sleeve back to show two swollen patches on his forearm. 'We decided in the end,' he continues, buttoning up again, 'that you can devise algorithms just as good from PIV.'

'PIV?'

Phocan holds a pinched thumb and finger to narrowly opened lips; for an instant Eldridge thinks he's miming toking on a joint, as was their wont back in South Ken – before, realising that Phocan's *blowing*, not drawing, he deciphers the charade:

'Ah – bubbles. You mentioned that – also in relation to helping model the final sequence, when the ship begins to … with the wind … Holland, right? Sledges …'

'Bobsleighs,' Phocan corrects him. 'Next week. I can sound them out about staging a break-up, get quotes, and so on.'

'I mean, we've got a basic model with the Berlin water people, as you know, but …'

'Sure. And with the bubbles: I'll be watching them through tug-, freighter- and drone-tinted lenses. If anything good comes up …'

He tips Eldridge a wink, to let him know their shared past buys him certain privileges, sneak peeks at material that, strictly speaking, should remain, like the *Sidereal*'s royal passenger, partitioned off, restricted. Eldridge nods gratitude, and moves them onwards past the next block of collaged source-pictures. Dressel and Herzberg, as one would expect, want the establishing shot's wide-frame to evolve into a slow zoom into the metropolis itself, mirroring Tszvetan's POV as the *Sidereal* is guided down to its assigned docking station. Then a ground-level pan across large swathes of processing bays, weighing houses, custom-filter basins … This horizontal realm is the domain of Doon Leer's chargers – 'chargers' being the name for the army of navvies and low-ranking port officials who load, unload, tariff-rate and zap ('charge') the contents of each vessel's manifest (and of course, anything else they might find stashed behind the floor- and ceiling-panels) with Argeral's own special brand of radium-tinged sub- or supra-electricity. In Argeral, energy is the unit of measure: goods, services, credit – all just names for, varying modes of, charge. Charge may now be galaxy-wide standard, exchangeable and leverageable all over; but only in Argeral can it be conferred upon an entity and thereby (as it were) 'minted', a transformation that's effected by its formal passage through Doon Leer – which passage's

74

most basic, sweaty, greasy nut-and-bolt work is conducted by the aforementioned dockworkers. These chargers are a race unto themselves – several races, several species: they're made up of itinerant labourers from all corners of the B-Roth system. Swarthy Arwaks, pointy-headed Tallians, three-handed Girodeans and such like: nomadic populations who've migrated here but never really settled; who sleep in Doon Leer's inns and brothels, or on mattresses in dosshouses, or in makeshift lean-tos purposed from discarded cargo shells. They work under the protection of their charismatic foreman Ourman, in whom Tszvetan will recognise a kindred spirit (a sequel, already in the pipeline, is to follow the heroic-but-conflicted Ourman as he conveys, amidst the chaos of a bloody uprising or coup, the entire charge-reserves of Argeral to safety). Although (not only in the obvious phylogenetic sense but also in a civil-legal one) aliens, these chargers are typical of Doon Leer's general population, which is also largely made up of outsiders – migrant traders, brokers, diplomats, spies, slaves, charge-drawn here from all over.

'That's the thing with great imperial capitals,' Berul, whose team have case-studied a trans-historical selection of these, is impressing just now on Briar, Herzberg and whoever else will listen. 'Empire, whether Roman, Inca or American, is always about movement, you see. If a place gives off a "rooted" vibe, if its inhabitants all look or talk the same ... well, then you're signalling to your audience its parochial, small-planet character. But if you want to convey real heart-of-the-beast centrality, engine-room levels of power – then you have to show a restless scrum of wildly different bodies: haggling, hustling, darting and colliding their way across every urban surface.' His hands haggle and dart about the air in illustration, before hovering beside his ears. 'And you have to lay down a soundtrack brimming with a cacophony of languages ...'

Berul, Dressler, Herzberg, granted the power to generate a universe, are gods. The rules governing all *Incarnation*'s actions and events, from most momentous plot reversal to least consequential background filler, are compiled in a big, fat tome entitled, quasi-biblically, *The Book of Incarnation*. The designers and coor-dinators are their priesthood; the modellers, their clergy. Briar's a kind of one-man Inquisition, wheedling out sacrilege and apostasy – though from time to time, when theological debate arises, it becomes clear to the true faithful that the Two Cultures man is (as he himself put it in as many words on his arrival here in London) acting as the enforcer of his own church's dogma. They may birth worlds, but these worlds must be underwritten by the possibili-ties laid out in the big Book of Physics he's constantly waving at them. Underwritten, too, in a more literal sense, by backers and producers, who'll oblige the crew to send them rushes at the end of each day's shooting, run barely edited scenes past button-pressing focus groups, then demand reshoots and re-edits, rewrites. They've already put the script through seven drafts. Gods or not, Dressler and co. have no illusions about this, know all too well that they exist in a closed feedback loop with baseness and stupidity. Their deck on the trireme might be a little higher, oars and benches softer, but they're galley slaves, just like the kids stuck in the outer room. Beneath their feet, the render farm hums, sending vibrations from the basement up through the whole floor, as though the entire building, like the *Sidereal*, were being held in the tractor beam of something larger than it, an inexorable, if opaque, process.

'For the thanadrine scene,' Eldridge is explaining now to Phocan, 'we'll need – I'm running ahead – some kind of mechanical rig.'

'To move around the performers' bodies?' Phocan asks.

'No. Well, yes and no: to move around their bodies and to move their bodies themselves around. It's to take place in zero gravity.'

'Cool.'

'The setting for it,' Herzberg says, diverting Phocan back to the styrofoam *Sidereal*, 'is the Observatory – this chamber here, with glass walls all round it. The lighting's the main thing: the space-ship's own lamps will all be off, but the two actors will be lit by the reflected glow from moons and other planets, coming through the glass. The scene takes place at the end of the voyage back to Kern; the end, too, of a long solar night, just as the predawn rays of Fidelus are creeping round the edge of Ardis Minor, into the home-planet's atmosphere. We want the light to glide around their bodies in a way that looks good *and* is consistent with the solar-planetary layout we've constructed.'

'In that case,' Phocan reasons, 'we should build two rigs: one for the human figures, and another for the light and camera. Car-plant robots are good for this. And we can model it all first with ray tracers.'

'What's that?' Briar wants to know.

'You fire rays from a camera,' Phocan explains, 'to a point you've designated as the light source in the take, and track the photons as they ricochet around whatever surfaces and objects you want in there. That way, you can see how light will spread and dissipate across the scene – by reading its path backwards.'

'You're going to put Joel Reney and Rosanna Wilmington into a car-building machine?' says Briar.

The Degree Zero gang and Phocan all giggle at this notion.

'No,' says Eldridge, 'we'll use mo-cap performers.'

'From Bergen,' Phocan adds. 'The Movement Underground.'

'From what?' Briar's confused now.

'Bergen. It's in Norway,' Phocan tells him.

Eldridge explains patiently to Briar: 'Most of the actual *filming* in a film like this is done with stand-in bodies – when we use real bodies at all, that is. Your Joel Reneys and Rosanna Wilmingtons just turn up at the shoot's end, speak a few lines, let us film their faces so that we can paste them over to the performers' craniums ...'

'... pick their cheque up ...' Herzberg adds; then, catching a glance from Eldridge, adds: 'Here, I meant to ask you ...' and leads Briar off to the room's far side.

'That guy's scary,' Eldridge confides *sotto voce* to Phocan and Berul.

'Special Technical Adviser?' Phocan whispers. 'And he doesn't know about ray tracers?'

'He's more Realism Tsar than STA. If NASA didn't use ray tracers on the Shuttle or the International Space Station, he doesn't want to know … Talking of craniums, though: we might need some help from you with the skull-blade alignment episode.'

When Phocan stares back at Eldridge blankly, Berul prompts: 'Scene 25 …' His listener's face showing no uptake, he adds: 'Please tell me that you've read my screenplay.'

'I don't believe,' says Phocan measuredly, 'that Pantarey were sent a copy …'

Berul turns away in frustration. Eldridge rolls his eyes. 'Paranoid retards. I'll take care of that.'

Unclipping a small walkie-talkie from his belt, he orders a subordinate to send him Soren, Degree Zero's runner, whom in turn he tells to go forth and amass the NDAs and restriction waivers requisite to the procurement, in a format either hard or soft, of *Incarnation*'s script for Phocan. Soren, who's got tiny whiskers on his upper lip, velveteen threads as yet untouched by any razor, scurries back off through the outer room, then through the lobby, out of the production building and across the courtyard to the mews in which the stable conversion that accommodates DZ's legal department is housed. On his way, he sees two junkies ambling towards the staircase leading to the render farm basement. He passes Deli Svevo's blue delivery cart, purveying the ranking staffers' lunchtime sandwiches, and passes also couriers wending their way by pushbike, motorbike and foot across the cobblestones, darting up and down narrow staircases leading to offices and workshops of DZ and other companies, picking up envelopes and packages, pulling others out of Velcro-fastened bags, scanning their barcodes, flashing e-pads up for signature, then radioing dispatch for their next assignment, haltingly conducting conversations over FaceTime and WhatsApp all the while in Russian, Polish, English, Arabic and Spanish. Amidst its transience, its impermanence, there is a durability to all this that Soren, if he wants to progress in this business, or perhaps simply in life, would do well to note. Empires will crumble, Death Stars will explode, but scurriers will always be there.

7. Ground Truth

Diamond, like Briar, has been tutored by Phocan on the ins and outs of moving photons around. She shadowed him her whole first week at Pantarey. On the Monday, as technicians set up a pommel horse in The Cell's gridded area, it was he who laid out for her the fundamentals of passive optical motion capture.

'What a marker does,' he pinched between his thumb and fingers the small, cream-coloured silken sphere he'd picked up from a table, one of thousands that seemed to sprout about the company's HQ like tiny mushrooms round a forest floor, 'is reflect light back to a camera. The camera's LEDs send the light out and the marker, the "nipple", bounces it back, thereby providing a position, or coordinate. One marker, one position; two markers, two positions; three, three; and so on. That's all it does: reflect – which is why we call it "passive". With me so far?'

She nodded. From a doorway on The Cell's far side a short, muscular gymnast was emerging.

'Here, though,' Phocan continued, 'is the paradox: the marked position's not the final goal. It's not the spot you want.'

'How do you mean?' she asked.

'The spot you're interested in, the one you *really* want, from a kinetic point of view, is the true pivot-point or centre – what we call the "root". In a human motion, this is almost always hidden from sight. The markers serve as stepping stones or way stations towards unearthing this elusive root. With four of them, we can build point-clouds round it, extrapolate it and reconstitute it.'

The abstract formulation began to make sense once the gym-nast, about whom Sennet had been busily attaching markers, mounted his horse and started swinging and scissoring around it. On the screen before which she and Phocan sat, Diamond watched lit dot-squares loop and gyrate in repeating sequences.

'You see them here.' Phocan's finger skipped from square to moving square. 'If we take these four, round his wrist, and draw them out' – his mouse clicked its way through these actions as he described them – 'then set this box up ...' With five or six more quick-fire clicks he'd built a rectangle out to the wrist's side and reproduced the dots (still moving, cutting out a small, repeating sub-step of the body's larger dance) inside this, their original arrangement expanded and enlarged; then, scurrying across a set of side bars, pull-down menus and the like, he made the dupli-cated dots fire out, like laser canons, four beams that, meeting at a fifth spot lying within their boundary, caused this last spot – itself moving on the screen, tugged back and forth by the four marker-derived dots' movement – to blaze into visibility, and Phocan to announce triumphantly to Diamond: 'There's our root. That's the wrist's core.'

He went on to unearth several more roots from various pas-sages and junctions of the gymnast's body, building rectangles off to the side, replicating marker point-clouds inside these, shooting rays out from them to bring to light new pivot-points.

'The goal, most of the time, in close-up body mo-cap,' he told her as he did this, 'is solved skeleton.'

'What's that?' she asked.

'Think of your clothes,' he told her, 'relative to the skin beneath them. A *person's*' – he corrected himself as he caught her peering, cross-eyed, at her own jumper – 'clothes. They're moving all the time. A marker on the former, on a T-shirt or whatever, won't give you a precise indication of the exact location of a mole on the surface of the latter. Just as a marker on the skin itself won't pinpoint a joint's coordinates beneath it, since skin's also highly mobile: as far as we're concerned, it's just another layer of clothing.

What we're after is the base, the bones under it all: solved skeleton. In clinical situations, at least. With entertainment, it's a little different: there the emphasis is more on augmented effect.'

'And here?' she asked him, pointing to the swivelling figure.

He had to think a little before answering:

'Here's somewhere in-between. It's not so much the *skeleton* we want as the whole circuit of force and counterforce, balance and its limits. Here the root's neither bone nor muscle, but something else, something more systemic ...'

Diamond, staring at the screen, let her gaze lose itself in the proliferating boxes. Shifting it back to the real gymnast, she was greeted by the sight of yet another box: the pommel horse around which he was circling, spindling and flairing. It was elongated, leather-finished, cambered on its upper surface, like a coffin. That all this motion, all these sequences, this ultra-formalised display, was orchestrated round positions that themselves remained interred ... The thought perplexed her; over the next weeks, it was to cloud her world view: everything she saw, each scene or situation she watched or participated in, she'd start extrapolating, reproducing, root-pinpointing, building boxes for, always off to the side ...

The Tuesday was spent off-site, down in London. In the basement of Guy's Hospital, Wing A, Lift C, she and Phocan were admitted to a gait lab on whose wall were painted sting rays, octopi and mermaids, all cavorting round a sunken treasure chest that Diamond at first glance misinterpreted as a flight recorder. Around an ethanol-dispensing tub and bandage box on a low table next to an examination couch were crowded soft-toy dinosaurs, ducks and gorillas; above them, half-depleted sheets of *Paw Patrol* and *Peppa Pig* stickers magnet-clamped to a whiteboard, figures peering in bemusement at its diagrams. The patient (in the management idiom printed on the dossier Dr Cromarty, Chief Clinical Scientist, was perusing as they prepped the room up, *client*), waiting outside when they arrived, was designated by the string *MA2703*.

'*MA*'s Male Adolescent,' Cromarty explained. 'This is his third visit.'

He handed Diamond the dossier. Flicking through it, she found page after page of episodic record, interspersed with boxes across which tricoloured contours (violet-orange-grey, now shadowing, now cross-cutting, now diverging from each other) depicted foot-progress angles and degrees of ankle torsion.

'I devised this format myself,' said Cromarty. 'The consultants who have to parse it to extract their cues for surgical decisions hate it. They just want a story, with a simple moral: *Do this, don't do that* ... But pathologies aren't fables. My task is to break each down to its constituent parts.'

MA2703's was pretty broken down: it contained dramatic peaks – femur-fracturing and calf-twisting interventions of the previous year, for instance – but these were few and far between: mostly it was subplots – abductor tension drop-off and knee-range expansion – whose bearing on the main arc, or even on each other, seemed quite tendentious; overall, it offered scant development, imparted no sense of heading to a climax or *dénouement*, happy or otherwise.

'Cerebral palsy's non-progressive. That's what makes it such a rich adversary, or quarry, or' – Cromarty looked around and lowered his voice to a whisper, as though not wanting to pronounce the word within the *client*'s earshot – 'muse.'

'Here, Lucy,' Phocan, sitting at a monitor-decked table with the gait lab's technologist, one Agnieszka Czajka, called her over. 'You can test the pick-up. Walk around waving this about.'

He threw her a calibrating baton, and she paced about the floor turning first one way then another, gyrating the baton's T-boned end in small loops through the air, as though to consecrate the space with holy water, or perhaps to dowse for water in the first place. As the corresponding loops and spirals etched themselves across the surface of their screens, Phocan talked Czajka through the pathways, shortcuts and (he seemed ready to admit this even if Pantarey's own help page wasn't) pitfalls of Physis 6™.

'The most important difference between this version and 5 is that you don't have to manually label each articulation point: the software does it for you. When it comes to the eventing, this will save you lots of time.'

'We ready for him?' Cromarty called out from beside his couch. Phocan gave the thumbs-up.

'Showtime!' Cromarty, turning ringmaster, raised and oscillated an imaginary top hat. His second, Dr Winter (same job title as him minus the *Chief*), exited the room, re-entering with a boy and (Diamond presumed) his mother.

'What's this?' Cromarty, turning from his couch, threw a mock double-take, and stared at the fourteen-year-old with friendly-astonished eyes. 'They must have sent Nathan's big brother!'

The boy smiled, blushing. Cromarty waved him over, and he left his mother's side to cross the floor on pointed, scissored toes. Cromarty kept his faux-shocked spiel up while MA2703 approached him, instructing Winter to check that they hadn't mis-prescribed super-strength growth hormones, screwing his face up Quint-like as he announced in his best sea-dog drawl *We're gonna need a bigger gait lab* ... Behind it all, though, Diamond, standing right next to him, could see his eyes running metrics, taking stock.

'Nathan,' he announced when the boy reached him, 'our eyes are giving science the lie. We're going to have to measure you, to bring your growth spurt back under the canopy of reason. Strip down to your underpants.'

Nathan, still reddening, obeyed. Cromarty steered him down on to the couch, extracting from his upper reaches waist-circumference and wrist-to-elbow figures with a measuring tape, while his second noted knee-to-foot and toe-abduction scores from the couch's base, where, like a surveyor hunkered in the shadow of a cantilever bridge, he crouched holding a goniometer between one opened eye and the bent legs which towered above him. This completed, they swabbed the boy's calves and thighs down and attached to these EMG electrodes, flesh-toned discs from each of which a miniature box hung, flashing intermittently, a tiny distress beacon. Their batteries, or perhaps his own nervousness converted into electricity, sent small local spasms through Nathan's leg muscles, rippling the skin's surface, and he reddened again, embarrassed by this subcutaneous excitation that was briefly, before Winter veiled its modesty with the bandages he coiled around his legs to hold the EMGs in place, visible to all – and even then still visible to Phocan and Czajka on the screen, across which they watched rows of fuzzy soundbars etch their way horizontally from left to right, jumping seismically with every quiver. Winter then, with Diamond's help, dotted about Nathan's metatarsals, thighs and kneecaps the Pantarey markers.

'To the Catwalk!' Cromarty commanded.

Winter now led Nathan to the gait lab's central area, a narrow strip or runway.

'If you pull the P6 window up,' Phocan was saying to Czajka over at their side table, 'you should see ...'

There it was, on her screen: a set of light-points moving in conjunction with each other, as they had with the pommel-horse gymnast.

'Now,' said Phocan, 'click on *spline fill*, and ...'

As soon as Czajka did this, lines – green, red and white – sprung up between the white dots, weaving a cat's cradle of intersecting, if irregular, triangles set on two perpendicularly adjoining planes; a configuration that, while purely geometric, nonetheless communicated unmistakably the hip-to-heel formation of MA2703's lower torso. When Cromarty, still playing ringmaster, had Nathan walk from one end of the runway to the other, this formation also ambulated: a complex pipe-cleaner figure, or the bottom half of one, whose constituent vertices and edges shifted and reconfigured with each movement. Occasionally, a line between two points would vanish, then flash up again between two other points, trying to forge a plausible connection that, in turn, would either stick or, overridden by the software, vanish again.

'I thought it knew which spot was which,' said Czajka as the figure's left thigh flickered out of visibility.

'Well, it does most of the time,' responded Phocan. 'Especially when it's been told once. If you just label that spot RTIB for right tibia, and that one LHEE for left heel, it should retain the designations as it moves on.'

Czajka pulled the labels from a menu on her screen's right, and dropped them on the dots tracking the positions of the markers that in turn showed the locations of the boy's tibia and heel; as his passage down the Catwalk continued, she performed the same click-and-drag manoeuvre for RTOE, LASI, RASI, LPSI ... Once MA2703 reached the strip's end, Cromarty, with a spinning gesture of the finger, turned him round and sent him back; then back again once he'd reached the other end; then ditto once more, and again. Phocan was right: after three or so passes, the lines joining the dots stopped fading, retaining their integrity instead from phase to phase.

'All labelled,' Czajka said, impressed. 'Can we go for strikes now?'

'Absolutely.' Phocan nodded. 'And it'll tell you when you've got a good one. Hit *Show Pads* ...'

When Czajka did this, the runway depicted on her monitor separated out into three rectangular sections, labelled *1*, *2*, *3*, each corresponding to a strike pad set in the real strip's floor. On MA2703's next pass, as his heel hit the first actual pad, on screen an arrow jumped out of the first rectangle, thrusting upwards from the floor in line with the stick figure's thigh.

'That's a hit,' said Phocan. 'You don't need to mark it; it'll auto-tag.'

'How are we doing?' Cromarty called pantomimishly across the room.

'One strike on that pass,' Czajka called back to him.

'Nathan,' Cromarty exhorted the boy, 'we're going to have to work you further. Keep it up. Imagine you're a sentry, pacing up and down before the palace gates.'

On the next pass they got strikes on Sections 1 and 3. The middle pad, though, didn't seem to want to register one: could have been reduced sensitivity from wear and tear, or how it lay within the boy's gait cycle ... Finally, after eight more to-and-fros, Section 2 pinged for them in concert with the others. Czajka, reprising Phocan's earlier gesture, held her thumb up to her boss; Cromarty informed Nathan that he was a star, instructed him to relax, to put his clothes back on, to take a bow, conducting all the others in the room in a round of applause that caused the child to redden yet again.

'Now,' Phocan, Diamond at his shoulder, told Czajka when the clapping had died down, 'you event it. Rerun the sequence; if you hit the notch marking each event, it'll prompt you with …'

She was already gliding the cursor to the first, most leftward-lying notch; as soon as this reached it, a *Create Event* box popped up, with *MA2703 right foot strike* pre-entered inside it.

'Click *Confirm* …' said Phocan.

Czajka did this; then confirmed the next *Create Event* box's default content as *MA2703 right foot lift*; and the next *MA2703 left foot strike*; and so on, moving rightwards down the runway, until the cycle was fully marked.

'Now we plug the holes,' said Phocan.

'There are still holes?' asked Czajka.

''Fraid so. Even Physis 6 can't prevent markers going into blind spots, clashing with each other, and the like,' he conceded. 'What it *can* do is give you the tools for overcoming this …'

For the next fifteen minutes he walked her through the program's various gap-filling options. While he murmured instructions, Czajka rotated the stick figure round on her screen like a clay pot on a wheel, combing it for parts where body-lines, despite the software's interventions, were still missing; when she found one, she swooped down on it, zooming in to enlarge single points, threading these with wavy filaments she fed through needle-eyes of cones and onwards to the next enlarged point, which she cone-threaded too, the frazzled braids floating around the figure in a loose gossamer web until, tightening the filament to pull it straight, she bridged the void between the paired points once again. On completing each fill, Czajka road-tested her fix, running the tibia- or thigh-formation of which it formed part backwards and forwards through sub-segments of the event in which they, in turn, played their own micro-role or function: the quarter-second following right foot-strike, while the metatarsal was straightening, or the two-tenths preceding lift off, when it was curving up again …

Diamond, not having much to do at this point, found herself staring at MA2703's mother, who'd been hovering around Phocan and Czajka's station, watching the accumulated data being fed into the gait lab's server, amalgamated with cached readings from his previous two sessions and fed forward to the online cataloguing systems of CMAS and ESMAC, to be worked through by the matrix of five continents' and heaven knows how many leading institutions' interlinked, cross-indexed CP research. Canopy of reason. Under this woman's gaze, the processors, blinking synaptically beneath the table, seemed to take on the status of boxed hierophants, oracles which she had ventured, suppliant, down to this grotto to consult; the wires linking them to one another to become black naval cords that, dipping from view behind gun metal, wound their way back to dark secrets, mysteries of origin, her child's sad incunabula. Her eyes, tracking them until they disappeared, were filled with a look not just inquisitive but also pleading – as though somewhere, among the labyrinths of circuitry, printed on some nanometric stretch of RAM-card, there lay the key to *fixing* Nathan, fixing the whole situation: something as simple as a switch that might be thrown, a feedback loop reversed, a line of code rewritten …

'So,' the mother haltingly asked Cromarty when he, too, sauntered across to the processing station, 'what's your current thinking?'

'On what?' he enquired back.

'Rhizomoty.' She spoke the word carefully, as though its very syllables contained an incantation.

Cromarty pulled a face. 'The trouble with SDR – rhizomoty,' he said, rolling out what Diamond could see was his standard lecture on the subject, 'is that it's based on the belief that you can simply isolate a problem from the body that it's part of. Edit it out, as it were. It doesn't work like that. Bodies are systems; complex networks; parts all interlinked. This is especially true in the neural field. Just slicing through the nerve-roots in the spinal cord won't stop the overstimulation in the upper brain: the ataxia's caused by a million other channels and transmitters, all of which are over-firing. Look, here's how ...'

He began to sketch her, in the margin of his dossier-pages, a motor neuron. When Diamond dropped back in on it two minutes later, the lecture had broadened out to embrace the entire history of hyperkinetic disorders – their social reception, the attendant attitudes and *mores* – through the eras.

'The Ancients held sufferers in esteem, thought them possessed of second sight; and the Medievals attributed to them the votive fervour of the followers of Vitus, shaking in rhapsody before his statue: *choreia,* choir, a chorus. You don't have to see it as a curse.'

'I don't,' the mother countered in a half-indignant, half-found-out tone.

'Besides,' Cromarty added, 'the surgical decision, ultimately, won't be mine ...'

His words trailed off, and he tapped his pencil's end against the paper, as though marking out a rhythm – to the process of decision-making, or of illness, or simply of time, its non-progression. His sketch's neuron had a core from which grew tentacles that trailed beneath it, like a jellyfish's. Diamond, feeling like an interloper, looked away, towards the gait lab's wall, where cephalopod limbs danced lithely with the fronds of seaweed woven all around them, with the happy crabs, the concupiscent mermaids.

Wednesday, it was back to HQ, where she progressed from single- to multi-body capture. Arriving in The Cell, she found its area divided by foam building blocks into a kind of floor-plan, with walls reduced to stubs that stopped at shin-height.

'It's an embassy,' Phocan explained.

'Which one?' she asked.

'Generic,' he said. 'SG are building a training tool for police forces around the world. The old embassy-storm scenario: terrorists, hostages, window-shattering abseils, boom, et cetera.'

SG was Serious Games plc, a regular Pantarey client. They'd brought both terrorists and captive embassy personnel with them – all, Diamond discovered when she chatted with them over greaseproof-wrapped brie and chutney sandwiches whose lustre was fast crusting over, junior SG staff.

'I feel like a dickhead,' a young man called Darren told her, standing beside the trestle table in a gluteally unflattering, nipple-studded black bodysuit. 'Pearly King in a gimp outfit.'

'It could be worse,' his colleague and her counterpart, the SG intern Michael, added. 'Last time it was loonies for ...'

'Mental health system users,' Darren corrected him.

'Mental health system users,' Michael, in mock naughty-schoolboy voice, repeated, 'wriggling and slithering about the walls and floor, to train nurses and orderlies to talk them into taking meds or standing still while straitjackets got pulled over their heads.'

'At least we don't have to do facials,' murmured Darren.

Diamond saw what he was getting at when, unfinished sandwiches abandoned, Darren, Michael and the other bodies were directed through their various routines, terrorists shuffling sideways across rooms with hostage-shields clasped tight in front of them, or jumping out of doorways to point guns at absent SWAT teams, or, touched by the latter's prospective bullets, crumpling to the floor. They executed these actions and others in a matter-of-fact, quite undramatic manner: dying, they expressed no shock or sorrow; threatening death, they exuded no menace; suicide vests, detonated with motions as banal as those deployed to release seat belts, produced no explosions. There were neither shouts nor screams: the actions all took place in studious silence punctuated only by the squeak of trainers on the floor, or SG's line manager and the ex-SAS man he'd brought with him calling out instructions. Since these were generally to repeat a certain shuffle, dart or crumple, or to move to another section of the floor, there to perform an action unrelated, or at least non-sequent, to the one they'd just been doing, there was no continuity, nor coherence, nor even any sense of anyone pretending, at a level either individual or collective, to be actually living out the situations and events they were depicting.

'The face stuff gets added later,' Phocan explained to Diamond when she asked about this. 'We have a trove of expressions – fear and anger, and so on – that we'll provide them with. For dialogue specific to this tool, we've got two actors coming in this afternoon.'

These actors, when they appeared, were transformed into overgrown teenagers, faces marker-pustuled, and then made to utter lines such as *Get back*, *I'll kill her*, *I've got a bomb* and *Save me*, all with the requisite look of desperation, terror and determination – but ultimately, since Phocan had instructed them to speak the words out clearly and, what's more, *slowly*, to facilitate good capture of mandibular and labial modulations, in a manner as strangely denatured as the morning's movements.

'It's not really acting, is it?' she commented to Phocan as he extracted roots from jowls, temples and cheekbones, reconstituting a snarl's pivot-points inside another box.

'Oh, it is, though,' he said – then, raising his voice to address the male performer, called out: 'Peter, come over here a minute.'

Peter, still silk-acned, ambled across and, when asked by Phocan to tell Diamond what he'd studied, announced proudly:

'German Expressionism. Did my thesis on it.'

Seeing her look blankly back at him, he added:

'The stuff you see in the old silent movies – how the villains scowl and cackle, and the heroines expand their mouths and eyes into huge gaping circles, to convey a state of mind that'll be recognised by any audience. That's what acting was about in those days: facial showjumping. You had to ride your skin and muscles through a course, negotiating obstacles, like troughs and fences: joy, shock, menace ...'

'Do you do theatre stuff as well?' she asked.

'You mean contemporary theatre? Do I act in it?'

She nodded.

'God no,' he snorted. 'Naturalist bullshit – like the *twentieth* century had never happened, let alone all ... this.' He gestured round The Cell. 'This,' he repeated, smiling at Phocan with what seemed to Diamond a mixture of affection and gratitude, 'is where the action's at. It's the real deal.'

'Faces,' Phocan explained to her as he manipulated Peter's feature-dots after the actor and his leading lady had retired, 'are landscapes. They've got peaks and ridges and ravines, which can be surveyed with absolute precision. Once you've got the contours, you can start manipulating them – like landscape architects ... you know, Capability Brown ... Anything's possible. Look ...'

A couple more clicks and Peter's upper lip started to curl back on itself, unwrapping his left cheek. Moving the pointer over to the right ear, Phocan then peeled back the other cheek, folding it down over what was left of the mouth and pinning its apex (now its nadir) to the long, underhanging ledge of the submaxillary passage where chin curves round into neck. He continued this origami until what had previously been Peter was no more than a cubistic scramble, resembling more a quarry or a bomb site than a face.

'For lots of applications,' he told Diamond, 'you don't need an actor in the first place. You can build the features up from scratch, then flesh it out. Look here ...'

Shuffling windows, he called up a file named *Annabel* and popped open a girl's face – a child's, no dot-point reconstitution but, it seemed, a gif filmed on a webcam: she was smiling, brushing hair out of her eyes and blinking shyly.

'This one was made for Interpol,' Phocan explained. 'A honey-trap for paedophiles. There was no original, for ethical and legal reasons. But she *looked* authentic; and she could even hold short conversations with the marks; so they thought that they were FaceTiming a real child, and would stay online for long enough for police to trace their IPs.' Closing the file, he added: 'Poor Annabel. She never got to exist, other than as a composite built around general metrics: long lashes, thin arms, brown hair, whatever ...'

He sat in silence for a while. Diamond watched him, waiting for him to continue with her priming. But he'd slipped into a kind of dazed hiatus, staring at something she couldn't discern, his mind trawling files inaccessible to her. The first time she'd been introduced to him, she'd misheard his name as *Focal*; and the elision, the corrupting metonym, had stuck – wasn't he, after all, inducing her into the world of focusing, of looking? His own look, she'd since noticed, was sometimes jumping between distances and depths of field, as though trying to lock on to two or more focal points at the same time – and, as a consequence, finding itself stranded between staging posts, lost in some interstice whose vagueness spurred it on towards new acts of focusing at once more strained and more vague; as though, like the earliest photographers out of whose bellowed, velvet-curtained clutter his whole discipline had hatched, he'd been conjuring his subject into visibility by use of multiple and staggered lenses, both inverting and reversing, and through not just apertures but also veils. He had that look now, seemed to be staring not so much at the actual screen in front of him as at some absent, offset one that floated spectrally a few inches in front of, or behind, this. She found it intriguing, and compelling, and somehow, in ways she couldn't quite articulate, as instructive of the pursuit to which she found herself apprenticed as any concrete or specific knowledge of it that he might confide to her.

Phocan, Phocus, hocus-pocus. They spent the last few hours of Wednesday cleaning. Multi-body capture turned out to be a nightmare in terms of its sight-lines. Limbs and torsos of one figure, passing in front of those of a second, or a third, as terrorists clasped to their breast or ducked and scuttled behind captives, produced weird and grotesque mergings: bodies seemed to mutate, sprouting organs and appendages in every which direction, then to slough them off again – a fluid orgy of construction and dismantling that ran simultaneously, at a range of speeds and rhythms that were unaligned yet still conjoined, processing at the same overall pace. Phocan's (and Diamond's) job, then, was to separate the bodies out again, to subjugate the schizoid carnage to the strictures of fixed individual identity, in which a leg, head or shoulder was assigned to a single person, and that person was determined as either an aggressor to be vanquished or a victim to be saved.

'We're like the rugby referee,' he said, 'who has to dive into the maul and strip the players from it one by one, to work out whose hand the ball's lying in, where another player's hand or leg is relative to that and to the ground, and so on. Come to think of it,' he went on, turning from the screen, 'sport's even worse than this. I've got to go and pitch our software at a sport-science trade fare in a few weeks from now, in Rome. We're supposed, before then, to have come up with a tool that can untangle football post-goal celebration pile-ups.'

'And will we?' she asked. 'Come up with it, I mean?'

'No,' he answered. 'It's impossible. What we can do, though, is fill the gaps, the unknown – unknowable – blank areas, with what, based on the possibilities, are the most plausible conjectures. So, with this hostage situation,' he turned screenward again, 'you've got – just as with the single-subject capture in the gait lab yester-day – your spline-fill, pattern-fill, rigid-body and kinematic-fills, then cyclic and quintic spine-fills ...'

Moving vertically along his drop-down, he ran all these options through their paces – one after the other, and with varying suc-cess. Sometimes a scrambled mass reorganised itself into the same number of clear, differentiated bodies as had entered the mix in the first place; at other times, though, the reconstituted figures would gain an accessory, hanging in the air beside them – neither gun nor handbag, nor any other prop that had been present earlier in the day, but such incongruous paraphernalia as umbrellas, party balloons and top hats.

'Artefacts,' smiled Phocan.

'Artefacts?' she repeated. 'Like handcrafted things?'

He nodded.

'But,' she said, 'aren't they the opposite of that? Not things at all, or even images of them ... Why do they call them that?'

'I don't know. I suppose because they're artificial – not there in reality, just generated, "crafted", in the interface between the object and its rendering. They're the mirages of our profession. You get them a lot in UAV work.'

'UAV?'

'Unmanned aerial vehicles. We're doing it tomorrow. I'll have to get you clearance.'

In fact, they spent both the Thursday and the Friday at BAE's headquarters outside Farnborough. The site was huge, ringed by two layers of reinforced green fencing; at the entrance, beside a security post whose personnel took fifteen minutes to admit (their preferred term, sent back and forth down radios, was 'verify') them, a Union Jack hung limp from a giant flagpole.

'Is this a company or a military base?' she asked him as they crawled past various fighter jets and helicopters planted in the verges and roundabout-islands.

'The distinction kind of blurs here, I'd say,' Phocan muttered as he parked by a gargantuan hangar. Pointing to two figures who'd emerged from a minute door at the foot of this, he added: 'Ah, here's Roger. He's our guy.'

Roger was the younger of the two; the other, smartly dressed, austere, the other side of sixty, wasn't introduced to them and, after murmuring some kind of order or instructions to Roger soon after they'd entered the building, retreated down a corridor into what Diamond took to be an even more restricted area. Unmanned aerial vehicles turned out to mean drones. In the sector of the hangar to which Roger led them, three or four of these were buzzing round a demarcated cube of airspace not unlike that of The Cell: black rubber floor, one fixed wall, string-mesh curtains making up three floating ones, HDI220 cameras clamped to rails establishing the control area's effective 'ceiling' (the hangar's actual ceiling was a good hundred feet higher). The drones were kite-sized, like the ones she'd see hovering above Port Meadow of a Sunday, playthings of children and hobbyists – only these ones came across as sharper and more waspish. They'd accelerate across the space then stop right on a speck of airborne dust without seeming to have to brake or slow down first; or turn one way then another in figure-of-eight patterns that recalled for her the gymnast's moves about his pommel horse. Their sound, undissipated here by any meadow's wind, was sharp too: an insistent and vindictive whine.

'With drones,' Phocan informed her as he hurled one roughly from his hand into the control zone's midst, where, after weaving around a little, discombobulated, it eventually re-stabilised itself, 'responsiveness is everything. Roots have to be recalculated several times a second – which removes much of the human interface.'

'How so?' she asked.

'We're too slow.' He smiled back at her, as though her question, and the computational inadequacy it betrayed, had furnished its own answer. 'These quadrators have IMUs to measure ...'

'Have what?'

'Sorry: inertial measurement units, to sense angular velocity. The idea is that they should be able to pitch and twist their way through doorways, vents and all manner of cavities, taking requisite decisions onboard, autonomously.'

'Hey,' called Roger from the far edge of the cube. 'Now the Ancient Mariner's gone, let's show your friend the Buzzby Berkeley skit.'

'Ancient Mariner?'

'Pilkington.' Roger jabbed his thumb over his shoulder in the vague direction of the inner warren into which his grey-haired boss had disappeared. 'What say?'

Phocan smiled indulgently. Roger and his sidekick Josh strolled over to a bunch of drones lying to the control zone's side and, crab-zagging around crouched, from one spot to another of the demarcated area's floor, arranged them symmetrically about this. Retiring back out past the white tape, they gathered round a laptop with a Beastie Boys sticker on it, Josh looking on with eager anticipation while Roger typed in commands.

'... and ... Enter! Now sit back, enjoy ...'

He stepped back, and the drones all lifted off in sync. Once airborne, they, too, started a crab-dance, a quadrille, with pairs cutting parallelogram-figures around other pairs, then splitting to form new pairs that in turn would cut new parallelograms, knitting intangible chain mail in the air as the block glided diagonally, overall shape intact, from one corner to another. That corner reached, the drones all wedged themselves into a tight-packed bud inside its right angle, then, like stamens of a wind-blown dandelion, turned outwards and detached again, one row after the other, shooting off to the cube's furthest reaches.

'That number's called "Little Web of Dreams",' Josh told her.

'And,' Roger, still in announcer mode, added as each of the web's dreams wended its way back to an assigned spot on the floor, there to await further orders, 'I'm afraid it's the finale as far as you're concerned.' Then, to Phocan, by way of explanation: 'Reaper guidance system next. This one's Level Two.'

Diamond, too, turned to Phocan, for a translation.

'I couldn't get you clearance beyond Level One,' he told her apologetically. 'You'll have to sit this bit out.'

'Try,' Roger chipped in as she traipsed down her path of exile, 'to pump Aidan in the next room for state secrets. He'll be happy to spill the beans.'

Aidan was, indeed, talkative. Like Josh and Roger, he was dressed in jeans and trainers; his demeanour, though, was slightly stiffer, less at ease – the consequence, it turned out, of a military background.

'I used to fly those things,' he told her.

'Quadrators?' she asked.

'No,' he said, opening his own, stickerless laptop. 'Predators – the predecessor of the Reapers you people are helping us with. They look like this ...'

Diamond peered past him at a picture of a long, windowless tube whose several short wings, like those of insects, were arranged about the thorax in a range of positions and angles, some pointing up, some down. If it was insect-like, it was aquatic too, its smooth, grey carapace reminding her of the skin of seals, or the large, featureless underbelly of a whale as it passes a tourist boat. There was, as with the whale-glimpse, something incomplete and unsatisfying about the sighting – as though, even when viewed in close-up, the creature's face, or character, its centre of intelligence, had stayed submerged.

'It doesn't have a head,' she said.

'I'm its head,' Aidan told her. 'We'd fly them from the ground.'

'Where?' she asked. 'In Afghanistan?'

'Yes,' he answered; 'I mean no. The *Predator* was in Afghanistan; but *I'd* be flying it from a field in Hampshire.'

'You'd be standing in a field?' She still had pictures of Port Meadow in her mind.

'A hangar in a field,' he said. 'Like this, but smaller. A box in a hangar; freight-container size. On a base, of course. I'd be there in full uniform, reporting to and liaising with various officers in other rooms: mission intelligence coordinator, director of operations, all the computer support personnel. But it was me and one co-pilot, or sensor-operator, in the box itself, flying the thing.'

'From a joystick?' she asked.

'Well, not just,' he said, sounding taken aback. 'We had six or seven screens around us: live-feed, instrumentation, flight data, terrain maps, ground-truth intel uploaded from the troops – photographs, basically ... Then chat boxes, so you could talk with the ground forces and with your own superiors – on the base, in London, Kandahar, wherever – directly, in real time. We'd be there at the controls for nine hours at a stretch.'

'Just watching?'

'Sometimes. Once I watched a house for a month straight, while people wandered in and out, or not; nothing important happened there. Or sometimes we'd scour roads for IEDs: hidden bombs, booby-traps. Troops can't see these, but we can, because metallic objects have a different temperature to the soil they're buried in. So do the cords that lead from them to detonators: they leave bright heat-signatures that run straight to the insurgents waiting to trigger

97

them off when a Humvee or squadron comes along. When you've pinpointed these guys, then you either tell the ground troops where they are or send a strike down yourself, from the bird.'

'What bird?'

'The drone. You whip a Hellfire missile off its rails, and take them out.'

'How long did you do this for?' she asked.

'Two years,' he answered. 'Then I got discharged.'

'Why?'

'PTSD,' he said. 'Pilkington took pity on me, brought me in here, and ...' He stopped and, mistaking her confused look for incomprehension, started annotating: 'Post-traumatic stress disor ...'

'I know what it means,' she said. 'But you weren't ...'

'Weren't what?'

'You weren't ... I mean ... in a war zone ...'

'Wasn't I?' He smiled, then added: 'Aren't we?'

Diamond made no response. From the restricted area next door a quadrator banked or accelerated, its tone crescendoing aggressively, then, just as suddenly, diminishing to no more than a liminal hum, like lights or fridges make. For half a minute, neither of them spoke. Then Aidan, keen to keep the exchange going, outed with:

'Guess how I and the other sensor-operators spent our out-of-theatre time.'

'What theatre?'

'The war zone. Guess how we passed our time between shifts.'

'I don't know,' she shrugged back. 'Sleeping? Drinking?'

'We played video games,' he told her.

'You're kidding.'

'Not at all,' he said. 'I'd even sometimes do a flight-simulator one. You could pick different eras: pilot a Handley Page Victor or a de Havilland Mosquito, all the way back to a Sopwith or an RE8. I found it relaxing; even therapeutic. Nobody was getting killed ...'

Silence, laced with modulating background whine, set in again. Then Aidan, suddenly animated, said to Diamond:

'Hey: you wanna see the Light of God?'

'I'm sorry?' she replied.

'Here, look.' He beckoned her towards his laptop, cursor skipping between folders. The file that he eventually clicked open was an mpeg; it showed a terrain, rendered in night-time vision: houses, trees, a deserted street ... The scene was being filmed from the ground, from something (she deduced from the slight movement, a slow heave and fall, as though the picture were breathing) like a body-camera. Nothing was happening – until a broad and brilliantly shining column burst out of the heavens and planted itself on the earth a hundred or so yards from the filmer.

'That's our beam,' Aidan announced. 'The laser that we send down from the sky. Our ground guys put their goggles on and *pow!* they see it, showing them the spot they need to hit. Only them: to the bad guys, it's invisible, but to our people it shines like a holy apparition: Light of God. When it reaches the floor, it blossoms.'

'Into what?'

'A square shape, usually.'

'God's a square?'

'Apparently. This is one of my own missions: I beamed the Light down on a sniper I'd located, and the Captain thanked me after they'd wiped the guy by sending me the video, a keepsake. Here, I've got another one that I can show you ...'

The new mpeg he opened had been shot in daytime, from the Predator itself – or rather, Aidan explained, from its Hellfire missile. Watching it, Diamond was at first reminded of generic YouTube parachuting clips: it showed, from POV a descending body that itself remained unseen, this same body's passage through the air. First there was blue sky, then, at the picture's base, the flat horizon line; then this last tilted upward like a trapdoor opening around a hinge set just beyond the frame, pushing the sky away as though the latter were a cushion or tarpaulin lying atop it, sliding off to be replaced by a single dry-brown surface that filled the whole screen. This new surface was approaching fast, and gaining definition as it did so, pixels refreshing at a rate that matched the speed of the descent. Eventually, out of its earthy gauze, a form emerged, an image: of a settlement or conurbation, perhaps no more than a village, whose white edifices were arranged around a central opening, a yard or plaza. In this opening a group of people in white robes stood, clustered loosely together, engaged in some kind of congregation. As the ground rose nearer it seemed to accelerate, and all the clearing's edges raced away, the opening opening further, flowing out, its borders running while its centre, too, expanded, growing ever clearer: white-robed men, locked in their confab, unaware that they were being observed – until the mpeg's final frames, in which they turned their heads up to look straight at the camera, and at Diamond, for the fraction of a second just before the screen went blank.

'I think that it's okay to show you this,' Aidan reflected. 'It's my own; never got classified. I say "my own", but actually, it was the software that rumbled the baddies this time: it detected sequences of movement and alignment that implied a probability of 95.6 per cent that something insurgent-linked was going on. Above 95, a strike usually ends up being called. All I did here was send the thing down, save its video-feed as a keepsake. I've got a whole bunch more that I could ... Are you staying in Farnborough tonight?'

Phocan arrived at that moment and whisked her to safety. She found herself excluded from the inner hangar's sanctum for a stretch of the next morning, too, but managed to confine Aidan to showing her pictures of artefacts (she had retained the term, and impressed him now by using it) thrown up by drones' remote-sensor software: of rainbow-cars and aeroplanes, their outlines doubled, tripled and quadrupled, daubed in glorious, RGB-separated technicolour; of the glacial and crystalline terrain-effects produced by vignetting and mosaic blurring, by relief displacement, colour balancing, chromatic aberration, bidirectional reflectance ... She spent what seemed like ages staring, captivated, at these glitches. It wasn't just that they were beautiful; beyond that, in their abstraction of a battlefield, of snipers, IEDs and doomed village summits into pointillistic billows, scumbled glazes, dribbles, splashes, smears, they offered her relief, a kind of psychic camouflage ...

Thus passed her first week. That was a month ago. Today, she finds herself doing PM analysis. The clients in this case are Ruff, an architecture firm, who've been commissioned by the City of Bedford to redesign one of the town's central shopping areas. Pantarey's brief is tripartite, and alliteratively so: transit, entanglement and tempo. The shopping strip is outdoors but, being divided from the street itself by retail outlets, steps and bollards, carless; whence today's mode of enquiry (PM stands for 'Pedestrian Motion', although in-house, they prefer the trade-term 'Pedestrian Flow in Urban Corridor', whose acronym, if you remove the linking preposition, never fails to prompt a giggle). They're to notate, in terms of not just route but also rhythm, the passage of self-selecting, if unwitting, subjects through the area of enquiry, translating every eddy and coagulation, every bump, swerve and dispersal into data-clusters that will form the basis of a model that in turn will inform Ruff's, and Bedford's, reconfig-uration of the space under investigation. In lieu of white tape, this space's borders are defined (although not marked) by T40Ss, nestled furtively under the eaves of facades and the bracket arms of lamp-posts – cameras that, instead of bouncing rays off reflectors stuck to the bodies of their subjects (who today, naturally, aren't wearing any), deploy laser-detectors to register depth of field. It's a new system, a new method, one in terms of whose hard- and software Pantarey have (as Garnett likes to boast) opened up clear blue water between them and their competitors, thus maintaining in their industry not only market advantage but, beyond that, a heroic status tinged with traces of the mystical. Markerless is the holy grail of mo-cap.

If she's progressed to markerless, she's become Markless too: Phocan's off purchasing gallons of bubble-mixture, to waft at a bobsleigh when they go to Holland next week. She's not tagged to him any more exclusively, in any case; these days she's farmed out to whoever needs an extra pair of hands. Today it's Sennet she's assigned to. He's had her climb a ladder, tweak a camera's angle, talk the cashiers in the precinct's Pret a Manger into letting them charge two iPads and a Mac whose batteries were running low and, now, dip back into the same Pret to buy Danishes and coffee so that she and he can ensconce themselves at the outdoor tables incognito: just two folks doing whatever they're doing here in St George's Walk, two grains of sand or pebbles on a beach, lost amidst all the others sitting, walking, idling, clicking, eating ... though, of course, they're not. These grains of sand also contain the world: their little screens, like the Quaker Oats packet in the hand of the Scot on the Quaker Oats packet, are feeding them the entire strip, captured and enclosed, from above ...

'What's interesting about the way people move in public space,' Sennet mumbles at her through pastry-flaked lips, 'is that they don't do what they're meant to. They don't follow the paths laid down for them. The planners envisaged shoppers leaving the Waitrose and the smaller concessions, then resting a while on those benches before moving on down the strip. But the benches get nabbed by the tramps, who take up residence there permanently, and create a natural exclusion zone around them; and besides, the spot under the willow tree's much nicer, as it's shaded in the summer – and warmed by low sun in winter, thanks to the gap between the supermarket and the cleaners to the south. Then the steps provided as the corridor's main exit: see how no one's using them. They like to cut between the bollards and the optician's instead ...'

On the laptop, the veracity of his claims, unascertainable to the naked eye, is instantly self-evident – all the more so when a heat-trace filter's applied, uncovering the accumulated smudge-tracks of each passage since recording started half an hour ago.

'By contrast,' Sennet continues, 'certain interventions produce certain predictable effects. Our trestle tables here, for instance: people don't climb over them, they go around. Even so, you notice how most of Pret's customers prefer to carry their snacks over to the empty market traders' stalls, and requisition these for picnic spots.' He cancels the filter before adding: 'That stuff we can all chart, though. What's really hard to get a handle on is self-congestion.'

'What's that?' asks Diamond.

'People instinctively move to spots where other people happen to be gathering. These spots are themselves as often as not inter-mediary – that is, they spring up in the gaps between "actual" or landmarked spots. But once they've sprung up they *become* a kind of landmark, temporarily at least. Which means that they, too, get offset on to other spots that spring up between them; and so on and so on, recursively. The only constant is the gap-structure, the "gapping". Outdoor life takes place in intervals.'

Sennet's got two hobby horses. One is talking down Phocan:

'Mark doesn't get this,' he continues. 'You can bring a joint or femur or torque-increment into definition, right down to the micrometre and beyond – but what does that tell you of the flux and reflux of the bigger-picture, the temporal-pattern set-up? I'm surprised Garnett can't see that. He loves Mark, treats him like his own son ...'

At times like these, she senses, with a tinge of excitement mixed with squeamishness, as though the vision were a secret whose unveiling is almost obscene, Pantarey's own solved skeleton creeping into focus. Sennet's other hobby horse is Markov chains. His conversation defaults to them in every second gap imaginable – and, the rhythmic sensitivity inculcated in her by today's task hints at her now, is about to again. 'A discrete-time Markov chain in countable state space is what we're dealing with here,' he tells her between sips of coffee. 'Although I suppose that you could argue for this corridor being viewed as a continuous or general state space ... Either way, the transition matrix is composed of the same jumps and holding times. If you take just one metric – length of pause between each burst of forward movement, for example ... Here, let me try to pull that one up ...'

Diamond, masticating leathery apricot, tunes out and runs her eye along the shopping precinct's floor. A section of its paving stones has been replaced by slabs – or not so much 'replaced by' as 'converted into', since the slabs have been cut from the paving stones themselves, in blocks whose edges don't align with theirs, placed in thin metal frames then returned to the paving, each block reset in its original position but removable so as to afford access, when required, to beneath-street-level pipework and cabling. Eight of these framed slabs run, one after the other, from a spot parallel to where her table ends to where the Waitrose starts: a strip within the strip, like old-style unspooled film, narrowing as it runs away from her, perspective accentuated by the rows of columns on each of the avenue's sides. A woman in a dress is entering this sub-strip now, being hit side-on by sunlight falling through the gap that Sennet pointed out a moment ago. From somewhere behind her, out of view, accordion music carries on the air: a slow, repeating tune that's full of minors. At the precinct's far end, by the bollards, a man leaves the optician's, holding the door open for a policewoman who's peering at a notebook as she enters. On the window by this door a diagram shows a cross-section of the eye, with sclera, retina, cornea, iris, aqueous humour, extra-ocular muscle and retinal blood vessels all labelled. Beside it, smaller diagrams contrast a healthy eyeball (spherical cornea, single focal point) with an astigmatic one (oval cornea, multiple focal points). A group of men in ties cuts between Diamond and this poster; as they pass her table, one of them says, *When I see that, it's time to go*; another answers, *It was time already*; they all laugh. The first man retorts something back, but the accordion music drowns his words out as they cross paths with the woman in the dress, replacing her within the sunlit zone . . .

Here's a strange one-two-three: a moment ago, a bald man with a backpack on his shoulder cut sideways through this zone towards the cleaners. As he entered it another man, bald but without a backpack, exited. Now, not half a minute later, a third man, also lacking a backpack although this time hirsute, is making his way in through the door. Diamond knows, because Sennet has told her, that the patterns they extrapolate from these comings and goings will be used not just by Ruff as they reshape the precinct; they'll also be harnessed, transformed and further monetised by Pantarey, deployed to other contexts and assignments, birthing algorithms for crowd scenes in movies, background movement in games ... But what's creeping into her mind now, metabolising with the sugar in a buzz of whimsical conjecture, is the apprehension, the suspicion, that some algo's at work here *already*, moulding this space's tempo, orchestrating all its paths and modulations; some source-code hiding not, like skeletons, beneath layers of skin and clothing but (quite the opposite) in the transience of its relay to the surface and beyond, the stealth of its convection up into ephemerality. She looks back at the ground. The paving to the framed slabs' right has painted signs and numbers running over it, instructions to the workers who will drill it up next week, or the one after that: algebra-strings of ciphers, as though it had come pre-annotated. She looks up again, right up towards one of the T40Ss, whose cold gaze tells her nothing. Beneath it, on a ledge, a pigeon's staring back, ostensibly at her and Sennet's Danishes; to Diamond, though, its concentration has a complicit air about it, as though, at some level, on some animal frequency, it (unlike her) had worked this stuff out, learnt to ride the streams and thermals of the algo's sequence – whence the superior, disdainful gaze it's sending back at her.

'They're memoryless, naturally,' Sennet's saying. 'That's the defining Markov property: absence of hysteresis. The amount of time between this movement-burst and the last one, or the one before that, has no bearing at all on how long we'll have to wait until the next. Only the present counts – or, if you want to be exact, the "stopping time" ...'

Diamond's not memoryless, though. Her thoughts are starting to ride back, like homing birds or web-dreams, to that first week, and Aidan's video: the second one, the mpeg with the village. It comes on suddenly, and quickly grows: the incongruous insertion, plane by plane and frame by frame, of the foreign scene into the precinct's tableau, to the point that soon it feels as though she were watching the former episode all over again – not on her screen but right here, in the space itself, replaying across its surfaces and textures, accelerating as it heads towards its lethal end. Is it some shared formal character that's causing the strange superposition, this overwriting of a Bedford plaza by some clearing in Afghanistan? It seems unlikely: that other space was square, while this is elongated; and the buildings were quite different, and the clothes ... Besides which, Aidan's mpeg had no audio: no human chatter, hum of background traffic or accordion notes emanating from behind the market stalls; and no smells, neither of Danish nor of tobacco, nor of the perfume coming at her from a woman stepping off the sub-strip now, out of the lateral light-block, depositing about the air a Roberto Cavalli vapour trail that spreads and dissipates ...

No: it's the above-thing, the above-ness, that's prompting this hysteresis in her. That she can see, with naked iris, cornea, etc., the whole doomed area from down here on her bench, and *at the same time* from on high, translated into topographic layout, sliced by the passage of its movements into clefted sections pieced together like some weird confection – this splitting, this doubling, is asking her mind to spindle and flair in ways it's just not trained to. Small tension-spasms start to scurry outwards from her spine. She senses her own presence as a threat: to buildings, people, life itself, to the whole atmosphere and habitat in which she finds herself embedded – unsuspected, deadly, fingers caressing the interface, the packet, the command-screen that's calling destruction down; senses in the very act of watching it this way a violence so ruinous that nothing, up to and including vision itself, will escape it. As the sequence playing out at the cleaners' entrance is brought to completion by the emergence of a new man with *both* hair *and* backpack, Diamond's mind supplies what neither file nor precinct has managed to show: the explosion – screams, cascades of glass and concrete, slabs and bodies opening, faces unravelling, space peeling and crumpling. Would this crowd, haphazardly assembled civic body of which she's just one small sensory organ, even *know* it had been hit? Or would these people carry with them to eternity this snapshot of drab market stalls and benches, perfume and accordion music, shopping trolleys being shunted by old ladies past the tramps, and eke out some kind of afterlife inside it? Who's to say that's not what's happening *right now* ... ?

Diamond's never had a panic attack before, and isn't sure this is one coming on – but there's a shortness to her breath, a need to tell someone, let them know ... know what? The policewoman's emerging from the optician's again, folding her notebook closed. She glances towards Diamond, and then up, towards the bird. Diamond, for her part, looks down, and fixes her gaze on the paper bag her Danish came in. Are you meant to breathe into it? Her right hand, reaching towards the table for this prop, detours (through either instinct for self-preservation or just hunger) at the final moment to the pastry – and it's this that saves her: raising it to her mouth again, she senses in its freighted texture and solidity, its leathery resistance, a guarantee of life that's strong enough to override the spectre of destruction, firm enough to steady now her breathing, calm her muscles; biting into it, she understands with growing confidence that whatever crisis she felt coming has been averted. By the time she's pushed the final mouthful in she's laughing inwardly: at the absurdity of the whole episode, perhaps, or perhaps with relief. She runs her gaze once more across the paving stones. Downtrodden wads of chewing gum in the illuminated areas glimmer like markers; in the darker patches they sit dullened, faded stars. Apricot tangs her lips. These, starting to move, mouth silently: *It's okay, nothing's happening, everything will carry on.*

8. The One Best Way

Skirting Lake Michigan beneath Chicago, Interstate 90 makes a Gilbrethian kink, veering eastwards to pass laterally through Gary, from whose junctionery Interstate 65 resumes the southbound line to Lafayette. Floating on an elevated section past the miles of ruined factories and boarded houses, Dean starts murmuring, in tune with the rental engine's hum-key, half-remembered snatches of a song from an old film she watched one rainy Sunday afternoon back in an era, more remote than childhood itself, of fixed-schedule programming: chirpy, folksy lines rhyming *Indiana* with *Louisiana*, *Rome* with *home*, *syncopation* with *hesitation* – or was it *explanation*? ... By Remington she's pieced together the pre-chorus and refrain:

> There is just one place that can light my face:
> Gary, Indiana, Gary Indiana ...

– but no more. The lyrics stick with her right down to West Lafayette; and, as she rides the lift up to the fourth floor of the Hilton, takes a bath, falls straight asleep and then, inevitably, wakes at 4 a.m. to watch predawn grey seeping through cheap lacquered drapes, they're still there, echoing within the rhythms of the hotel's heating system, void spaces and interstices of her jet-lag: *syncopation, hesitation, ana, ana, home* ...

Dorley has sent her out here, to consult the Gilbreth archive, with a view to ascertaining ... what, exactly? Her remit's vague: to dig around the holdings, see whether the idiosyncratic modelling technique devised by an industrial time-and-motion pioneer a century ago might be construed to constitute, its iterations to lay out, a set of 'first citations' – might be construed to do this to the extent that these could form a legal basis for … for something. On whose behalf is she conducting this enquiry? Client A … via Peacock … although her first, and indeed only, point of contact, the post she reports to, mothership, control, is D&G, on to whose server she's to upload daily all her research files, the paragraphs and pages of her interim report …

Her remit is so vague, in fact, as to preclude, in terms of methodology, the rigour into which a Dip Eng Law, a clerkship and a junior associateship have trained her. In this rigour's absence, she's jumped randomly, as off a pier into a lake, into a wide expanse of Gilbrethness. This Gilbrethness washes and laps across her desk, sequence determined by the order in which folders happen to arrive. Here are four things she's learnt about Lillian Gilbreth in her first three days:

1. That her family spent their summer holidays in Nantucket. Her husband Frank taught their children to sail by marking out a boat-shape on the ground, etching gunwale, bow and stern into dry earth, laying pieces of rope for main- and jib-sheets, moveable poles for boom and tiller, and drilled them in the art of jibing, tacking, heeling and running before the wind until they'd attained an advanced level of seamanship without ever having set foot in an actual boat. The local drugstore, where they'd go for ice cream, was called Coffins.

2. That she had the idea for the cyclegraph technique while hired by Remington (firm not city) to devise methods of increasing typing speed and accuracy: looking at the way the typists' fingers flexed, extended and contracted, jumping up a row or two before recoiling back to rest above

their home-keys – never along a simple up-down vector but (she suspected, and the cyclegraphs confirmed to her) in circuits, buckled loops in which no single position other than the resting one was passed through twice; how entire hands shot up to platen knobs and carriage-release levers then fell back again, in similarly asymmetric and yet fluent, self-enclosing paths ... Later, on the back of this, she would be hired to work on more efficient firing of machine guns, which Remington made too. The mechanism, it turns out, is pretty much the same.

3. That she was a lifelong Republican, who even flirted with eugenics – but that, despite these rightward leanings, Lenin so admired her methods that he rolled them out across the Soviet Union, hoping they'd help smooth the way towards state socialism. She met Russian delegations, and American trade unionists. *If everyone just worked together*, she opined with a flourish lost on almost all her readers, *class conflict would melt into air, into thin air.*

4. That, as a child, she went to school with Isadora Duncan, Jack London and Gertrude Stein –

– this last fact being divulged, to Dean's amazement, by a school yearbook: Oakland High, 1891. One of its pages bears a photograph of a prize-giving ceremony: there's a rickety-looking stage, and a gowned lady handing medals out to children, three girls and a boy. *From Left: Gertrude Stein (rhetoric), Lillian Moller (grammar), Isadora Duncan (gymnastics), Jack London (math).* The girls are bunched together, in a kind of huddle; the boy, smaller, stands facing them, holding his medal outwards, as though deciding which of them to dedicate it to – less London than Paris, dumbstruck by three goddesses. He looks ill at ease, as though the lines of a short life-script had been pre-stamped on his face: the restless yearning, the stumbling around backwoods, the search for a moment never quite possessed, for some lost eighteenth century ... The girls, meanwhile, look confident, as though they know already that, departing this photo, they'll call into bloom the twentieth.

Here, in File 27, is a letter to her sister Vera, written a few days after Lillian's wedding:

I've exchanged,

she muses,

not only my name but, it seems, a whole *mise-en-scène* – high-ceilinged rooms with gilt-framed mirrors, stiff black sofas stuffed with horsehair, music boxes and wax flowers under glass domes, our *hoch-Deutsch* Moller *habitus* – for this new upstart world. Frank *is* America.

What does she mean? Frank is an upstart, to be sure: a short and self-made man who had no business courting her; bricklayer who so infuriated his successive bosses with his disquisitions into the efficiency or lack thereof of each hod-carrying style, of every path of trowel to wall and hand to brick and brick to wall, etc., that they kept promoting him just to get rid of him until he found himself devising streamlined operation protocols for entire sites, then companies, and now already, at just twenty-seven, industries. They're honeymooning in the St Francis, just off Union Square. She recounts to Vera, in some detail, how the bellboy, carrying in the breakfast tray, tripped on the door sill and spilled the tray's contents:

I retain a picture of it in my head: the tray flying through space, the cups and coffee jug, glasses of orange juice, plates of egg and bacon all gliding away from it, bodies no longer glued into a unit, each following its own trajectory.

III

Frank's in the middle of a contract with the New England Butt Company; he decides on the spot to remove sills from all shop floors within his purvey. Lillian continues:

> The strange thing is that, every time I call the episode to mind, I see it not in motion but quite still, as though each part were frozen, hanging in the air, above the threshold ...

The marriage produces thirteen children, of whom twelve survive. Frank runs the household like a training camp, like a laboratory – a showroom, too – for his cult of time management. He films the children eating, table-laying and -clearing and, on analysing the developed footage, devises more efficient methods for these tasks; methods which, once instituted, he films too. He films their tonsil and appendix operations, extracting new surgical protocol: nurses should act as 'caddies', placing requisite woods and putters in the doctors' hands, ensuring that play runs uninterrupted, tee-box to fairway to green, incision to resection to suture ... Various-sized Gilbreth offspring, blinking in magnesium glare, slide out on to Dean's desk now and again; but mostly it's pictures from the 'betterment rooms' set up by Frank and Lillian in their employers' factories, or their own Purdue lab, shop floors' and workstations' meticulous duplicates. Here, in File 14, are some blown-up film frames showing workers – seamstresses, meat packers, telephone-exchange operators, each wearing a light-ring – performing their tasks against a grid: in some cases an actual gridded backdrop, in others a penetrating screen imprinted on the film through multiple exposure. They're heavily annotated, snags circled, arrows injecting comments – *work rhythm broken here* – into the spots, the 'knots', that need untangling. A handwritten draft passage is attached by paper clip to one of these:

> Each unit divided into subdivisions/cycles of performance.
> Each cycle then divided into subcycle = micromotion.

The full, typewritten draft, contained in File 31, continues:

> Once all micromotions are identified and modelled, methods
> of least waste can then be synthesised.

The sentence will end up in *The Quest for the One Best Way*,
Lillian's magnum opus. Frank likes to film his subjects at full speed,
a clock-hand racing in the background, measuring off hundredths
of a second. But Lillian has understood the paradox that's central
to their entire project: that motion can be mined – interrogated,
made to spill its secrets – only when its territory, its dark interior,
has been colonised by its inverse, by stasis.

Here's another scene of arrested motion, in File 7: a photograph
showing a roadside picnic. The Gilbreths' open-top Pierce-Arrow
has pulled up in a small clearing by a wood; hampers and rugs
and children, like so many micromotions, have been unpacked, laid
out across the grass. Lillian describes this picnic, or one like it, in
another letter, also to Vera, from File 9: Frank, map-reading, getting them lost, she murmuring behind the steering wheel beneath
her breath:

> *Nel mezzo del cammin di nostra vita*
> *mi ritrovai per una selva oscura*
> *ché la diritta via era smarrita ...*

Beside the blankets, they find an enormous anthill. Frank
presents it to them as a paragon of streamlined labour. Lillian
counterbalances his sermon with her own, more nuanced portrait
of a highly complex social structure held together, ultimately, not
so much by efficiency as by belief – in service to the queen, in
colony's totality; belief that's wired in, pulsing at an irreducible,
base level, neural electricity itself ...

Frank, on his own base level, hates waste. He abhors it, an
abomination in the eyes of his one god, efficiency. Wasted food,
wasted water, wasted energy, money or motions: all these offend

him, sting him to the core. Waste is pollution; waste is dirt. A large portion of his time-management rituals turn around cleaning, cleanliness. At home, the bathroom walls are hung with instructions for washing:

> Soap in right hand, on left shoulder; run down top of left arm back up bottom of left arm to armpit; down side, down outside of left leg, then up inside of same leg; then ditto in mirror-version for the other side ...

If, afterwards, one of the children leaves a tap dripping and the tub fills up again, they're made to take a second bath, *teach them about wasting water* ... One summer, in Nantucket, they're all set to work on a research project into the best way to pack tins of detergent. Deliberations about whether or not to buy a family dog turn around calculations of the reduction in garbage-man-motions to be brought about by lowered household food-waste levels. For bodily evacuations they're allotted a fixed time to purge themselves. Here at this picnic, they'll be banished, when they need to unload their own waste, in twos, into the woods that loom silver-gelatinous behind them: clearings must be kept clear, unwholesome motions buried down in earth and darkness. Lillian, summarising Frank's thought, writes that the elimination of waste will result in 'Happy Minutes', in time 'saved'. Saved for what? *From* what? *Might Frank's real drive*, Dean finds herself jotting down in her notes,

> not be towards some kind of time so sanitised it's empty – time devoid of motion, of all content other than itself? – And would this empty, voided time be *pure* time, or just ... void?

The archivist who's taking care of Dean is one Ms Bernadette Richards, MA, MLIS, CA, Processing and Public Services Officer (Archives and Special Collections). Portly and black, cast in the timeless mould of middle age, she treats Dean like an aunt who hasn't seen her for a decade: calls her *Honey*, expresses amazement that she's high-tailed it *all the way over from England!*; ushers her each day into the dedicated reading space she's reserved for her. She serves up to her additional material not held in the Gilbreth files, more general-circulation items. There's a book, long out of print but a bestseller in its time, written by two of the grown-up children, Frank Jr. and Ernestine; also (as Dean informed the Peacocks) a film. Both are as folksy as the 'Gary, Indiana' ditty, full of quirky anecdotes and screwball vignettes – run-ins with exasperated servants; toll-booth attendants, wide-eyed at the sight of twelve kids packed into a car, waving them through *gratis* ... And both play up Frank, presenting him and him alone as source of the whole Gilbreth *Weltanschauung*, artesian well whence its initiative and dynamism gush. But Dean can see after her first hour in the holdings that it's Lillian, all Lillian, who upscaled Frank's narrow ergonomic vision, teased it out across fields and dimensions that he didn't even know existed. After her first day she can see, too, that it was Lillian, not Frank, who penned the essays and the books for which, sometimes with her, sometimes alone, he's credited as author. Could Frank have come up with this passage:

> Growing to realise the importance of the slightest change from a straight line or smooth curve, the worker comes to think in elementary motions. Tracing and retracing, with our models' help, these motions – motions refined through changes to chair and work-bench placement, table height and inclination angles, through study of the most efficient workers' models (other workers running their own hands along the model's wireframe track, over and over), and through further refinement even of these – all this will bring about a transformation from awkwardness to grace, from hesitation to decision ... ?

Of course not. A psychology degree's made Lillian understand that operators have to *own* the movements they perform. Frank never got this; he's a Taylorist, thinks that the employee has to be shown – told – what to do. But she can see the value in a machinist *knowing*, both kinetically and intimately, through repetition, like a lover, every curve and bend and twist of their own action, in aspiring to the perfect line, *desiring* it. Again, could Frank have written:

> The importance of rhythm was recognised in the Assyrian and Babylonian pictorial records, which perpetuate the methods of their best managers. By the same logic of perpetuation must the machinist be trained until his eye can follow paths of motions, judge their length, speed and duration, and thus cultivate an innate timing sense, aided by silent rhythmic counting, that can estimate the times and routes of movement with instinctive accuracy … ?

Überhaupt nicht. She's learnt this through studying poetry: ranges of metre, cadence, rest. Before psychology, her BA was (like Dean's) Eng Lit; MA dissertation on *Bartholomew Fair*. Literature's threaded through the fabric of all her deliberations. When she writes, in *The Quest*'s first waste-attacking chapter, that *true conservation contains thought of neither waste nor niggardliness*, she's got Shakespeare's *mak'st waste in niggarding*, from *Sonnet One*, pulsing, surround-sound, in the background. When designing for workers the relaxation areas she's identified as vital to output's beat, she fills them with books – a different selection for each space, but always one that includes a dual-text *Divine Comedy* (she slots this into all her waiting rooms too, picturing impatient or distracted eyes falling and lingering on Purgatorio IV's *attendi tu iscorta, o pur lo modo usato t' ha' ripriso?*). She writes her own poems. Here, in File 27, is an elegy to Gantt:

> He preached the Gospel of real leadership,
> In quiet words, with stress on facts and laws
> Showing the goal and pointing out the way,
> Nor dreamed his words would found a Fellowship
> Of those who held him Leader in a Cause, —
> The winning of a new Industrial Day.

It's rubbish, sure – too corseted, too measured – but that's not the point. It's the *mechanics* of the process she appreciates. Writing's an operation, just like sewing, cutting steel plates or assembling boxes. Lillian has studied Marey, knows that *le père de la chronophotographie*'s work began with sphygmographs, pulse-writers, etching blood's own cadences and meters on smoke-blackened glass; that some of his earliest motion photographs, alongside ones of bayonet points swirling as they traced the outlines of the perfect thrust, recorded cursive hand-styles, carved in air. Killing and writing. Her annotations in the margins of her battered copy (File 20) of le Prof's *Du Mouvement dans les Fonctions de la Vie* try out various translations for his neologism *chronostylographie*: *the writing of time … time-writing … time*-as-*writing …* During their first Remington contract, when Frank guinea-pigs the children into testing out his touch-type learning system, covering the keys with a blank sheet to force them to internalise the letters' layout, he gets them to copy out a passage of *Moby-Dick*. He's never read the book – just seized on a Harper & Brothers edition he's found in their rented holiday lean-to, vaguely aware that it has something to do with Nantucket and the sea. But Lillian has, and spends two days dissecting in her mind the episode on which the tome, by chance, has fallen open in Frank's hands: the Polynesian harpoonist Queequeg, also transcribing – in his case the tattoo-pattern from his skin over on to his (for now) redundant coffin:

> Many spare hours he spent, in carving the lid with all manner of grotesque figures and drawings; and it seemed that hereby he was striving, in his rude way, to copy parts of the twisted tattooing on his body. And this tattooing had been the work of a departed prophet and seer of his island, who, by those hieroglyphic marks, had written out on his body a complete theory of the heavens and the earth, and a mystical treatise on the art of attaining truth; so that Queequeg in his own proper person was a riddle to unfold; a wondrous work

in one volume; but whose mysteries not even himself could read, though his own live heart beat against them; and these mysteries were therefore destined in the end to moulder away with the living parchment whereon they were inscribed, and so be unsolved to the last …

Needle, harpoon, pen; white whale, white paper … That summer, concurrently, they're also working for the Automatic Pencil Company. Frank stages a publicity stunt, filming the children building a casket, filling it with old-school, fixed-lead pencils and, with decorous and solemn faces, burying it in the sand. They all get double scoops as a reward for this one, lining the bar at Coffins, shooting thumb-propelled graphite at each other between licks. The druggist's name, Lillian learns in conversation with him, has been passed down from carpenter-undertaker forebears. Nantucket wood has a distinctive colouration, its own shade of black. Back in the house, too busy to keep notebooks as she darts from bedroom to pantry, porch to bathroom, she has a Dictaphone installed on every floor; the tape-rolls, emptied daily, are sent down to two stenographers installed in a small room beside the lounge. This prompts a small epiphany about a book that's long been part of Lillian's mental landscape: *Dracula*. 'There is,' File 34, a letter to her mother,

> so much *secretarial* work in that novel – all that typing out and duplicating of the other characters' notes and confessions that Mina busies herself with, even as her vampire-tainted blood turns on her. I always wondered, when you read it to me as a child: How does she find the time?

Now, though (June 1924), she *gets* it; gets that this is what the story is really about; that all the earth-boxes inside which the Count walls up and ships his territory and domain from Transylvania to London via Whitby, death-lair crates with which he sends himself from half-life to revived un-deadness, serve as doubles, satellites orbiting the *real* box within whose walls life becomes deadened and revived:

> This, Mother, I now see: the true vampire's casket is Dr John Seward's Dictaphone.

Three days after this letter's postmark, Frank, standing in the phone box from which he's just spoken to her, suffers a massive heart attack. After the funeral, Lillian pens another too-stiff elegy:

> Go on, My Dear, I shall not faint or fall,
> I cannot know, but I can sense your way.
> God speed! You must not swerve or wait for me.

She thinks back to that summer, all its typewriters and secretarial pools, three decades later when she's hired by Macy's. Beneath floors stacked full of toasters, stoves, refrigerators (the demand for automated kitchens has exploded, due in no small part to her own work), she installs felt padding round the long pneumatic tubes through which notes shuttle from the ground-floor tills up to the safe room and change clatters in the opposite direction – eight hundred of them, powered by air drums whose vibration was sending a constant roar around the shop floor. *Pneuma*, breath of God; now muffled. Filming the cashiers at work day after day, week after week, extracting first one then another of them from the line-up to isolate and metal-cast their motion in the on-site betterment room, then tweaking the positions of the tubes, the chairs, the tills, then gazing down, from the store's mezzanine, over her new configuration, she perceives, once more, a kind of secretariat, expanded twenty-fold: these women rhythmically striking their keys, transcribing some great work, a book taking on shape, right here, before her very eyes. If Borel's monkeys are destined, eventually, to write *Hamlet*, what would the character and content of the cashiers' opus be? Perhaps this one will never have a name, is bound to hover just beyond the edge of legibility, eternally suspended in the act of being composed ...

And then there are the boxes. On her fourth day of research, Dean's led by the kindly Ms Richards down to the stacks from which the files have been brought up to her; and then beyond these, out into a courtyard – a sizeable one, more like a loading bay or depot – inside which sit rows of corrugated-iron containers of the type used on giant cargo ships.

'This is where we keep oversize holdings,' the archivist confides with a wink, as though letting her in on a secret. 'You'll want Number 7.'

Ms Richards fumbles in the pocket of her skirt, pulls out a plastic fob and holds this to a corresponding plastic-coated patch on Number 7's door. The patch, or possibly the fob, emits a small beep; the soft, rubberised sound of smart cylinders and latches disengaging follows, and the door pushes back automatically to allow them ingress. There they are, in rows and layers and columns, as in the storeroom of a shoe shop: a supply of little boxes sitting in a big one. They look at once the same as in the pictures Dean saw back in London and completely different. Same because they're plain back boxes with two sides and the roof cut away and, rising from the floor of each, a thin metal track that crotchets and streaks about the air to loop back round to where it starts, its bows and swerves thrown into relief by grid squares marked across the box's whole interior. Different because here, amidst dust flakes idling through weak shafts of sunlight, the twisting bars' implied speed, their kinetic vibrancy, has been both retained and (as it were) stood down, switched into standby mode. They're flaking too, grown bulbous with oxidising, like old skin. In the physical objects, she can see not just the hooks that anchor the wireframes to the boxes' floors but also, in the more elaborate or 'off-balanced' of these wireframes, thin vertical support armatures tucked away behind them. The painted background squares, so luminescent in the photos' black and white, seem fainter in the real air's chromatism; besides which, they're genuinely faded with time. But as soon as Dean steps forward and scrutinises one and then another from close up, the tubular iterations, as though reactivated by proximity alone, seem to zing back into life; she can not only see but almost viscerally *sense* light-rings' trajectories: so many lathemen's or seamstresses' action-signatures retained, fragments of time and motion held against oblivion ... Lillian's preferred term was *embodied data* ... Instinctively, Dean finds herself, like the models' first users, looping her thumb and fingers round the tracks, gliding her hand along their winding path, repeating some hundred-year-old moment – reinhabiting, perhaps even re-*living* it, skin stroking metal ...

'How many of these are there here?' she asks.

'Says in the record three hundred and eighty-five,' Ms Richards answers, flipping through a print-off. 'That's here. The Gilbreths' own inventory lists more, in other archives ...'

It does indeed. Lillian has been meticulous in indexing each one. The Smithsonian has eighty or so; MIT a score; Stanford a handful, in the Muybridge archive. Hundreds more have been lost or destroyed – but they're still inventorised. They all are: every box the Gilbreths ever made. Lillian was quite unflinching in her determination to capture each movement, not to let a single one slip her recording net. Once an action was wire-modelled, the model was photographed – in stereoscope once more, reverse-engineered into a little pair of thumbnail snapshots, photographs of models made from photographs, that in turn were assigned a number and, along with a short title or description of each action ('shelf-assembling', 'switchboard operating', etc.), entered in the record whose print-off Ms Richards has in her hands now. *That*'s what was represented by the squiggle-strings scrawled at the base of the photos that Dean showed the Peacocks: one riddle, at least, solved. Dean spends the next two days working out which of the eight hundred and fourteen inventorised movements have their corresponding models extant here, in Oversize Holdings 7, matching them up, thumbnail double-photograph to box – task helped by the inclusion of each number on the boxes themselves, written in white paint, also now faded but still legible, on their floors, near the front edge ...

There's a Five Guys on the strip-mall just off campus, and, next door but one to it, a Tender Greens. Breaking off, alternately in one or the other of these, each day for lunch, Dean finds she's watching people eat – or carry food across the restaurant, settle themselves at tables, remove coats, hang bags on backs of chairs, head to the bathroom, open doors – through penetrating screens and chronocyclegraphs now grafted to her visual faculties, invisible prostheses. The passage of fork to mouth, of hand to napkin, arm to sleeve or hip to door-jamb – all becomes ergonomics, choreography. In spinning hems and shawls, amidst the smell of burgers and seared tuna, she sees, once more, Julius's grainy and post-coloured Loie Fuller gif re-looping. Isadora Duncan: Lillian stays intermittently in touch with her until she (Isadora) dies. File 24 contains a 1913 letter in which the diva thanks her old friend for the condolence note after her children's drowning. *You would like their father: he's the scion of machinists* ... So does File 25, from 1927: *Down in le Midi, cheri, frolicking with Desti and Chatov* ... Lillian, in her own journal from that year (also File 25), comments that it's Chatov's scarf that, catching in an Amilcar's rear axle two weeks after the postmark on this one, snaps Isadora's neck and sends her *à la gloire* ... Gertrude Stein stays on her radar too – hard for her not to: by the thirties she's packing out concert halls around America, intoning publicly to rapt audiences

what was the use of my having come from Oakland it was not natural to have come from there yes write about if I like or anything if I like but not there, there is no there there

and privately to Lillian

You'd love what they've turned our old neighbourhood into: an industrial park ...

There's reams of other correspondence. Dean returns to it when her matching of inventory to boxes gets held up. Here, in

Files 42–5, are Soviet-stamped envelopes bearing tributes from the Russian Taylorist Alexsei Gastev, telling her she's

> set the worker on the path to the one best way; helped unleash him from the shackles of his body; through your light-rings consecrated his new matrimony with the liberating dynamism of the great machine ...

Or here, File 46, from Vassar's President, inviting her to the opening of a hall of residence named after her

> the better to inspire our students to find the one best way through the great challenges that face them ...

This phrase, *the one best way*, crops up time and again throughout the articles, the books, the letters. As the projects scale up, and as Lillian grows older, the words appear to change their meaning, or at least their range, until it seems that she's no longer looking for the one best way to pack five hundred toys into a crate or move a thousand chocolate lumps from a conveyor belt into the variegated moulds of an assortment tray: she's after bigger fish. *Might there not be*, she writes (File 61) to Powel Crosley, autumn '54 from Sarajevo, *a one – a truly one – best way? For everything, I mean ... ?* The more she delves through these Purdue files, the more Dean starts discerning – in the writings or, perhaps, between them – the outline of an idea taking shape in Lillian's mind, as though the archive were itself, in its totality, a wireframe model down whose kinking path Dean's thought-hand, little palmer-pilgrim, is now gliding:

> From the mid-forties,

she writes in her report to Dorley,

> terms such as 'perfect movement' and 'pure original motion' start cropping up in Ms Gilbreth's notebooks – often

free-standing, out of context, but nonetheless (to my mind) indicating a turn in her thinking towards the possibility of some form of 'higher' or 'absolute' movement not yet modelled, perhaps even (if such a thing may be imagined) derived from no source other than itself. This turn coincides with Ms Gilbreth's newfound fascination with the sightless workers she was helping train. Having started from the premise that such physically disadvantaged people could, with help, be brought up to the capability levels of the able-bodied and thus granted assembly-line and even artisanal roles, Ms Gilbreth ended up believing that, despite appearances, blind people stood at an *advantage*, not a disadvantage, to their fellows.

(Dean likes 'fellows': it's a Gilbreth kind of word.)

For the blind, she reasoned, all movement is *de facto* already abstracted from extraneous context and surroundings; and, at the same time, embodied as action that has no exterior correlative it's imitating. From the late fifties, when she found herself consulting for first NACA, then that agency's successor NASA, Ms Gilbreth's utterances, growing rarer, started drifting in more fanciful directions, as though the prospect of entering outer space had expanded the frontiers of the possible, or thinkable. Towards the end . . .

Dorley calls her from London two hours after she dispatches this email, audibly excited. 'NASA?' he barks. 'You mean this lady, Gilbreth, is instructing *astronauts* on how to *space-walk?*'

'Not exactly space-walk,' Dean replies, voice full of sleep (it's 3 a.m. West Lafayette time). 'More like just move about the module, whose designers had drawn heavily from her work on domestic ergonomics. From the early days, she'd get her children to follow her around the kitchen with balls of string and pin-tacks, marking her passage from sink to bin to cutting board, or cupboard to bin to door to bin again, until the room became its own cat's-cradle model box.'

'That's insane,' chuffs Dorley. 'Neighbours should have called in Child Protection …'

'Not really,' replies Dean defensively. 'It worked: it led to her designing better kitchens. Later, after her blind work, she made modified ones for people with reduced mobility: simplified, refined, more closed-in and all-surrounding. So the progression on to NASA-consultancy makes sense: if you think about it, a space module is just a kitchen or a living room for people whose motility has been conditionally altered.'

There's a long pause while Dorley takes this in. The line, too, seems to stop its crackling and hold, like a breath, the scratch and buzz that has been riding with their voices like a dirty aura. Then, smudging the quiet's cleanness with new static-bearing speech, he says:

'You told me there's an inventory of all the motions that she and her husband modelled?'

'Yes,' she confirms.

'Send it to me,' he orders her. 'By the way, stop sending unencrypted files. Use CounterMail or Proton from now on.'

'Okay,' she tells him. 'I'll do that tomorrow. I'm matching the numbered inventory entries to the physical models in this collection. There's a little glitch, but it should be cleared up by then.'

In fact, there are two glitches: Dean's path through the archive has acquired its own pair of snags, its 'knots'. The first seems trivial: the inventory's entry-numbers skip from 807 to 809 – there's no 808. Clerical error perhaps – uncharacteristic, though, from the diligent Lillian. Dean wouldn't get too hung up on this, if it didn't come in tandem with the second snag-knot. This one's vaguer, harder to pinpoint: it consists of a change in the demeanour of the holdings' staff. Ms Richards, so benevolent and helpful for the first few days, has grown more distant – or, to be precise, evasive. She's still there, tending to Dean, supervising files' delivery to her; but a reticence has crept into her manner. Twice, in the last two days, request forms have come back with 'in use' stamped across them. When Dean asked 'by whom?' the archivist seemed to recoil, snatching the chit away as though even allowing her to see it were too much. Bizarrely, as they left the building after the second of these episodes, Dean heading off through the dark car park back towards the Hilton to file her daily report to London, Ms Richards called after her:

'Take care!'

The words weren't spoken in an offhand tone of voice, nor colloquially proffered; it sounded as though the archivist were actually warning her to be careful, as though she'd perceived some imminent threat lurking among Purdue's lawns and footpaths – ejaculation strange enough to make Dean turn around to ask what she meant. Too late: Ms Richards' hairbun, coat-wrapped frame and stuffed leather bag had slipped away into the darkness, and the question died in Dean's throat. The next day, when she raised the issue of the missing 808-entry, Ms Richards answered, almost curtly:

'I can't help you.'

No *Honey*; no beamed smiles; Dean was left to stare morosely at the gap on the page (there is one, a double return – she pictures a hand at the typewriter's lever, Lillian's or one of her secretaries', undulating in a double fishtail side-swipe, left to right and back again) between the photographs and short movement-descriptions of Box 807 and those of Box 809. It could well have been a simple error, after all: these entries are among the last ones, made at a point when Lillian's eyesight, like her memory, is fading, letters and notebook entries starting to wander off on their own divagating courses, handwriting kinking and wavering as the end, in all its shapelessness, heaves into view ...

Lillian spends her final three years in a retirement home in Phoenix, Arizona. It's called The Beatitudes. The name suggests to Dean some kind of girded region, like the Temperate or Torrid Zones, the Tropics or Antipodes, Indies or Maritimes; it's not until she looks it up that she realises it comes from the Gospels. Matt. 5:3–11: *Blessed are those who ... etc. ... etc.* Lillian, nominally, is agnostic – but she nonetheless believes in upward passages, apotheoses, transformations: hesitation to decision, awkwardness to grace. By this time she's phenomenally famous. Invitations (all declined) to speak, or at least to come and pick up honorary degrees, are pouring in from all around the world; there's talk of statues being erected, of becoming the first woman (Liberty aside) stamped on a US banknote ... In the Soviet Union, Lenin's veneration of her has taken deep root, outlived Lenin and moved on two or three generations, beyond Gastev, on to Rozmirovich, rationalisation associations, *ob'edineniia* ... Her children visit her, tell her about the moon landing for which her work has been so instrumental, but she doesn't really understand. She makes final, sporadic entries in the notebooks, though, and keeps up intermittent correspondence. It's among the tail end of this latter category, spread over the final two files, that Dean comes across the Vanins letters.

There are two of them, folded up in envelopes that, like Gastev's, bear Soviet postmarks – in Vanins' case, from 1969 and 1970. The paper inside is letterheaded with Cyrillic writing and an image that seems to depict some kind of university or research centre. The writing itself's in Latin script, though: handwritten English. It's quite hard to follow, partly by dint of not being very neat, partly due to a propensity to give over to diagrams or algebraic shorthand. The letters' author is one Raivis Vanins – name already familiar to Dean: Lillian has mentioned meeting him a few years earlier, in ... a quick flip back to File 32 retrieves this datum: Zürich, the Fourth International Symposium on Applied Kinetics. Lillian's diary entry of 26/2/65 records her being impressed by the young physicist, whom she saw as *taking my work somewhere interesting, quite unexpected* ... The letters seem to be part of a series; they refer to previous correspondence (not contained here); on top of which, they're incomplete, missing whole pages.

In the first letter, deploying a familiar tone (he uses her first name), Vanins thanks Lillian for her enthusiastic response to the work he's 'been conducting in light of the T.T. episode'. He outlines, through sketches and calculations so incomprehensible to

Dean that they might, with equal plausibility, represent a formulaic disquisition on the nature of dark matter or the flightpath of some kind of insect (there's a kind of cone, two directional arrows corkscrewing around a straight vertical line and, beside them, the same letters, *T.T.*), his thoughts about said 'episode', and informs her that, with her permission, he'll attempt to model it. Of the second letter, only page two is preserved inside the envelope: beginning and ending mid-sentence, it communicates what Vanins calls 'my shock – amazement, and perhaps delay ...' *delay*? No, there's a dot and then a cross: the word's *delight* ... 'my shock – amazement, and perhaps delight – at the implications of this labour, which would seem to transform all the tenets and' (illegible: *assumptions*?) 'of our ...'

Here the page ends. Paper-clipped to it, though, is a photo of a wireframe model – a little snapshot, like the others Dean has seen, the thumbnails in the Gilbreth inventory; but in contrast to these just a single, not a stereoscope, image; slightly skewed too, since it's been taken (presumably by Vanins) in a different setting, from a different angle, and printed with different chemicals on different paper. In the model, in its open-sided box, the metal track rises and turns first anticlockwise and then clockwise before plunging once more to the floor. At the top, on to the photograph itself, are written, once more, the doubled initials *T.T.*; at its base, *Box 808*.

It's not the air conditioning that sends a chill down Dean's back as she looks at this photo – more the sudden recognition, morphed into a physical awareness, of a missing part's insertion. She finds herself flipping back and forth between the files now with real vigour, driven by the sense that something's taking shape here: something solid, perhaps almost *sayable* – but, if so, only silently, in this scrawled idiom of pictorial and alphabetic cipher, doodle-hieroglyphics ... nonetheless, by virtue of these same, somehow *recoverable* ...

In the last file, there's a journal that she hasn't thumbed through yet, Lillian's final one. It, too, is full of doodles, letters, symbols that might, together, amount to some form of mathematical notation, or might simply represent the dying unravelling of a mind whose frame has lost all traction, warp- and cloth beams tumbled from their axes, fallen prey to woodworm and decay. Even amidst this fuzz and visual shipwreck, though, there are still words: fragments, snatches of recalled or uncompleted thoughts … *name for force that holds all things in motion? … praxis (energeia), work (ergon), potential (dynamis) – but contemplation … ?* A jumble of these snatch-fragments appears in the notebook's final entry, peppered about (as though to annotate) a drawing that Dean recognises as a shaky copying of one of the cone-and-corkscrew sketches from Vanins' first letter. Some of the words that Lillian has added, perched amidst the springs and arrows, look like names: *de Honnecourt, Maricourt, Bessler* … Others, lower down, seem to be written in an archaic form of Italian: *fattore … farsi … fattura … legato con amove in un volume … geomètra misurar lo cerchio … l'amov che move* … Three crayon-drawn circles cut across these lower fragments, each circle gradiently coloured so as to partially reflect the others. Below these, in English, runs, in bold, penned letters, like a kind of tag, the line: *Box 808 –* is that *charges?* No, it's *changes – Box 808 changes everything.*

In the time it takes Dean to flip forward through nine unused, virgin pages to the notebook's cover and then back again to this page, one thing at least has become clear to her: the inventory's omission of the eight hundred and eighth box is no accident or oversight, no numeric typo. There's a thing – a something, or an *everything* – behind it. That something has a name, or rather number – 808 – and an embodiment, a box, a low-grade photograph of which she, Dean, is holding in her hand. It's in her right hand; her left, meanwhile, is hungrily (and blindly) padding the desk around it, feeling for a copy-permission sheet – vainly too, it turns out: she's used up all the ones Ms Richards gave her. She considers going over to the archivist's station to ask her for a new one, but holds back, as though afraid of leaving these open files alone, of letting the alignment into which she's nudged and coaxed them – alignment that, like that of stars, seems to portend some great event, some revelation, but just fleetingly, when viewed at the right moment from a certain point and angle – slip away again. She stays there until closing time, first noting all the words down, then just staring at the pages, eyes darting from diary to photograph to letter, letter to diary to photograph, as though to string-and-tack them, to cat's cradle the whole set of scenes and movements, or at least their traces, on to which they open – and, in the same movement, close again ...

After being kicked out, she races straight back to the Hilton, and stays up most of the night drafting a new report for Dorley:

Somewhere,

she writes, excitement and the lateness of the hour extending her a license for rhetorical indulgence that she wouldn't normally permit herself,

in the relay between Ms Gilbreth and her young adherent on the far side of the world, the far side of the Iron Curtain; in the transfers and translations, in the unexpected redirections of the type that only geographic distance and generational difference and, above all, chance's vagaries can occasion, something cropped up that seems to have beguiled, fixated and surprised them both – certainly, to have consumed Ms Gilbreth to the point that, in a final and quite counterintuitive move, she redacted it from the index of her life's endeavour. The significance attached by her to Box 808 is, despite the host of unknowns hemming it in on every side, beyond all contestation. For her, and in her own words, it 'changed every-thing'. For my part, I'm convinced that, despite the enfeebled

too strong – and prejudicial

that, despite her weakening general state around this time, the recognition on her part of some kind of breakthrough

achieved by her cohort Vanins (himself at the peak of his professional and intellectual powers) was effected from a robust
inner mental enclave, a castle keep of absolute lucidity ...

Does Dean really believe this? She does. Despite the shakiness, the
incoherence, there's a conviction emanating from the penstrokes,
from the words, a certainty that no doubt, not even the confusion
of senility, can undermine. The question follows, though –

The question follows: what new ground did this box breach,
that hundreds of other boxes hadn't? A course-shifting event,
insight or understanding must have emerged from what first
Vanins and then Ms Gilbreth called 'the T.T. episode'. As
to the nature of this episode, I remain entirely in the dark.
Perhaps more research, this time into Vanins' own archive,
should such exist, is called for. How this last might be tracked
down, given the disintegration of the state under whose
auspices he worked, is ...

She sends this, as instructed, in encrypted form, over the firm's
safe line. She then steals a few hours' sleep beneath whose surface
dreams – of boxes sent by ocean liner to the wrong location,
Five-Guy and Tender-Button shake-straws twisted into wireframes
modelling some momentous action taking place offstage (behind
the counter, in the kitchen or some other non-specific backroom),
tardily submitted copy-request slips that, doubling as hotel-guest
towels, blot, sog and disintegrate – are never far submerged.
Morning finds her in the strip mall's Au Bon Pain, then, ten minutes prior to opening, staking out the Holding Center's entrance,
willing its staff – custodians and doormen, even janitors, but principally Ms Richards – to appear round the corner, jangling keys.
Her willing doesn't work: Ms Richards doesn't come today. In
her place, when the Holding Center does eventually open, there's a
man: a little younger, possibly late thirties, white, neat moustache
sitting on a grey, clean-shaven face. She senses, as soon as she nears

his workstation (he's reordered it; it's *his* today), a new charge in the air. He rises to meet her, but it's not a friendly rising; more like – *almost* like – a blocking of her route.

'Can I help you?' He utters the words coldly, in a tone that makes it clear that helping her's the last thing he intends to do.

'Oh,' says Dean. 'I'm working here. I mean …'

'You're staff?' he asks.

'No, no,' she starts to tell him. 'I'm a reader. A researcher. I've been here – just here …'

As she tentatively points over his shoulder to her little desk, she sees that her nest of files and papers, which Ms Richards usually leaves out for her, has been cleared up.

'Oh …' she says again.

'You have a pass?' he asks.

'What? Yes, of course,' she answers, feeling for it in the pocket of her handbag. As she does this, the man's face, despite its attempts to remain expressionless, is briefly lit up by a micro-smile, a flicker of pleasure furnished by a foreknowledge of what's about to happen.

'Please touch in,' he instructs her.

Ms Richards issued her the pass and showed her how to do this on her first day here, but subsequently always buzzed her through herself, so Dean has never used it. Pressed to the electronic reader now, the card's met with a sour beep that, if she'd been sinaes-thetic, would have presented to her vision the same colour and tone as this man's skin.

'Oh …' Dean mutters for a third time. 'Shall I … ?'

The man doesn't answer, doesn't help her out in any way. After what seems like an interminable pause, he says to her:

'Your card's not good for entry to this centre.'

'What can I … ?' she begins; then, again, 'Maybe I can …' But these efforts don't get any uptake. Eventually she tries: 'I mean, I'm a registered visitor.'

This last clause he latches on to. 'Any visiting privileges you had,' he informs her, 'have been rescinded.'

'How do you mean?' she asks.

'You are no longer welcome here. You'll have to leave the building.'

The next few minutes, when she'll look back on them, will remain stubbornly blank, as unretained in memory as long-past movements never modelled. She must have turned and walked back down the corridor, past the concierge's booth, opened the door and exited – but these actions seem to have evaporated along with her access to the world of Lillian and Frank and Vanins and the curves of sculpted light and moulded time and all the other magic toys that have been placed beyond her reach. All she'll remember is standing alone in the Holding Center's outsize car park in the bright indifferent sunshine, listening to the middle-distance trundle and whirr of vehicles passing by on Interstate 52.

Book Two

1. And Down We Went

You don't hear the fan start. There's no slow and ponderous *thwop ... thwop* notching up to *thwop-thwop-thwop*, then accelerating through the *thwopthwopthwopthwop* layer before emerging on the other side as an undifferentiated liquid roar. This is due, in part, to the positioning of motors and compressor at the point of the circuit furthest from the test section and the control room; in part also to the electric buzz that, spilling from the motors' dedicated substation, covers the whole site. The engineers know when the fan is on, though. The first thing they pick up is the ripple-pattern on the surface of their tea; then comes the windows' rattle, and a general blurring (or is it a *sharpening*? van Boezem duck-rabbits from side to side on this one) of all edges: desktops, monitors, drawers, whiteboards. A few seconds after this, flesh joins the vibratory awakening: you feel it in your gut, in pressure waves, like bass – only, you realise as the frequency now finally resolves itself into a sound, it's high, not low; soprano, an urgent and indefinitely prolonged *fermata*, drawn from the fraught diaphragm of some mechanical Rhinemaiden.

Most wind tunnels have two control rooms: one for synchronising the activities of the various aerodynamic subsystems, the other for model-handling. Here at Nederlans Wind NV (formerly Nederlans Lucht- en Ruimtevaartlaboratorium Luttelgeest), these functions are amalgamated in a single space, which, consequently, has assumed almost cathedral-like proportions. Under a giant halo light that seems to hover, flat and round as a benevolent spaceship, are two rows of pews, all white, with screens interpolated down their length at regular intervals like prayer books. Right now, several of these screens are showing temperature readings from the stilling chamber, second throat and contractor, pressure readings from the strain gauge balances and blow off, or voltage readings from the heat assembly, all topographically arrayed. Others show the outline, geometric and abstracted, of the model. The actual model, the physical object, is being nudged and shuffled into place atop a force plate set in the test section's floor, which is raised by half a metre from that of the control room and separated from it by a partition wall whose central stretch is inlaid with a thick window. The elevation and the framing, not to mention the illumination from the lights embedded in the test section's surfaces, infuse the model and the men around it with the look of figures in an altar scene or stained-glass panel: a master image to which the smaller, lowlier boxed pictures votively refer. The model seems (and not entirely without cause) to give off its own light – no model at all in lay terms but the thing itself, full-scale, fully dirigible, fibreglass cowling and steel parabolic runners (eu.4,000 a pop) freshly scored by the Igls ice it shot down just two days ago: a bright-red bob-sleigh, BMW, fifth generation, and the Österreichischer Bob- und Skeletonverband (Zweierbobdivision)'s pride and joy.

'There will be no movement.' *Cheftrainer* Otto Ebner, ITK, M.Sc. (Linz), peers nervously towards the precious vehicle as the NW engineers lock the force plate's crown into position.

'Well,' van Boezem grants him, 'the *bobsleigh* won't move. The air will move around it.'

'*Ja, natürlich,*' Ebner says impatiently. 'That part I understand. But what I mean is that there'll be no *Friktion. Reibung.* It only stands above the board, with runners still on the same place. On the *authentisch* track, over the ice, the runners move.'

Van Boezem pinches the bridge of his nose. No Lorentz-transformation algebra required to work out that this session will be long. 'Ground friction was not one of our parameters,' he gently informs Ebner. 'Only air drag. If you'd requested it, we could have placed a moving belt under the model, although not one made of ice – and then, the speeds at which ...'

'No, no: is fine,' Sven Medosch, the Verband's *Statistiker*, slips his svelte arm across Ebner's shoulders and leads him away from van Boezem towards a spread of clipboards, casting the Chief Technician a wink as he does so. Ebner won't be that easily bought off, though; he still peers out, hawk-like, at the bob, the engineers, his half-naked riders, upper portions of Elastan suits hung from their waists, the spread arms lolling downwards, limp and sacrificial ... From the moment this Dutch visit was first mooted, he insisted on verisimilitude. He's told the riders not to look at or even think about the wind-tunnel environment around them, but to fill their heads instead with sights, sounds, smells of the *Bobbahn*: rushing white walls, rooftops of Badhaussiedlung flashing into view beyond them, scrapes and crashes, the refrigeration plant's ammonia ... Everything counts. They're dealing in thousandths and ten-thousandths on overall times, which translates, at any isolated moment within that continuum, to micro-, even nanoseconds. At this level, the molecular comes into play: of this he's sure. Just thinking something (*Here's a banked turn ... It is cold ... Ice whips my cheeks ...*) will fire off neurons that will cause changes in muscle tension, inflate neck and thigh nerves, trigger a contraction of the shoulders; and these things, all these voluminous, if to the naked eye invisible, arrangements, reassemblies – well, these too must register at some scale, present surfaces and edges to be touched, resisted, dragged, no? ... *Wer weiß?* It all forms part of the picture.

And here's Phocan, set back by several rows of monitors and NW or OBSV personnel from the test section's glowing shrine. He's standing guard, with Lucy Diamond, over a trolley on which several large cases are stacked. PIV: particle image velocimetry. It's new, for Pantarey at least, assayed successfully with ventilation fans, about as powerful as a stack of hairdryers, back in The Cell, but otherwise as yet un-road-, or rather tunnel-, tested; this will be its first real application. Phocan, running this thought through his mind, finds himself tripping, or at least stumbling, over the word 'real' – not for the obvious reasons (setting's artifice, speed's simulation, etc., etc.) but because it forms the tail end of the space-ship's name that's wedged itself into his various mental door frames ever since that jaunt to Berners Street, to Degree Zero's office, the whole *Incarnation* project. *Sidereal*. He had to look it up (*adj*: of or pertaining to the stars; time measured relative to same; motion as well; from *sidus*, star) and even press the online dictionary's little *speak me* button for the right pronunciation. *Side-ear-ial*, stress on the *ear*. In his own ear, though, in its echo-chamber, he still hears it as *side-real*: two words, standing beside each other, speaking of adjacency – their own, sure, but also of adjacency in general, of things set to the side of other things. Would that, he muses as he, too, watches the riders kit up, mean *un*real things, turfed out of the real's kingdom, made to stand in some ignominious corner of deceptiveness and falsehood? Or might it mean real things *themselves* cast aside, rerouted, drifted leeward, hiding in a kind of quantum sidebar to the world, to time? At the film's climax, the ship's supposed to start disintegrating: *that's* what he's meant to be asking van Boezem about today, when the right moment drifts by, an aside: *Would it be viable to model the disintegration sequence here?* They're already doing it in water, in Berlin; but a wind tunnel would give them another POV on it – it is wind, after all, that's meant to tear the thing apart ... And if the answer's *Yes*, he'd not only be helping his friend Eldridge; in drumming up more business for the firm, he'd also be earning Brownie points with Garnett: two birds, one stone. Meanwhile, there are the lasers and the delay generators – and, most importantly, the bubbles ...

Suits have been pulled fully on now, BMW and OBSV logos puffed up into legibility by forearms, pectorals and deltoids. When the riders stoop to gather up their helmets, Katja Avanessian, team *Krankengymnast*, extracts two small plastic packets from her tracksuit pocket and hands one to each. They're ear-plugs, polyu-rethane, designed to compress then re-expand to fit the contours of a given ear canal. As Oskar Luksch squeezes his in, he feels their noses slide over cartilaginous *Startkurven*, ride up fibrous walls of first, then second *Hohes S*-turns, before getting wedged somewhere in acoustic-meatal speed traps. It prompts him to begin his visualisation: for the next 54.25 seconds, while Brakeman Eward Miessen performs box jumps and calf raises, Avanessian clears away discarded water flasks and Engineer de Veen preps up his smoke gun, Navigator Luksch stands in the same spot, eyes closed, hands clasping spectral rings that hover just before his waist, swaying first one way then another as inclining shoulders set a line for chest and stomach to pursue, hips twist and calibrate, then the whole torso twitches, readjusts, pursues another line … To van Boezem and his staff, Phocan and Diamond too, he has the look of a *sensei*, or *senpai*, an adept or apprentice in some esoteric martial art; or maybe just a madman.

'High speed leg good; compressor good; vanes positioned; temperature stable …' Second Technician Roussel's eyes hopscotch about three screens as he checks off the functions.

'Wind-flow up to .4,' van Boezem instructs him.

A palpable excitement spreads across the Austrian contingent; they all look at the test section, expecting … expecting what? Leaves to scurry along the ground, branches to whip and dance, riders to grab at lamp-posts as their umbrellas evert and fly away? None of these events, of course, occur. But there's a stirring – one that seems to come, like the visceral tremblings and the singing (which they clock as something not *new*, but rather familiar yet until now unnoticed), as much from *within* as from the tunnel's recesses: an eerie and exhilarating apprehension that what's meant to happen here is happening already, all around, invisible.

Van Boezem nods to Medosch, Ebner, Avanessian. 'We'll start slow.'

Ebner holds his index finger up towards his riders: First Position. Luksch, standing at the bob's left side, retracts the push-bar from its slit and holds his open hands eight or so centimetres from this, as though warming his palms on it. Miessen stations himself half a metre behind and slightly to the right of him at the bob's rear, hands similarly raised above the fixed twin push-bars on its fins. The riders remain still and silent for a good half-minute, letting their breathing synchronise. Then Luksch starts intoning the cadence:

> *Ach, du lieber Augustin,*
> *Augustin, Augustin*

After the first two lines, Miessen joins in, and the two of them rock back and forth in unison as they chant:

> *Ach, du lieber Augustin,*
> *Alles ist hin!*

– their voices rising more and more with every beat until they hit both *hin!* and bars with a loud shout, throwing the full force of their minds and bodies at the word, the metal and – ultimate target, to be rushed, ambushed, blasted to oblivion before it has a chance to scramble its counterforces – stasis. Or that's what they *would* do if they were on the starting ramp at Igls; here at Luttelgeest they can't *actually* push. They know exactly how to manage the discrepancy, though; Ebner has been very precise in his instructions: they're still to fling every last joule of energy towards the bars – but then, at the precise juncture where the force would (in the normal sequence of things) pass from hand to metal, they're to freeze the instant. Not relax, *versteht ihr – gar nicht!* – but to freeze, or to arrest (*verhaften*) the action, keeping it in such a state that the force remains present, concentrated, even active; but restrained. The two men do this now, and hold the posture, the required exertion doubled by the dual demands of pushing *and* holding back.

'Now,' van Boezem tells the Austrians, 'we seed the air.'

He nods to Engineer de Veen, stationed by the tunnel's wall two metres upwind of the riders. De Veen presses a switch on his smoke gun and holds its wand out so its nozzle sits right in the centre of the flow. The propylene glycol vapour first emerges from it as a wispy dribble, unsure where to go – then, elongating as it slithers from the aperture, raises and weaves its head from side to side as it advances, a snake charmed by the tunnel-*pungi*'s single, drawn-out note, its body rippling along behind until, taken complete control of by the stream, it hurries in a straight, brisk thread towards the model. When it meets the bobsleigh's nose it curves around and hugs this closely, without losing either form or (it seems) speed; to the Austrians' untrained eyes, the cowling even appears, in raising and kinking the vapour, to accelerate it. Hitting first Luksch's and then Miessen's bodies, though, the thread – halted, rebounding, crushed by its own continued onrush – frays into a jumble of irregular patches which in turn break up and dissipate into a formless cloud around the riders' helmets.

'You can see,' van Boezem commentates unnecessarily, 'that standing is not aerodynamic.'

'*Ja*,' says Medosch, 'but is unavoidable. How else can they get quickly moving? And besides, the speed is low in this phase – so they are not creating much resistance, I think. *Oder* . . . ?'

The Chief Technician gives him an approving pedagogic nod. 'The Reynolds number round the bodies at this point is . . .' The statement floats, unfinished, towards Roussel, who, plucking the figure from his left screen's right-hand column, tells them:

'1×10^2.'

'What's Reynolds?' Medosch asks.

'Inertia-to-viscosity ratio,' van Boezem answers. 'It's a dimensionless quantity, so we can use it to scale up or down a given situation, or to establish dynamic similitude between different positions – in this instance, of the riders . . .'

Luksch and Miessen, in their test section, know nothing of Reynolds numbers. Luksch, as per Ebner's instructions, is gathering mountain peaks around him – Patscherkofel, Serles, Kreusspitze, Speckkarspitze – stacking them, nearer and further, in the smoke-haze. Miessen, meanwhile, is running through his split-times: .1 seconds off the leading pace at fifty metres means .3 over the course; .2 at fifty stretches to .7; .3 to a gaping 1.5 . . . This, too, is seeding: by the time you've hit the first mark, the eventual delay's already bedded in the present moment's soil, the end-time's genetic destiny written in the roots and tendrils that grow out of this, a code that no twisting contingencies of skill or luck will ever fully manage to erase or override. Miessen, like all brakemen, has grown strong under the load of this responsibility. It weighs on him regressively: if the jump-on spot is where, handing the reins to Luksch, he gifts to the navigator a future that, *at the hand-on point itself*, is largely set, then this point, too, is seeded, predetermined – by the first steps of the push, the tightness of the cadence prior to that, his limbering-up before that too, the training before even that; regimes of exercise, nutrition, general formation stretching back for weeks, months, years. Gripping the push-bars tighter still, he summons through the vapour memories of his first ever descent: his cousin's fourteenth birthday party, Königssee run glowing in winter darkness under arc lights whose meter had been well fed by the coins of Onkel Lukas (*privat vermietet* for a whole two hours: Tobias's branch of the family, flashing across his horizon in biannual starbursts of Audis, dressage horses and Antiguan holidays, always seemed like aristocrats next to his); and he, not knowing the other guests (all Kalksburg classmates of Tobias), lurked in the background, poor relation – until Tobias, on his fourth or fifth go, pushed a boy wearing a brand-new Schöffel ski suit from the sleigh and beckoned him instead into the back seat, shouting pink-faced *Hold tight, Eward ... Hold on tight ...*

Ebner, level with and perpendicular-facing to his riders on the far side of the viewing window, lets his gaze slide from their visored faces and Elastan-coated shoulders, hips and knees, on upstream (down imaginary run) into the smoke-flow. His lips, cracked and blue-veined, are open, moving almost imperceptibly, intoning what van Boezem, glancing sideways at him, presumes are his own quantities and scales, the Reynolds numbers of his discipline's arcana. Wrongly: what's actually being mouthed into the air is the continuation of the cadence:

> *Geld ist weg, Mensch ist weg,*
> *Alles hin, Augustin!*

Ach, du lieber Augustin,
Alles ist hin!

The words, both carried and smothered by the tunnel's song, start colouring the scene's bizarre abstraction: its transposition of sleigh and riders from their ice-groove twelve hundred kilometres away to this empty tube; their simultaneous doing and not-doing of their actions; their frozenness in time while time still visibly flows on past them … As folk-rhythm and arrhythmic, monotonal fan-note fold into and out of one another in the space around his ears, Ebner senses, seeping out from the test area with a consistency against which no thickness of glass could insulate, infusing the control room's air, filling his lungs with every breath, a kind of melancholy. He pictures the cadence's author, the drunk minstrel Marx Augustin, set down (as recounted by the stanzas) in a grave that isn't his, a plague pit, stripped of money, friends, clothes, even a floor to lie on, clutching the only object he has left: the bagpipe, outlandish paraphernalia of his errant craft, this plaintive sack of wind …

'Otto. Hey, Otto!' Medosch has been saying his name for a few seconds now. Ebner grunts, shuddering himself back to attentiveness.

'What?'

'Ready for Second Position?'

'*Ja, selbstverständlich.*' He waves to Luksch and Miessen; when, seeing this gesture, they uncrouch and loosen, shaking hands and feet and rolling heads, he holds two fingers up. Obediently, they climb into the sleigh, Luksch at the front, Miessen behind. Once in, the brakeman doubles over, bowing his head forwards till it's buried in the small of Luksch's back; the navigator, meanwhile, slides his legs down the interior of the vehicle's front cowling, right down to the nose, hands feeling for the steering rings while torso sinks until only the visor and the helmet's crown protrude above the fibreglass's rim.

'You can increase the speed now,' Medosch tells van Boezem. The Chief Technician nods and instructs Roussel to ramp wind-flow up to 1.5. Again the Austrians all peer expectantly towards the test section, inside which (again) nothing looks any different – until de Veen once more fires up his smoke gun and holds out its wand: this time the wind snatches the thread immediately, whips it straight along to the sleigh's nose and over its upper body towards Luksch's helmet – meeting which it kinks a second time, as smoothly and continuously as the first; then, curving back downwards as it clears the crown, traces the outline of his upper back for a few centimetres before peeling off, re-finding its horizontal and, ignoring Miessen crouching far below it, racing on unfrayed to the tunnel's diffuser.

'Like a silk tight over a waxed leg, no?' van Boezem smiles to Medosch.

Unobserved by any of the men, the eyes of the two women present, Avanessian and Diamond, meet and roll.

'What groundspeed is this simulating?' Medosch asks.

'About seventy kilometres per hour,' replies van Boezem.

'They do this speed,' the *Statistiker* tells him, 'for the run's first half only. By the second they're at 120, even 140.'

Van Boezem half-turns towards Roussel, floating this figure onward to him too. Roussel's hands slide about three keyboards, pipe-organist fingers pressing keys, initiating tracker actions, pumping bellows, pulling stops. Inside the test section, de Veen plants his front leg more firmly and leans back into the wall. The smoke is hurtling over model and riders now, honing them, like a belt sander perfectly aligned with razor's edge. The Rhinemaiden's becoming more and more worked up: her pitch, still emanating from all quarters – walls, desks, objects, air – is growing higher, louder, faster. A minute or so into this new flow-rate (3.1, Roussel announces to the room), an effect so eerie and (it seems) miraculous occurs that all but the NW personnel turn and cast about them looks of bewildered fascination, like enchanted sailors.

'Where are those coming from?' Ebner speaks for all of them; 'those' being the voices (plural, contrapuntal) into which the single note is separating out and multiplying. More than a duet, it's a madrigal, with Aeolian minors, tritones and ascending sixths – all slightly *off*, but off by intervals that, while not uniform, seem coordinated, each one's notch of off-ness corresponding, by some system which no earthly musicology could parse or measure, to that of the others. The image comes to him of electric pylons singing in the wind: lattices, cages, gantries, crossarms, wires all oscillating, voices humming each at their own frequency but intertwining, a hermetic *cantus firmus.*

'From the fins,' van Boezem answers Ebner, pointing. Directing their gaze back at the test section now, they see the smoke-thread being chopped up around the bobsleigh's tail into short snippets, each of which twists and cringes, as though trying to flex its way back upstream, to a time before the cut, the sudden birth, this traumatic discontinuity, but succeeding only in taking up its place as one more in a set of disconnected, curling vortices.

'*Le tourbillon,*' Roussel says knowingly.

'What?' Medosch asks.

'The engineer's old friend the whirlpool,' annotates van Boezem. 'Your bobsleigh's strolling down von Kármán Street.'

'Reynolds is up to 90,' Roussel states, much too contentedly for Medosch's liking; 'which means drag coefficient .075.'

This figure Medosch understands. Turning towards van Boezem, he mutters: 'Not good ...'

'No, no,' the Chief Technician answers soothingly. 'It is good. This turbulence you must think of as the sand in which the treasure you've come here in search of has been buried. Here is where we start to dig, take readings, help you make improvements ... Our machine' – the helix-swirl his hand makes at this point expands the reference area of this rather old-fashioned term, *machine*, so that it circumscribes both the test section and the out-of-view stretches of the tunnel; also the control room, the entire site and, beyond all these, some mysterious, or perhaps dimensionless, quantity forever destined to exceed the sum of its constituent figures – 'will be your map and shovel all in one. We even do the digging for you ...' NW has paid a brand consultancy firm eu.50,000 to come up with this analogy. It seems to get some purchase on the Austrian.

'Yes. Yes, of course,' he says. 'What do they need to do?'

'The riders?' asks van Boezem. 'Nothing. We will run the wind-flow right up to the top speeds the sleigh reaches, and keep it up there for as long as they can hold position. During this time, we vary the angle of attack, by changing ...'

Medosch begins to frame a question, but van Boezem whips the answer out before a word is uttered:

'The angle, that is, between the model's reference line – its chord – and the oncoming flow. This we achieve by changing the inclination of the force pad. Thus we can ascertain not only drag but also lift, lateral force, yaw, roll and pitching moments over a range of attack angles.'

'You can *see* all these?' Medosch asks.

'Some of them we will see in the smoke and on the chalk; and' – here he nods towards the British delegation – 'the bubbles. But what we see with the eye will be a sketch, no more. The gold will come to the surface later, when the data's processed.'

Roussel digests the figure that van Boezem proceeds to murmur to him – 5.2 – with a kind of avarice. As he opens the valve yet further, they all feel the gut-roll growing, waves spreading outwards from their abdomens, across the room, the air, the other people's bodies – and inwards too, vibrating down through muscles, fluid, bone. The choir are screaming now, fugue-permutations veering and careening to the outer limits of the field where *any* ratio of intervals or pitches might hold sway: tonics swapping with sub-dominants within the space of single notes that seem to play out in three octaves all at once, false entries, inversions, retrogrades and diminutions running riot through all keys – until, suddenly, these fall away, like clouds, and the accompanying mute throbbing in their inner ears lets them know, like the calm, triumphant silence that fills airline cabins in the first few seconds after take-off and ascent have been successfully completed, that they've passed the hearing threshold.

Phocan and Diamond took the early flight today: Stansted, 5.45. With no duties to perform yet, Phocan's gazing at Roussel's screens, their digit-clusters and their thermal patches, outlines and auras pulsing in peristaltic rhythm as the feed-data replenishes itself. If Roussel is sifting lines and figures, sorting shuffling movements into groupings and translating colour-swarms to information, Phocan's simply hypnotised, Medusaed. On the central monitor the bobsleigh's silhouette crouches in vivid blue, innermost doll of a *matryoshka* set, with ever-larger silhouettes repeating all around it and each other, grading from green to yellow as they multiply. No fixed shells, though, these dolls are living – or maybe dying. Their bodies, as they tumble escalating outwards, are forever breaking open, pixel life-blood gushing from one level to the next, which ruptures too, ditto the next layer – on and on up, in lurid flows that radiate towards some vague periphery, then, when it seems all form and structure *must* have ebbed away, turn round and radiate back in again, the two-way current generating in its midst small, transitory islands, intermediate thresholds that, no sooner than they're formed, start bleeding too. Somewhere, around the borders of his own dazzled thought-screen, he senses an intuition trying to stake out a provisional ground, or at least drop into the flood tide a sea anchor; senses at work within these flows some kind of *logic*. Not the fixed one under whose protectorate Roussel's operating and within whose jurisdiction the processors and hard-drives are accumulating rates and indices ... No, Phocan's starting to suspect the presence of some *other* kind – an *illogical* logic, whose nebulous, endlessly mutating grammar would be formed not of fixed terms but of its own very mutability, pure drift ... One, though, at whose core, or outer border (since these two are shifting places constantly), there lies a proposition ...

Which – elusive and perhaps ridiculous, but this morning, in NW's gargantuan contraption, filtered through the gauze of his cognitive dissonance, no less insistent – proposition, plainly stated, is: that this display, this lurid animation, has been crafted, tailor-made, for him, specifically *for him* – if only he might ...

if he had the wherewithal to ... It's the acetate effect again, the overlaying, simultaneity: this looped drama of shape-finding and shape-loss, of coagulation and disintegration, seems to gather and disperse, to draw into discernibility even as, in the same motion, it scrambles it again, a process – is it too much to say a *struggle?* – to which Phocan, though he never willed or planned it this way, has been dedicating his whole life. The pixellated dumbshow, pregnant with itself, seems to affirm this to him on repeat, performing, in encrypted, mute language of shade and contour, a long quest he's never quite managed to *name*, all its encounters glimpsed in passing but not realised, some seduction whose full consummation might be glorious but would (the rupture and the blood-gush hint) necessitate, or at least stand *adjacent* to, a scene of monumental and inexorable violence. Now Phocan senses, tingling in his gut with the great fan's vibrations, a dual feeling of purpose and of guilt – guilt for an act of which, even if he's never *executed* it as such, he's been, since long ago, entirely culpable.

'Mark?' asks Diamond. 'What are you ... ?'

And just as suddenly the intuition and the understanding which it seemed to be drawing, in pulses, to the edge of clarity both dissipate, spilling past the on-screen *matryoshka* bobsleighs' and his own mind's outer lip, conjectures carried and transmuted beyond recognition by the unforgiving lines, inferences all unravelling into their dance ...

' *'ch habe eine Frage.*' Ebner, three feet closer to the test section than Phocan, has been similarly lost in musings – in his case directed to or prompted by his contemplation, through the glass sheet, of the actual bobsleigh, or rather of the smoke-laced air flowing around it. He murmurs his remark in German as he's really just thinking aloud; but, since a question's signalled, van Boezem asks him what he wants to know. The *Cheftrainer* hesitates at first; then, switching to English, outs with it. 'If I am understanding right, your' – he opts for that quaint word again – '*machine* ... is leading back round to itself.'

The Chief Technician, despite the obtuse phrasing, understands what he's getting at. 'Yes,' he answers, 'it's a Prandtl tunnel. A fixed loop.'

'This means,' Ebner continues, 'that the wind that passes my men turns a corner, and another, and another, and eventually passes them again a second time; and then a third; a fourth; a fifth ...'

'Well, yes,' van Boezem says.

'Then, my question: once it contacts with their bodies, with the sleigh, it is changed. It is ... marked. Its shape, as the smoke shows us, has been altered; and this alteration is a point of information.'

'Yes, exactly,' van Boezem's face beams teacherly benevolence again.

'So this bit of wind then moves onwards, down the tunnel, *all the time still shaped this way*. It is no longer just a neutral piece of air: it is an *Abdruck*, an ...'

'Imprint. Impression,' Avanessian prompts.

'*Genau*: impression, of my navigator's elbow or my brakeman's cheek, or of the bobsleigh's nose, or of this whirlpool by its fins. And not just of that body: it's a *Stempel*, also, a "stamp", of that moment, of that point in time, *nicht wahr?*'

'Yes, but ...'

'So: when it comes around the second time, already shaped and *stempelt* this way, and it hits the nose or cheek or elbow once more, which once more should make a mark, an information-point – well, I am thinking ...'

The others wait indulgently for him to formulate this – his own team, too. He's won three Olympic golds, four silvers, six bronzes. Method in madness; he has leeway.

'... I am thinking that this second *Abdruck* cannot be a pure one. It is not imprinting on to blank, but on to an already-imprint. After it has gone round the first time, every particle of air is like this: a two-, or three-, or thousand-time already-imprint. And the moment-*Stempel*, too, is carried round to the next moment, which so then is *stempelt* on already-moment ... which is a big problem for me, because ... because when ...'

This one, medals or not, he can't quite formulate. It's there, though, lucid in his head: the vertiginous suspicion that this instant of perception on the riders' part (of coldness, being whipped by ice, seeing the turn's edges loom), and, with it, a newly generated piece of *now*-ness, is being funnel-looped round, folded back in on itself, to replay, like Marx Augustin, from the hollow spot of its wrongful interment.

'But,' van Boezem breaks the awkward pause, 'it's not like that. There are the honeycombs in both the settling chamber and contraction area, and meshes, which remove swirl and lateral variation as the air passes through their cells. And the diffuser's screens, that break down eddies into smaller ones, which decay faster. All these are turbulence-suppressing mechanisms; through them, we are able to deliver to the test section consistently clean air.'

Ebner digests this sceptically, then asks:

'Where do *you* get the air from?'

'In the first place, you mean?'

Ebner nods.

'We take it from the ambient, just like an open Eiffel tunnel does.'

'The ambient?'

'Outside: the fields, the sky ...'

'From the ambient it comes and to the ambient it returns,' Roussel intones, lifting his eyes up to the halo-light.

Van Boezem fixes Ebner with a reassuring smile, which is half-heartedly returned. The physics lesson's settled the *Cheftrainer* for now; but small, undecayed pockets of disquiet are still there, swirling downstream in the honeyed silence. Van Boezem senses a tiny perturbation in his own mind, too: something to do with his elision, unchallenged by Ebner and so let stand by him, that casts the Luttelgeest air as the ultimate blank slate: uncompressed, unfiltered, free as the birds that dart about it. Disingenuously: he knows all too well – as engineer and *polderburger* – that the air about these fields, this sky, is anything but neutral. It, too, is *stempelt*. This landscape has been made: lines laid down, sections divided by right angles, flows turned and diverted down braced channels. *God*, as the old saying (unattributed) would have it, *created the Earth – but the Dutch created Holland*. A century ago there wasn't any earth, or even air, here; only water. Lying three metres lower than the sea it has (for now) evicted, polder land is scooped-out, hollow land: one giant wind tunnel. And in all Dutch polders, right from the beginning, it was wind that did the scooping and the empty-ing: cap-mounted sails pumping water through *duikertjes*, into Archimedes screws the windmills also powered ... And when the polders grew and bumped against each other, and the water bailed out of one threatened to overrun its neighbour, rather than fighting and sabotaging one another's works (as villages in Bangladesh still do), municipalities, like children pooling Lego, let their individual polders become chambers in a huge, amalgamated polder-circuit – which, in turn, called for joined-up governance, a national control room operating subsystems of *baljuws*, *heemraden* and *dijkgraafs*. Three of van Boezem's ancestors were *baljuws*; one of them is mentioned in Leeghwater's *Dagboek;* his paternal grandfather, the one he knew, worked directly under Lely. Environmental manage-ment is in the blood that pumps around his body: regulated flows, each cycle marking out a generation ...

And so is disquiet – or, to give it a simpler name: fear. For there's that other wind, even less neutral, whistling off the Noordsee, from Rhein-, Maas-, Schedlt- and Eems-nymphs all conglomerated (gods, too, can pool Lego) into a monstrous Zuidermaiden, furious and vengeful. You can't always hear her, but she's still transmitting on some frequency or other, even when the storm-fan's idle: in previ-ous triumphs written on the ground, circular *wielen* scored by the screwing movement of inland-boring water; or carved, like the name of van Boezem's maternal grandfather, the one he never knew, into memorial-stone beside those of the grandmother and two uncles he never knew either, drowned in their sleep in '53; or in the dreams that, despite the Delta Project's realisation and the sealing of all exits to the sea (the polder-circuit, too, is closed-loop now), despite the EUMETSTAT- and FOAM-linked, MPP-enabled weather-tracking systems to which every *stadhuis* in the whole of Flevoland is hooked up, still come to him, as to all *polderburgers*, at least once a year – dreams of water rushing, vertical as the dyke-wall it's just breached, thundering and boiling as it spreads out at its base, a giant brush lifting trees, cattle, houses, people, sweeping them away …

The tunnel has been running at 5.2 for half an hour. Roussel turns from his screens and signals to his boss that he's got what he wants for now; van Boezem does the same to Medosch; Medosch looks enquiringly to Ebner, who nods back at him, then signals to his riders to stand down – or, rather, up. All their ears pop as they drop back through the hearing threshold. De Veen has downed his smoke gun and picked up a camera; he's taking side-on photographs of the bobsleigh's rear section, on to which he painted, just before the session started, a monochrome layer of kerosene mixed with fluorescent chalk. The wind has evaporated the former and coaxed the latter out into a boldly contrasting set of vortices and sinusoids smeared luminously over each fin, abstract geometric paintings. Van Boezem, turning to the Pantarey duo, announces:

'Bubble time!'

This is Phocan and Diamond's cue to unpack their trolley-mounted cases. They extract, from cut foam lining in which the objects sit like the articulated parts of saxophones or rifles, a range of angle-poise arms, cameras, lasers, goggles and a plastic bottle of car-battery size from which a pipe protrudes and inside which a greenish liquid sloshes as it's carried to the test section. While Phocan helps de Veen fix lasers and cameras to the tunnel's walls and ceiling, van Boezem explains to the Austrians:

'You will be the first NW clients to benefit from this particular flow tracer.'

'The goggles are for us?' Avanessian ask Diamond.

'No,' she answers. 'They're for the riders. But if anyone is epileptic, you might want to leave the room.'

The wisdom of these words becomes apparent when, be-goggled Luksch and Miessen crouched back in their cabin and the wind flow ramped up once more, Phocan activates the lasers, which strobe purple round the bobsleigh and, more strangely, green round the periphery of the observers' vision. Still stranger is the way the beam, in the test section, separates into three sharply defined, if porous, walls: one at the bobsleigh's nose, another at its tail and a third half a metre downstream of it, each one a thin light-plane cutting the flow crossways, like a sluice gate. Strangest of all, though, is the spawn of bubbles that the plastic bottle, sitting upstream of the model, tirelessly brings forth and launches on the air: a bubble-throng of biblical proportions – exodus, horde, frantic pilgrimage – more and more of them, all rushing and stampeding down the tunnel, bouncing off the cowling, skipping over Luksch's helmet, dancing reels and circles in the wake-turbulence before eventually scurrying, like a crowd of lemmings, to cast themselves from the diffuser's cliff-edge to its meshes' rocks, on which they burst.

'Why the three laser planes?' Medosch asks Phocan.

'They translate the drag field down the tunnel,' he explains. 'Each plane is an interrogation area. The bubbles give specific index points from which value can be derived across a diachronic stretch.' Leaning over de Veen's shoulder, he starts talking him through the tomographic software, the lasers' bandpass filter presets, the delay generators' resolution-timing scales ...

Ebner, staring into these translation planes, which seem to catch the helium spheres even as they zap unpausing through them, coquettishly offering his eyes presence and stasis while with the same gesture whipping the illusion away again, dissolving it back into wind, sees something ghostly in their *Nachglut*. Van Boezem, noticing the *Cheftrainer*'s gaze lost in the bubbles, smiles:

'It's like a children's party, no?'

Ebner makes no response. He never had children. Athletes young enough to be his offspring, then his offspring's offspring, have passed through his arms, a new batch every three or four years: he's got them, then they're gone, down the ramp, out of sight round the first bend, leaving as after-image trophies, photographs, the next batch in whose faces their faces are ghost-stamped, like the previous batch's were in theirs. Now it's the bubbles' dance that's tapping out the folk-song's rhythm in his head, twitching his cracked lips into silent motion once more:

> *Jeder Tag war ein Fest,*
> *Und was jetzt? Pest, die Pest!*
> *Nur ein großes Leichenfest,*
> *Das ist der Rest.*

– and he sees, framed and dissolving in each plane, day after day, the remnants of the last day's party: held in stillness but rushing headlong nonetheless to the next day, the next party; till all planes, ghoulishly aligned, present the spectacle of plague-corpses feasting on plague-corpses, pausing in their chewing now and then to gaze straight back at him, their new companion, and to chant in undead voices:

> *Augustin, Augustin,*
> *Leg' nur in Grab dich hin!*
> *Ach, du lieber Augustin,*
> *Alles ist hin!*

Navigator Luksch's visions, too, are reaching a finale, or at least a coda. He's gone down the Igls circuit – threaded both needle-eye and labyrinth, set a line through Höcker, Fuchsloch, Hexenkessel, Weckauf – in his imagination at least twenty times in the last ninety minutes, slide-carouselled his way through every mountain range in Austria. He's physically and mentally exhausted – but the bubbles, infusing the air with lightness, are granting him a little uplift: he finds his thoughts wandering, not from the Hafelekarspitze and the Patscherkofel, but from winter to spring and summer. Although the exercise does not, strictly speaking, fall within the remit of Ebner's instructions, he starts dotting the pictured Tyrolean hills with flowers, whose names he reels off from a list that he was made to learn by heart in fourth grade: Alpine aster, lady's-slipper orchid, purple saxifrage and two-leaf squill; true lover's knot, anemone, blue moonwort and the stemless gentian stamped on the back of one-cent coins ... then lady's mantle, wolf's-bane arnica and eyebright augentrost; spring gentian, yellow dock, globeflower, false helleborine, mouse-ear hawkweed, maidenstears, bitterwort and (rarest of all, jewel of the Sonnenspitze with its own, dedicated folk song) edelweiss ...

What machine, operating at what scale or dimension, through what overlay of planes, could tell this congregation – render or make visible to them, carved into what flow tracer or the undulating contours of which screen – the following: that the litany which Luksch is silently reciting was originally written, back in 1583, by one Carolus Clusius? What of that? More than a little. There's a closed-loop circuit at work here, conveying the Low Lands to the heights of Austria and Austria back here to Holland, slipstreams in whose turbulence this afternoon's whole episode is held, all passing through the needle-eye of Luksch's reverie. For the Flemish-born Clusius not only compiled, while serving Maximilian as Prefect of the Imperial Medicinal Garden in Vienna, the definitive taxonomy of Austrian flora; he also, summarily dismissed by Maximilian's successor Rudolf, wended his way to Leyden, in whose *hortus botanicus* he set to work studying the strange permutations of a new variety of flower. Plucked from the Himalayan fortieth parallel – the slopes of Pamir, foothills and valleys of Tian Shan, Kunlun, Karakoram – and meandering its way, via the silk undergarments of Ottoman warriors, the double-tasking executioner-gardeners of Süleyman the Magnificent, and Ogier Ghislain de Busbecq, Dutch ambassador to his court – or alternatively (the data's weak here) via Ceylon, through the usurping offices of Governor Lopo Vaz de Sampaio – to the unknown Flemish merchant who, finding a set of bulbs tucked in a fabric shipment, mistook them for onions but didn't like the taste so planted some instead, inviting to admire the bloom come spring his neighbour Joris Rye, a botanist, who wrote immediately to Clusius ... Riding whatever magic carpet of history it was that wafted it down here, the tulip, with its long stem, large leaves and boldly woven petals (*tulipan*, like a turban, the Turks said), elicited from gaping Hollanders a reaction so immediate that cod-psychologists would later speculate that the flower's form, through a quirk of chance or fate, presented to the 'national mind' some kind of visual cipher to which it was just *programmed* to respond ...

Respond, of course (this part's well known), it did, teasing the genus out into a range of species – *Admiral Liefken*, *Admiral van der Eijck*, *Viceroy*, the eponymous *Tulipa Clusiana* – which, being Dutch, they traded. It was 'breaking' they prized: erupting trans-formations, brilliant scarlets and swarthy almost-blacks running in sharp-edged stripes, or flames, or flares, along the centre of each petal, staking out clear borders round its edges, rendering the genus supreme among flowers *in the same way* (Charles de la Chesnée Monstereul now) *that humans are lords of the animals, diamonds eclipse all other precious stones, and the sun rules the stars.* The thing was, that no breaking pattern could be duplicated, nor, despite the tricks the nurseries deployed (grafting, soil-depth variation, manure-starving, manure-glutting, freezing, scorching; some even turned to alchemy), breaking induced: it happened, or it didn't, and it ran its course. It was, Monstereul mused, as though the flowers, in finding their true lines, were *self-perfecting* – the logic of the occidental horticulturalist cross-fertilising at this point with that of the oriental poet (Khayyam's tulips sup, as do we all, on Heavenly Vintage until Heaven chooses to invert us back to Earth, like empty cups) or, indeed, theologian, for whom the tulip (*lale*: same Arabic letters as *Allah*), bowing its head when in full bloom, embodies the essential virtue of modesty before God ...

But not before the market. By 1634, a *Viceroy* bulb is fetching 3,000 florins, a *Liefken* 4,400. The famous tulip-trading marts are set up on the Stock Exchanges of Amsterdam, Rotterdam, Haarlem, Alkmaar, Hoorn. As the Revolt sends waves of bulb-packing immi-grants and refugees up from the south Netherlands to the United Provinces, the pool swells; traders grow rich; their *handelhuisen* start investing in land-reclamation schemes, carving out room for gardens in which new bulbs can be cultivated, reinvesting profit from these in more polder-schemes; round and round, the centripetal cycle pushing outward: space, money, space, all held in an expanding membrane of liquidity ... Thus Clusius, Father of the Tulip, fathers Holland.

Breaking will later turn out to be caused by the Mosaic Virus. Aphid-borne, it may make lovely patterns – but it reduces the flower's reproduction rate at the same time. Which means fewer flame-streaked tulips – which, *natuurlijk*, makes them all the more valuable. By 1637 a *Rosen* bulb is going for ten times a craftsman's annual salary. Bigwig investor Adriaen Pauw's got a giant bed of them blooming in his castle grounds, or so it seems – but it's a layout of earth-mounted mirrors, angled to multiply half-bunch into cornucopia. Do you, Pauw wonders one day as he directs his gardener in shifting the mirrors around for greater effect, even need the half-bunch to create the illusion? Do you need *one*? After all (he tells himself), the rarest and most precious *Rosen*, *Semper Augustus*, has grown so scarce that no one has actually *seen* one in three years. There are supposed to be twelve of them in existence, all held by ... by this *man*, this man who's meant to live in Amsterdam, but whose *identity* ... No matter: we don't need the flowers or bulbs, the traders say; we'll sign contracts for future delivery. The buyer doesn't need the cash; the seller doesn't need the goods; nor will they when the date comes round – they'll just exchange the price-difference between now and then. With prices fluctuating daily, and these fluctuations having rhythms that, to cannier traders, are discernible (and, it goes without saying, manipulable), you're trading in the pattern not on the flower, but *of the fluctuation*. Same thing: it's still pattern. Index and value. Might there be a navigator, crouched down in the *Beurs'* cowling, tweaking with imperceptible mastery the steering rings? Might its lines, too, be self-perfecting? The traders reckon so; they dance around its slipstream, spinning out options, futures – even as the plague, the human one, starts cutting their own reproduction rate, their stock ...

And then the slipstream turns into a vortex. Shorting, bear-raids, rumours swirling left and right … Here's some motherfucker selling *risk on credit*! Here are angry 'florists' hammering at the *Eerste Kamer*'s doors, demanding payment on all contracts executed before 30 November; then pleading for twenty per cent buyouts; then (*come on, guys!*) for at least *ten* … No dice, the politicians say: enough's enough. We've got a name for what you *klootzaks* have been playing at: *windhandel*, trading in the wind. We're banning it. All contracts (sub- and forward-contracts, swaps, exchanges) void. At which point, as you can imagine, pandemonium breaks out: you've got speculators chasing each other through the cobbled streets, ripping up contracts, dropping the shreds from bridges into the canals; and you can't even give the bulbs (the common types of bulb, the only ones in actual circulation) away; the true line, all lines lost, steep-banking turns and labyrinths now unnavigable, the crash's inevitability finally revealed in all its naked obviousness as seeded from the very push-off, its anticipation the only thing that lets you know it hasn't come quite yet, until … *Pop!*

The fan has been switched off now; the riders dispatched to the storage room to change back into civvies; lasers dismounted, angle-poise arms unscrewed from the walls; bobsleigh zip-bagged and borne off to a waiting van. Roussel's screens are still lit, but they're static. Beneath them, under the desk, the hard drives hum. They know stuff, but they don't know what they know yet; it will be a week before the fully processed findings are presented to the OBSV. De Veen has got a mop out, and is cleaning up the viscous film that's sticking to the tunnel's floor. The bubbles have marked the diffuser's vanes too, peppering their mesh with dull grey patches that, over the following weeks, and months, and years, will grow duller and greyer as they merge with one another and with newer patches; a thickened and composited stain ledger that will never be read, even if someone were to try (why would they?), but will nonetheless record, in muffled, incoherent scrawl, that something, at some time or times, has taken place.

2. Love Philtre

Aboard the KFS *Sidereal*, things are hotting up. Tild, the ship's royal passenger, upon whose safe conveyance to her fiancé hopes for the future well-being and security of Kern, Argeral and pretty much the entire B-Roth star system largely rest – as, too, does the honour of Commander Tszvetan, her conveyor – is voyaging (as protocol demands) in an isolation that is splendid but no less solitary for that. For the first moon cycle or so of the long trip, she flops around the immaculately contoured repos, ottomans and hanging eggs that deck her suite. Now and again she ventures out to traipse the *Sidereal*'s long, empty corridors; if a crew member tries obsequiously to return her to her quarters, she rebukes him for presuming to tell *her* where she may wander, tossing back as she spits the words at him black hair that's streaked with radium-coloured zigzags. Despite her haughtiness, the crew are all in awe of her – star-struck by not her status, but her spunk. Early on, soon after they'd left Doon Leer, she would turn up in the engine rooms, play Atcheque with the stokers and swap some of her philtres for the amphoras of 'kwavit they're carrying back to Kern ('back' as in back again: the liquor, native to their planet, only acquires its character when it's transported twice across the Kwador boundary line, one time in each direction, the resulting chemical mutation generating its distinctive taste and potency). When informed by blu-text that such fraternising was forbidden to the crew, she merely shrugged; but on learning that the stoker who'd been friendliest to her had received a beating for his kindness, she halted the visits. So now she just flops and lounges, lonely, homesick and, above all, bored.

It's not until the middle of the second cycle that she finds her way to the Observatory. This chamber sits above the *Sidereal*'s uppermost starboard trusses – hovers almost, an appendage, communicating with the main body of the vessel only through a spiral staircase coiled around the fixing arm that alone prevents it from detaching itself and drifting into space. The chamber is perfectly spherical: a cyst, or fishbowl, or giant helmet, floating eyeball, whose wall (feat of engineering) is formed of a single tempered sapphire-glass sheet. Inside, torquetums, dioptras, astrolabes and spectrohelioscopes nestle in soft velveteen moulds around a central standing console to whose upper surface is affixed a second and much smaller vitreous globe, a 'reader' capable of both ascertaining star positions and ascribing to newly encountered constellations, when its memory's up to the task, tentative designations, whose names it, when required, projects across the larger dome's interior, thereby aligning territory and map. On stumbling across this room, Tild, not one for reticence, starts making free with instruments and console, holding to her eyes and twiddling the discs and flanges of the former, slowly moving downturned hands above the latter, as though warming them (the reader's operated like a theremin). It's while standing thus cocooned by astral coordinates both actual and projected, light sliding across her face and adding new transversals to her hair's angular geometry, that her immersive reverie is rudely broken into by a male voice issuing, it seems, from space itself:

'You're not supposed to be here.'

Tild spins round. He's standing behind her, near the hatchway to the staircase – although not that near: he must have been observing her unnoticed for some time. Counterweighing shock at his presence, fury at his voyeurism and a need to reassert authority, the Princess, raising back to her right eye the astrolabe her hands almost let drop when he first spoke, enquires disinterestedly:

'Says who?'

The question is rhetorical: the voice was Tszvetan's. He, too, has spent much of the last moon cycle flopping about the *Sidereal*'s navigation deck and wandering its corridors, the most recently trekked of which has brought him to this eyrie. Is it anxiety about fulfilling his obligation to his 'uncle' (in fact, uncle) Louis Q, or lingering grief at his parents' loss, or simply solitude induced by years of long celestial voyaging, that lends him such a sad and contemplative air? Or is it something more immediate? Taking a step forwards, he tells Tild:

'You're holding it wrong. Here, let me show you ...'

Thus begins the first Observatory Summit. He explains to her the reader's software, talks her through rotation of styluses, alignment of tabulae quinoctialis, interconversion between horizontals and ecliptics ... To his surprise, she demonstrates a complete understanding of the mathematics involved, even correcting him when he mis-states the off-set of the axis of rotation of the planet closest to which they happen to be passing just now, Gallon, as 25 degrees (it's 23.5).

'Your computation's weak,' she scolds him teasingly.

'It served me fine during the Saraõnic War,' he quips back.

The atmosphere inside the chamber changes instantly, as though the thermo-gauge had yanked the temperature down several notches.

'The Third one?' Tild asks.

'I was too young to fight in the other two,' he answers.

'My uncle died in that war,' she tells him.

He pauses for a while, then says, without any affect or inflection:

'I'm sorry.'

'Are you?' She sets the sextant she's got in her hand down roughly, hairline fracturing its index mirror. Looking for some other object to take up, her hand's drawn towards the rapier he removed (the better to facilitate his taking up position right against the reader's console stand) from his waist and laid down moments ago, which is now humming softly on the deck.

'Don't touch my rapier,' he says measuredly and quietly – and the Princess, despite being unused to obeying orders, even less interdictions, freezes inches from the weapon. Sensing his control of the situation, Tszvetan presses his advantage home by adding, in a voice tinged with cruelty: 'It's killed people.'

These lines bring the Summit to an abrupt close. Tild storms from the Observatory, and spends the next three or four diurnals beaming large 3-D projections into her suite's stale air. She beams two Atcheque pieces she finds in her pocket, prisoners held over from an uncompleted and now uncompletable engine-room game. She beams a dead cigala she finds rigor-mortised amidst pumps and sandals in a desiccated wardrobe. She beams scans (of objects, faces, scenes) that friends have blu-texted from Argeral. The *Sidereal* turns out to have a good on-board projecting system, capable of both fast streaming and high-magnitude upscaling without sacrificing definition. Placing her text-compact, or just any object, on the jack-pad, Tild moves around the simulacrum it builds hovering before her, gazing at it from all sides and angles, even underneath: she spends hours splayed on the floor in dreamy study of various forms, their curves and masses – study made still dreamier by her ingestion of the contents of the philtres she's brought with her. Back on Argeral, Tild was both wild child and decorated student, first of all her year in quadrive and alkimia; until Tszvetan and his crew turned up to head off her diploma-path with Louis Q's proposal, she'd been a magisterial candidate at the Academy, investigating for her *disertatiõ* the mineral and molecular composition of her planet's signature power source and medium, breaking charge's field down into components, teasing from these integrants derivatives several of which turned out, when ingested, to produce effects that, from a psychoactive point of view, could be called *interesting* ...

Nor is she all brain, though. It might seem like whimsy, or a fascination with its structure and articulation, that prompts her to spend more time perusing the projection of the pendant hanging by her neck than she does the beamed likeness of anything else – but there's a darker reason for this. The pendant casts, in intimate anatomic detail, the skull of her uncle Merhalt – uncle who, as she has just had cause to inform Tszvetan, perished in the most recent conflict between their respective planets. Merhalt was just three years older than her, more a brother than an uncle: they grew up together, frolicking in royal *brinquedotecques* and *gzhiardini*. When she learnt that he'd taken his place among the millions of other victims of this pointless space-grab out in Saraõ, she cried for weeks on end, refusing to leave her boudoir, shunning all visitors. What brought her out eventually was news that Merhalt's body had arrived back, in full state, to be accorded its due funerary rites – prior to which she obtained from the crown pathologist a skull scan (he had died – unusually – in close combat, his skull's staving by an enemy rapier bringing about his demise), which she had the royal *mettalourgon* cast for her in rare blue osmium.

There's no precedent for this in Argeralian custom; it was her own eccentric plan entirely, realised by operating way beyond the limits of her royal prerogative. But realise it she did, and the pendant, intricately modelled relic, has hung from her neck ever since. Here in the *Sidereal's* ambassadorial suite, she sets it down on the jack-pad and beams it out again, breaking the seal on one more philtre, the contents of which she swallows (the philtre's aperture being small and narrow) in small, pucker-lipped sips. Then, as the skull sculpts itself out once more at waist height, larger than life-size in the room, she again sits, then lies, then slides around it, staring at the meticulously rendered set of planes, plates and panels all conjoined around a central suture running down it like a stitch before abruptly giving off to a large crater, a concavity that seems to suck into its void all planes, all lines – and yet, being formed of beamed light no less than the projection's other areas, is as 'present' as them, as filled in as this whole luminous sphere that, were she to beam her own face in like detail, she would see reflected not only in her eye's curved outer membrane but also in the tear forming against this now, just on the verge of dropping . . .

For the stretch following the first Observatory Summit, then, a stand-off sets in and takes hold, a kind of stalemate or (as with Tild's Atcheque match) hiatus, interregnum, period of suspended play. The Princess mopes about her suite, gazing at formless forms; Tszvetan mopes about the upper quarters, fiddling redundantly with cockpit settings (for the most part automated), meandering along corridors that seem to multiply and grow the more he treads them, heading back again and again to the even more isolated Observatory, leaning his face against the cupole's glass and staring into space, letting his eye rest on one point, on a planet or a vulcanoid, a tiny giant or hypergiant or subgiant, then moving it backwards to a further-outlying, tinier-still detached binary or nebula, with the effect that all the stars and clusters seem to be in constant retreat from him, from the *Sidereal*, each other ...

'Chill of intergalactic distance,' murmurs Herzberg, leaning over the shoulder of Eldridge, who himself leans over that of his star coder Charlie, working keyboard and glide-pad down beneath them at his table. 'Is there some way to, you know, *accentuate* ...?'

'What if you take each one of the star points,' Eldridge suggests, 'and increase the space between it and the next by a measure proportional to ... I don't know ... time elapsed or something ...'

'We can do that,' says Charlie. 'With Parergon you can set relational distance-augment/time-diminish gradients. It gives you a kind of infinite perspective.'

'But ...' Herzberg isn't entirely happy with this idea. 'It's not so much *infinity* we want; not disappearance at the edges or the limit. More like ... an *invasion* of what's near by far-ness ... Like all surfaces and edges are retracting, dwindling even from their own position ...'

He's thinking, partly, of the staircase scene in *Vertigo*, or the reverse-pull shot of Brody on the beach in *Jaws*. But even more he's dredging up deep-sedimented memories of childhood meningitis: how the room, his little bedroom, seemed to fill with a voluminous expanse that simultaneously emptied it, ate it away, as though some cosmic road digger were scooping out whole chunks of *there*-ness, filling them with *not-there* craters. These craters would swell, pregnant with an absence to which his delirium acted as midwife, birthing it in sweat and whimpers right above the carpet – and then cupboard, desk, toybox and even bedside lamp would take on the aspect of unmanageably distant objects, even though they were right next to him. The illness seemed to open up a peephole on a universe of expanded vacancy, laid out somehow beside or maybe even *within* this one, waiting for its opportunity, its chink, its moment . . .

'. . . a monstrous remoteness that has got all close-up,' he's telling Charlie. 'Outer reaches transposed to the inner sanctums . . . Or as though eternity had wormed its way into each second – that's the look I want: helpless, cold and neutral. Definitely cold.'

'Parergon can do that, too,' Charlie says confidently; 'no probs.' He types *c-o-l-d* in his sidebar.

The onset of the third moon cycle brings with it a change of mood. Tszvetan and Tild, quite separately but in sync, as though the course their surges, ebbs and bores will take were set by mechanisms they're no more aware of than a tidal body is, find themselves – almost literally – crossing swords once more in the Observatory. It's she who interlopes on him this time; unlike her, though, he notices her entry straight away, but lets her circle him a couple of times before addressing her:

'Not far to go now,' he comments, pointing through the chamber's glass wall to a spot lying somewhere beyond her left ear. 'We're passing Acephalus already.'

She turns round and sees the planet, with its signature blue ring, but ventures nothing in reply. Eventually he adds:

'You must be happy.'

To this line, too, she offers nothing back. Her silence, like their terse earlier exchange, seems to dictate the chamber's gravity: the air feels heavy. After a long time she turns back from the glass to face him.

'Are you married?' she asks.

Tszvetan shakes his head. 'To my work, maybe.'

'And just what's that?'

He gestures round the chamber, or perhaps beyond it, as though indicating all the galaxies and nebulae. 'I navigate.'

'And smuggle,' she adds with a smirk that is aggressive but not hostile. 'Your hold's full of zeletrion and 'kwavit.'

'It's all charged,' he says. 'I've got the manifest.'

'Sure,' she laughs. 'And if ...'

The second Observatory Summit is cut short at this point by the loud wail of the *Sidereal*'s alarm system. It will turn out to be triggered by a short in the composting tank, easily fixed. But Tszvetan's not to know that yet; he hurries from the chamber – leaving, as Tild notices when she, too, makes towards the hatch, his rapier on the floor. Of course, she picks it up. And, after turning it over in her hands just as she did the torquetums and dioptras during her first visit to this room, she takes it with her, back down to her suite.

Why does she do this? Hard to say. Perhaps because, since childhood, she's got used to taking what she likes. Or perhaps, on the contrary, as not a manifestation of her birthright's license but a reaction against circumstantial powerlessness: if she's, effectively, a hostage to diplomacy, to realpolitik's exchanges, then she'll take her own sub-hostage, turn this glowing, humming thing into an object as symbolic as the Atcheque pieces. Or perhaps ... perhaps because the object *itself* fascinates her. It's not just the aura lent it by its lethal function; there's something else, too, something about its shape that speaks to her, that seems to whisper the familiar, even the intimate ...

In this last intuition, she turns out to be half-right – or (more correctly phrased) *exactly* wrong. It's not the rapier's *form* that she was recognising, but the *inverse* of this. When she lays it on the jack-pad and beams it out all big and holographic in her suite's dry air, the blade's physical qualities – its pronounced distal taper and the deep off-centre fuller running from its point of balance to its centre of percussion, or the grainy, light-martensite *niye* jagging in layered contours down its side – take on the aspect of the imprint left by something else. Or, rather, of the block that *made* that something else's imprint in the first place, of the negative of all its pleats, folds and declivities. Instinct tells her immediately what that 'something else' might be. Tugging at her neck, she sweeps the rapier aside and lays the blue osmium pendant on the jack-pad in its place. Scaling up the projection, homing straight in on the skull's fracture, she can see straight off that its topology's the same – that is, the unequivocally corresponding opposite. And if she slides the rapier back next to it, and aligns the two together . . . just so . . . There it is, an exact fit: all of the dents and shards and pockmarks that define the skull's deep crater, its fatal concavity, slot in precisely (*amphichirally* – the term jumps out at her from ghosts of lecture notes abandoned back on Argeral) to the visible units that together make the blade; they're mirror images of one another. This is the weapon that killed Merhalt; and the hand that wielded it belonged, and still belongs, to none other than her pilot and protector Tszvetan.

This is the plot's first crisis. And its second: it's a double-crisis. Why? Because it's been growing glaringly self-evident to Tild, despite all efforts to camouflage awareness of the fact amidst the billow of projected objects and the fuzz of philtre-daze, that she's in love with Tszvetan. It started as they left Doon Leer, among the pageantry and splendour of departure, courtiers lined up in gold and scarlet robes, hautboys and tombours filling the bay with noise: the way this self-possessed but sad figure stood alone on the ramp of his vessel, half-detached, like the room in which she's since met with him twice, from the whole ceremony, and (by extension, as though the ceremony acted as a baroque stand-in for this) from life itself. In her long, drawn-out pacing of the *Sidereal*'s labyrinth, she's been both trying to lose the object of her fixation and, at the same time (as if by chance, round the next corner, on the far side of an airlock), to run into it. As has he. It's mutual: Tszvetan, too, has grown fixated with this jag-haired princess who acts like some sister he never had, who seems to hold all rules and custom in contempt but who nonetheless can see a higher value in this royal marriage, her submission to it almost, at some scale or level, a defiance. His roaming, and her roaming, de-centre the labyrinth, have turned the *Sidereal*'s corridors into a Kepler field in which binary planets waltz round each other in anxious ellipses, each seeking the elusive focal point that would, if ever actually reached, result in a collision guaranteeing its cataclysmic end. Now, though, an extra weight, a Schwarzschild element, has been thrown into the mix: she's got the rapier. At some point he's going to have to come and get it, from her suite ...

And when he does, she'll be obliged to kill him. To do anything less would be to spit on Merhalt's grave. As far as Tszvetan's concerned: to follow his desire for her to its conclusion would, same thing, defile *his* uncle, feed him through a mangle worse even than death's. Still, the ambassadorial quarters' draw on him is irresistible. He reasons, knowing even as he runs the argument through his head that it's plain bullshit, that he *has* to go and get the rapier, and do it discreetly; that to send one of his crew, or in any manner formally acknowledge her theft of it, risks sparking a diplomatic incident. That part is true; what's spurious, bullshit, about it is that he knows all too well that if he goes down there and allows the inevitable to take place, a situation will blow up that's ten times worse politically than any rapier-snatching episode ...

Consequently, a second stand-off sets in, one far more charged than the last, as the stakes are now much higher – and are about to increase, since Tild, among her ottomans and eggs, has taken a decision. Out beyond Acephalus, out past even Gorgon and the Lethe Nebula, there lies a planet called Nocturnis. Beneath the hydrogen clouds of its atmosphere and the kaolinite layer of its topsoil sit compacted (and eponymous) mineral belts of noctural. Since 742 (ironically, as a consequence of the Third Saraõnic War, a sub-clause to the Landis Armistice that brought it to a close that year), Argeral has held the exploitation licence for these belts, revamping the small mining concession (noc-tural has niche industrial uses) that was sitting all dilapidated on the Granchap Fields, sole foothold of life, let alone civilisation, on the uninhabited outcrop. It was in Tild's own research group at the Academy that noctural was first seriously analysed, its elements identified; and Tild herself who baptised the previously unknown one 'thanadrine'. This compound – denser even than the osmium she wears around her neck – turned out to contain an admixture of thebanum and chalcanthitus so concentrated that its ingestion, even in trace quantities, would be guaranteed to bring about a dreamy, carefree and perhaps even fantastic but for that no less inevitable death; whence the name Tild assigned to it. Ever the student, or perhaps the danger-seeker, she's brought an extract of it with her, a philtre-pent tincture that she's kept, for safety reasons, separate from all the others. Digging this out now and laying it on the jack-pad, beaming it up large, moving around its replica and marvelling at its strange colouration – dense black laced with blue, not unlike the swathes of interstellar void extending all around her out beyond the *Sidereal*'s walls – she wonders if she'll gain some kind of experience of these abyssal spaces, some *awareness* of her entering and merging with them, of oblivion itself, when she ingests it. For this is her decision: to drink the thanadrine, to rejoin Merhalt, thereby staying faithful to both her brother-uncle and, since she can neither kill nor love him, Tszvetan.

It's back to the Observatory that she repairs in order to see the plan through. She doesn't want to do it in the confines of her suite; far better here, amidst the constellations she'll soon join. Stripping the philtre's seal, popping its cap, she holds it up towards the galaxies and clusters and blank patches, toasting them all with her final gesture; then (unable, due to the philtre's shape, its narrow aperture, to down its contents in one gulp), begins to suck-sip the thanadrine. It's yet another sign of the extent to which their thinking, not to mention moving, has become entwined that Tszvetan bursts in on her as she's halfway through this, and immediately (from her pallor, or the fatalistic and determined look on her face, or if not those then the convulsions starting to rack her lower body) understands exactly what she's up to. As she stares straight at him, piercingly, defiantly, he rushes up to her and, snatching the philtre from her fingers, suck-sips its undrunk half. Even in what she takes to be her death throes, she's astonished by this act. The two of them stand face-to-face for a few seconds; then, as Tszvetan's calves and thighs start shaking to the same irregular beat as hers, they throw themselves into each other's arms to wait for death.

Death, though, has other things to do. It will be several cycles before Tild, from a chance conversation she'll have with one of Louis Q's barons at a banquet during which her royal health is toasted repeatedly with 'kwavit, realises what has (at a bio-chemical level at least) occurred: just as the ship's transit through the Kwador boundary line alters the composition of that liquor, so, too, has it changed the make-up of the thanadrine they've just imbibed. While the thebanum element seems to have been unaffected, the chalcanthitus has become, not exactly neutralised, but rather *catalysed* into something more akin to cantharidinus or rhodotoxina – to put it in lay terms, into an aphrodisiac. As the *Sidereal* rounds Ardis Minor, moon of its destination planet, and as Kern itself, sunk in the final stretch of the long night from which the rays of Fidelus will soon awaken it, heaves slowly into view, Tszvetan and Tild find themselves floating naked, clasping at each other, joining, separating, joining again as they tumble slowly through the chamber from which, Tszvetan having disabled the charge, gravity has, like duty and concern, been exiled.

This is the difficult bit. Modelling it all was relatively easy: you just build the room in CAD, drop in two bodies, set the parameters for movement, and the program does the rest. As far as lighting goes: the ray tracers have done their job, marking (in reverse) the trajectory of photons as they squirt from Fidelus, bounce off Ardis Minor and the by now far-away Acephalus, wash around the sapphire glass of the Observatory's dome, then pass through this to be deflected or occluded by the console and the moulds of various instruments, or by the floor, or by discarded clothes that drift, course logarithm-plotted, about the chamber's air; plus, naturally, by the floating and migrating limbs and torsos of the dis- and re-entwining lovers. That all works just fine. The difficulties start when you go analogue; when human bodies, with their flesh that knows nothing of asymptotes and their parabolas, enter the picture and start wobbling and flapping over the whole equation. They've brought in the finest, the industry apex: mo-cap performers from the fjords, from Bergen, whom they've rigged up and manipulated through the movement sequences the software scripted. But it looks awful, even if you discount all the straps and cages. For one thing, their skin and muscle, toned though these may be, still sag downwards at every opportunity – we're not in zero gravity *here*, after all. The A.D.s have tried all kinds of fixes, even stitching threads into flesh-coloured leotards and pulling upwards at the spots where droops are most egregious; but this just gives you a chicken-skin look whose repulsiveness runs counter to the scene's required eroticism. For another thing, even when they've adhered to their assigned paths with what to the naked eye may seem complete precision, there's still massive deviation. Actual bodies just won't do what's asked of them; even complying, they set up folds and kinks and barriers in all the wrong places, which plays havoc with the light path, which in turn trashes the whole set-up that Eldridge's guys have been, meticulously and at great expense, constructing for the last few weeks. And then, above and beyond all that, it just doesn't seem *right*; the movement, taken as a whole, doesn't in any way suggest that all this tumbling and twining's *really* orbiting around a central and impassioned act of coitus.

'Looks like a puppet porn show!' Herzberg shouted when he saw the rushes.

'The window of a butcher's shop during an earthquake,' Eldridge concurred. 'Haunches and carcasses all bumping up against each other!'

'Rag-dolls spinning' – Herzberg again – 'in a dryer!'

So they've defaulted, on the sly, back to the virtual; or at least to the virtual archive of a pre-existing scene they never them-selves staged, nor even witnessed. No one did – discounting the participants, who didn't really 'witness' it as such. Phocan has slipped them, in the strictest confidence, some files that he said were gathering dust on the Pantarey server, out-takes from a previous job whose purpose Eldridge and his team can only guess at. What they show, in fully captured and evented detail, is two human figures, male and female, copulating in every position that might be imagined, plus a few that none of them ever thought possible before viewing this cache. What's so useful about it from the DZ team's perspective is that, rather than try to push two floating bodies, virtual or real, together – that is, to do this from a starting-point of their not being conjoined, and to make their conjunction seem convincing – they can instead, like the ray tracer, work backwards, throwing the whole process, its causation, into reverse: *start* with bodies plausibly (because actually) joined in coital union, and work *outwards* from that point in order to extrapolate approach and exit angles and trajectories, a bit like they did with vessels entering and leaving Doon Leer's harbour. It's a canny move: since they'll only be using Pantarey's off-cuts as a foundation stone, embedding their core moments beneath layer after layer of morph and render until the original's completely (in terms of recognisability) buried, there's no danger of anyone crying IP-infringement foul downriver. The team isolate positions, movements, thrusts, and build outwards from these, constructing graceful, tender sequences, elaborated to the point that they can drop both Bergen mo-cappers' and CAD-programmed bodies, or at least parts of them, back in. *Then* comes the light: twenty coders are right now, in one way or another, helping to reintroduce this into the newly configured mix, splash it back over fresh topologies, a newfound land of curves and edges either roving on their own or set in motion by the POV that roams in loops and gyres round the Observatory's chamber and beyond the dome of this, out into space, now looking in on the two lovers through the glass, now turning outwards, flaring into rings and starbursts as it rotates to face Helio-D directly, now graining up as it rolls onwards away, back round towards the *Sidereal*, Kern's arced and hazy surface in the background ...

'Hang on a minute,' Ben Briar smells another rat here. 'What the fuck is that?'

'Lens effect,' Herzberg informs him.

'It looks really good,' adds Charlie.

Briar purses his lips, as though he, too, had been necking some bitter philtre. Choosing his words carefully, he enquires:

'And why ... ?'

It falls to Herzberg to step up and defend the visual aberrations:

'I'd have thought you would approve: it's realistic – these blemishes are what you'd actually get if you stationed a camera just there.'

'So,' Briar snatches at these incriminating words, 'we're to suppose that there's a *camera*, a real, actual camera, in space, floating conveniently next to these two lovebirds' nest? Is that part of the plot? If so, then why not show its gantry, or its stabiliser, or just have the time-code flashing on the image?'

In fact, he's not a million miles off here, although not in the way he thinks. A camera *is* part of the plot – several cameras, some protruding bulbously from ceilings of the *Sidereal*'s corridors, their presence plain for all to see, others less evident, or not evident at all, secreted grub-like inside wall panels and rivets, rails and hanging tubes, or even hovering in plain sight yet, being nanoscopic, underneath perception's radar. Tszvetan's no fool; he knows that the Kern authorities, and Louis Q himself, are keeping tabs on him – and knows, too, that his uncle has turned a blind eye to most, if not all, of his previous misdemeanours, that a degree of wilful ignorance has always oiled the cogs of their relationship. But this ... He sensed something quite strange about this mission from the outset, almost as though it had been set up, planned, like some kind of experiment in which both he and Tild would serve as lab rats, their maze-navigations constantly observed. Later, lying in quiet post-coital reverie beside her on the floor of the Observatory to which gravity has been restored, he'll even wonder whether Louis Q was *willing* this to happen; whether he's actually watching in real time and, if so, whether it's in fury or benevolence, like a kind, indulgent god gazing down on his creatures who, imperfect (since He made them that way), have (as His great plan prescribed) screwed up ... That's later, though. Right now (to the bemusement of the crew, who know when not to reason why) he's turned all charge off: there's no energy, no recording or transmitting capacity; the vessel's powerless, hanging suspended between Ardis Minor's pull and that of Kern, whose outer atmosphere it's grazing. Everything's suspended – not least time, which seems to partake of the quality of light, groundless or levitated, far-flung, outcast ...

Diamond, during that long week of technical induction, got all hung up on the question of instantaneity. As Phocan talked her in more detail through Pantarey's cameras, with their four circular rows of LEDS emitting infrared at 850 nanometers, he explained the principle of 120-degree illumination, and of passive optical motion capture generally:

'You've got to *throw* the light out and then catch it back again,' he told her. 'These LEDs pulse at the frame-rate of the camera, which is anything from thirty to two thousand frames per second. The speed doesn't matter: what's important is that whatever speed it's running at, the pulse-rate of the LEDs is set the same.'

'Why?' she asked.

'Think about it,' he said. 'The camera throws the infrared out to the markers, and the markers bounce it back at the exact rate as that at which it's thrown out; *and* at the exact same rate as that with which the camera snaps the light back and records it. That makes for ... makes for ...'

This was a prompt: he was waiting for an answer. She knew the one he wanted, and supplied it:

'Instantaneous capture?'

'Instantaneous capture, spot on. You don't look convinced.'

She didn't – wasn't. After chewing on her tongue for a few seconds (a trait her girlfriend liked; it opened up a window, she said, on her cogitative processes), she ventured:

'It's just … If the light has to travel out towards the object, then bounce off it again, then travel back towards the camera … Well, doesn't that take, you know, time?'

Phocan laughed.

'But Lucy, it's travelling at the speed of *light*. That makes it instantaneous.'

He'd still said *then* and *back*, though. And *again*: throw the light out, *then* catch it *back*, *again* … But that was just words. To all intents and purposes, he was right: she saw that. Yes. And yet … it worked fine, the logic held tight if you were capturing the motion of a gymnast swinging round a pommel horse two yards in front of you, or hostage-taking extras dragging hostage stand-ins round a simulated embassy, or even a control drone in the sky two miles up. But what if you went deeper than the sky, further away? Each photon from the sun takes eight minutes and twenty seconds to reach Earth; sixteen-forty to bounce back. So light from Sagittarius, Auriga, Cassiopeia … ? Years, centuries, millennia, immeasurable stretches: by the time *those* LED-ringed cameras have snapped their bounce-rays up again the Earth probably won't even *be* there any more. The principle's no different with the gymnast; the distance may be shorter, but the mechanics are the same: emission, then recapture, all conducted at a pace that's ultimately no less limited than that of sound, or of molasses, or cars crawling up Finns Business Park's drive, over the bumps … She kept her counsel, but retained the quibble henceforth as a grit of secret certainty: that structural delay is built into the process; that, even when it's playing out at a level beneath the detectable, the measurable, it's still *there* …

This is the level Tszvetan and Tild are occupying right now, the time-zone they're inhabiting: the zone of the delay, of light's slow transit. Since there has been no bed, nor couch, nor even floor beneath her during this magnificent and weightless tryst, Tild's had the impression that what's supporting her, providing base and traction every time she pulls Tszvetan down towards and into her or, hovering above him, descends once again to dock on his set body, is nothing other than the planes and cushions of the light that's reconfiguring itself around them so accommodatingly. It hardens into banks and columns when required, or billows out, when that's what their movements and positions ask of it, into soft, downless pillows, undulating waves that in turn dissipate when heads or arcing backs no longer need them. The light's both prop and medium of their lovemaking; at one point, opening her eyes suddenly as she throws her head back, seeing a beam shoot out through the dome's sapphire glass and break into a fine scintilla-dust beyond it, she's struck by a conviction that this light is pleasure itself, reified. If it plays that role for her, it also plays the role of safety: swaddling them, holding and hiding them inside its dazzle, it keeps consequence at bay. What law requiring plain, diurnal optics could penetrate this fine-mesh cradle to disturb its frequency, undo its tangled luminescence? In the last moments before Kern's tractor beam locks on to the *Sidereal*, as she drifts off into sleep, this luminescence seems to open up still more around her, and grow deeper: an abyss that, even as she sinks into it, bears her up.

3. The Norbert Wiener Appreciation Society

They do this thing at Canard where they wrap a poached duck in soft clay and fire it in a kiln for half an hour. To liberate the roasted bird, whose juices the tightly fitted carapace has kept intact, removing any need for basting, they smash the hardened earthenware embalming with a hammer – right before you, at your table. It's a Celtic recipe. The clay comes from the Evenlode by Charlbury a mile away, thick mud borne down there from the Cotswolds, sedimenting as the river winds its way past Ascott-under-Wychwood, Chadlington, Stow-on-the-Wold ... The waiting list for tables seems to wind for just as long; Garnett tried once to get a reservation, and was offered an early-evening slot six months away. But Pilkington ... Pilkington's managed to grab a place for them in the two days since dropping him a line, asking to 'pick his brains'. The man's hooked up in many ways, through channels Garnett has learnt over the years not to enquire about too much. He's waiting for him in a quiet little enclave, a snug almost, in the corner. It's the best spot in the restaurant; they won't be overheard.

'My Anthony. Still tying paintbrushes to sheep?'

'Things have progressed a little since then – as you know ...'

Their hands unclasp and they sit down. A waiter passes by with bread. After he's gone, Garnett enquires:

'How's Thérèse?'

No small talk, this – more of a plunge in at the deep end. Pilkington's wife was diagnosed two years ago with Parkinson's. Her state is not improving: tremors, cogwheel rigidity, pill-rolling fingers, festination ... Pilkington uses the medical term for each of these symptoms, not bothering to translate or annotate, since he knows full well that Garnett understands them.

'It's ironic,' he says when the list's exhausted, 'us two talking about this.'

Here, too, Garnett can follow perfectly, no need to gloss: they're on the same page – same pages. *The Human Use of Human Beings*: the passages devoted to Parkinsonianism. Voluntary feedback regulating a main motion fails to establish equilibrium with postural feedback working in the opposite direction ... oscillation levels spiral out of control ... the patient reaches for a glass of water, and his hand overcorrects, swings too much, draws a too-wide arc ... For Wiener, everything was feedback. When I pick up a cigar, I translate into action nothing other than a feedback mechanism, a reflex turning the amount by which I've not yet picked up the cigar into an order to the lagging muscles. When I shoot down a plane, my limbs on the ack-ack gun and the wire along which the firing order hums its way towards the earphones clamped round my head, the vacuum tubes that plot the plane's path on a radar screen, and thus the timeline from which approach gradients to the spot of air it's occupying right now can be extrapolated to predict the spot that it will occupy two seconds hence: all these make up an integrated circuit, in which servo-mechanism isn't just the mode of mankind, but his measure also. And not just of mankind: elevators, steamboat engines, jellyfish amalgams, the whole architecture of abstracted systems such as economics or the law – these, too, are birthed and structured by (and therefore legible within) the matrix-womb of cybernetics. They were so excited by it, he and Pilkington: atheists both, it was as close as either of them came to having a religion. Spectres float between the two men now, kinking round curves of wineglasses and side plates: ghosts of two young engineering postgrads with wide collars, bushy sideburns, flaring cords, all fired up by the new world leaping at them from the pages of Nash, Bateson, Geyer and von Glasersfeld. But it was him they came back to, again and again

– prophet, messiah and apostle, all contained within a single name and figure: Norbert Wiener. There was something in his vision that transcended informatics, systems- or game-theory; something Garnett thought he'd left behind with Aeschylus, Catullus, Sappho: a condition best denoted by the old, unscientific label *poetry*. *We are* (Garnett had this line taped to the wall above his ZX Spectrum's screen) *but whirlpools in a river of ever-flowing water; not stuff that abides, but patterns that perpetuate themselves ...* Or (this one from a passage that was read at his and Amber's wedding): *To be alive is to participate in a continuous stream of influences from the outer world and acts on the outer world in which we are merely the transitional stage ...*

'It seemed so optimistic, then,' Pilkington muses as he swills Malbec around his large-bowled Waterford. 'Wiener was offering us a path to justice, knowledge, the unlocking of closed structures ... What did he call it? *Irreversible entry into a ...*'

'*Irreversible movement into a contingent future which is the true con-dition of human life,*' Garnett supplies the words.

'Exactly. Man as open system. Society as an endless process of unfurling and cross-pollination. Life itself as file-sharing *avant la lettre.*'

'Yes – to an extent ...' Garnett inspects his wine too, as though it, and not the proposition, were the suspect element. 'But ...'

'But ...'

'Wasn't the vision always tinted darkly, blood-tinged? All that Manichaean talk: the universe abandoned, running itself down ... technocracy casting human responsibility to the winds, to have it come back seated on the whirlwind ... the arms race, business, adver-tising rowing us into a maelstrom of destruction, or just floating us quietly on downstream, to the waterfall ... He called us *shipwrecked passengers on a doomed planet.* You look like you're about to kill us.'

These last words are spoken to the waiter who's raising a mallet just beside their heads. Used to such quips, the latter brings his weapon down to fracture the upturned hold of the duck that's lying on the tray stand he's unfolded by their table. The casing falls away, as do succulent legs and wings and fillet at his carving knife's light touch. With tonged fork and spoon he serves these to them, lays some sprout tops on the side, refills their glasses and departs again.

'For Wiener,' Garnett mumbles after a few moments through cheeks filled with sweet brown flesh, 'life was all about denying death. God's, Santa Claus's or your own: the need to alleviate the disaster of mortality is what fuels belief in progress, and the endless generation of bigger and better things, or "products" ... The death-drive offset on to the assembly line ...'

'This,' says Pilkington, 'is what I wanted to ask you about.'

'Death?'

'Assembly lines.'

Garnett, mouth refilled, whirrs his knife-hand mechanically: *Go on* ... Pilkington, setting his own knife and fork down, asks:

'Do you recall the work of Lillian Gilbreth?'

'Yes, of course,' Garnett responds. 'I looked at all her time-and-motion studies when I was setting up Pantarey.'

'Lillian and Frank ...'

'Lillian and Frank: correct. Their methods laid the groundwork for what people like us do. Our Norbert even mentions them, in passing. They bridge the gap between the nineteenth-century – Marey, Taylor – and the world that would emerge with Ford: mass automatisation and, later, digitisation. Without them, there'd be no mo-cap.'

'She made boxes, didn't she?'

'That's right: light tracks sculpted in metal and set in cutaway black boxes. Each one showed the path of a worker's movement cycle. I've got one at home.'

'An actual Gilbreth box?' asks Pilkington.

'I presume so. I found it in a storage cupboard in an old Birmingham factory that ...'

'Does it have a number on it?'

The urgency of his old friend's tone takes Garnett aback. He, too, sets his fork down, and answers:

'I don't think so. Never looked. She made scores of the things. Hundreds, probably.'

'Eight hundred and fourteen.' Pilkington flashes a bridge-player's smile, the type that might accompany the partial revelation of a hand.

'Well,' Garnett smiles back. 'Seems like it's I who should be asking you the questions. Are these extant?'

'The boxes?'

'Yes: the eight hundred and fourteen boxes – the eight hundred and thirteen I don't have ...'

'Not all in physical form,' says Pilkington. 'Some are in collections; others will be knocking about basements, like yours was. Others just got thrown out once they'd served their purpose. But she catalogued them all. Itemised them.'

'How?'

'Stereoscope. Essentially, by reverse-engineering the process that she'd used to build them in the first place. And these records, almost all of them, are "extant". Every motion, every iteration she cast has been "stated", as it were ...'

Pilkington's cards take on material embodiment now, as he pulls from a folder nestled in his corner's recess a set of papers which he spreads across the tablecloth.

'Have a look ...'

There are two stapled stacks. Garnett leafs through the one with pictures on it: column after column of black-and-white double-photographs of Gilbreth boxes, all numbered and labelled, much as Pilkington has just described. The other's full of text: the paragraphs of some kind of report in which the name 'Gilbreth' pops up every five or so lines. Its diction's not quite academic, not quite scientific, certainly not journalistic – closer in style to a government white paper or internal dossier that might circulate within a corporation ... *Bearing in mind the importance Ms Gilbreth attached to the abstraction, or perhaps better to say extraction, of kinetic sequences, we might speculate that* ... Typeface is Times New Roman ... text is broken into sections, the division following a logic less of subject, theme or chapter than of patchwork assembly, legible blocks alternating with long strings of ciphers, or commands, or code, typed in a different font that reminds him of old JavaScript or ASCII: *01mdean02cdorley03crypt04decrypt7text102* ...

'We came across this,' Pilkington comments after letting Garnett flip for a while through the pages, 'last week. I'd be intrigued to know your thoughts.'

'*Came across?*'

'Yes: noticed, stumbled on to, picked up, were appraised of ...'

'You make it sound passive.'

'It is. Just like what you do: passive ... what do you call it?'

'Passive optical motion capture.'

'Right. We passively captured this communication while it was in motion.'

'You people ...' Garnett tries to strike up a mock-chiding tone; but duck and greens start to taste different in his mouth; the air seems to take on an altered texture, infused now with obligations, with embargo, with the shadow of officialdom. Is it called *MI5* or *MI6* now? Or some other name that's never even written down or spoken? 'First thing I'm going to do when I get home is get my IT guy Hossain to upgrade my security, install a better firewall ...'

'My friend,' Pilkington fixes him with a pitiful gaze, 'use a typewriter.'

With a quiet nod he invites Garnett to skim his way on further through the stack. The first few pages precis Gilbreth's life and work; they contain nothing not already known to him, bar a few details about family circumstances (*twelve* children); her husband's abhorrence of dirt; the extent to which NASA leant on her work; her penchant for writing sub-par verse ... It's several sections in, after a range of ASCII interjections (the *mdean* part of the cipher-string keeps popping up), that the meat of the report starts peeping through, passages highlighted in yellow marker, either by Pilkington or by whatever *us* is lurking behind him, behind these pages' digital purloining, this whole afternoon's encounter ...

It seems to involve correspondence carried out by Gilbreth with a young Latvian physicist around 1970. Parts of the correspondence, two letters from him to her, have been scanned – by now, double- or triple-scanned, print much degraded. More scans, of what Garnett understands to be pages from Gilbreth's jotter book or journal, are reproduced beside these. Here, too, the handwriting is hard to parse – all the more so due to its tendency to give over now and again to doodles; the physicist's letters also break off intermittently for diagrams or sketches. The report's author has tried to summarise the correspondence (no mean task, since even the physicist's side of it, the only side included in the file, is incomplete); also to gauge this correspondence's effect on Gilbreth, as surmised from her reactions to it contained in this same jotter book or journal. *The significance attached by Gilbreth to Box 808 … what he persisted in calling 'the T.T. episode' … what the acronym 'T.T.' might …* This acronym's recurrence sends Garnett flipping back to where he first encountered it: the partial scan (it begins with the second or perhaps third page) of the first letter, whose author also refers to 'the T.T. episode', proposing to model it according to Gilbreth's own light-track wireframe technique (for good measure, he includes a kind of drawing showing a cone-shaped object swinging round some type of pole, though in the absence of the letter's opening page, or maybe pages, the actual, un-abstracted or -extracted content of the 'episode' remains obscure). It's only then that Garnett registers the name of Gilbreth's correspondent, though his eye must have flitted across it several times.

'Vanins? Raivis Vanins? I knew Vanins.'

Pilkington's still fixing him with his bridge-player's smile. Of course …

'Oh,' says Garnett meekly. 'You knew that already. Is that what … ?'

'In part,' Pilkington answers. 'Why not? Let's start there. Tell me about Vanins.'

'Well …' Garnett sighs resignedly. 'I met him twice. Once at a Paris congress in the mid seventies … Then in Delft, ICAM, 1988 or so … We had a drink together, corresponded for a little afterwards … He was director of the Solid-State Physics Department in Vilnius or Tallinn or – what's the capital of Latvia?'

'Riga.'

'Right: at Riga's Technical University – a post he got at the ripe age of thirty-eight or thirty-nine.'

'Something of a whizz-kid?'

'He was viewed that way, certainly,' says Garnett. 'He seemed to have a whole body of papers to his name ... light-particle sound pulses, shear-wave imaging, self-focusing, the work of Askaryan, Sarvazyan, Osipyan ... He was one of the few Russian – Latvian, Eastern Bloc, whatever – scientists allowed to travel; I guess he acted for us as a kind of peephole on to the whole world of Soviet physics. Not a particularly open one ...'

'Even after perestroika?'

'He went quiet around that time; I think he'd retired. But rumours seemed to swirl around him, even in his absence: a kind of mythomania born of ignorance instilled by decades of the Cold War; all that weird shit we'd imagined going on in Soviet labs and research institutes – I don't need to tell you ...'

Pilkington grunts acknowledgement. It was weird shit: para-magnetic resonance, synchotron radiation, superconductivity ... They knew, from leaks, defections, propaganda, that advances, even breakthroughs, were being made – but sifting all this traffic, trying to separate the signal from the noise, to work out which develop-ment was actual, which just paranoid projection ... The speculation, at its outer reaches, skewed weirder than weird, veered into the realm of sci-fi: bioradiation, pondemotor forces, Z-rays, ESP ... In the late eighties, after Albatross, Pilkington was loosely involved with a counter-research unit that had been set up in Cambridge for the sole purpose of establishing the efficacy or otherwise of 'instrumental psychotronics' à la Beridze-Stakhovsky, just in case ... And then, when the whole Soviet house of cards collapsed, this, rather than bringing clarity, a giant reveal, just saw the archives dissipated – shredded, lost or siphoned off to private holdings ...

'One of Vanins' big things, like mine, was kinaesthetics,' Garnett's saying. 'He was Gastev's heir, essentially. Saw the ends of practices like Gilbreth's stretching far beyond assembly lines, or even spaceships. Once his writing started getting out, translated, circulated, well, it struck – like Wiener's had – a chord with people in all kinds of areas, not only physics.'

'And the rumours?'

Garnett shrugs. 'The usual type – in the biomechanics world, at least; that township's age-old urban legends: that he'd come up, behind his institute's walls, with a means of generating torsion fields, or proof of Tryon's zero-energy hypothesis, or some such philosopher's stone ... Perhaps nobody quite believed these *literally* – but on states of equilibrium, particularly, he was streets ahead.'

'That subject,' confides Pilkington, 'or one like it, seems to provide the topic of his correspondence with Ms Gilbreth. Here, on page twenty-four ...'

He helps Garnett leaf through to the nominated page, which contains, set side by side as before, printed scans of two handwritten papers: on the left, a page from a further letter, or perhaps the same one, from Vanins to Gilbreth; on the right, another page from the jotter book/journal of the latter. In the left-hand scan, Vanins describes his *shock – amazement, and perhaps* (illegible) *– at the implications of this labour, which would seem to transform all the tenets and* (assertions?) *of our* ... In the right-hand one, Gilbreth seems to have copied in her own hand the diagram that appeared on Vanins' previous letter-page. Here, once again, shakily rendered, is the cone, or cone-shaped object, or perhaps just cone-shaped field of vectors, circling the upright line, or pole. The circling movement's bi-directional: double-headed arrows at the cone's base, its swing-zone's lower rim-circumference, make this clear. About the figure Gilbreth has added several other little sketches: of cogged mechanisms, mill-wheels, spoked and levered automata; also some coloured circles. Across the whole page are dotted a few words and phrases in Latin or Spanish, and some names.

'*Maricourt?*' Garnett reads. '*Bessler? De Honnecourt?* The wheel-and-hammer, spinning-rings-that-need-no-winding, pendulum-decked-gravity-disc charlatans? Is Gilbreth in her addled dotage starting to buy into the old perpetual-motion scam?'

'Not at all.' Pilkington lets out a short laugh. 'Although you'd be surprised how many of physics' big beasts jumped down that rabbit hole before: Wolff, Bernouilli, even Leibniz ... They set out to demonstrate the notion's folly and, somewhere along the line, flipped over into obsessive believers, drunk on a conviction that the very work they'd done to dispel any credence in the possibility of endless movement proved its viability ... which "proof" the next scientist in line set out to debunk, only to find himself converted – while the first, meanwhile, had apostasised back again. You could say the perpetual motion's there: these self-renewing waves of scepticism and credulity, reason and fantasy ...'

He takes another sip of wine. Watching him, Garnett pictures a toy, a gizmo he once gave to his young nephew: a Sullivan drinking-bird that, as methylene chloride rose up its long neck-tube, tilted its felt-covered beak into a glass of water, the absorption of which caused the cooling chloride to sink down its neck again, which in turn pulled its head up for a breath of air before the process started over.

'I've become convinced,' Pilkington dabs his lips, 'in my own state of addled dotage, that our work, at base ... The great contraptions we come up with, all the engines and the interfaces and the operating codes – that these are nothing more than prompts for our own supposition and projection, stand-ins for some ultimate machine we'll never build but nonetheless can't stop ourselves from trying to ... Jacquard looms, the Internet, crackpot time-travelling patents or those influencing engines sketched by generations of psychotics: whether they get made or simply trawled up from the depths of some delusion is beside the point. All machines are imaginary. Doesn't our Norbert say as much, somewhere?'

'He does,' Garnett murmurs distractedly; he's scrutinising still the copied journal pages. From the shakily redrawn sketch, the coloured circles, the scrawled names and Latin / Spanish words, an arrow leads down to the page's base, where, in a hand that appears purposeful and strained, as though accomplished only through a monumental act of will, more words, in bold, are written:

'*Box 808 charges ...*'

'It's *changes* ...'

'... *changes everything.* Which one is 808?'

'Have a look,' Pilkington answers knowingly, pushing the other paper-stack towards him once more. Garnett flicks through the pages, eye moving top to bottom, down the photographed and numbered motion boxes, through the seven hundreds, then into the eights, 805, 806, 807 ...

'Oh!'

'Exactly.'

There's no 808: it's missing. The stretch of paper where it should be leers back blank and empty, glaring as a razed section of forest or a patch of wall from which a painting's been removed.

'Why,' Garnett wonders aloud after a few moments' silence, 'does she go on about it so much when – this other person too ... ?' He's flipping through the pages of the second stack again, the scanned notes, letters, journal pages, the anonymous author's summary and gloss of these. It's everywhere: ... *that Vanins' experience of 'the T.T. episode' led to the creation of Box 808 is highly* ... page nine; *808 seems to have excited her so much that she revised her entire* ... ten; eleven: *Box 808's supreme importance to her project is attested by* ... 'What do you think it ... ?'

'That,' Pilkington responds, 'is the big question. That's what's generated all the noise.'

'Noise?'

'In my ... community. We're not the only ones to have picked up on this. There seems to be a general buzz all round. Consensus is that there's something worth looking into ...'

'What kind of something?'

Pilkington reflects a little, then continues:

'Vanins was, *inter alia*, an important figure in the field of Soviet aeronautics. I've seen files, whole stacks of files, on him. If he did, as your colleagues liked to fancy, chisel a Northwest Passage through a stretch of the hitherto theoretical-physically impossible, even if it didn't lead to any direct application we became aware of, but got lost amidst the clear-out, overlooked, misplaced ...

Well, MOD will want to know about it – as will several other outfits we could think of ...'

'But why would he tell Gilbreth? She wasn't a *physicist*.'

'No. But she, more than anyone else, understood kinesis. Bodies in motion. And she'd used this understanding to transform the world – feat for which he, and many of his ilk, revered her. I think they saw her as a kind of Darwin or Linnaeus, capturing and freezing movement's every sub-species and class and phylum: folding napkins, pulling levers, loading guns ... all part of the same general ballet. With the boxes, she'd attempted to amass a general taxonomy of act and gesture. To amass, and to improve – for practical reasons, partly: efficiency, well-being of factory workers, housewives, astronauts ... She always wanted to work out ...'

'The "one best way".'

'The one best way,' says Pilkington, 'exactly. But – as the author of the report you're holding explains so lucidly – the meaning of those words changes with time. It starts out signalling the leanest path, the most economic and productive route a worker's hand or body can cut through the space around it in the execution of its task. Later, though ... Later, the idea sprouts wings, grows all-encompassing and vague at the same time. There's something abstract – almost devotional – about it all. She seems to come to believe that there exists, somewhere, hidden from our view, a *perfect* shape for every act – essential, almost preordained. And beyond even that, that there might be a kind of *absolutely* perfect motion-circuit hovering concealed behind even the perfect ones – the kingdom, as it were, containing all the phylums; sum of their possibilities, their infinite- and zero-point, alpha and omega ...'

'So she *was* a mystic,' Garnett murmurs.

'Yes and no,' says Pilkington. 'Isn't that what ... ?'

'Isn't what what?'

'Isn't that what you do?'

'Me?'

'Pantarey. All your kinetic typologies, which you scale up and down from keyhole surgery to war to silly films ...'

'I wanted to ask you something about silly films. We want to use a wind tunnel to stage ...' Garnett begins, but Pilkington waves the interjection off:

'Isn't your work – our work – all about accessing and deploying underlying sequences and patterns? Mapping particulars on to great universals? Isn't that the art to which, in one way or another, we've both devoted our best years?'

Garnett, out-argued, grants the point in silence.

'And our Norbert, his Augustine visions – isn't that a form of mysticism too? He saw inductive logic as a supreme act of faith. Call it physics, metaphysics or theology: it doesn't matter ... And I'm wandering. We want to know what Box 808 is, and what *everything* it changes.'

'You really think there is one?' Garnett asks.

'A Box 808?'

'An *everything* to be changed by it.'

'Gilbreth,' Pilkington deflects the question, 'clearly thought so. But then, she was very old; the diaries and the notebooks show a mind stumbling. Besides, whether there *is* or not – an *everything*, a box, an either – is beside the point. There's noise. Which means our view on this, like Gilbreth's photographs, is stereoscopic: focus is partly on the actual givens, the reality, whatever this might be, and partly on gaming the speculation. If someone else thinks *we* think it's important, or if a third party thinks that we think *they* think it's important, then ...'

Garnett can see this: it's straight von Neumann, basic game theory ...

'Even,' continues Pilkington, 'if this box had nothing in it but a pair of old shoes, or was empty – if it exists, we want it to be us that has it and not one of the someone-elses and third-parties ...'

The waiter comes to take their plates and hand them dessert menus. Garnett orders a crème brûlée, Pilkington a slice of chocolate tart, and brandies for them both.

'It's a pity,' Garnett muses when they're left alone again, 'that you can't ask Vanins what it's all about.'

Pilkington's face, the flow of its expressions, shudders to a sudden halt; he looks at Garnett's own face now intently, scrutinising it. Garnett, uncomfortable, adds:

'He is dead, I presume.'

'Not at all!' Pilkington sits back suddenly. 'I thought you knew that.'

'No. I hadn't heard from, or about, him in so many years, I just imagined ...'

'He's living,' Pilkington informs him, 'on a dacha outside Riga. In his upper eighties, but still ... *extant*.'

'Then why don't you ... ?'

The other's look as the sentence trails off underscores the thought's naivety. In a tactful, almost diplomatic tone of voice Pilkington tells him:

'A head-on approach from *us* doesn't seem, in this instance, quite appropriate.'

Garnett can see that as well – but not what's coming next. Pilkington picks up his dessert fork, taps its tines against the tablecloth – twice, a little Morse-code rap – and says:

'We thought that maybe you ...'

'Me? How on earth could I ... ? I mean, if your own people couldn't ...'

'Precisely because,' purrs Pilkington, 'you're not one of our people. Or anyone else's. With Pantarey, you struck off on your own. Makes you a *bona fide* member of the same old guard as him: the pioneers, trailblazers ...'

Garnett looks down modestly, bathing in praise's warmth. His friend continues:

'You could renew contact with him: shared field of interest – states of equilibrium, perhaps ... revisiting an old line of enquiry ... compare notes ... steer it onwards from there ... He'd respect you. He'd *trust* you.'

'And,' Garnett looks back up, 'I'd betray that trust?'

'For a purpose. For a purpose. And it's not even betraying. If this 808 stuff was nothing, a delusion of Gilbreth's senility, then what harm is done? If it was something, then that's knowledge shared – *un*boxed, brought out into the light. That's a good thing, surely – scientifically speaking ...'

'I'm not sure I view it the same way as ...' Garnett starts, but Pilkington cuts him off.

'Your man Mark Phocan has been visiting us at Farnborough.'

'Well, yes,' says Garnett, not quite seeing the connection. 'After all, you're a client.'

'For now,' Pilkington says. 'The contract's coming to an end. There's been talk of renewing it, taking it to another level, with markerless tracking ...'

Garnett stares at his friend, trying to work out what he's getting at – as though his words, like a report encrypted, were keeping their essential content wrapped, embalmed, sarcophagaed beneath a carapace of manner; leaking out, though, now, through cracks skilfully wrought, with just the right amount of pressure ... Mixing together too: imaginary machines, markerless tracking – and now this: beyond the perfect movement, beyond movement itself, some kind of 'absolute', a disembodied circuit, hovering, concealed, everything-changing. Taken together, what would it all bode? The 'kingdom', as Pilkington would have Gilbreth hoping? Or another type of dispensation, far less kind or to be wished for: a regime of total capture – one with which he, Garnett, is, always has been, complicit ... Latching on to Pilkington's *un-boxed* and groping into memory's back reaches, to some passage filed away with deer and sherry, he now pieces together half-remembered shards of Hesiod, *Works and Days*: ἐκ γαίης πλάσσεν κλυτὸς Ἀμφιγυήεις παρθένῳ αἰδοίῃ ἴκελον, *moulded clay in the likeness of a modest maid* ... Pandora ... *took off the great lid of* πίθου, *the box* ... *then earth was full*, πλείη μὲν γὰρ γαῖα κακῶν, *of evils, and sea too* ... Aloud now, he recites:

'μούνη δ' αὐτόθι Ἐλπὶς ἐν ἀρρήκτοισι δόμοισιν ἔνδον ἔμμνε: *Only hope remained* ...'

'What's that?' asks Pilkington.

At this point in their meeting, before Garnett can respond, a strange interlude occurs. Swing-doors arc open, wafting smells of melted chocolate and burnt sugar to them, prelude to their waiter who glides, back first, through the entry to the kitchen then rotates mid-floor to guide their desserts smoothly down towards their tabletop. As Pilkington's plate taxis across the last few centimetres to its assigned slot beside the small fork he's still playing with, Garnett notices his friend's hands tensing suddenly, fingertips simultaneously digging into and pushing away from the tablecloth.

'What's this?' Pilkington's voice has real aggression in it, tinged with what sounds to Garnett like fear.

'Chocolate tart,' answers the waiter. 'Isn't that what you ordered?'

'Yes,' Pilkington responds; 'but not with this ... this ...'

Both Garnett and the waiter peer down at his plate. It's white, and circular, as plates generally are. A portion of its surface area has been filled by the dark slice of tart – a sector whose two radii are connected at their separated ends by an arc inset from but aligned with that of the plate's circumference, while their meeting point precisely coincides with the plate's centre. Coming from the plate's far hemisphere to intersect this tart-slice sector at an obtuse angle – intersecting it so as to rest partially atop it – is a wafer: light-brown, slightly smaller than the slice itself and shaped not as a sector, even a displaced one, but a triangle whose base sits on a chord the endpoints of which lie at roughly three and six o'clock (POV Pilkington). This wafer, like most wafers, bears the mark of the iron in which it was formed, a grid pattern stamped across its surface. To its side, lying in the final sector of the plate, the one covered or crossed by neither slice nor wafer, sits a scoop of ice cream – high-end, in-house-fabricated ice cream within whose spherical mass fragments of ground vanilla are embedded, like small graphite flecks in marble.

'... *assemblage!*' Pilkington, alighting on the right word, almost hurls it at the waiter. 'I ordered the tart! There was no mention of ice cream or wafer.'

'We mark it with both *D* and *G* on the menu, Sir. If you're dairy- or gluten-averse, I could ...'

'That's not the point!' Pilkington cuts him off angrily. 'I just want to know what's ... what's coming to me ... without these ...'

His sentence fades out, possibly because he realises as he speaks it that it makes as little sense to him as to the waiter or his friend. These two both stare at him, wanting to help remediate the situation while quite unable to because they're at a loss to understand it.

'I can have it,' Garnett offers. 'We can swap.'

'No.' Pilkington nixes the idea gruffly. 'It's not that. I'd rather you just ...'

'I'll take it away,' the waiter picks his cue up here. 'We'll take it off the bill, of course. And if there's anything else we can offer you to ...'

'Nothing. The brandies. Make them doubles.'

'Absolutely,' says the waiter. 'On the way.' As smoothly as he set it down he whisks the plate off the table and guides it back through the kitchen's swing doors out of sight. Garnett makes to say something, but Pilkington, regaining his composure, waves the episode away.

'Vanins,' he says. 'You'd be helping me immensely. Have a think; let me know.'

Tentatively, Garnett shatters his crème brûlée's glaze and starts to eat it. Brandies come; they drink them. Pilkington, relaxed and meditative again, muses:

'Shipwrecked passengers on a doomed planet ... I remember that bit now. But – doesn't he say something about salvation, too?'

'Not exactly,' Garnett answers. 'He says that even in a shipwreck, human decencies and values don't all necessarily vanish.'

'That's it. It's true: not *necessarily* ...'

'We're going down, he says; but we can do it *in a manner worthy of our dignity.*'

'To dignity!' cries Pilkington. He drains the remnants of his brandy, then announces: 'I'm paying. Let's go.'

Outside, there's a car waiting – smart, executive, unliveried. Pilkington instructs the driver to go first to Charlebury Station, where they drop Garnett. As the car pulls off again, he winds the window down and calls out:

'Use a typewriter! And burn the ribbon afterwards.'

195

4. The Girl with Kaleidoscope Eyes

Noam Webster, keeper of the skulls, runs his hands up and down the row of crania lined up on the shelf. His fingers tap the parietal bone of one, linger on the orbital plate of another, jump past two more and touch down on the zygomatic arches of a third: his little warm-up, loosening the ivories, prodding them into attentiveness while he decides which tune to play, which key to play in. Lucy Diamond, standing just behind him, scours them with her eyes. Their shapes and sizes are so variant that it's hard to see them – and Webster, and her – as belonging to one species. Some have bulging frontals, others flat ones – straight-up, windscreen-slanted ... some temporal lines are raised, others regressed ... sutures each scrawl their eccentric signature, their wavering graph-curves, on calvarial parchment. Plus, each one is damaged – chipped, indented, notched, trepanned, depressed – in its own way ...

'The thing with high-velocity impact – say, when a bullet travels through a skull, especially when dispatched from up close, what we might call the "execution scenario" ...' Pinching the sphenoids of the skull on which it's currently resting between thumb and little finger, Webster's right hand lifts it; the fore and middle fingers of his left, meanwhile, turn into a gun's barrel jammed against the occipital bone. 'The skull's so fragile,' he continues, 'that, as soon as the bullet' – his cocked thumb-hammer crooks in simulated pin-strike – 'enters it, it starts to splinter, with the lines of fracture spreading out in all directions, in proliferating branches, like a railway network sprawling over a whole territory – to the point that there's no territory any more: it's all just fracture network. When the splinter lines run up against each other, they remake the skull in their own image, as a set of void channels, of fissures; at which point the skull disintegrates. This process takes place with extraordinary speed. It sometimes runs its course, entry to disintegration, more quickly than the bullet travels: the cracks tear around the cranium's circumference so fast they beat the bullet to the other side. By the time it arrives at the frontal plate, there *is* no frontal plate there any more, hence nothing left for it to exit through. Which poses certain challenges to subsequent investigators ...'

'I see,' says Diamond, trying from the off to strike a balance in her tone between receptive and imperious. This is her first solo outing since being upgraded to full Pantarey staff member (Associate Technology Officer, ATO: she's just handed him her card). Last time she visited Forensics, it was as Phocan's sidekick; now, she has to signal brief-command, client entitlement. She informs Webster: 'But in this case, it's not a bullet. It's a rapier. The character's already got a model of her uncle's staved-in skull, and when she finds the rapier that did it, she's able to ...'

'What's a rapier?' Webster asks.

'It's a long, hand-held weapon for close-quarter combat. In this film, they're full of energy. They glow.'

'Like a lightsaber.'

'Kind of. But it's solid, made of martensite. Maybe the closest approximation would be a samurai sword – one infused with plutonium or some like form of radiation.'

Tokyo: Chofu. Images of dogwood spray in Jindai Botanical Gardens spread round Diamond's own cranium, of *ume* flowers, whose long filaments, extending radially from deep-red central stigma to wave laden anthers at incoming airborne traffic while bright petals fanned open around them, seemed to duplicate in softer form the satellites that she and Phocan were helping JAXA to configure. Their hosts took them, one afternoon, to visit the Yoshihara swordsmith workshop: endless rhythmic hammering and bashing of the smelted *tamahagane*, breathing of the wood-fires, rasping of the bellows, fire-spark blossom drifting through the air, about the floor … Even when drawn out into billets in which the *katana*'s final shape could be discerned in embryonic form, the steel still held within its body molten pockets, hot as planetary mantle. *Charge.* From the Creston's high windows she'd look out over the night-time city, its unquenchable illumination, the magmatic neon flows, and see a unit – like a battery-pack or memory plug-in of unspeakable complexity – continually recharging. And the people … She read on the plane an article describing Fukushima's after-math: whole populations radio-iodinised, buzzing with enough isotopic discharge to work Geiger counters up into a frenzy. If the Yoshihara visit stuck with her it was, perhaps, because the precious, volatile bars plucked from the furnace seemed to reify that sense of chargedness – that, and the way bandanaed and kimonoed sword-smiths held them up for reverential scrutiny, or passed them on between themselves, from tong to tong, or laid them out to cool, polished and dusted them, less artisanal than ceremonial, forensic …

'This,' Webster has set the skull down now and moved to a com-puter, 'is a PBR, made with our latest toy, a Faro laser scanner, of one of these specimens – the third one from the right, to be precise. We could provide you and your movie people, Double Zero, with …'

'It's Degree Zero,' she corrects him.

'… Degree Zero, with this very scan, or one much like it. It's made with the same flyover method we use with the Pitt Rivers and British Museums, digitising ethnographic artefacts.'

'Artefacts as in … ?'

'Statues, fetishes or handmade bowls, what have you …' he tells her without taking his eyes from the screen or fingers from the glide-pad, moving about which they spin the radiant green cranium around, enabling multiple flyovers, each from a new angle, of its wound-crater, a detailed survey of its pleats and ridges.

'This is more or less exactly what the character does,' Diamond says.

'She has a Faro scanner too?'

'Version 20.0,' Diamond smiles back, 'with screen-independent holographic render … Hey, what's that?'

She can't help herself slipping back into ingénue mode: the printouts covering the wall behind the monitor are too intriguing. They seem to depict a kind of urban grid: an irregular one, with arrows indicating various jagging trajectories across it.

'What's … ? Oh, that: Sarajevo,' answers Webster. 'Twenty-eighth June 1914. It's the route that Archduke Ferdinand's car took across the city. Collaboration with the History Department at UCL. Apparently, the century since the assassination has produced a thousand theories as to why the anarchist Princip did it, or why this particular event sparked off the biggest tinderbox in human history – but no one's ever thought to carry out a basic time-and-motion study.'

'And … ?'

'And what?'

'And what has it revealed?'

'It has revealed,' Webster proudly announces, 'that it all boils down to a three-point turn.'

'A three-point turn – like in a car?'

'Indeed: not *like* but *actually* in a car. The Archduke's motor-cade, driving down Appel Quay, here' – he's over at the wall now, pointing out the road in question – 'turns right toward Franz Josef Street so as to deviate from the back-up route to which it has, as a precaution, switched (a bomb has been thrown earlier, and hit a secondary car; the pages of the speech Franz Ferdinand reads just prior to his assassination are flecked with blood) – a double-deviation, back to its initially announced route. Which isn't very safe, given the day's threat level. So, when the security implications of this dawn on the Archduke's bodyguards, they decide to switch back a second time; which re-rerouting neces-sitates a three-point turn. Now, think of three-point turns: what do they all, no matter how swiftly or deftly they're executed, entail?'

Diamond thinks back to her driving test: angles and distances, protocols and sequences, mirror-signal-manoeuvre … 'Toggling between forward and reverse?' she tries.

'Well, yes ... But that dictates another basic quality: that every three-point turn contains, at – *as* – its pivot-point, a static moment. Here in Appel Quay, this moment takes place right by where Princip is standing. So, naturally, he pulls his pistol out and offs his sitting-duck duke quarry.'

'What are the chances?' Diamond murmurs.

'Chance,' says Webster, 'is a can of worms this project has pried open. The more you look at it, the more you start to see a sort of correspondence – of *symmetry* almost – not only in the layout of the streets, the doubled routes, the switchbacks and retracings and so on, but also in the larger field of the event's contingencies. Take just one sample area, for example: the lead actors' titles. On one side, you've got Franz Ferdinand, the Archduke; on the other, Princip, the anarchist. *Archduke*, like *princip*, means 'prince' – from *arc* or *arche*: prime authority, but also curve plotted in space; and *dux*, or leader, plotter of a route. The Archduke's people plot a route through space; the anarchists launch their counterplot, a plot against arch order, against structure. But their plotting is defective – as you might expect: they don't believe in arcs or arches, that's the whole point. But – here's the twist, which perhaps isn't such a twist after all – an arc comes to their aid: a double-arc, embodied in a three-point turn. It's like a kind of doubling-up, a folding. And the street towards which the Archduke is heading doubles his own name, halfway at least: Franz Josef is his uncle, who's dispatched him off to Sarajevo – like a double, to die in his place.'

'So are you saying ... ?' Diamond begins; but Webster cuts her off:

'I'm not saying anything. Just tracing out a set of lines; a fracture network. That's all I do. I have a hat in this ring, too.'

'Professionally?' she asks.

'Titularly. Staying within the same interrogation boundaries, names and their meanings: *arc* comes from the Greek *arkheion*, house' – he opens up his hand to indicate their environs – 'of records. In Ancient Athens, they had *archons*, magistrates, guardians and interpreters of the public archive; through their collective analyses and deliberations, the *archons* oversaw the workings of democracy and justice.' He pauses for a while, then adds: 'Archives were held in chest or *arks*, made of acacia wood.' His finger gently slides down from the diagrams and route maps and swings back towards the skulls as he continues: '*Arca* can mean *coffin* too ...'

Diamond's middle name is Sky. It was her mother's maiden name. Her parents were second-wave hippies, early-nineties flower children. In tribute to the tangerine streets and marmalade skies, the plasticine porters with looking-glass ties of the song – as well (she suspects, reading between the lines of the foundation myth they fondly peddled her) as the fact that they were both tripping when they met – they named her Lucy. Are there arches at work there, too, plotting, from base coordinates of nomenclature, the paths and switchbacks, folds and doublings, assignations both fortuitous and unfortunate, even catastrophic, that her life will follow? Or is it something older, routes laid down prior even to that, some vast mechanism as inevitable as the engine movements of open-top motorcars, or newspaper taxis appearing on the shore, waiting to take you away? Here, in Forensis plc's back office, one of the many darkened rooms that she now seems to spend the lion's share of her time in, Diamond finds herself struck by a pervasive sense of powerlessness, of freedom from volition. It's neither a particularly bad feeling nor a good and liberating one – it just is what it is. It comes to her, she shrugs it off and turns to Webster as he says:

'This is the other thing I meant to show you.'

He's back beside her at the screen, shutting down the luminous green cranium and popping open in its place a LiDAR file depicting, in equally rotatable projection, a modern urban or suburban living room. The space is illustrated colourfully and schematically, in architect-diagram style. Between orange and yellow blocks and cuboids labelled *closet*, *bench press*, *TV*, and so on, a green human avatar lies stretched out, the circle of its head distended into a long oval seeping red across the floor. Cutting aslant the room, a conic section, also red, depicts a projectile's flight path, door to facing wall, passing above the backrest of an armchair at whose base the human figure's feet lie, pivot-points around which it, too, has been doubled, folded out and downward, vertical to horizontal. Diamond recognises the scenario at once: it's a case Pantarey have taken on for a humanitarian NGO, the shooting of a Guatemalan dissident. They modelled the whole thing two weeks ago back in The Cell, with markered extras moving through various scenarios, the files then being passed to Forensis who, like them, are offering their services *pro bono*.

'This is a sneak preview,' Webster tells her. 'We're still working on it. But – spoiler alert – the *Policia Nacional*'s account is holding up about as well as this politician's hairstyle.'

'Trade unionist, I think,' she corrects him again. 'How can you tell?'

'If it had been a random break-in, as they claim, the victim would have moved either towards or away from the point of entry, to confront (if he was feeling feisty) or (if he was minded for self-preservation) flee from his assailant. On top of which, objects and furniture would be displaced. If they'd even wanted to make it look as though it *might* have been a break-in, they could have knocked over the stereo or bench press, or rifled the closet. But they didn't. The position of the victim's feet – hinged round but otherwise unmoved from by the armchair – suggest he had no inkling of his killer's presence in the house. And then the gunman has chosen the angle most propitious for a straight-up take-out: a clear line of sight, good reference points in the door frame and far wall's cornice boundary. If I apply all the axes, you can see ...'

He clicks a side-bar option, and the depicted room becomes a kind of loom all of whose yarns converge on the shooter's position, as though its contents and dimensions were being knitted by, from or around this single point, the muzzle of his gun. The geometry's so clear, so perfect, that it seems to Diamond inconceivable that the space, the living room, could ever have been designed for anything other than this one event; seems that the converging warp-lines were all there already, and the conic section too – not over- but *underlay*, integral design-key announcing: *This is the bullet's trajectory, and always has been; this is the point at which Plane A is intersected by Line B* ... If this trade unionist has died, it's for the simple reason that he drifted into this trajectory, transgressed the plane, the point of intersection – occupied, however transiently, a certain spot within the grid.

'Their timeline's off, too,' Webster's telling her.

'Sorry? How do you mean?'

'The *policía*'s. From their crime-scene photos that they say were taken two hours after the supposed break-in,' he pulls up a screen of thumbnail snaps in which the loom's symmetry and order have been lost, neutralised or at least camouflaged by the actual room's banal grey surfaces, 'you can see, through the window, the exact lie of the shadow cast on to the ground by the house's outer wall. Cross-referencing that with the building's original architectural plans, which we got hold of, and with Street View, and with easily obtainable sun-tracking tables for Guatemala City on that date, March the fifteenth ... Well, you get a time-reading of more than three hours earlier. It's clear the time code on the photographs is falsified, or at least wrong ...'

Now Diamond's thinking of another room, with freesias, and *ume* flowers; of a bed, a furnace, stars, a spaceship, Chofu, Sarajevo ... In the Creston's bedroom, on the wall, a line from Basho had been printed: *Days and months are travellers of eternity.* As thumbnails, blowing up and shrinking, follow one another in quick, flickering procession, she sees once again the pulsing lights, synaptic spectacle of death and continuity, flat screen in which all actions are contemporaneous, replenishing each other endlessly.

'These people,' Webster clucks, 'don't get it: everything is information. It's being sensed, being recorded, stored and studied all the time. The entire world's an arc ...'

He's picked up the skull that he was holding earlier; it's resting, like a sleeping kitten, in the cradle of his left hand held to his warm stomach while the index finger of his right hand runs and reruns down its suture, like a blind man's scanning lines of Braille.

5. Critical Interval

On the apron, as the Alitalia Airbus A320 is being pushed back, Phocan watches a small drama playing out. Beside a jet bridge that's accordioned down almost flat against a terminal itself shrinking with increasing distance is a hawk. It's hovering about the corrugated metal, almost, but not quite, in place; every few seconds it tweaks its position, shifting two or three feet to the right, or left, or up or down, returning to a spot it occupied a moment earlier, or else establishing a new one in the gaps between all these. It does this neither languidly nor playfully but with intent, wings beating fiercely, head and neck twitching their way through minute readjustments that keep its vision locked on the same focal point.

Working his own gaze backwards down the eye beams, Phocan sees what's in the cross-hairs here: a sparrow flapping gracelessly against the tarmac, making abortive take-off bids in one direction, then another. At first he thinks the sparrow must be wounded, grounded by a broken wing; that the hawk has picked it out and is just waiting for its energy and will to ebb away, for surrender to set in, before swooping down for the kill. When the sparrow rises ten or more feet in the air, though, he realises he's wrong: this ascent was perfectly competent; calling it off and turning back again was a decision, as deliberate as the hawk's studied readjustments. It takes a few more strike-outs by the sparrow and adjustments by the hawk before he understands what's going on: the hawk's controlling the whole area without needing to patrol around it; closing off vectors of airspace, blocking swathes and columns of potential flight, each mooted escape path, simply by angling itself towards them. The two birds understand each other, and are operating in well-calibrated synchrony; a chess game they'll carry on playing, move and countermove, the one snuffing the other's future out, until the sequences have all been run through, endgame drifting on to the inevitable resignation, just a matter of time ...

A few feet from the sparrow, there's another scene unfolding. A luggage cart's trundling across the pavement, four dolly compartments coupled up into a train pulled by a small tractor. As the driver plies the narrow staging-area channel hemmed in by red restraint lines to his left, white vehicle-corridor and yield lines up ahead of him and, to his right, the aeroplane, perched on its yellow taxi lane, to which his consignment is to be delivered, then pulls a tight U and draws to a halt across (but not within) the red and white rectangle of the loading box, the dollies snake from side to side, each taking its cue from the one in front, so that the carriage as a whole seems to be partly following, partly digressing from, routes of the boundary markings over which it's slithering. *Bedbug, moth*: the words take shape amidst the verbal babble spilling out of cabin speakers and the open in-flight magazine. Yesterday in Finns, Garnett called Phocan to his office again. Entering, he discovered his boss watching a YouTube clip. It was an old one, digitised TV footage from the sixties or even fifties; it showed a man advanced in years demonstrating to an awkward, crew-cut child the operation of some kind of robot with a painted insect carapace.

'Palomilla.' Garnett's tone was full of fondness – for the insect, or the boy, or Phocan; or, perhaps, for the avuncular, robot-controlling man. This last was holding a small flashlight in his hand, directing its beam straight on to the dog-sized, beetle-mimicking contraption, which responded by advancing with a whirring sound across the studio floor. But not in a straight line: it meandered drunkenly, turning a little one way then the other in a kind of ponderous slalom, as though undecided which of two approach angles to pursue towards a beacon-wielding summoner who, like the wind, could not be steered directly into but demanded constant tacking.

'It's his Tropism Machine,' said Garnett. 'He built it – that's Wiener there – with Singleton at MIT in '49. They called it Bedbug-Moth, or Palomilla.'

'Funny names,' said Phocan, to say something.

'The Bedbug-Moth's because it's phototropic. There's a tiller,' Garnett beckoned him near, as though explaining a model train set's workings to him, 'underneath the cover, which controls the single steering wheel beneath its nose. The tiller's set up with two modes of action: one positively phototropic – programmed to do nothing more than seek light out, like a moth – the other negatively phototropic, as monomaniacally' – he cut the word into insectoid segments, *mono-ma-nia-cally* – 'intent on fleeing any and every light source, like a bedbug. See?'

On screen, the cyber-beetle carried on its restless battle with itself, veering first, dog-to-bone, towards the torch, then in revulsion, Superman from kryptonite, away again, which made the positive impulse kick in once more, which in turn triggered the counter-impulse – on *ad infinitum*, or at least the mpeg's end.

'He built it to help army neurologists.' Garnett's voice was meditative. 'Battle-worn troops were coming home displaying pathologies ranging from the shakes to full-blown neurasthenia . . .'

On his desk, between the keypad and the monitor, there was a kind of shoebox. It was old, black and wooden – more the type of box you'd keep brushes and tins of polish in than shoes themselves. Two of its sides, and the roof, were missing, thus affording (whether by chance or design) a view on to an abstract diorama: from the floor rose a kind of sculpture, a thin metal tube that veered and swerved about before dovetailing back to its beginning spot. This misshapen diadem was held in place, at its lowest point, by a crude staple and, at a point not its highest but presumably the most propitious balance-wise, by a column planted unobtrusively in the scene's background, a dark obelisk whose pinnacle rose to meet it. The interiors of the sides that hadn't been removed were covered with white grid squares like

The Cell's; on the floor, near the front edge, the number 374 was handwritten in thin white paint.

'It's my own,' said Garnett, watching him eyeing it. 'A Gilbreth box.'

Phocan, drawing a blank with this name, stared at the twisting metal loop some more. The supporting obelisk made him think of Cleopatra's Needle on the Victoria Embankment; by extension, of a raft of funerary, sphinx-like forms, as though the floating circuit had been mounted on some monumental, if miniaturised, riddle.

'It seems,' Garnett continued, 'that they've started to become collectible.'

'What have?' asked Phocan.

'Sit down,' Garnett instructed him.

When he emerged from the office two hours later, he'd been handed a bunch of papers, and told he was going to be dispatched to Riga (*It's the capital of Latvia*, Garnett informed him helpfully) to hunt down a box – a box much like the one he'd just been shown, but with a different number. He'd also been chastised for knowing nothing about his own discipline's pre-history.

'But,' he objected, letting the rebuke, unjust though it was, slide in order to address the more pressing implications of the order he'd been given, 'I've got Rome' – phone out, fingers leapt into action, swiping and expanding iCal entries, summoning up schedules – 'then Bergen, then ...'

But Garnett's hand, raised in paternalistic override, cut him short.

'You've got time,' he reassured him, soothingly but for that no less authoritatively. 'I still have to prepare the ground for such a visit. You'll need a plausible excuse; some line of enquiry not linked to the box itself – not directly, at least. In the meantime ...'

In the meantime, Phocan has been reading up on Raivis Vanins. Seems that the guy came of age during the height of 'Soviet Taylorism' – or, to use its more generic name, of 'scientific management': the wholesale adoption, and adaption, of the capitalist

West's newest industrial labour protocols, not least universal stand-ardisation of not only shop floors but all metrics by which work was both conducted and assessed. A million steelworkers, shipbuilders, car, washing-machine or aeroplane constructors stretching and reaching, bending and swivelling their way through sequences so near-identical as to be assessable at scales macro and micro, Omsk to Ufa, Krasnodar to Tolyatti ... If the deviating tendency of a single Voronezh double-roll rotary-press operator or Chelyabinsk MINSK-2 circuit board assembler could be nixed the moment it arose, ironed back into ergonomic conformity with the actions of the other ten-thousand-odd rotary-press operators or circuit board assemblers, so, too, could deviations – good ones, beneficial tweaks and upgrades, from the minutiae of belt speed or switch position right up to complete equipment overhauls, metrification, even digitisation – be rolled out in unison across the Euro-Asiatic board, and, once unrolled, evaluated with complete precision, increased yield-to-man-hour (-week, -month, -year or -five-year) ratio deter-mined to the third decimal figure. Where Taylor's only frame and *telos* had been growing factory-owner and shareholder profit, his Soviet cheerleader Alexsei Gastev saw in Taylorism's rise an opportunity to liberate the worker from long serfdom, from an evo-lution trapped in nineteenth-century neoteny; to release him from the shackles of his very body, or at least the bourgeois-humanist conception thereof, its small-minded designation as a skin-bound monad separated from the roaring and erupting dynamism of the great machine. The first unlocked by, multiplied and networked through the second, though, a new man (this, as far as Phocan can make out, was Gastev's main thrust) would arise, and with him a new proletarian culture – singing, joyous, epic, in which noisy cavalcade of work will bring about both individual self-oblivion and collective self-determination; where in generators' running transmissions, furnaces' gurgle and hiss, the rhythmic clang of blows, our thirst for life will gain titanic force. *Comrades,* he bel-lowed in 1920 on being handed the Central Institute of Labour's inaugural directorship, *raise up your hammers to forge a new world!*

Gastev fell foul of Stalin, and was shot in the Great Purge of '36–'38. Vanins, luckily, was still in nappies then; he entered adulthood and, not long after, took his master's degree as the second Soviet-Taylorist wave was breaking, implemented through the Ordzhonikidze EEI, in plans for a new Statewide Automated System, *Obshche-gosudarstvennaia avtomatizirovannaia sistema* ... Safer, if soberer, times. Besides which, Vanins was a scientist – physics, pure and, if not neutral (nothing was), then at least emanating from a source so far above syndicalism or the vagaries of party faction as to occupy an abstract plane of absolute relations from which Soviet science and industry were compelled, by destiny as much as edict, to take their cue. He seems, though, to have shared his predecessor's zeal for ergonomic transformation, to have been convinced that something bigger than production figures was at stake in the labourer–tool coupling. Phocan's reading a selection of his papers now, as Norman beaches slide beneath the wing:

Work, therefore, should best be understood as a state of kinetic absorption in which the operative's entire essence is given over to the rhythm of his apparatus – and, in being thus surrendered, is remade as an unbound potentiality: fluid, morphing, never finished; spirit realised as rhythm ...

The rhythm motif's big; it keeps on cropping up: *rhythm of historic sublimation ... rhythm and time ...*

Thus we, as the work terminal's architect, create – in the true revolutionary tradition – a new mode of world-time, one in which the flux of being pulsates ...

'That's bullshit,' Sennet, peering over Phocan's shoulder, annotates. 'You can't impose a tempo at the scale of history: only detect it.'

'You're not really meant to see this,' Phocan tells him, turning the page window-ward. It's true: Garnett was quite stern about this – uncharacteristically, since Pantarey staff always operate under professional *omertà* anyhow, research, data, files all covered by a large NDA-shroud that each of them has signed, if not in actual blood, at least in lifeblood of continued salaried employment-prospects. That's external, though: the company culture, generally speaking, positively encourages in-house chatter, note-comparing, the cross-pollination of ideas and applications. But *internal* muzzling? Phocan's only guess – two guesses – are that either it's a personal matter, Garnett's indulgence of a box-collecting hobby about which he's slightly coy, or else that Garnett, here, is playing the role of gauze or interface, screening off other players in a game whose stakes are higher than whatever level to which he, Garnett, let alone he-Phocan, has been cleared … There was an urgency to his employer's tone, a sense that he was passing to him (yes: to *him*, not Sennet) an important baton, harnessing him with a task allotted not so much by Garnett, or even by whomever it might be that he was hiding, as by some abstract force of pure necessity – that Phocan was, like Soviet science and industry, being assigned a *destiny*: to find this box elided from a cataloguing system fifty years ago. This urgency, which he dismissed at first – just as he dismissed, for the first few days he swotted up on it, the box number's elision as a small clerical error – has been infecting him, too, merging with the sense of purpose he experienced in Holland, in the wind tunnel, and (by association although there's no rational reason for this) with the intimation of guilt that, like a vapour-outline, swirled into shape and dissipated again around that. Encountering Vanins' utopianism now, the physicist's gaze fixed on a bright, pulsating future, compounds this intimation: Phocan's own future, by contrast, seems to somehow lie already in his past – to loop back through it like a Gilbreth motion circuit, to some point, some stretch of time, some *act*, lodged there even if yet to be passed over … And encountering the Latvian's clarity of insight, now, reprises his own sense of nebulousness, of occupying a field of vision that's at once both luminescent and as opaque as these thickly packed, sun-impregnated clouds they're flying through …

Sennet blows a silent raspberry and turns back to the talk that he's to give tomorrow. Phocan has a presentation to make too, but he'll do that on auto-pilot: it's just software demonstration, sales-pitching. This stack is more enticing. It's infused with a real fervour. At one point Vanins casts himself and his colleagues as *the new Phidiases, sculpting and modelling the fine ivory of Soviet man* ... He seems to have had his fingers in a range of pies, not least that of aeronautics: several of the papers Phocan's been handed by Garnett are concerned with flows – compressible, transonic, incompressible; with aeroelasticity and flutter; with divergence and control ... Clouds fade out over Northern France; Paris scrolls past; later, Alps. Their pleats and folds, for Phocan, chime with the words *sculpting and modelling*, make him think of topography, of CAD and LiDAR ... Here's the old AI, Aeroplane Introspection, kicking in again: the other week, in Berners Street, he felt *old*, felt that he and Eldridge were like dying magi, sole repositories of their subject's mysteries. Now, though ... Now, after Garnett's (perhaps, after all, not so unjust) admonishment and errand-assigning, and while reading Vanins, he's struck by a feeling of *youngness*, of being granted a geological view across a landscape that was formed generations before his arrival, strata crinkled and stacked, each one atop the other, like the plates and ridges of these mountain ranges over which they're flying; or, perhaps, an *archae*ological view, as of the sedimented levels of the city towards which the plane's beginning its descent now, new announcements spilling from the speakers triggering a scurry of tray folding and seat repositioning, of paper stashing, leaving just time before the bump-down for a last unanswered question to pass through his mind: *Why Palomilla?*

They're booked into Hotel Cardano, in the Celio. Lots of the IACSS delegates seem to be holed up here; an easel-mounted noticeboard stands in the lobby, giving dedicated shuttle-bus departure times. The graphics, this year, depict a CGI footballer levitating upended in mid overhead-kick, the letters *I-A-C-S-S* flying from his feet like clods of turf – stellar rather than dirty clods, as bold and glittering as movie-poster titling, with smaller subtitling below word-fleshing out the organiser's acronym: *International Association of Computer Science in Sport*. The player is fictitious, image-source generic – politic on the part of the Association, who can't be seen to promote or favour any one of the many brands and outfits represented by the conference's attendees; although the level of the membership subscription taken out by each of these does, not unreasonably, bring concomitant dividends in terms of line-up and slot-allocation, sideline hospitality, favourable stall-positioning and dinner-seating, and so on. Generic or not, Phocan can instantly identify the picture's provenance: a project Pantarey worked on for FIFA 18. It was Ribaldo who came in, blacked-out limo bouncing its way up Finns, to do the mo-cap for the special moves (run-of-the-mill dribbling and passing and formation-holding had been grabbed weeks previously in Vancouver, from the UBC varsity team). He was uncooperative to the point of obstreperousness: didn't want to do the tricks he thought of as his 'own'; even tore the markers off and stormed out to sulk in the car while panicked handlers whispered into phones. Electronic Arts' lawyers prevailed: a mo-cap obligation clause was written into the contract that in turn underwrote the revenue-stream keeping his car parked, motor idling, outside HQ right then. Someone must have explained this to Ribaldo; after an hour he re-emerged scowling, submitted himself to nipple reattachment, and, eventually, performed stepover, chop and scissors – but badly. It was obvious he was doing it half-arsedly: a little *fuck you* that he'd thought up in the back seat. Phocan and co. had to spend the next two weeks patching the moves over from match footage, pixel by pixel, thread by thread and fill by fill ...

The conference centre's in the Borgo – close enough to walk, which Phocan does. The first morning's sessions are all about pattern analysis. In the spirit of supportive comradeship, or adherence to its motions maybe, he drops in on Sennet's. It's a panel discussion; besides Sennet, there's a German *Informatik* guy, a statistician from Slovenia and (as chair) a Texan dynamical systems theory prof – all male. It's Sennet holding forth when Phocan slips, coffee in hand, into the side-room:

'... into four main schools of thought: perturbation (Hughes, Dawkins, David), relative phase (Walter), chaos (Lames) and, lastly – and conversely – self-organisation (McGarry). What my team at Pantarey, in collaboration with Loughborough's Sports Science Department, have been developing in relation to football – soccer – both draws from and supersedes all these conceptual frameworks ...'

Phocan has heard this before: complex human-behaviour streams, of which those found in football are exemplary ... hidden temporal-sequential structure ... detection beyond the 'narrow reach' of standard statistical analysis ... whence ...

'Whence,' Sennet's rounding the pitch off now, 'Pantarey's new T-pattern model.'

The statistician, understandably, has been bristling at these assertions. As soon as the chair signals open discussion he jumps in:

'We have a good track record. Since the advent of sabermetrics to the world of baseball, statistics – even in what you call its "standard" form – has managed to ... I mean, you won't find a major-league team that's not signed up to PITCHf/x. The diamond's been transformed into a mathematical matrix; strikes, singles, doubles, home runs into data points; coaches can reset their field to account for such-and-such a batter's tendencies, to leverage the probabilities ... I'd call that pretty *wide* reach ...'

'I'm not,' Sennet cuts back in, 'denying any of that. But the *time* element ...'

'The "time element" just happens,' the Slovenian scoffs. 'It's a set of dots and clusters laid out in a line.'

Now it's the *Informatik* man who's taking umbrage.

'I cannot agree with this. Frequency of occurrence – even probability – is not coterminous with, much less equivalent to, relationships between discrete events within a sport performance; or any other type either ...'

'Exactly!' Sennet bows his gratitude across the table's velvet, bypassing the chair, who's happy to let play run on uninterrupted. 'And that's where our T-pattern analysis comes in. If I could demonstrate …' He fiddles with his desktop, still the projector's prime feed; a string of letters pops up on the screen behind the panellists. 'Here's a short stretch of play, extracted from an English Premiership match last season. Each event type – pass, tackle, interception, shot, save, throw-in – has been assigned an alphabetic value: a letter, in other words. So here, you get the sequence *p a n b p j c n j d p n p a p j p b n c n d n j p j a b n n c p n d*. No pattern there, you might say – but you'd be wrong. There *is* one, but it's hidden by redundant letters. When you extrapolate it on a lower line' – he does this with the next slide – 'and strip out all the *n*s and *p*s and *j*s, you get the sequence *a b c d* – repeating twice.' He pauses, to allow his listeners to see the truth of this claim for themselves, before continuing: 'Frequency counts wouldn't have detected this; neither would lag-sequential or time-series analysis. T-pattern, though, allows us to unearth repeated temporal strings, even when various other event types pop up in-between the pattern's elements.'

The Slovenian's stumped. The German is impressed. Sennet presses home his advantage with a third slide:

'You can see here that, after an occurrence of *a* at moment *t*, there's an interval $[t+d1, t+d2]$ $(d2>\_ d1 >\_ 0)$ that tends to contain at least one more instance of *b* than you'd expect from chance alone. We call the temporal relationship between *a* and *b* the *critical interval* – a concept that lies at the centre of T-pattern thinking. Determining or ascertaining it – plotting, that is, both critical interval itself and also interval between each of this interval's instantiations – will place a manager at a distinct advantage. In a nutshell, that's where the extra goal's going to come from.'

Now the chair enters the fray:

'How is it different from the algorithms that the hedge-fund wonks are running?'

'It's the same principle,' Sennet concurs. 'Mapping chance over a temporal continuum, deducing from that map a strategy for profitable intervention. The difference is that, unlike trading, football is zero-sum: one side's successful intervention is the other's catastrophic loss.' Shifting in his seat, he adds: 'Of course "chance", being circumstantial, isn't actually chance at all. What we discovered is that, even when there's *no* pattern, there's still a pattern. The small patterns no longer in evidence have been subsumed by larger and more complex ones – that's why they've disappeared. Which is good: you *want* to constantly upscale your detection from partial to larger strings. So here,' he clicks his next slide up to reveal new letter-chains, 'if $Q = (ABCDE)$ could be partially detected as, for example, *(BCDE)* or *(BDE)* or *(ABCE)*, you discard the *A*s to *E*s and scale to Q; after which you'll have to consider a newly detected pattern – Qx, say – to be equally or less complete than an already detected pattern, Qy, *if* Qx and Qy occur *equally* often and *all* Qx's event-elements are *also* present in Qy (but not vice versa). At which point, you eliminate Qx. We call it "completeness competition". It's a kind of brutal evolution – Darwin on steroids, a fight to the death: the only pattern standing at the end is the one for which no critically related pairings can be found to feed the hungry Moloch of a larger pattern.'

Sennet's won the room: people are scribbling notes. He drinks his victory in, then adds:

'Some patterns are acyclical. In other words, the temporal distances between their occurrences – the patterns', not their events' – may be irregular. The *within*-pattern intervals between events can still remain invariant, or not: it doesn't matter. What counts is the *overall* pattern occurrence ...'

Phocan's attention's drifting now: he's looking at the delegates, their lanyard-mounted name-tags, the IACSS tote bags hanging from their chair backs, draped across their knees ... Gilbreth and Gastev met one another at a conference: Prague, 1924, ICSM – the Industrial Congress of Scientific Management. He was head of the Soviet delegation; she part of a forty-strong American one. Did they have tote bags then? Or lanyards? Did attendees cultivate a studied air of boredom as the default look to bring into each room, or scan the rows of seating ranking delegates according to desirability? And what of 1965, Zürich, where a now-ancient

Gilbreth met a Raivis Vanins not yet thirty but already throwing quite a swell out from his MIPT lab? Had he felt bold enough to stride across, announce himself, start holding forth about kinetic hypostasis? Or had he edged up to her nervously, threaded his way between rings of minders and admirers, meekly pressed a paper or a card into her hands? However it occurred, he'd got her attention: their correspondence started soon afterwards, and lasted five years, until she was too gaga to write anything to anyone. Phocan's got, in his own tote bag, the passages of it that Garnett passed him, copies of surviving scraps, incomplete sub-strings of a larger pattern time and loss have rendered undetectable; he was up half of last night reading and rereading them. *T.T.* ... That doubled character, like the ones on the screen now, seems to have codified some sequence or event, what Vanins and Gilbreth both referred to as an 'episode' ... And then the mention of a box, the number, 808 – the same number absent from the stereoscoped inventory. There does, as Garnett took pains in his office to convince him, seem to be some link: the two terms – *808, T.T.* – keep popping up together. But it's what accompanies them that's intriguing: *changes everything* ... There's an apperception, from Gilbreth's end at least, of some grand divulgence taking shape, its form and outline growing lucid, even as her mind fuzzed over ...

The chair's opened the panel up to contributions from the floor – all of which, confirming Sennet's clean sweep of the session (panel discussions are as zero-sum as football matches), are directed to him. A sharp-faced young man's asking a nerdish question about completeness-competition equations; Phocan tunes out again, and looks through the window. The jalousies, controlled from the same master panel as the beamer, were angled so as to render the room dark enough for slides to be discernible, although not so dark as to obscure the speakers; now, with the onset of the Q&A phase, the technician has notched the slats another fifteen-odd degrees towards the horizontal, to illuminate the questioners. Their upward slant sends Phocan's gaze into the sky above the Prati, where starlings are flocking in large numbers. There's a name for it, which he can't remember. Back inside the room, Sennet's explicatory voice has given over to a woman's – an Italian woman with (Phocan discovers when he turns back inwards) black glasses and a headband. She's asking Sennet about something she's describing as the 'event border':

'Where do you set this?'

'Set it?' he asks back.

'Yes,' she responds. 'Where is it? What's inside the event field, and what's not?'

Now Sennet understands the question. 'The groundsman has kindly set this border for us,' he answers, 'in bold, white, painted lines. When players and the ball lie within these, they're pattern-legible; outside them, they're anathema. They don't exist.'

He looks around the room for the next question, but the woman's not done yet:

'This cannot be so,' she informs him. 'Even with one of your own event examples – *la rimessa*, "throw-in" – this border is surpassed or ruptured by both ball and player. Besides, think of the stadium layout. Beyond the touchline are the dugouts. The substitutes sit here; and the manager, effecting active interventions. And behind this, more importantly, *la folla* – the crowd. You'll know as well as I that home-field, home-crowd advantage generates, within the English Premier League, a sixty-four per cent home-win rate.'

Sennet, initially dismissive of her quibble, is brought to attention by her command of this statistic.

'And then,' she's warming up here, 'there are other factors. How long before the game did the team eat? Did they arrive together at the stadium? Did the Catholic players pray ... ?'

'Ah,' Sennet thinks he's seen a weakness in her attack line, 'T-pattern makes no judgement on causality – not at the gastronomic scale, nor at the theological. It merely detects patterns.'

'*Si, si,*' a conference-centre staffer's holding out his hand to take the mike from her, but she's not surrendering it. 'This issue of causality's a *falsa pista;* it has no bearing on my point. My point is that these factors, too, stand in relation to the *as* and *bs* and *cs*.

They, too, are in the pattern. If we can highlight' – she pronounces this word with the Italian *h*-drop: *eye-light* – 'one particular event type – say, the goal kick ... What is the "event" here? Kicking the ball up the field? Okay. But what about the bouncing of the ball before the kick? Three bounces? Four? Does the goalkeeper wipe his glove against his forehead, to clear away perspiration? Does he evacuate his throat, mutter a phrase, or even speak the phrase's words inside his head as he starts on his little run-in to the kick? Or does he glance at the stadium's seating, towards where he knows his girlfriend or his mother or his son is sitting? What if he catches sight of a particular banner in the stands, or recognises, just before his foot touches the ball, the odour of an hot' – the dropped *h* again – 'dog ...'

'Are you suggesting,' Sennet asks her, 'that we should assign values to each of these ... *micro*-events?'

Now it's her turn to smile.

'*Perché no?*' she shrugs.

'But then ...' Sennet's victory lap has turned into a marathon, in which he's starting to show telltale signs of exhaustion, of cramp's onset. 'If you brought all those in, your equations would be hopelessly unwieldy. I mean, where would it *end*?'

Nobody seems to have an answer to this question; for an uncomfortably long stretch, the room is quiet; then the chair, the Texan systems-theory man, outs with a quip about *this* event field's end, its border, being dictated by the schedule, the odour of biscuits waiting for them in the lobby, etc. There are chuckles, but the atmosphere's deflated. Delegates shuffle out. Over amaretti, Phocan gets talking to the awkward questioner. Her name's Rafaella Farinati, and she's with the Università degli studi di Milani, *Dipartimento di Psicologia dello Sport*.

'Were you just trying to knock him off his horse?' he asks her.

'An *orse*?' she asks.

'To take him down a notch. Demote him.'

'Ah! *Affatto non*,' she answers. 'We are also making our equations for completeness – though I think we understand the term in different ways. Five years ago, we started to examine the cases of *nevrotic* sportsmen and sportswomen, ones who can't hit the ball until they've gone through a routine: of touching some part of their body, for example, or brushing their eyes on one spot of the stadium, then on another – same sequence again, each time. We have concluded that these people were *non aberranti ma esemplari* – not perverse, but typical. Through them, we come to understand the field and range of data that a player's processing at any given moment.'

'Don't they shut that out, though?' Phocan asks. 'The excess stuff?'

'Exactly wrong.' Rafaella Farinati pokes his shoulder with a floury finger. 'It is central to the data-architecture of their whole performance. Like yours now.'

'Mine? What performance?'

'You're exchanging conversation with me,' she says, 'but what's really in your mind? The taste of your *biscotti*, and the colour and texture of this carpet that we're standing on; the various other carpets it reminds you of; the rooms they lay in, what you experienced in those rooms; your anxiety about which *sessione* to attend next, or where to go for lunch – that's what you're thinking, what's determining your actions and decisions. If we want to understand event fields then we have to be *olistic*, start appreciating all the channels on which information is being processed, not a fraction of these only ...'

Actually, what Phocan's thinking is that Rafaella Farinati's cool. It's not just what she's saying, or gratitude to her for having granted him this dose of *Schadenfreude* over Sennet; there's something about her whole demeanour, her ensemble – most of all the headband, which is stirring vague associations round the peripheries of his own recall, ones that he can't quite assign a value to, not yet, *rimesse* held up just beyond the touchline ...

'Where are *you* going to lunch?' he asks.

She snorts derisively, as though to say: Anyone could have seen *that* event type coming. 'I visit the Forum and the Palatino each time I'm in Rome,' she tells him. 'I'll take something on the way there. I think you have your *presentazione* on body-separation now, though ... no?'

He wonders if she's memorised the schedule, or if she harbours a professional curiosity for kinematic-filling software, or ... or what? She's giving off an air not just of knowing Phocan's business, but, beyond that, of knowing it in a *knowing* way, as though aware of more than she's been letting on. Before he can reply, she brushes off his shirt the micro-crumbs, but not the flour, left by her finger's prod, then smiles – not at him, it seems, but at something over his shoulder – turns on her heels and disappears into the general IACSS throng.

He cranks out his own talk distractedly. Artefact reduction ... quintic interpolation ... Pantarey ... Physis 6™ ... and done. He lunches with Sennet, bad linguine in a tourist trap on the bank of the Tiber, then decides to skip the afternoon session and head to the Forum too, even if he won't be able to pass off bumping into Rafaella Farinati as a quirk of chance. The bumping-into doesn't happen anyway; she's departed by the time he gets there, if she ever went there in the first place. A meeting does occur, though. Phocan's leaning on a railing by the sunken water garden of the Domus Augustana, looking down on its fuzzed labyrinth whose shape reminds him of a QR code, when he becomes aware of someone at his side. It's the kind of proximity that straddles the border between normal and invasive, measurable not in standard inches but through incremental calculi that would relate the distance between people to amount of space available around them. This guy's three or so feet away from Phocan – on the tube or at a football game, T-pattern parsed or not, this would be plenty. But they're not on the tube; there's hardly anyone about now; three feet is too close. What's more, the guy is looking at him, smiling. Pick-up? No: Phocan sees, peeping from his jacket-front's top pocket, a plastic protuberance that he recognises from its colouration as the upper corner of an IACSS delegate card.

'Quintic filling,' his companion murmurs. 'Liked your presentation.'

The accent's Italian, or maybe Swiss. Phocan doesn't recall seeing him in his talk.

'Just standard stuff,' he answers unambassadorially. 'Who are you with?'

The interloper smiles again, his gaze directed ever so slightly to the side of Phocan's face this time, pulls a card from the same top pocket and passes it over. It reads: *Alain Pirotti*; then, below this: *Cassius First Motion*. No job title, nor logo, nor company tag-line with obligatory present participle (*making, bringing, streamlining . . .*); just these words, an email address and a phone number.

'Your project touched,' Pirotti tells him, 'on an issue spanning our discipline's whole field.'

Phocan waits, politely, for the thought's completion, the reveal, which Pirotti now provides:

'I mean,' he says, 'the gaps. They've plagued our business since the outset.'

'What,' asks Phocan, eyeing the card, 'does Cassius do?'

Pirotti, still smiling slightly off-centredly, waves away the question.

'For decades – long before the markers and the processors arrived; as you know . . .'

'I'm not quite sure I follow . . .'

Pirotti fixes his eyes firmly back on Phocan's face.

'It's in the report.'

'Which report? Mine?'

Pirotti smiles back silently by way of answer. 'For almost a century now,' he says eventually, 'the capacity has been in place to plot the curves and stretches of a movement-segment at its outset; to describe its structure; to enclose it in a form that's folded back into itself, contained and perfect; like . . . let's say, a figure-eight. And then to do the same for the same segment's end-stage: another *eight* . . .'

He pauses, gaze still fixed on Phocan as he speaks, observing his reaction.

'So,' he resumes, 'we have two bookends, carved with an artisan's precision: start and finish, *eight* and *eight*. But then, between these, at some point – between two given points within that stretch, the more we zoom in and interrogate it – there will always be a patch of unmapped territory: a hole, big and round, or oval, or who-knows-what shape: a *zero* ... What are we to do?'

A breeze, rising up from the sunken garden, ruffles Phocan's neck. Pirotti, seeing him tense up, presses:

'Eight; zero; eight ...'

Phocan stares back at him, uncertain what to say. Up in the sky, the birds are at it again: starlings, clustering in spheres, columns and conjoining funnels – giant masses that billow and contract elastically as their internal volume redistributes itself. Pirotti, still smiling at him, asks:

'We live in a time of information-sharing, do we not?'

He pauses again, waiting for an answer. Hesitantly, Phocan says:

'It depends what information's being solicited, by whom.'

'Okay,' concedes Pirotti. 'Of information ... *exchange*: an *economy* of knowledge. Our world, unfortunately, is not open-source. But people will pay well for much sought-after insights, or packages.' Then, as though it were an afterthought: 'Or boxes ...'

There's that breeze again, that ruffling. Phocan looks down at the labyrinth, trying to discern its source. Pirotti, at his ear, continues:

'We should keep in touch. We understand, my people just as yours, that correspondence can be ... fruitful.'

My people? Now he's feeling dizzy. It must be the height, the angle or the labyrinth's pattern, triggering some reader-response in him, some reaction. Phocan closes his eyes for a while, head resting on the rail. When he looks up again, Pirotti's gone; the Palatine is empty; then a group of Chinese tourists in bright anoraks starts trickling across the hilltop's green. Before he, too, leaves, Phocan's granted two small, if sudden, insights. Firstly, that Pirotti's smile was not so much intended for *him* as responding, albeit with a certain delay, to another smile directed at its bearer earlier: Rafaella Farinati's. He couldn't explain how he knows this, but he does: the second smile fitted the first – *completed* it, as both prompt and response, Phocan's shoulder a mere way-station or relay post across which it was beamed. Secondly, that it's *murmuration*: the word for starlings' clustering and flocking. He should have had it on his tongue-tip: it's been modelled over and over, after all ... Reynolds ... Delgado-Mata ... Hartman ... Benes ... Hildenbrandt ... subjected to bin-lattice spatial subdivision, transposed to a spread of fields: multi-channel radio-station programming, weather-simulation software, dispersal/concentration ratios of crowds fleeing in panic from the source of gunfire ... What's this instantiation of it, this bird ink-blot, murmur-modelling for him? It's hovering above the Basilica now, thickening over Caesar's temple, elongating over Vesta's, before trickling up the facing hillside to pulse in the air above the Tarpeian Rock, which sits denuded, awaiting new traitors.

6. DYCAST

In the next room, Thérèse is sleeping. She sleeps several times a day now. At first it was structured – *morning nap*, 10.30 to 11.15; *afternoon rest*, 2.15 to 3.30 – but as things advanced it started to just happen when it happened. Where it happened, too: chair, sofa, bench … It's almost narcolepsy. This time, at least, she looked vaguely comfortable, propped up by cushions in a window seat, well covered by a shawl, and the heating's on. Pilkington, post-prandial, thought he'd catch some himself, but got diverted, *intercepted*, passively or not, en route through his study, where, best part of an hour later, he still finds himself. He's trying to compose an email, response to a request that Garnett's sent him: his old friend wants pointers as to how a spaceship might start to collapse when placed inside a 'solar wind'. *For comparison*, Garnett has written, *think of a fighter plane in a Mach 25 environment: what panels would give first? How would they peel away? Is there a formula for determining the brittleness of sheet-metal and rivets relative to age, stress factors, pressure? Etc. …* It's for a film Pantarey's working on, some sci-fi blockbuster. A little quid pro quo. He's jotted a few notes down, but for the last twenty minutes he's been ruminating, letting his thoughts glide idly back to last week's Canard meeting: the clay-wrapped duck … the ice cream … the damn ice cream … with the wafer-grid, no less … That kind of detail always brings it on: old Project Albatross. It's as if people knew. *Do* they? Those little jabs and accusations seem to follow him around, to hang or coalesce around him, rumour-cloud of smirks and whispers, words so familiar they don't even need vocalising: *How do you lose an aeroplane … ?*

He's seated at the secretary. Both the object and the term have come down to him from his grandfather. As a child, he'd spend hours playing with the cubbies and the drawers, the slant-front opening, the small under-the-counter catch that, once depressed, released the hidden recess from mahogany depths. In the first weeks of their marriage, when they moved into the house, shuffled the furniture around, it confused Thérèse when he spoke about it. *You make it sound like a person – like a mistress with whom you slink off to spend your time,* she told him. *Call it an* escritoire *instead. Or just plain* desk. But he persisted stubbornly with *secretary.* The word, for him, is less suggestive of humans – stenographers, PAs, what have you – than of secrets, recessed, catch-protected; or, perhaps, at some more bodily scale, of secretion, moist, dirty and shameful. Pilkington's hand slides furtively around above his knees, making its way towards the button. It still works: he feels the spring-load mechanism give, hears sprockets, rods and chain crank through their paces, waits for the small compartment to slide out from behind its thin facade, Potemkin panel … About once a year he undertakes this ritual, akin to prelate flagellation or to Filipino auto-crucifixion. *This* is why he thinks that, on the balance of probabilities, it's a good bet that Vanins has some notes, some records, *something* of the sort Thames House are so keen to get hold of, stashed away: because *he* does, in defiance of all acts and contracts, interdictions, vows … This residue he's held out or held back, held *to* him, siphoned off and buried like toxic waste, or dark, disgusting treasure, serves as his private autobiography, his unpublished confession, scrawled in code, a hieroglyphic alphabet of sine and cosine, channel-filter frequencies, glide-path degrees, strain-gauge transducer settings and transmitted pelvic loads …

He sets the disgorged recess on the desktop, covering Parkinson's carer support information packages, reunion invitations and phone bills, and lifts the notebook from it. It's a Silvine memo pad, red, 10 by 16, the brand name slicing cursively across an empty shield around whose sides two laurel branches curl on the front cover;

pages lined, not graphed, inside. Pilkington's surprised, each time he thumbs them, at how un-aged they are: thirty-plus years on, they should be yellow, crinkled, like old parchment. But, as though the secret drawer contained a humidor, the paper, the card binding, the whole book is soft and pliant to both touch and eye; the jottings could be yesterday's, today's ... The agelessness brings on a double recognition: not just of the notes, but of the nature of the memory for which they serve as peg and cipher. Hasn't it, too, stayed forever young? Rather than obeying the rear-view mirror optics that dictate all mental objects must retreat down one-point avenues of time, dwindling and fading, the whole thing has become fixed by the perspective, drawn into sharper focus – not shrunk but compressed, infused with greater density; through concentration, made to loom larger. Wasn't that the whole point in the first place? A compression that was also an expansion? Four years into a single second – a second that contained a million others, and as many lives and deaths ...

He got the gig six months into his posting. Not through the normal chain, his MOD line-manager or the one above him; no, it was McReady, his old supervisor back at Edinburgh, who tapped him on the shoulder, took him to tea in the Four Seasons, introduced him to Sir Ronald, figure who loomed large, if spectral, in the military-aeronautical imagination: MOD's Chief Scientific Adviser, full member of both Defence Management Board and Defence Council ... And to Dashell, Langley's Vice Principle of Research Projects, who found tiered cucumber sandwiches and scones perplexing.

'Are you meant to eat bottom-to-top or top-to-bottom? Why do they cut the crusts off, anyway?'

'For symmetry, I think,' opined Sir Ronald. 'Given that they're triangular, two sides with crust and one without would seem a tad off-balance ...'

Then they got down to cases: a collaboration, hook-up, joint-planned and -conducted, between NASA, British Aerospace, the FAA, Marconi Avionics ... There were others, junior partners, outliers, subsidiary parties ... The idea was to stage a CID – the first of a civilian aircraft. Dashell's people in Virginia were interested in acquiring baseline structural crash-dynamics data; BA and FAA in testing out an antimisting kerosene they hoped could not just fuel a plane but also prevent fireballing when spilled at impact; Marconi in the validation and improvement of their nascent structural-mathematical aircraft model; all parties in load measurements and load transmissions, fuselage acceleration, occupant human tolerance and the various sliders linking these to one another and a host of subcats, all interrelated. CID stood for *Controlled Impact Demonstration*. Simply put, they were to crash a plane, deliberately, on a beach out in the Indian Ocean.

'Project Albatross,' Sir Ronald informed Pilkington, cleaning a spot of clotted cream from his cheek with the back of his little finger. 'So named for the bird's wingspan, and the Tristan of that family's presence – admittedly quite rare, often through misadventure, which you could say complements the one-off nature of our test – in the region.'

'And what role would I ... ?'

'Navigation,' replied Sir Ronald. 'It's quite simple – just a big remote control, really. We need to guide a Boeing 720 safely to its doom.'

'Emphasis,' Dashell leant in, 'on *safely*. The impact footprint will be tiny. And the interrogation window – the one *we're* interested in – is the first second after impact.'

'The first *second*? But the fuel ... the antimisting agent ...' Pilkington turned to McReady for professorial support – and was met with a look of detachment, the three years of tutelage, the entire scaffolding of academia revealed now as a sideline to the *real* work the Prof. Emeritus had been doing when he reared his charges, falling away now as the intellectual vessel was delivered to the orbit of this higher purpose. On his own, he turned back to the other two, and asked: 'Won't that play out over an extended period – say, half a minute or so? And the load transmissions too, as they react to one another while the plane ...'

'Exactly,' Dashell told him. 'There's so many factors that it's basically random, or as good as, two, three links down the event chain. Our good friends can throw their private-sector money on that bonfire if they want. That initial second, though … We're banking on it giving us a pretty stable metric in terms of the data traces it could generate, if intelligently primed.'

Thus began the next four years – four years which, if their destiny was to be swallowed and consumed by just one second, prepared for this fate by gorging themselves on the previous two decades. All transport accident files, company and govt., from Boeing, Lockheed-California, McDonnell Douglas, the FAA, the CAA and all the rest, were gathered, sifted, strained; each passenger jet crash between '58 and '79 broken down, stripped, fed into the accumulative database that in turn produced, after eight months, a Venn diagram revealing that, of 993 disasters in this period, 176 were both well documented and within the catchment area for survivability; which special crashes were then evaluated in great detail: context, cause, collision-nature, outcome … Every wing detachment and tail break-up, every stabiliser loss and slat retraction, tail strike, stall, fuel-tank explosion, pressure bulkhead failure; the whole spectrum of fuselage deformation following impact, conflagration timeline, crumple pattern and debris trajectory, injury-type distribution and row-based survival odds – all these were cross-indexed, each factor bringing with it, like so many plane shards, patches of its originating context and scenario, the pieces joining together in the manner of a jigsaw puzzle made from piles of other puzzles, mixed, scrambled perhaps but now quite neatly reassembling into a new image that, instead of just remaking one of the originals, creates a new composite in which each of the old ones stays recognisable even as it's wiped. Call it the *Ur-crash* (or, in Gilbrethian style it occurs to Pilkington in reverie beside his secretary now, the *one best crash*); the one that hasn't happened yet *as such*, but that nonetheless has underlain each of the ones that *has*, rulebook and blueprint, sum of possibilities, totality that hovers spectral above every partial iteration, haloed blur or maybe heat mirage – and hovers, too, above the spectres of its victims, past and future, open ledger always full yet always holding space back for new entries.

By March '82 this ur-disaster had been planned and plotted. Statistics, magicked up through rounds of filtering and cross-indexing, revealed that 54.5 per cent of mishaps happen during approach and landing, which dovetailed neatly with the practical requirement that the thing descend on to a strip of beach. Glide slope would be a representative 3.3° to 4.0°; nose-up attitude 1.0°; sink rate 17 ft/sec; no roll or yaw attitude; longitudinal velocity 150 knots ... It got so Pilkington could actually *see* it, see the plane descending, again and again, guided by nothing other than his own volition, held in the phase-lock of his mind's variable frequency; and hear, on repeat too, not just the roar of its approach, but also static crackling around this channel's edges, taking on the character of voices – hundreds, thousands of them, filling the bandwidth with their cries ...

His first visit to Septentrion was in the autumn of '82. He was flown commercially via Lagos to Mauritius; onwards on a military plane, a giant propellered Atlas, to the Diego Garcia base; from there, on a Short C-23 Sherpa to the atoll, touching down in the footprint itself. You see it long before you reach it: this distended pretzel floating in the sea, emerging in a patch you could have sworn you'd stared at for some time already and had thought was empty, like an anamorphic image in a painting or germ culture in a petri dish. Its shape, folded and curled round a central lagoon, earns it its designation as an atoll, but to all intents and purposes it's a bank – a set of sandbanks ringed together, elongated white-tack lumps pressed on to a blue wall. Ground-side, the white takes on an even whiter quality. Grabbing a handful of beach as he stepped out of the Sherpa, letting it trickle back between his fingers, Pilkington noticed the people waiting to greet him exchange appreciative glances, observing the eager act of a professional – material analysis, soil-sampling – and felt fraudulent: in reality, his gesture was simply an attempt to clasp, to get to grips with this consuming *whiteness*, with the pigment not so much of a mineral as of a concept, a condition. The sunlight was white, not yellow; the sea-glare too; and so, apart from one black private, were the personnel, American and British servicemen and engineers. No locals: they'd been shipped out forcibly two decades earlier; their own catastrophe, a crash no one would model. White: sand, people, light itself were blank and virgin, plasmic surfaces awaiting first impression. Then blue: sky, sea, electric matrix of emergence, of potentiality – blueprint indeed . . . If this small, narrow strip would be Ground Zero, then this moment he was engineering two years hence, this charged and stretched-out second, would be not only his, but (it seemed to him, somehow) his whole epoch's founding instant, the explosive *now* from which the futures of both would billow, find their mass and shape . . .

'We'll be acquiring,' Dashell was also on the atoll with a spotty-faced assistant, Briar, overseeing the NASA side of things, 'over three hundred and thirty time histories. Fuselage accelerations normal, transverse, longitudinal; wing (inner, outer, bridge and tip) accelerations normal and spar longitudinal; bending moments wing and fuselage vertical . . . Then loads: seat, dummy, lap-belt, shoulder-harness, bin-support link . . . Dummy accelerations normal, transverse, longitudinal – head, chest and pelvis . . .'

'Pelvis?'

'It's where most of the body load goes, typically. The plane crash-lands, and everyone performs a giant synchronised hip-thrust.'

He wandered off whistling 'Ain't Nothing but a Hound Dog', leaving the Marconi man, Anderson, to bring Pilkington up to speed on anthropometric modelling:

'Thirteen of the dummies will be instrumented – triaxial accelerometers, restraint load cells and the like buried in their various cavities, to ascertain whether the load transmissions and accelerations stay within parameters of human tolerance – of liveability, in other words. These ones will be diffused about the cabin, to maximise coverage; some upright, others set in brace position. Then seventeen more, non-instrumented ones, your basic CPR types, will make up the numbers, keep the smart ones company; just like in life.'

'And how will they relay their intel?' Pilkington asked.

'Transducers,' answered Anderson. 'Four hundred of them, transmitting from the dummies, engines, fuselage, you name it … Gain ranges from one to one thousand, with full-scale output of 5V into the pulse code modulation system, which has a frame format: 129 8-bit words per frame at one megabit per second; 60 words assigned to the 180-Hz channels and 58 words to the 100- and 60-Hz ones. We keep word size down at 8 bits to allow for the high sample rates, and send the whole thing through a low-pass four-pole Butterworth filter before sampling, to stop aliasing errors …'

Anderson had lost him with *pulse code modulation* … Daydreaming, Pilkington found himself mixing the term in his mind with *human tolerance*: the idea of a pulse, a pulse-beat, persisting amidst all the wreckage, sending out its signals past the barriers that death, aliasing errors and all other weapons stockpiled in oblivion's arsenal have set up in a bid to stifle it … It was when Anderson got on to describing the aircraft structural mathematical model they were developing that his attention was reined back:

'… that this will be the takeaway: whether DYCAST gives us an accurate view, or not …'

'What was that?'

'Whether it gives us an accurate …'

'No, the bit before: die cast …'

'It's the finite-element code the model runs on: DYnamic Crash Analysis of STructures. If this little outing ends up validating it, we won't need to keep smashing aircraft on to beaches.'

Pilkington tracked back to the Four Seasons meeting, Dashell's spiel: *so many factors … basically random … two, three links down the event chain* … Now, in his mind's eye, he saw a pair of dice, flung down on to a table of white sand, striking and bouncing, glancing one another, every new collision upsetting whatever spin axes they'd – if just for a millisecond – settled into, diverting roll paths into new ones which would lead to new collisions, on and on, chance multiplying, mushrooming exponentially, infinity reached by the first tenth ... It was, indeed, random. But that *first* strike, that initial contact ... *that* could be willed: the angle that the dice are held at, how hard they're thrown, which side is upwards-, downwards-, sideways-facing ... So it was with the plane's impact: scale the dice-throw up a thousand-fold, milli- to second, and you've got the time-frame of the crash – the same proportional relations, same progression into randomness, but also the same window for control. Glide slope, velocity, sink rate: if well primed, these could, as Dashell said, provide a stable metric, generate a set of numbers that were unique, finite, *true* ...

Whence his own role: die-primer, off-vessel helmsman. *Kubernetes*: wasn't that where Wiener dug up the name *cybernetics* in the first place? If McReady, playing pilot himself, had steered Sir Ronald to him it was because he knew that the Ph.D. he'd midwifed into being contained the most up-to-date overview of the field. *On the Use of Emulator Software in Remote Navigation Systems*: most cited thesis in the department's history; earned Pilkington his stripes – and now this. Armed with Sir Ronald's seal, he got to hand-pick his team. Back in the UK, they designed this project's tailored remote navigation system – thirteen channels, one per servo – plotted the 720's path from NSF Diego Garcia's runway (Septentrion's strip wasn't long enough for take-off) over the sea, the banking turns – first left, then right – that it would make, worked out the wiggle-room it had to dampen oscillations, realign with target centreline, the final approach angle. Like (it strikes him now here in the study, duck and wafer still crowding his mind's stage) a Gilbreth wireframe, yes ... Then Vanins. Garnett said that he'd put a man on it already. Others are on the trail: Thames House knows that, through its own various feedbacks. Everything leaks. Typewriters and ribbons, word-size, sample-rates ... The pulse code modulation data on four of the channels of the airborne tape recorders, Anderson informed him, would be digitally delayed by 256 milliseconds, to ensure data acquisition in the event of a momentary tape-speed perturbation during impact.

'Think of it,' the Marconi man said, 'as a kind of memory glitch, but in real time.'

Pilkington did, and more: wasn't the entire project like this? An instant held back or diverted from itself; a second that's both more and less? Where *was* that second, then? Where is it, now – where did it go? Nowhere and everywhere, perhaps: for him, it's turned into an overwhelming presence that's eternally ungraspable; totality that's incomplete; destination missed, elided; moment cut out from the flow of time and exponentially enlarged, like some eternal frame ...

A small disturbance comes from the next room: a murmur, breaking the surface of Thérèse's sleep. The pamphlets, the online support groups say anxiety can be precursor to dementia. Maybe it's just the heat: the radiators are on full. Out on the atoll, it was always hot, even at night. On his return there, February '84, he found the strip transformed: cameras, landing lights, lines like yard-markers on American football pitches or shove-ha'penny-board guillotine slats ... Two rows of heavy steel wing-openers had sprouted in the landing corridor itself, ten or so metres past the tyre-kiss spot.

'They're slicers,' Anderson, on whom the intervening eighteen months had incised their own trace, a slight jowl-lengthening, announced. 'They'll cut the thing wide open, spill the AMK fuel at a guaranteed rate of between twenty and a hundred gallons per second. Here, have one of these ...'

He opened a pull-top metal beer tin and handed it to him. To Pilkington's amazement, it was cold. Last time round, they'd spent all day glugging warm water out of Osprey bottles that, if you could be bothered, you could tie up, trail in the lagoon and reel back like a fishing line to drink tepid at best. Now, the Americans had fridges. Besides beer, they kept ice cream in them, industrial-sized tubs of vanilla, strawberry and mint-choc chip, which they gallantly shared with their English partners. Among all the men (they were all men), both officer and private, military and civilian, a mood of camaraderie gave over, as April approached, to one of palpable excitement, laced through with a lubricating joviality, with transatlantic banter about cricket, baseball, hockeys field and ice (relative merits of), the edibility or in- of Marmite, what in heaven's name hominy grits were, speculation about why dummies were orange, why Septentrion was so named when its constituent sandbanks clearly numbered six, why the first of April had been chosen for Impact Day ... *April Fool!* they took to calling out to one another, to the sky, horizon, or whatever surface they could find to hurl the call at. It became their password, their shared in-joke, unofficial project title. *Who're we foolin'?* they'd bark and howl over beers and ice cream of an evening, endless stars spread out across the blue-black dome that seemed to curl not just above but around and even below them as well, as though their atoll were set in the middle of a glass-ball paperweight, a snow-globe, bone-chip particles still riding thermals generated by a contact, a shaking, that had taken place long ago, before time began ...

The joke, of course, turned out to be on them. Preventing accidents indeed ... The most enduring laugh, the bitterest one, would be Pilkington's, and his alone. They didn't, they still don't know: it was *him* ...

7. The Movement Underground

There's a joke all Bergeners know: a tourist and a ten-year-old local kid find themselves next to one another at a bus stop/shop counter/cafe table – in whichever version, staring through rain-bleared glass at streets along which rivers of rainwater gush. The tourist asks the kid:

'What's it like here when it's not raining?'

The kid looks back at him as though the question were the stupidest he'd ever heard.

'How would I know?' he says. 'I'm only ten.'

Rain here is post-Newtonian: it can fall down, sideways, even upward. Stepping out, first morning in town, Phocan picked up an umbrella in the hotel lobby, and was puzzled by the receptionist's enigmatic, slightly condescending glance. The riddle was resolved within two minutes. No one carries the things here; they're useless. The rainwater swirls in hazy streams, auratic drifts around you, finding out your every port of entry: gaps between coat fasten-ings or shirt buttons, between sleeve and wrist or trouser-leg and ankle, weft and warp of jumper-knit. By the time he'd reached Sardinen he was saturated: not just clothes but (it felt) skin as well, as though some strange inversion of this country's vaunted sauna ritual had just taken place, a reverse sweating, and the atmosphere, not he, had shed its moisture, millions of nebulised drops that his body, like a sponge, had thirstily absorbed. His hosts' first act was to have one of their number, an acrobat named Trine, lead him to a *klær buttikk* to purchase a full-body anorak that, like a scientist in a film involving mass-contagion or (as with *Incarnation*, although Ben Briar – oddly – hasn't flagged this up and called for the characters to wear similarly prophylactic outfits) alien contact, he now dons automatically each time he ventures outside.

MU's housed in an old canning factory, whence its informal title. MU stands for the Movement Underground, but everyone just calls it (building, company, employees) Sardinen. In the vaulted workshops, hooks from which the daily catch was hoisted by the barrelful before being upended, sloshed down ramps on to conveyors that led millions of fish a merry dance through grading, brining, nobbing, seaming and eventual cartoning now secure ropes and bungees, aerial straps and nets, *cordes lisses* and *volantes* to and from which acrobats hang, swing, split, piston and basqule, while up towards and even sometimes on beyond them other bodies rise, shot from the trampolines with which patches of floor have been inlaid. Still others fall, from beams and loading doors, in dives by turns gracious and willed, evocative of Acapulco cliffs, and (conversely) passive and unshaped, as though the faller had been shot or pushed or simply lost their footing, on to blue crash-mats that boom as they implode under each impact, upper surface crumpling before rising once more, yeast-rich dough on speed-play, to assume its previous volume although not topography (the exact distribution through the plastic of folds and creases never, Phocan's concluded, the same twice) as they await the next free-falling mass. In one corner of the room a human pyramid reaches almost to beam level: a misshapen one that's crumbling and collapsing even as it forms, discarded body-blocks scrambling to their feet and stumbling on across the floor to form new, smaller mastabas as they clamber over other fallen, stumbling bodies, groping their way forward . . .

The scenario's as follows: Tszvetan and Tild have been found out. It was always bound to happen; even at the state reception in Kern's harbour, as the *Sidereal*'s doors groaned open and the bride-to-be was led down the long, rose-draped walkway, face emerging from the clouds of dry ice with which the vehicle had been doused (Herzberg's, not Briar's, idea) – the way her escort led her by the hand, the way he *held* her hand, a lack of stiffness

to the grip exuding more familiarity than ceremony ... Courtiers'
tongues started wagging right then, and haven't stopped since. One
of their number, a weaselly commandant named Marloe who's
long harboured a grudge against Louis Q's protégé (they're the
same age; Tszvetan was a better racer than him, and outnotched his
kills during the War by two-to-one), has been constantly dreaming
up ways to blow their cover. He's activated route tracers and communications spyware, body-signature detectors, crypto-shadows;
he's let slip, Iago-like, insinuations at each opportunity – none of
which ruses have achieved their goal, partly because the lovers
have been on to him and taken appropriate precautions (trace-
erasure software, phoneme-scramblers, shadow-diffractors, etc.,
etc.), partly due to Louis Q's unwillingness to see, or to acknowledge having seen, what's obvious to everyone else.

And obvious it is: no one-off, the thanadrine-fuelled episode has
tapped, in Tild and Tszvetan, inexhaustible reserves of passion. It's
an addiction; they get actual, i.e. somatic, withdrawal symptoms if
the tryst isn't re-consummated every day or so – high temperature,
nausea, the shakes ... For venues they've been using semi-public
spaces: the Botanical Garden, Natural Science Museum, Tentirn
Tower – assignations thought up on the hoof and messaged via
ad-hoc interfaces immune to deciphering because devised by the
lovers themselves, intuitively, idiolects almost. He'll drop chips
into her blu-ray stream at certain frequencies, or project flickering
laser-beams on to low-hanging clouds above the palace, or flash
over an iconogram showing a *caprifolio* tree, none of which symbols have been pre-infused with a fixed meaning by them – but
each time, she knows exactly what he's signalling. The others –
courtiers, servants, populace-at-large – know merely *that* they're
signalling, and trysting, but can't place this knowledge in the forum
of decodable enunciation, hence of record ...

Marloe, no fool, has thought the situation through, and tweaked
his strategy accordingly. He's come to understand that, as far as his
aims are concerned, his goal isn't the *uncovering* of the affair, since
this was hardly covered in the first place. Nor is it convincing Louis

Q that the affair is taking place: if what the ruler's seen already isn't evidence enough, then nothing will be – they're virtually screwing right in front of him. No: what he, Marloe, needs to do is to uncover to the *populace* Louis Q's awareness of the state of play; and beyond that, to uncover to him, Louis Q, the populace's knowledge of his knowledge of their knowledge of the tryst – a loop of knowing feeding back into and energising itself, galvanising the whole situation from its stupor. Once all separating curtains, all snug-walls have been torn down, all blind alleys razed, the partitioning of acknowledgement eradicated, then ... *Then* Louis Q will *have* to act: his own head, crown, sceptre, his *authority*, will be on the block. Marloe's been dreaming up some fitting form of *mise-en-scène* through which the requisite tripartite viewing – Louis Q of lovers, public of lovers-and-Louis-Q, Louis Q of public-viewing-him-viewing-lovers – might be orchestrated ...

Events, or at least the court calendar, conspire with him: on Kern, from the Second Kingdom onward, to mark each new moon cycle a royal hunt's been undertaken. With much sounding of tambours and waving of draps, the regent and his entourage mount an armada of five-cylinders and *kjarabancs* and chase down the *radjars* that proliferate around Kern's veldt and wetlands. The excursion lasts a whole diurnal – an all-male affair, one in which Tszvetan, in the normal run of things, would not only feature but also star, bagging more of the elegant, antlered beasts than anyone else (though, as protocol demands, tributing to Louis Q the excess of his tally over and above that of his liege). But this time he's crying off, pleading an old injury, a Saraõnic shoulder-wound that's playing up – which is (to use the old Kern idiom) *kwatsch*: he and Tild will take his uncle's absence as free pass for an uninterrupted nocturnal of *couping*. This they do, imbibing between bouts a range of cocktails that Tild's mixed for them – nothing so all-consuming as thanadrine, none of which in any case remains (they knocked it off in one go that night on the ship), but nicely complementary to such drawn-out sessions nonetheless: rhodontrine, porphyridion, mandragal, draughts that double the effects of darkness, swathe them in the intimacy and security of what seems the first, or maybe final, night, inducing a forgetfulness, obliviousness even – to danger, to the risks of discovery and of forgetfulness itself. Eventually, passion and bodies spent, they drift seamlessly off into a deep and peaceful sleep. When Louis Q, led on by Marloe (who is easily, once Tszvetan's DF software's been reactivated, capable of tracking them) and with the entire hunting party in tow, arms laden with *radjars* in a state (it seems) no more limpid or inanimate than that of the two lovers, stumbles into the *palazzo's* Sala Rosa just as dawn, once more, peeps round Ardis Minor and creeps over the Kernwinal Hills, projecting Fidelus's light on to the golden threads of the room's darkened tapestries, it takes a full minute of shouting, prodding, tugging and, eventually, slapping to wake Tild and Tszvetan up.

This, then, is the state of play: Louis Q, apoplectic at his bride's and nephew's joint betrayal of him; at having himself been found out finding out; at having (consequently) to do something about it; at the tawdry symbolism of the antlers being clasped all around him, proffered like so many mocking mirrors – and Tszvetan and Tild, blinking in the hostile daylight, shamed and naked but at the same time silently defiant. They stare back at the assembled company with eyes so piercing that courtiers avert theirs; to Louis Q, the eyes say: *Yes. You willed it, and it happened. What are you going to do?* The regent has no choice. He decrees that Tszvetan and Tild be executed in the public square come the diurnal's zenith. Marloe, though, who truly is a shit, ventures to suggest to him that Tild instead be handed over, straight away, to Kern's *leperosi* – poor sub-citizens who, afflicted by a meteor-borne virus that both disfigures and cripples them, causing rank lesions to erupt across their skin before eating its way down into their flesh, which in turn causes toes, fingers, sometimes entire limbs to auto-amputate ... These creatures, shunned by employers, landlords and just about everyone else due to the highly infectious character of their disease, find themselves condemned to endless wandering about Kern's empty precincts, waste grounds, marsh- and border-zones, from which they emerge intermittently, en masse, to shove mendicant, insufficiently digited hands at passers-by who recoil in revulsion from them. Why not, urges Marloe, hand Tild straight over to the group of them that they saw camped out in the disused old port as they rode back from the wetlands, and let them have their way with her?

In this, too, Louis Q is cornered: any temperance of his ire, ebbing to humble love of his revenge's violent pace, would be viewed as a sign of weakness – from a political, never mind personal, POV, ill-advised messaging. Tszvetan is popular, and the *plebeiani* seem to be taking Tild to their collective heart as well; a delay or commutation that leaves the two intact could birth a dangerous ambivalence in terms of public loyalties, open an interregnum in which fealty might start swinging, see the younger couple take on the aspect of a parallel royal household, a new court-in-waiting ... No: it behoves Louis Q to be swift and brutal, and accept Marloe's baroque proposal. So it is: Tszvetan to be burned, today, in the *piazzo*; Tild to be gang-banged to death, gangrenously, by Kern's *leperosi*.

'You're sure you want them climbing over each other like this?' Phocan asks Herzberg as the two men watch Sardinen's *akrobater* mounting one another's backs and shoulders, then, formations grown top-heavy, tumbling off again to roll about the floor before once more finding their feet and seeking out newly forming masses to join up with.

'Absolutely,' the AD decisively responds. 'It's what Lukas wants. The *leperosi* manifest as a collective body. They *represent* collectiveness – a counterpoint to the heroic individualism of the main characters; and ... there was something else too ...'

'Okay,' Phocan says. 'It's just a little difficult to ...'

'Also,' Herzberg continues, recalling Dressel's involved lecture on the matter, delivered to him by the great director back in London on the eve of his departure here, 'disease, infection and affliction: these are low embodiments of the desire that's overtaken the two lovers. He mentioned *Death in Venice*: how the plague, you know, all the collapsing bodies, symbolise the moral downfall of the upright and respectable composer, his "abandonment to longing's putrefaction" ...'

Phocan hasn't seen *Death in Venice*. But he knows that markering and mo-capping a 'collective body' is going to be a headache – paradoxically, since a gangling, multi-limbed monster is precisely what you often get before you extricate and allocate the portions; that latter task (extricating, allocating) being the very one to which he's just last week been trying to convince the IACSS crowd that Pantarey's Physis 6™ is perfectly suited. Here, though, the sequence is reversed. The production *to order* of an artefact, of tangle and confusion, isn't as simple as you might presume – unpredictable or indeterminate conglomerations being characterised, after all, by indeterminacy, unpredictability ...

'Let's,' he tells Herzberg after thinking for a moment, 'get them markered up, and have them do their tumbling and re-amalgamating as per your directions, and we'll just see what we get, take it from there.'

Watching the sequences three hours later, rain playing against Sardinen's corrugated roof the only background noise now *akrobater* have been stood down and decamped, collectively, to a bar round the corner named *Sardinkan* (with effusive hospitality as buoyant as their leaps and bounces, they urged Phocan and Herzberg to come join them once they'd finished what they 'had to do'), Phocan is pleasantly surprised at the results. The mass of future *leperosi*, as yet featureless and unadorned with poxed and lacerated skin, limb-stumps, lecherous grins, and so on – they'll acquire those in London, at DZ – do indeed seem to function as one single, if unusually configured, organism, whose decentralised intelligence flows around it in a current as it, too, wends simultaneously one way and another, coalescing like continuous rainfall round the body of the girl – as it happens, Phocan's raincoat-selecting assistant Trine – who's standing in for Tild, or rather for Rosanna Wilmington.

'I like it.' Herzberg nods approval over Phocan's shoulder. 'I think Lukas will too. Let's go join our friends in the Sardine Can.'

Herzberg's satisfaction with his little pun deflates as soon as they arrive to find that *Sardinkan* does indeed mean 'sardine can': a graphic of one, hanging over the bar's entrance, leaves no room for doubt on this front. Inside, it's as packed as one, acrobats crammed around tables, perched on barrels, windowsills and ledges, straddling the wooden beams that run beneath the hostelry's low ceiling. They seem to have quite a heat on already; there's a jovial air about them; some of them are singing; others laugh as they pass phones around. Drinks are ordered for their guests, along with a new round for the Sardinen. When Phocan asks Trine, who's made space for him beside her, what they're looking at on the phones, she hands the one she's holding to him, and he scrolls through scores of snaps of acrobats in various states and shapes: crumpled, starred, falling, swallow-diving, flailing, rising, soaring, catapulting ...

'How do you know who's who?' he asks. Most of the jpegs show them in bodysuits, or with head tucked under legs, or stretched back upwards so the face is turned away.

'We don't,' she shrugs. 'It doesn't really matter. What's important is to find new figures and new permutations.'

'But ...' he starts – then finds he can't find the words for his quibble.

'Yes ... ?' Trine prompts, wiping a giant beer-head tidemark from around her mouth.

'I mean ... Aren't you proud when it's *you* who's found one?'

'That's not how we think,' she tells him. 'It's never about *us* finding something, or *us* owning a particular action ... We're trained to see our bodies as the place where the action occurs.'

'And your face?' he asks.

'What about it?' Trine asks back.

'When Rosanna Wilmington's is plastered over it ... Won't you feel, you know, kind of cancelled out?'

'I was never "in" in the first place,' Trine replies.

Phocan's about to ask her what she means, but just then another round arrives, ordered this time by Herzberg.

'Half the film's budget gone right there!' he shouts as he passes out the tankards. 'Pantarey can get the next one.'

This Pantarey does – after which Phocan's at least half-cut, as are the company in general: their bodies seem to glide from beam to ledge to chair to bar counter more fluidly, without definite outlines; bar counter and beam seem to be gliding too, their borders shifting, realigning. Then it's out again into the acrobatic rain, surging and turning, hovering and bouncing. Trine's beside him, holding his arm, and the cobblestones are running till they're back at his hotel; then somehow he, like Bergen's rain, has managed to fall up two flights of stairs to his second-floor bedroom, sadly without Trine it seems, although someone is holding forth to him on the subject of anonymity – or is it just him, talking to himself, lying face down, forehead intersected by the raised wooden threshold between lounge and bathroom ... ?

The threshold mark will stay with him, forehead-imprinted, for most of the following day; in his scrambled state he'll associate it, every time he glimpses it in rain-blurred glass, not simply with Trine – that is, with Trine's absence – but also with vaguer, modulating sequences, chains of imperfectly reflected episodes that regress backward, passing through Rafaella Farinati, telescoping off into some dark recess that memory, at least his right now, isn't up to the task of illuminating. Now, waking up still splayed across the doorway, the rain still crackling out a constant background static on the walls and windowpanes, its aquacity crowing at his dehydration, he drinks all the bottled water in his minibar, then refills the container from his bathroom tap. Flipping his laptop open, he finds awaiting him amidst the inbox clutter two emails of note. One has a *.lv* address: Latvia. It's from Raivis Vanins' office, and it bears, prefaced by a *re:*, the header (*Possibility of Jumelans visit?*) of his own email from four days previously. It reads:

Dear Dr Phocan,

Professor Vanins thanks you for your interest in his work. His research into states of equilibrium was principally conducted several decades ago, and has not until quite recently elicited the type of curiosity you communicate. The Professor draws your attention to the holdings of Rīgas Tehniskā Univerisitāte's Solid-State Physics Department, where the bulk of his archive is kept, and suggests you begin by consulting these. He asks me to add that, should you still wish to meet with him in person, he will, in deference to his old acquaintance your patron Dr Garnett, be prepared to make time for you. Should such an interview be desired, he suggests a date after 13 September.

Yours,

Lazda Krūmiņa
pp Professor Vanins

Patron? Nice word: paternal. No mention of black boxes: why would there be? They weren't alluded to in the overtures to Vanins made by first Garnett and then, once the channel of communication had been opened, him. Reading this Lazda Krūmiņa's response, Phocan feels fraudulent, borderline criminal – an impostor, even if he's not, his sense of alienation from the straight path of his calling amplified by this appalling hangover. Maybe he played up his strategic fascination with the states-of-equilibrium stuff too much: is there an edge of suspicion to the surprise expressed by her, or perhaps through her by the Professor, about his Trojan horse, his *violon d'ingres?* He's not able, this morning, to gauge innuendo levels. What does *until quite recently* mean . . . ? The second message comes from a generic account, no national suffix – but the address grabs his attention straight away: it's a.pirotti@gmail.com. The header: *808.* It opens with the same salutation as the other:

Dear Dr Phocan,

It was edifying and encouraging to meet you in Rome. I wonder how your enquiries into the subject we discussed up on the hillside are proceeding. Do keep me up to date. Perhaps we could connect in Riga, should you find yourself in that neck of the woods at any point in the near future.

I remain your friend and well-wisher,

A.P.

Now, just as when he met Pirotti in the flesh a week ago, Phocan feels disoriented, vertiginous. It's more than just the toxins and potassium depletion: it's the sudden groundlessness induced by overlap of territories that should find themselves far apart, unconnected – as though, in their fibre-optic relay to him, or perhaps within the very silver casing of his laptop, two separate fields had intersected, *read* each other, breached whatever barriers had been put in place, by geography, technology and just plain reality, to keep them separate and unrelated. *Riga*: how on earth … ? In London, as soon as he'd returned from Rome, he looked up Cassius First Motion, and found nothing; he scoured online directories of mo-cap companies, not that this was necessary: the industry is small, he knows them all, but there are always fledglings, start-ups … nothing; then of general tech, CGI outfits *à la* Degree Zero, sports-science labs, data-security firms – still nothing. Cassius didn't exist. There was, of course, the number on the card – but to phone *that* would have entailed a step beyond another threshold, the betrayal one. Industrial espionage. Why didn't he report the tapping-up to Garnett or Hossain immediately on his return? He doesn't know the answer to that; but for some reason, he didn't. It seemed too intimate, a *peccadillo* almost. And then Farinati's role, if she was part of it … Should he have read her over-the-shoulder smile? Her pointed marking of his lapel? Or seen through her proffered not-quite-assignation on the Palatino, the most obvious place in all of Rome? Now this … He throws on his anorak and heads out into the rain.

The day at Sardinen is spent, once more, capturing tumbling, dis- and reassembling bodies. Once his nausea's been quashed by sugar-intake, Phocan settles into a quiet rhythm, watching leprous forms advance with an irregular regularity, a faceless multitude that seems to sense and think and measure time through its collective body: Lukas's formulation, planted in his mind by Herzberg, repeats itself for him as he sits editing sequences after the live-capture session's finished, playing the same short stretches over and over … *liberating dynamism of the great machine* … in the rain's crackle and his laptop's hum, Gastev's lines take shape too. Or was it *erupting*? The more Phocan watches, the more abstract the sequences grow: pixels, shearing from the mass's body to form new blocks, take on the aspect of cells, plasmatic units in search of new clusters and new designations. *Non aberranti ma esemplari* … Farinati's words to him also seem to ricochet around the cannery's airspace. In his addled state, reason all but capsized by great waves of glucose-level fluctuation, Phocan, for some reason, finds his mind drifting back to the extensive disquisitions that Diamond, when she was still wet behind the ears, Pantarey intern, drew from him on artefacts, subject that seemed to fascinate her. No matter how much he tried to impress on her that these were nothing more than the result of glitches, bugs, shortcomings in the code, she kept pushing her homespun thesis that they might in fact be caches for 'a type of information that we haven't yet learnt to interpret'.

'How do you mean?' he asked, bemused.

'You know, like in the old days, when rheumatics' knee-joints foretold thunder-storms. Or with PTSD'd veterans like my friend Aidan' – this man's name, ever since Phocan's knightly rescue of her from his clutches, had become a kind of bonding joke between them – 'how some weird, neurotic quirk they keep repeating, that makes no sense, is really a symptom that encodes a trauma-scene too awful to be captured as "official" memory but, thanks to the, you know, encoding, manages to sit right in the open, hidden in plain sight …'

He mock-swatted at her head with the data wand he was holding.

'Doesn't work like that. They're glitches. Software failure. End of story.'

Today, though, he's suddenly not so sure, finds himself prey to an inversion as total as that of yesterday's Acapulcan plungers. What if ... what if artefacts, rather than marking a limitation, an inadequacy, were ... What if, contrary to all evidence, to logic itself ... if they were the very thing most *true* in all configurations – tokens, splinters of a stratum of reality so deep, so sedimented, that it hasn't yet been charted, let alone assigned grid-coordinates, a vessel or a form, but ... ? And if ... then ...

No, the thought won't take shape, probably because it's *kwatsch* as well. Fuckin' kids: Eldridge was right. Phocan closes the *leperosi* file and pops open another, *falling.vp*. There are those plungers: a body, male or female, tightly clad in a black, marker-studded bodysuit, is dropping from one of the loading doors towards a mat. Phocan's got seven versions of the plunge: some clumsy, others more streamlined and aerodynamic, some neither-nor; same body, or different ones, performing each – impossible to tell, and doesn't matter. It will eventually become a fleeing Tild, plummeting flailing from a cliff edge to be caught in mid-air by a pirogue-riding Tszvetan; also *leperosi* One, Two and Three, and perhaps Four and Five, too, hurtling to their deaths as they lunge and grope after her. Phocan runs the flailingest dive-sequence through several times; then a more placid one; then, for no reason besides whimsy, he freezes this second dive in mid-fall, runs it backwards, then forwards, then backwards again, so that the figure yo-yos up and down, before eventually freezing it once more in mid-air. Thus arrested, its kinetic panic is transformed, communicating now a kind of serene unconcern that Phocan finds soothing. Spreading outwards from his screen, it seems to overtake not just the space here in Sardinen but beyond too – Rome, London, Riga; to usher in a general state in which things, all things, find themselves caught up in the same general, if unnameable, contraption, and the world, its stakes, its struggles, all hang in the balance.

Book Three

1. *Cidonija*

Like the cracked skin of *leperosi*, the Gulf of Livonia's surface is stretched by the wind and furrowed by the wakes of ferries plying their corridors between Riga and Stockholm, Riga and Helsinki, Riga and St Petersburg. There are larger ships too – tankers bearing freight-stacks, corrugated blue and red and yellow boxes piled five-high. In one of her dispatches, this woman (he presumes that it's a woman for some reason) whose name has been blacked out in the *01mdean02cdorley* printouts he's been handed mentions *Dracula*: Lillian Gilbreth's fascination with the novel's boxes, with the Count shipping his earth-lair in a set of crates from Transylvania to England … Phocan's got boxes on his mind. The first Latvian houses that slip into view beneath the wing, laid out across a strip of sandy beach or dotted amid trees and inland waterways, look like the cargoes' freight containers, colourful and wrinkled through their overlay of plank strips. The same type of wooden house lines the road into town, strangely anachronistic next to glass towers of banks and international hotels. Above his taxi, like the streaked track of a wireframe, tram cables run – always in duplicate, a double line bending and kinking as it traces, in advance, his one best way towards this assignation with Vanins, with Lazda Krūmiņa, with (whisper it) the possibility, the spectre, of Box 808.

But not all the way; not yet. The vagaries of airline scheduling have deposited him in Riga two days before he's to be received at Vanins' dacha, which seems to lie a few miles out of town on a commuter train line. Lazda, with whom he's by now had enough rounds of correspondence to be on first-name terms, has given him detailed instructions for getting there, and even mooted the possibility of a night's stay, but on the date she's been inflexible: the Professor will be available on 14 September, not a day before. As soon as he's dumped his suitcase in his eighth-floor room at the Intercontinental, Phocan makes his way, through empty squares guarded by old orthodox churches whose gold roofing seems to splay itself out, disco-ball-style, in the yellow of autumn foliage on branches, lawns, paths, steps and gutters, past ornately corniced civic buildings alternating with dilapidated work yards, telecoms outlets with vacant lots, towards Tehniskā Universitāte's archival and administrative building. It's a dark grey edifice with opaque windows, sitting on a square that's given over to a Red Guard monument, several bus stations and a taxi stand, and separated from the city's broad and charmless river by a four-lane carriage-way. The lobby's full of frescoed portraits, men Phocan has never heard of: Konstantīns Pēkšēns, Vilhelms Ostvalds, Etjēns Laspeiress, Eižens Laube, August Toeplers, Alvils Buholcs ... There's a frescoed map, too, charting these savants' diaspora to the Americas, Australia, the vast swathes of Soviet Europe, Soviet Asia ... None of them seems to have stayed in Latvia.

A lone receptionist in a glass booth is unsure where to send him; after a few calls on her internal phone she directs him to a third-floor office. But he gets lost on his way there, finds him-self wandering long, empty corridors whose marble slabs embed what looks like a circuit-pattern, pared down and abstracted, stripped of all resistors and inductors, switches and capacitors and any component that might impede its linearly superimposable advance along the floor, past vacant leather armchairs, unappre-ciated plants and columns both of plaster and of dusty sunlight. Occasionally, emboldened by the solitude, the absence of mounted cameras, Phocan interprets a door's ajarness as an invitation, and intrudes soft-footedly on empty studies in which test tubes and retorts, loop tracers and lab flumes, interferometers, resonance tube apparatuses, polarimeters, ballistic galvanometers, Van de Graaff generators, pipettes, burettes and barometers lie around workbenches beside open notebooks whose pages give off in mid-scribble, as though suddenly abandoned – not a half-hour ago, nor a day, or week, or even year: these rooms are musty, full of age and obsolescence, of hypotheses and theorems dissipated without being distilled, embryonic worlds that never found their frequency or form. In one room a chipped wooden ladder leans against shelves that seem to have been ransacked, their books strewn across the floor or toppled, domino-like, over one another, box files tipped back, spilling photos, letters, pamphlets. On another's windowsill, old Soviet quarterlies are precariously stacked. Phocan palms through them, finds an English one, flips open to an article: *Electrolyte Solutions: Literature Data on Thermodynamic and Transport Properties*, by Victor M. M. Lobos and I. Quaresma, 1956. Beside the windowsill an old machine keeps watch, a buttoned, dialled and tubed contraption at whose function he can't even guess; it has gauges and needles on it, maybe a sonometer – but there's nothing that might serve as pick-up. To its upper surface has been taped a kind of crib-sheet, but the lettering's Cyrillic ...

The archivist, when he finally locates her and hands her his card, reacts with surprise not only to his visit but also to the idea that there might be archives, in this building, of the sort he's looking for. Vanins? Phocan's dropping of the name, by now infused for him – as, it seems, for quite a few others – with magical, totemic qualities, falls flat. Perhaps it was the way that he pronounced it. He tries *Var-neenz*, but to no avail. The archivist, if that's what she is, prods about her own internal phone (like the receptionist's, an old push-button auto-dialler) and, after two short dialogues in Latvian, informs him that most faculty documents from the sixties and seventies have been moved to a storage facility on the outskirts of town. She gives him an address, which he then thrusts at one of the taxi drivers waiting at the Red Guards' feet.

It starts to rain during the drive – a rain more gravity-observant than Bergen's. Soviet-era housing blocks run into one another, streaking and reforming in the windscreen wipers' screen-save. The facility, lying off a road that turns to mud as prefab office blocks give over to decrepit warehouses and car breakers, is fenced, barriered and gated; but there's no one at the gatepost and the barrier is up, so they drive straight into the compound and crawl hesitantly past ramped loading bays and shuttered entrance windows. Above these, and them, a bunker-type building rises five storeys tall; large metal signage, battened to its roof, spells out the storage firm's name: RIGASTOCK. Beneath the letters, draped all the way back down to the first floor, a billboard optimistically flashes Rigastock's phone number and URL to passing trade. A woman walking, umbrella-less, from one of the building's side doors towards her parked car scurries past Phocan when he jumps out of the taxi to accost her; a large man in overalls smoking a cigarette, though, similarly unprotected from but seemingly untroubled by the rain, cranes his head down to listen a minute later. He appears not to understand a word that Phocan says to him – but, answering in what sounds like Russian, leads him up one of the loading ramps, then through another side entrance, then down a corridor towards a lift. This conveys them to a fifth-floor storage space whose concrete walls are lined with ventilation ducting, fire extinguishers and buckets, two of which have been moved out to spots around the floor, also concrete, to catch the drips falling from the ceiling. Eventually, they arrive at a wooden door; the large man knocks on this; a woman, opening it, welcomes Phocan into a carpeted office hung with pastoral-idyllic paintings showing *radjar*-like antlered deer cavorting around forests of a lurid, almost psychedelic colouration. The large overalled worker bows his head and retreats, leaving them alone.

This woman turns out to speak no more English than the worker did. She asks Phocan if he understands Russian; he tells her he doesn't. They eventually establish that they both have a few words of German – enough for him to convey what it is he's after and for her to tell him that if that's the case he's not allowed to be here: it's a private storage company; and besides, if the archives he wants to consult come from a Soviet-era state facility they'll have a seventy-five-year embargo slapped on them; on top of all which, she now has to close the office, to go pick her daughter up from school. She more or less frogmarches him downstairs and outside again; but, seeing him scour the compound for his taxi, which by now is long departed, she takes pity on him and, telling him he'll never manage to summon a new one out here, offers to drive him back to town. Thus he returns, wetter but no wiser than he was when he left it three hours ago, to the Intercontinental.

'Why're state archives being held in commercial storage spaces?' he asks an American tech worker on to whom, two drinks in, he's unloading – in generic, unspecific form yet still perhaps, it strikes him the next morning, in view of the tendency of Pirottis to pop up in places where you're least expecting them, imprudently – his frustration in the hotel's bar. 'Or, more to the point: why are they being held in private storage, but still covered by the censorship laws of a state that no longer exists?'

'This place is kind of schizophrenic,' Kyle (the name's still pinned to the guy's T-shirt) tells him. 'After independence, they privatised everything, but didn't overhaul the infrastructure or even the personnel. A third of the banks went bankrupt; the owners of another third are now in jail; and the last third are making hay as money-laundromats. *Their* owners would be in jail too if they weren't in government, or at least pally with it. The censorship is from the new regime: they don't want all the dirt on who was shopping whom to come out while the shoppers are still skipping around in public. Plus,' Kyle, also at least two drinks in, is warming to his subject, 'what you have to appreciate is that almost half the population here are ethnic Russians. They speak Russian, call the Latvians "Nazis" – which, during the War, they were – see the Soviet Union's collapse as a catastrophe and keep nagging Putin to send back the tanks.'

'I can't work out,' Phocan twists his straw reflectively, as though the answer lay amidst the ice cubes, 'whether the vibe here's ultra-modern or just retro, left behind.'

'Both at once,' Kyle says decisively. 'Riga's always looked both ways, ever since its Hanseatic League days, when it served Peter the Great as gateway to an open, i.e. unfrozen, seaboard. It's skimming distance now from Scandinavian comm-techs, and at the same time still tied umbilically to swathes of Steppe and centuries of peasantry. If you go down to the covered markets by the train station, you'll see old women from the countryside sitting all day long, each at their own little table or beside a tattered quilt their grandmother made, trying to sell five shrivelled turnips, staring into space.'

He turns to the barman and orders more vodka tonics. When they come he picks up where he left off: 'During the Cold War, Riga was an intersection point for spies. This hotel,' he lowers his voice, 'would have been rigged up with microphones – not to mention pretty girls to drink with, take up to your room, whisper restricted info to. Now,' he concludes, scrutinising him through vodka spectacles, 'it's just us.'

Phocan excuses himself and retires, alone, to bed. Next morning, as he's heading to the market to see for himself the Stoic turnip sellers, he receives a call from the first archivist, the Tehniskā Universitāte's one, who has not only kept his card but also gone to the bother of doing some ferreting around for him. They have some Vanins-related items in their building after all; he's welcome to come look at them. These transpire to be mainly articles he's authored: *Resistance Gradients in Mesospheric Flight*, 1968; *Benefits and Disadvantages of Delta Wing Configuration*, 1964; plus several more in Russian. There's a folder full of notes, too – drawings, sketches, jottings, and so forth. No letters from Lillian; no sudden *T.T.* enigma-solving key or cipher; but – gold dust it seems at first, then, as time wears on without any actual revelation, let alone *eureka!* moment, ensuing, just dust – he does come across the number *808*. It's written – more exactly, drawn – beneath a chart listing dynamic properties of the Tu-144 aircraft: the two figure-eights separated by the not-quite circle (Pirotti was right: it's more of an ellipsoid). 'Drawn' as in doodled – whimsically, as though Vanins had been daydreaming during a meeting, let his mind drift in the middle of some computations ... And repeatedly: as it progresses, it rotates until each of its digits is lying horizontal on the page, one beneath the other, *0* under *8*, two

8s beneath each *0*, the whole sequence hanging vertically, like a flourish underneath a signature, a spring, or possibly (perhaps he wasn't daydreaming at all) the type of flight-path that the figures given in the chart might produce in the Tu-144. For an instant, Phocan's back at Farnborough, surrounded by the whine of Roger's air-decorating drones. They called it *Buzzby Berkeley*, two zs: 'Little Web of Dreams' ... That Aidan character hitting on Diamond in the outer room ... the austere and elusive Pilkington ... Phocan's alone: the archivist's left him the side-room to her office. Glancing at the door, he slips his phone out, turns the sound off, takes a quick snap of the page and pockets it again; then steps out, thanks her for her help and heads back down the circuit-patterned marble corridor feeling cheap and treacherous, a spy in a hotel ...

Next morning, finally, he hops on a commuter train to Jumelans. The carriages are quaint: blue-yellow-orange on the outside with steep steps to their high doors, decked out with wooden seats wide as park benches inside. The conductor can't be more than eighteen; he's got up, *Saturday Night Fever* style, in a uniform consisting of side-lapel skinny blazer and large-collar shirt unbuttoned to the base of his ribcage. They trundle out along a spit of land bordered by inlets, past old wooden houses camouflaged by foliage of spruces, ferns and taller trees he can't identity, past fishing dinghies lost in reeds, stopping at single-platform stations for two, or four, or no passengers to board and alight. Most have wooden ticket offices or waiting rooms, the same plank-strip overlay he noticed from the plane, with faded signage in both Latin and Cyrillic. One, though, the last stop before Jumelans, a place called Siliciems, sports a new, asymmetrical steel station house topped with a racing quiff or 'accent', whose implied speed matches the building's slant – a construction of the type that calls attention to itself as architecture, as commission.

'It's for the super-rich who come from Russia to Siliciems for the New Wave Festival each year,' Lazda will tell him when he comments on it in the car. 'A waste of money, since most of them arrive by limousine, with chauffeurs, or even by helicopter; never train. They stay in the spas, which get guards at their entrances, and the town's suddenly full of plastic lips and boobies, and for one week of the year a cappuccino costs ten euros. The whole festival's a cover; no one's interested in New Wave; they come here to do business deals off Moscow's radar.'

Lazda speaks near-perfect English with a heavy Baltic accent. She's the only person waiting at Jumelans for the Riga train. She's wearing jeans and a light army-surplus jacket, standing beside a Skoda's open driver-side door.

'Phocan,' she says, pulling off, pronouncing the two syllables inquisitively. 'It is a typical English name?'

'It's anglicised,' he answers. 'It refers to Phocis, a region in Greece – to Phocans, who come from there. I suppose I must be ...'

'I read your papers,' she cuts him off, changing gear.

'My papers? I haven't ...'

'*Bodily Differentiation in Haptic Event-Modelling.* Also: *Sequence Layout for Generic Simulations* ...'

'Wow. I didn't think anyone knew about those. That first one was my thesis.'

'It's all online,' she tells him as they pass a small, derelict factory whose brickworks are being reclaimed by the forest. 'I like to know who comes to see my grandfather.'

'He's your grandfather? I thought you were just ...' But this thought is swallowed by his second question, which, turning to face her, he lets loose too quickly: 'Many people come?'

She pauses before answering, scanning the rear-view mirror. 'Sometimes they come, and go again. Then others come; then no one for some time, then several close together. I don't think they find what they're looking for.'

Is there a mocking tenor to the words? An accusation in them? Her voice isn't hostile; there's a kind of knowing irony to it, though. It prompts him to defend himself pre-emptively:

'I'm interested in his work on states of equilibrium. Are you a scientist too?'

'No,' she says. 'Art History. I'm an assistant professor here in Riga.'

'But you serve as his secretary?'

'No one else provided him with one,' she says – then, turning the tables, asks: 'Who are you working for?'

'Pantarey,' he replies defensively. 'I laid it all out in our first email exchange; and the research param ...'

'Yes,' she cuts him off dismissively. 'I know. Who are they working for?'

It's as though she'd slammed the brakes on, or they'd pulled up at some kind of road block or control point. The conversation restarts, but a threshold has been passed.

'Several clients,' he says, feeling paradoxically less, not more, defensive – not because the question's not aggressive but because, in this instance at least, he genuinely doesn't know. 'We have partners of all types – universities, medical research firms, sports science, entertainment, aerospace ...'

'Partners,' she bounces the term back at him.

'Our founder,' he tells her, both illogically (since it doesn't follow) and (since she already knows) redundantly, 'knew the ... your grandfather.'

She sniffs and turns off the main road on to a small track lined with narrow ditches and with houses, some no larger than allotment cabins, others more elaborate, but all bearing the marks of having been assembled on the hoof, as patchworked as the foliage whose colours blend and jar around them. The track intersects another, similarly ditch- and house-lined, then, almost immediately, a third, into which Lazda makes a right turn before pulling off, just opposite a tiny and abandoned-looking children's playground, into what he takes to be the Vanins property.

It's an old place – several places, more a complex than a single building – built around a garden. There's a two-storey main house of light blue wood, to which a one-floor brick extension has been added; lying across a lawn from this, a kind of hybrid barn or greenhouse whose unpainted wood strips alternate with glass and corrugated plastic rises as high as the house it faces. Further in, at the garden's far end, its base obscured by an overgrown vegetable patch, a treehouse stands, cubistic and irregularly proportioned, its undulating roof of small wood tiles inset with non-aligned, oddly shaped skylights. Phocan's eye darts, as he steps from the car on to grass whose texture has a softness his shoes haven't felt for a long time, from one place to another, wondering which opening, which plane or vista Vanins will appear from; wondering beyond that just how this *name*, this presence that till now has manifested itself to him only in sentences on paper, as report and rumour, ubiquitous but unlocatable reverberation, might be translated into and embodied in a frame of roughly, give or take a little, the same size as his. It seems almost unthinkable ... There's movement in the greenhouse-barn – is that him? It's in the upper stretches of the glass and plastic; and the lower, and all over: dark patches flapping, shadows sweeping and retreating, at a scale too big, it seems, to issue from a single human, a formation too dispersed and mutable to come from humans at all ...

'He's sleeping,' Lazda says. For a moment Phocan confuses this snippet of information with the shadow-puppet show he's watching, the strange silhouettes – as though the flickering were Vanins' dream, the glass and plastic membranes his translucent mind-scrim. They're both wrong, though: Vanins is awake, and walking from the low-lying part of the main house towards them. Phocan knows it's him and not a gardener or housekeeper from the wave of care that sweeps through Lazda's body once she's caught sight of the thin man in the light-brown pullover, diminutive against the bricks: the way she opens her whole stance towards him, takes a half-step forwards, as though to assist him as he steps on to uneven lawn, then, catching herself, holds the motion, keeping it in check or in reserve, her muscles still alert, on call in case they're needed. They're not: the old man proceeds steadily, diminutive against the grass his feet don't seem to flatten, diminutive still as he reaches Phocan and holds out a light and fragile hand.

'You are Garnett's missile.'

The voice, too, is light; if not exactly fragile, it's still textured, grained by age.

'Missile?' asks Phocan.

'I mean missive. Garnett's envoy.'

Phocan nods. 'He sends best wishes to you.'

Vanins unclasps his hand, then, prompted by the sight of some-thing beyond Phocan's shoulder, asks:

'You like *cidonija?*'

'I'm sorry ... ?'

Vanins says something in Latvian to Lazda. She disappears into the house. The old man holds his arm out, inviting Phocan to follow her; they traipse inside. *Cidonija* turns out to be quince, dried, sliced and sugared. They eat them from a china bowl, with milkless black tea, also sugared. Lazda is quiet while Vanins floats Phocan general enquiries about Pantarey's projects, his own back-ground, the state of kinaesthetic and fluid-dynamic research in the UK ... About the more specific reasons for Phocan's visit, the equilibrium-state stuff, he asks nothing – either because he's taking it as understood, established between them already, or perhaps because he senses, on some frequency, that, like the New Wave Festival, it's just a front, a cover. Behind her look of disengagement, Lazda's listening carefully: Phocan can tell, can feel her scanning his responses as though they formed a long, unbroken printout being cranked out by a polygraph. Eventually Vanins rises and says:

'Come with me to the aviary. We can talk there.'

Back across the lawn, the greenhouse-barn reveals its secret, or at least one of them: the patches and silhouettes are made by birds' wings flapping against the glass and plastic. There must be scores of them in here, large and small: swifts, plovers, waxwings, crakes and sandpipers and wrens, wagtails and pipits, all the way down to the common thrush and sparrow, flitting from wall to shelf or darting in and out of the small birdhouses dotted about the beams. There are plants, too, pushing against windows, trailing twines from rafters, drawing finely woven curtains round two or three armchairs and a sofa spread about the floor.

'I built it myself, in the sixties,' Vanins tells him. 'It was not easy. In Soviet times you couldn't buy materials; but you could *get* them. You had to negotiate: you went to a sawmill with your own wood and asked them to cut it for you in exchange for three litres of homemade apple brandy, or a kilogram of courgettes. Now,' he adds with a laugh beneath whose sugar coating bitterness is stored, 'you can buy anything; but no one can afford it.'

'How long,' asks Phocan, 'have you had this dacha?'

'It was my father's,' Vanins answers. 'Normally, under communism, it would have been confiscated; I could even have been exiled or shot for owning private property. In my case, the state took it, but they let me lease it back, since I had dispensation: my position at the Universitāte ... The *aviary* I said I needed in order to carry out research into bird flight, in the tradition of Marey.'

'Did you carry it out?' *Marey*: Phocan's been learning about him these last few weeks, since he in turn loomed big (as *01mdeanetc.* also records) in Gilbreth's formative prehistory – first person to translate into sinuous curves captured on paper, glass or, later, photographic plate the movements of soldiers, patients, cats and all manner of subjects locomoting, pulsing, flowing, flying. Diagrams of birds rigged up with harnesses and *stylographs*, hallucinatory negatives of each stage of the wing's transit superimposed in single-frame simultaneity, float now from the textbooks Garnett pressed into his hand and flap around his mind.

'I observed them,' Vanins smiles wryly. 'I looked after them, and still do.'

His hand sweeps a few seeds scattered about a counter into a small pile, which he then pinches in his fingers and holds up to feed two wagtails and a thrush who perch just long enough to snatch one each before darting away again. Vanins' eyes follow them as they disappear into one of the birdhouses, then turn back to Phocan as he declaims, in frail but steady tones:

'*How do you know but ev'ry Bird that cuts the airy way / Is an immense world of delight, clos'd by your senses five?*'

'I'm sorry?' Phocan asks.

'Marey's biographer chose those lines as epigraph. Do you like birds?'

'I like movement,' says Phocan. 'And I like equilibrium.'

'So you have said,' Vanins replies. 'I invite you to stay for supper. In which case, you should remain here overnight; there are no trains back into Riga after seven. You can stay in the treehouse.'

'I would be delighted,' Phocan answers. 'Perhaps then we can talk a little more about your work on ...'

'Later,' Vanins tells him. 'Now, I'm tired.'

He motions Phocan to the aviary's door, and out across the lawn. On the far side of this, the treehouse's skylights are lit up. Lazda emerges from beneath them, folded pillowcase in hand. Has she been preparing the place for him? Was the decision to have him stay already made? As they approach the main house Vanins stops in his tracks and says:

'Marey, as you know, was fascinated by it.'

'States of equilibrium?'

'No,' Vanins looks bemused; 'tiredness. That was one of the main goals of all his research: to eliminate fatigue. He saw it as a moral – as a *spiritual* – affliction, scourge of a nation exhausted by defeat to Germany, by absinthe and hashish, by *ennui* ... His *Station Physiologique* was set up to re-galvanise the youth, to bring the clerk or manual labourer into alignment with the soldier and the gymnast, infuse them, and the body politic in general, with the energy and dynamism of the locomotive – or the bird ...'

He closes the aviary's door gently behind them, before adding: 'But me, I'm tired.'

Later, as he lies with Lazda on the aviary's sofa, sweat cooling on their skin, Phocan will ponder this exchange again, wondering if Vanins' words held some kind of accusation, or acknowledgement, or resignation ... Wondering, too, again, on whose behalf he's been sent here. *Missile*: was the malaprop really an error? Like his granddaughter, the old man speaks English with a heavy Baltic accent, but the grammar's perfect ... These reflections are for later, though: tomorrow afternoon. Now, grainy and imprecise as the gloaming that surrounds the house's faint but warm electric haze, Vanins' utterance doesn't solicit a response.

263

2. Frisch Weht der Wind

'You can get away,' Herzberg finds himself explaining, 'with a lot more in a situation that's unfamiliar than in one that's familiar. A spaceship is not – to most people, most *other* people – familiar.'

Ben Briar, his addressee, holds fire, contrarian impulse overridden by the qualifiers *most* and *other*. Herzberg, sensing a few more seconds of indulgence unfolding in front of him, continues:

'Now, you might think that this lack of a comparator, of an experiential reference point or authority, would whip the rug out from beneath the possibility of empathic identification. On the part of the audience, I mean. But, paradoxically, it doesn't. Or rather, it creates an opening, the chance for a swift one-two. What I mean is, that you counteract the defamiliarisation by introducing, however incongruous they may seem, the *most* familiar, mundane objects of all, to make the whole scenario credible. So, here, we've thrown a simple fork in ...'

On the BenQ PV3200PT 32-inch 4K IPS Post-Production Monitor at which the two men, and a host of others grouped around them, stare, the fork, CGI rendering of your basic IKEA Livnära (chosen, for its generic tine spread and wood handle, over the more narrowly Scandi-connoting Förnuft), drifts languidly in midair down the *Sidereal*'s engine-room corridor, rotating as it passes the POV.

'*This* object, though,' Herzberg cautions in a stern tone, '*has* to be convincing. You must really go to town in terms of detail: where it shines, the metal's granularity, how aged it looks ...'

The fork continues its slow passage down its gravityless vector, emitting, like an isotopic sheen, the memory of every *castaplane* and *stoumpot* mouthful it has borne from plate to mouth – and not just those of surly and unmannered stokers, nor even the refined crockery and lips of such as Tild and Tszvetan, but also of each of its viewers here in this room and, beyond that, in the world at large, the universe outside these walls to which it seems to slowly inch, awaiting its launch through some hatch as yet unseen.

'The best lies,' Herzberg commentates as soon as he feels the allure of the fork's lustre fading, 'are ninety per cent truth.'

He teaches a design course at St Martins; it's a line he feeds his students. Here, though, the dynamic's different, the authority reversed. It's like a viva, or tenure-track meeting, or even disciplinary hearing. It's as though he were *pleading* for Briar's approval – framing everything in the man's terms, his Aristotelian metrics. *Realism Tsar*. He gets more nervous about, sleeps less each night before, having to interface with the adviser than he does when making presentations to people with actual executive power over him, the power of contract-termination, fingers resting on the levers of professional life and death: *they* treat him with the reverence due to a craftsman, defer to his artisanal expertise, whereas this guy ... The Two Cultures man is like a gruff version of Yoda. He may not be the Emperor, nor even a Sith Lord or Darth, but he's the keeper of the Force – and in this universe the Force, like charge in Argeral, is everything. Now Yoda's gearing up to speak, rolling his shoulders, grunting, as though inconveniently roused from a deep sleep.

'Before we start with forks,' he croaks, 'perhaps we could establish where this "wind" is coming from.'

It's a fair question. Herzberg has an answer, though:

'It's coming from the *Sidereal*'s prow, and rushing down towards its stern.'

'But how's it moving *down* it? Wouldn't it just sweep the *Sidereal* along *with* it, like a piece of chaff?'

'That isn't the effect we . . .' Herzberg starts – then, self-censoring, tries again: 'Tszvetan is driving against the wind, head-on, engines full blast. He's also using the C-Anchors, which lock on to a coordinate and set the ship's position to that, rather than just relative to . . .'

'Do you even know what solar wind is?' Briar witheringly interrupts.

'Well, sure. It's a . . . it's a discharge,' Herzberg desperately tries to reconstruct the Wikipedia entry he glanced at a month ago, 'a stream of electrons, particles, and so on, discharged by a star when it . . . when it, you know . . .'

Briar cruelly lets the silence ring for a few seconds, before stating, in a casual, almost bored voice:

'It's a plasma-stream released by a sun's upper atmosphere. Its corona. As you say – correctly, if incompletely – a discharge of electrons, protons, alpha particles and other agents that have managed to amass escape velocity. It travels supersonically across the heliosphere until it runs into the termination shock – hitting which, and despite dropping to subsonic speeds, it propagates in front of it a bow wave that wreaks havoc with magnetic fields and gravitational configuration and incoming cosmic rays of any planetary atmospheres unlucky enough to find themselves in its path – indeed, that subjects planets without strong magnetospheres to complete atmospheric stripping.'

'That,' Herzberg jumps back in eagerly, 'is kind of what we're going for: stripping. We want the solar wind from Fidelus to *strip* the *Sidereal*, take it apart. That's why it needs to stay in place: so that the wind can unpick it, right down to its skeleton – and beyond, to nothing.'

Briar ponders this statement for a moment, then, surprisingly and to Herzberg's enormous relief, pronounces:

'That can work. Your ship would have to approach Fidelius . . .'

'Fidelus.'

'. . . would travel through Fidelus's heliosphere, inwards from the heliopause towards the heliosheath, until it nears the termination

266

shock. That's when the wind will hit it. But you have to understand: it isn't just a wind. As I've just intimated, it's a general cosmic fucking with all terms and values: gravity, polarity, attraction, radio-wave intensity, light ...'

'That's even better.' Herzberg's really happy now. 'Exactly what we want.' His hand moves across the desktop to *Incarnation*'s leather-bound, Post-it marker-swollen treatment and rests for a while atop it. It's not there for consultation or for prompting – the whole team know it by now almost by rote – but rather as a prop, a crook, a totem whose mere presence can gird and stabilise all realms, even the ones in which disastrous destabilisations are to play out ...

Tszvetan is indeed driving against the wind, in every sense. At the end of a string of plot-twists no less acrobatic than the MU acrobats performing in them – leaping, still shackled, from the flames licking at his feet from the lit pyre in Kern's *piazzo* on to the pirogue on which his friend and sidekick Govnal, gatecrashing the execution, whisks him away to safety; scything his rapier through scores of horny *leperosi* as he clears a path for, and then plucks from free-fall, Tild; fleeing with her to the Marais wildlands where, befriended by the hermit O. G. Rin, they live, royal clothes worn down to Tarzan-and-Jane strips, as hunter-foragers; then, as Louis Q's DF drones close in on them, making a bid for lasting freedom, re-entering Kern's citadel disguised as (what else?) *leperosi*, breaking into the docking-bay in which the *Sidereal* has been impounded, rapier-scything a few pound guards in the process (Govnal, meanwhile, has spread word among Tszvetan's loyal stokers, who are standing by to reman the vessel – after, naturally, doing a little scything of their own); and, finally, blasting their way (the harbour's tractor beams having been sabotaged by these same stokers) free of Kern's atmosphere, back up past Acephalus, beyond Ardis Minor, out into deep space.

Or, more precisely, towards Fidelus. The crew, preparing to set course for Patagon or maybe Nova Z once they've passed through the Sirin belt, are caught off-guard by Tszvetan's orders to keep bearing straight ahead. Tild, too – but neither she nor they say anything. With each passing diurnal a tacit understanding grows; and with it a complicity, a fatalist conviction, sets in. There's no habitable planet out there: only more asteroid belts, then empty interstellar medium, then, at the end of this, the heliosphere around the massive star. To enter that, to drive on through deple- tion and stagnation regions to the termination shock, can only be a one-way ticket – no one on the *Sidereal*'s in any doubt about that. If they go along with it, if they decline to mutiny or even comment on the starship's ill-boding trajectory, it's because their minds all seem to have coalesced around, been drawn into align- ment by, a single intuition – unarticulated, perhaps inarticulable, but nonetheless as forceful and attractive as the monstrous confla- gration towards which they're hurtling. It's tied in with the whole set-up of their tryst: its history, its circumstances and condition. For Tild, coupling with Tszvetan wasn't simply an *alternative* to being faithful to Louis Q, one possibility or option among others; it was a rejection of *all* options, of all possibilities, the very category – a plunge into the impossible. For Tszvetan, reciprocally, Tild was never just a quarry, Argeralan *radjar* to be hunted down, new entry to be jotted in his amorous kill list. Nor would it be correct to say that his desire for her was simply 'bigger' or 'stronger' than his sense of duty towards Louis Q, than his adherence to conven- tion, his respect for codes of honour and the like. No: it, too, involved a bound beyond all binds and codes and underpinnings; it required the crossing of a threshold past which there exists no stable ground – just void. The void called them, and they came. What new ground, then, what planetary terrain, what minerality of soil and subsoil, could sustain this shadow-coupling, feed this love birthed through, of and into groundlessness? None: only the void might host it. If, on the voyage from Argeral to Kern, they found a habitus in light's delay, amidst the ultraviolet and the infrared of its obstruction, now, once more, it's to the spectrum's break-up, to the ravaging and disentanglement of light itself, of photons separated and expelled, transformed into a material force, to wind, that they will turn to find the non-place of their dwelling, found their kingdom of non-being. After the tenth diurnal they can spy, from the Observatory, diffracted through the viewfinders of astrolabe and spectrohelioscope, the strange flickerings of Fidelus's current sheet, rippling like a ballerina's skirt; then, with naked eye two diurnals later, aurora, swirling ghostly in the star's magnetosphere, celestial will-o'-the-wisps, beckoning ...

The modelling here's complex – even more than for the first seduction scene. Light-waves will need to be not only bounced around but also separated, broken down, unthreaded. That will come later. For now, the DZ crew just need to figure out how the *Sidereal*'s to be stripped. They've started with a gross model – with three, in fact: one digital, CAD, low-spec, the basic form and outline of the vessel; the other two physical, if equally basic, iterations, duplicates each of which has been immersed in its own fluid-mechanical environment. NW have allowed use of their wind tunnel for flow tracing and yaw/roll/pitching-moment measurement, but they flat refused to submit the thing to wind speeds that would actually break it up, since flying parts of a spaceship, even a scaled-down one, would have dented, gnarled and lacerated delicate, expensive honeycombs and vanes (van Boezem's indignant email, sent via Phocan, informed them that they'd 'have to meet all costs for the destruction of not just your spaceship but also our livelihood!'). So, for the full, catastrophic sequence, or at least its gross, undetailed version (analogue), they've stuck with the Germans, who dunked into the *Versuchsanstalt für Wasserbau und Schiffbau*'s Berlin cavitation tank a month or two ago a 1:96 *Sidereal*, VWS being less squeamish about such propositions due to a long history of simulating nautical mishaps, their UT2 containing strong, debris-catching nets affixed downstream of measurement section but up-flow of pump and filter parts. ('The irony,' Eldridge told Herzberg, who tells Briar now, passing the quip off as his own, 'is that, to simulate wind, even when wind's itself a simulation – or, let's say, approximation – you need water.') Eldridge has got sequences from all three of these first, tentative modellings up on the BenQ now, running in multi-screen. In the left-hand-side video, the tank one, broken water-flecks dance furiously round the ship's hull, rising to form lips and wedges as they run across its winglets, landing struts, disruptor banks and stabilisers. The watery medium in which the camera also sits, in tandem with the unabbreviated proprietorial label, *Versuchsanstalt für Wasserbau und Schiffbau*, overlaid across the film's upper-right section, makes Herzberg, every time he watches it, think of U-boats chugging through the depths of the Atlantic. The right-hand-side video, the CAD one, shows an analogous, or rather non-analogue, version of the process taking place in the cavitation tank, pixel-flecks and lips and wedges forming and dispersing, flaring and contracting round the *Sidereal* as they pass it in a stuttered virtual flux from which fury, this time, seems quite absent. In the middle video, the NW one, the wind tunnel's smoke tracer wraps the ship in a fine-mesh cocoon while bubbles bounce and ricochet about its slipstream.

'We've established,' Eldridge says, 'the movement round the vessel's hull. In both the CAD and the water tank we ran the sequence on until it starts to break up, as you'll see. But in a way, that's a red herring. It might give us prompts, suggestions; but our task here's not so much to record the way an actual or simmed vessel broke apart on such-and-such a day, as to decide how *we* want *our* one to do this, in a way that maxes the event's spectacular potentiality *and* is consistent with the flow-parameters enveloping the object – and, of course,' he finds it politic to round off with this small gesture of tribute, 'all the laws of physics that, in turn, envelop those.'

The gesture works. Briar slowly nods assent, but asks:

'How will you decide, when you haven't got all the details there yet? It could be that it's the tiniest piece of a truss segment, EVA rail or radiator panel that gives first – which fragment then tears a small rip in down-hull cowling, which causes depressurisation in the avionics or the storage bays, which ...'

'Ken Pilkington,' says Herzberg, 'thought – he's at the MOD, in aeronautics – that it would most likely be ...'

'Ken Pilkington?' Briar repeats, incredulous. 'How in heaven's ...?'

'He slipped us some advice, through Pantarey ...'

Briar's gaze, for a brief moment, seems to disengage – from them, the screens, the room, the task at hand – and to transfer itself on to some other figure that, like a ghost at a private feast he's hosting, only he can see. Eventually he murmurs:

'If anyone knows about dematerialising aircraft ...'

He doesn't complete the sentence. Herzberg, cautiously, continues:

'He suggested having something towards the front give first: a payload bay door or forward bulkhead ...'

'Pilkington!' Briar whispers – then, realising that the others are all staring at him now, shakes off whatever phantom he's confronting and, authoritative voice restored, informs them:

'Yes: bay door or bulkhead are both possible. But it could equally be near the back, if there's more drag there: say, an aft body flap or stabiliser could pull a whole segment of fuselage off with it as it ...'

'We like front best,' Herzberg tells him. 'That way, you can see the event-chain progressing down the vessel, both structurally and dramatically: people racing around as the damage spreads, trying to batten down communicating hatches, seal the airlock modules and so on ...'

'Yes – but for that, surely, you need details.'

'To a degree. You just have to be Jesuit about it. What happens if we start by making this communication mast snap off and plough on through the solar sail, then having sections of the engine blow? You start the run that takes the ship apart from there, or there, or *there* – just "peel" a bit back, let the computer do the rest. But you do this in gross, not fine. You don't need every ventilator duct and odour-filter canister factored into the model at this point. That would take months to work out, even with the procs we've got. You only need to fake a bit of detail – which is where our fork comes in. So, here, we've primed up three scenarios ...'

Charlie, who like a faithful stoker has been waiting for this moment, pulls up now on the BenQ the first of these. It depicts, as intimated, a front-to-rear event-chain of destruction: nose sensor, gyrodynes, elevons, correction engines, thrusters peeling off the simulated model one by one, colliding with each other and the hull.

'We've put seams through the structure,' Eldridge explains, 'and assigned each surface properties: tensile strength, brittleness, elasticity, and so forth. Just to get an idea ...'

'Doesn't look very realistic,' Briar says.

'Well, not yet. There's no part-sim in it at this stage, and ...'

'Part-sim?'

'No particle simulation: smoke, metal confetti, things that go *pow* and *pouf*, like dust from beaten rugs. And, of course, no light. Those come in at the render stage. Now, here's Scenario Two ...'

This one, not wildly different, starts by unpicking a thin telemetry, or perhaps approach and rendezvous, antenna from the *Sidereal*'s upper fuselage; the antenna then embeds itself, like a knife thrower's decorated blade, in the ship's starboard solar panel, which begins to shred, decompositing itself as its shards rush on downwind. The third scenario begins with the same initial detachment, only this time the antenna, like a twig being fed into a shredder, finds its way into the port-side engine, which explodes, not only ripping out whole segments of the cargo bay and armoury but also sending what's left of the ship careening sideways, fishtailing as it tries to right itself.

'The great thing with Houdini,' the screenward-facing Charlie tells them, 'is that it knows the wind's not constant: you can factor in the gyre and gimble. And the spaceship will correct as it gets buffeted – which, in turn, informs what part it exposes and, by extension, what might go wrong next.'

Briar nods more, acquiescent if not humbled.

'Of course,' Herzberg jumps back in, 'we won't show the whole thing. Just some moments from its progression, to narrate its timeline – the best bits. With wide-shots, you don't need to get all details right – on close-ups, though, you do. That's where physical modelling's useful: showing how a screw works its way loose, or how cracks spread across a heat-tile ...'

'There we can take cues,' Eldridge adds, 'from the cavitation tank, and feed them into the simulation.'

'Where's this extra sail appearing from?' asks Briar as, on Charlie's screen, a new wing flickers into view out of abyssal darkness and adapts itself spectrally to the span of the first one which is listing down to meet it.

'Glitches,' Charlie answers.

'We'll catch them all in rendering too,' says Eldridge. 'We'll have wranglers round the clock, twenty-four/seven.'

Now the scenario's gone interior: we've got fire extinguishers, pneumatic panels, contents of medicine chests all drifting loose inside the module – plus, again, the fork. Herzberg, sensing a kind of truce with Briar, starts telling him a story.

'There was once, a few years back – not here at Degree Zero but at one of our competitors, in London perhaps, or perhaps it was in the US, I can't remember – a man named Decebal Călugăreanu.'

Eldridge, Charlie and all the others smile; they know the story. Briar nods again, awaiting the next part.

'Călugăreanu,' Herzberg continues, 'was Romanian, a whizz-kid coder, brought in by this post-prod company for a specific purpose: plotting the passage of an object (a royal sceptre or magic crystal or Moses basket or something along those lines) down a stream, a strait of quick-flowing water in a scene in some big-budget fantasy or other ...'

The day (so the story goes) Călugăreanu arrived in London/LA/Wherever, the FX department's head – Herzberg's counterpart – introduced him by rolling his eyes and saying 'I'm not even going to *try* to pronounce this guy's name ...' The staffers looked at their feet awkwardly, embarrassed by their boss's xenophobic boorishness; over the next day or two, they learnt to pronounce the name without much problem. It's not that hard: Decebal, like *decibel*; Călugăreanu, like the Sardinian city. The dept head never learnt it, though – for the next few weeks he kept the eye-roll up, called Călugăreanu *D.C.* each time he addressed him, and so on. Călugăreanu, meanwhile, set about plotting the sceptre/crystal/Moses basket's passage downstream. Let's imagine that the sequence was to run for about twenty seconds: it's a matter of defining a trajectory that's both dramatic and consistent with the givens – water flows at such-and-such a pace, rocks here and here, object dropped here …

'Like Poohsticks,' Briar says.

'Exactly,' Herzberg concurs. 'Same as what we're doing: fluid simulation. With rapids, or with wind, a thousand micro-factors come into effect with every frame. The better the simulator, the better you can calculate where the thing is in twenty seconds; and the better you can do that, the better your water will look. So Călugăreanu gets to work. He works alone. He's a hard worker: always at his desk, first in, last out. In fact, he's never out. They find him in the office every morning, punching the keys, clearly not having slept all night. The weird thing is …'

The weird thing was, he never invoiced for his overtime. The FX dept head would prompt him, ungraciously, calling across the floor *Hey, D.C., don't you guys* want *to be paid?* 'You guys' perhaps being coders, or Romanians, or just people with non-waspy names. Călugăreanu would just smile back quietly. He knew why he wasn't invoicing for the night-time labour. A day or so into his coding, the thought had struck him that, if he could work out where a sceptre/staff/Moses basket will be in twenty seconds in a river, he could also work out where pork-belly futures will be in the morning on the Chinese Stock Exchange, and spent his nights building an algo to do just that. On the day before he signed off on his Poohstick task, he sold his algo to Salomon Smith Barney for 500,000,000 dollars. It was all over the feeds; the staffers cheered him to the door. But Călugăreanu wasn't quite done: on his way out, he paid a quick last call on the dept head, and made him an offer: if he, the head, could say his, Călugăreanu's, name, right now, then he, Călugăreanu again, would pay him, head, ten million pounds/dollars/euros – instant transfer, on the spot.

'The guy actually tried,' Herzberg rounds off the anecdote. '*Cala-gear-something … no, Kalloogerena … Calarea …*'

'*Supercalifragilistic …*' Charlie joins in.

Even Briar is smiling. There's a coda to the story, though.

'The really interesting bit about it all,' Herzberg in full-on lecturer mode, authority restored now, adds reflectively, 'is that Salomon Smith Barney only got three or so months' use out of Călugăreanu's algorithm. Which was fine – they made their 500,000,000 back several times over. But it turned out to be so good that it influenced the entire pork-belly future-trading system. It became *part of* the system, its macro-machinery – like a lock, a weir …'

His gaze, and Briar's, turn back to the BenQ. The model videos are playing again now, snips from further down the files. In the Berlin cavitation-tank one, angry lips and wedges have now prised struts loose, caused stabilisers to hang off like broken wings, the hull to flap autocorrectively from side to side – which, in turn, hastens its destruction. Below this, the CAD simulation runs through the same scene disinterestedly, flecks moving without rancour or intent around the shredding ship. The wind-tunnel footage, as before, shows a smoke-swaddled *Sidereal*, cradled by the flows that hold destruction, and it, in abeyance. Inside the vessel, similarly passive, Tild and Tszvetan stand amidst untethered medicine boxes, fire extinguishers and fork tines, awaiting their consumption, their apotheosis.

3. Jamalac Scoop

Gloucestershire in September: willowherb drooping and flaking in weak sun against the wall, meadowsweet's last flowering in the ditch, cut grass composting in the pile, and Thérèse sleeping. Now she sleeps more than she doesn't. At some point in the summer it flipped over; he didn't record it then, nor could he put his finger, now, on the precise week, let alone day, on which it happened – but a tipping point has been reached, passed, left behind, and sleeping has become her main state, her default mode. Doctors are hopelessly reluctant to commit, endlessly pussyfoot around his questions, no matter how circuitously phrased (*How might we begin to plot ... ? In terms of temporal parameters ... So what type of trajectory ... ? ... timeline from here on in ... ?*) – but the chatrooms, the support groups seem to give her three to six months. Speech is going; so is taste; smell's gone already. She doesn't admit it, but she's seeing and hearing things, hallucinations: he can tell that from the way her eyes, last part of her that's still alert and active, fix on the empty space above his head, or on a spot of wall beside the door-jamb, then dart off again towards an edge of cornicing or stretch of carpet and hover there, fiercely attentive, by turns frightened, bewildered and enchanted. What are they saying to her? What magic lantern shows is she being treated to? They've upped her Levodopa levels, to deal with the cramps and neuralgia, but her dopaminergic transmission is degenerating, and toxicity is setting in. Incontinence, too. Human tolerance finds its own boundaries, its limits: illness is a way of tracing, rubbing and redrawing these, over and over, an endless experiment, blueprint drafted on the body's foolscap ...

Pilkington's in his study, and he's got it out again: his secret ledger, laurel wreath that brings with it no public office, manifesto that no joyous crowds will ever hold aloft, Red Book destined to remain unread. Strangely, his anxious dreams nowadays concern it, and Albatross, as much as her. The two scenes seem to have merged together: it's her arm, her shoulder, or the casters of her wheelchair that he's trying to steer round, realign with target cen-treline, guide safely to their landing corridor, their kiss-spot on the sand. *RLOS*: the acronym's scrawled on the page open in front of him, above a sketch showing the signal-command chain he set up to lead the 720 from Diego Garcia to Septentrion. Radio line of sight: a terrestrial-oceanic network, simple as Ancient Greek bea-con towers or games of pass-the-parcel, with each post receiving from the last one temporary jurisdiction over the plane, giving it a little airborne left-and-right to check the telemetry, keep the old thing responsive, then handing it onwards to the next one. There they are, each station's sign: *DG, LV Siren, RPS Sept* ... the letters float about the page, reanimating for him metal pylons rising from cement set into sand, or from the deck of the light vessel bobbing just beyond the fourteenth parallel, the *Siren*. The mast beside the landing strip, beside home base, Ground Zero, was a triangular guyed lattice, red and white, with tensioned steel cables set at various angles, Lilliputian bindings pinning it down to the beach. Beneath it, the green tents; the generators; the recording vans; the instrument stations of Marconi, BA and the rest, arrayed in complex subdivisions like a desert sheik's encampment ...

And, between all these, orienting their scatter, attracting them around it like so many shavings round a magnetised lead bar, the landing strip, evacuated main street of a western town awaiting its high noon. With static cameras planted all about so as to cover every angle, to provide shot-reverse-shot capacity for each phase, each moment of the action, the beach reminded Pilkington (who'd never seen one but held in his mind the same popular image of them as everyone else) of movie sets. And the plane heading towards it … that, too, was like a film set: less protagonist than mobile studio, equipped with its own cameras and mikes, lead players, extras, props, all bound by their adherence to a script whose first draft was – is – written down right here; whose final typescript, shooting version, had been photostatted and distributed in various modified, partial forms, like an orchestral score adapted to each instrument. Turning the page, he finds, spread out across the next two, a block diagram of the data acquisition system: Time Code Generator (IRIG A) feeding Tape Recorders #1 and #2, Camera (IRIG B) and Syst 1 PCM, which last box is also fed into by Signal Conditioner and in its turn feeds two more Tape Recorders, #3 and #4, Delay Memory and S-band … The arrow-headed flow lines bi- and trifurcate as they run left to right, verso to recto, kink as they dip into the notebook's central gutter. The plane, too, was meant to slide across the boundary between each control zone, pass eventually the margin separating sea from land, and hurtle in, an arrow to its mark, transducing multi-channelled secrets to the giant IBM housed in Dashell's and Sir Ronald's tent, the largest, greenest, shadiest one: master converter that would process all the multiplexing input cards' sequential data, filter and sample and make legible once more – to them, to him, the world and all posterity – the millions of words hurtling their way, 8 bits at 129 per frame, across the great unworded silence, the blank space.

Outside the study, a small gust draws from the meadowsweets white spray eruptions, puffs that hang about the air like smoke when canons have been fired. Above them, birch trees rustle and shed leaves. First breath of winter, of a future with no Thérèse in it. On the first of April 1984, a light breeze skimmed Septentrion, fuzzing the atoll's sand. Beaufort would have ranked it 2: the vane beside the landing strip was stirred but not priapic; wavelets on the sea were glassy but not broken. By quarter past nine, everyone was at their posts, although there were still two hours to go until the kiss-down; mood was busy but informal, people calmly and good-humouredly getting on with what they had to do, zapping about by jeep and foot, or radioing from one station to another, or, when stations were adjacent, just calling across: *Hey, fool, get your ass over here ...*

The beers, at such an early hour on this day of all days, were confined to their fridge-barracks, cooling beside champagne bottles that they'd had to bribe (with other champagne bottles) Diego's quartermaster to enter in the manifest as 'technical hardware'; but ice creams were out in force. No one in the command chain had objected: they kept the men cool, and happy; Dashell was himself partial to them. Anderson, some time in February, had started experimenting: now, beside the pre-fab chocolate and vanilla, there were mango and papaya, coconut and litchi, guava, starfruit and jamalac on the menu, scooped out of a Gaggia gelatiera (inventoried as 'counter-antifreeze device') that, like a commercial airliner with instant turnaround, was kept in non-stop operation. *Albatross Ice Cream*, Anderson called it; *Comes in seven deadly flavours ...* Pilkington, like most of the other senior personnel, had a scoop in front of him more often than not: working his way through the sins, sloth to envy, litchi to guava, one at a time, held in a small glass beside his console, although not for long; in these temperatures, you had to polish them off quickly. Today, he was downing more than normal – out of nervousness, perhaps, or perhaps because he garnered comfort, reassurance even, not so much from the ice creams' taste as from their form. With an old Japanese Nevco serving spoon on the inner cranium of whose aluminium scoop-head flaking blue paint had produced a surface that resembled, it struck Pilkington, that of the atoll-flecked Indian Ocean if viewed in gnomonic projection from on high, the Marconi man, like a cosmic magician pulling newly formed planets from his hat, managed to turn out compact globes of coloured coldness that, time after time, came up impeccably, exquisitely spherical. Pilkington must have gone back for a new serving every half-hour, small rewards to help him tick off each task: copying the pre-fires, clearing the frequencies with each guidance station, checking flight-path coordinates yet once more

... In the last stretch, the final minutes just before Hour Zero, it was a jamalac scoop that stood in front of him – most exotic of all the flavours: wax apple, *syzygium samarangense*, white with a pink blush. Beyond this scoop, his radar screen, gridded, green and empty; beside these, the book.

At two minutes past eleven, on Diego Garcia, the Boeing took off. Twenty-one and a half minutes later, it was handed over to the *Siren*. In another twenty-three, it would come within range of Septentrion. Pilkington was to bring it down himself. Any of his team could probably have done it, but the final approach seemed, from a symbolic point of view, consistent with the rites and pro-tocols of nautical tradition, to demand his individual pilotage, his personal conveyance. *Kubernetes*: he'd plotted its route and relay; he would carry this Olympic torch through its last few steps, sink it in the bowl, the cauldron of its final conflagration. On the landing strip, the heavy steel wing-opening blocks gazed seawards, impassive as Easter Island statues. On his screen, the plan-position indicator's radial trace swept its way round the grid's concentric circles, drawing swathes and segments out into an afterglow that faded and returned with each new sweep. At 11:45:32 he glanced at the scoop: it needed eating, but he didn't dare divert his hand, his eye, one jot of his attention from the console on which, from one instant to the next, a new dot would appear, and grow into an outlined shape: wingspanned, an albatross, his very own one, coming home to roost ...

'Hey Pilko!' Anderson hailed him from the Marconi tent. 'Turning up fashionably late. Is that an English thing?'

They were a little past handover time: forty-five seconds ... now a minute ... now two ... Pilkington felt, for the first time since coming here, effect even the ice cream never gave him, a chill spreading outwards from his skull, down the back of his neck. He radioed to LV *Siren*, who said the plane had left their zone four minutes ago.

'But you can see it on your radar still?'

'Negative that.'

'Then why can't we?'

In the loud silence riding the waves back to him, he heard fear massing, finding its inchoate frequency. His walkie-talkie buzzed: it was Sir Ronald, 'checking in', voice calm and measured, deep bass over which Dashell's more dramatic baritone soon cut in:

'Where's our fucking airplane?'

On Pilkington's second monitor, a message appeared: *Integrity Event.* Could mean just about anything: antenna obscuration, interference, doppler shift, clock error, or some kind of drift ... They were using extended Kalman filter; nowadays, it would have been unscented, with all arbitrary non-linear functions replaced by derivative-free higher-order approximations and their Gaussian distributions, sigma points furnishing state vectors and uncertainties, all propagated via state transition model. The drones at Farnborough have IMUs and built-in geodetic systems, little onboard globes with their own prime meridians and tropics ... That's now, though; this was then. A big remote control, just like Sir Ronald had said. On his main monitor, the radial trace continued sweeping, drawing into luminescence the plane's absence, the grid's emptiness. In front of it, the scoop was melting: sagging, crumpling, sloughing off its symmetry. Out on the runway, slicers stood brutal in their unusedness. Over the next few minutes, hours and days, they, like the pylon and the generators, like the vehicles and the tents, would transform themselves in his eyes, without actually changing their form or appearance, from idols issuing exultant summons to their god, a living deity who any second now would manifest himself, into mute testaments to their, or to the world's, abandonment. It was the physics, though, not metaphysics, that would imprint itself on and stay with him. Not the advanced aerodynamics of forces and moments, of wind axes and velocity, of drag and side-force coefficients; but the simple physics, so child-simple it was colour-coded, of the radar screen's vacant web (green), the sky's undotted upper plane (blue) and the beach's undisturbed lower one (white), all arranged around this pink-blush sphere that was dissolving, and dissolving with it all the other shapes too, running them into a flat, continuous surface on which nothing was and always would be taking place.

There was an inquiry, of course. It took two years; and, like Albatross itself, it kind of fizzled out. It was in no one's interest to bruit the affair about. All documents and drives, all screeds and scripts and transcripts touching on, feeding into or output by each phase of the operation were commandeered. His own station, every monitor and floppy disc of it, was impounded; the red notebook, though, remained, like the 720, off-radar. Hiding in the light, perhaps: everyone had grown so used to seeing him clasping it that it had become, for them, a part of him, not of the project, like a pair of glasses hanging by a strap around a person's neck, a wallet in their hand – or, in previous centuries, a monocle or ladies' fan. Irony of all ironies: the inquiry reproduced the fatal error of its subject of interrogation, as though ritually replaying, in a blind spot, its own blind spot. They pored over the printouts, looked at the transmitting hardware, at the sampling rates, the signal-to-noise ratios, the onboard sensor-switching frameworks … They checked and rechecked the flight-path coordinates, tracing the chain of copies and transferrals all the way back to the first typed pages. But the error, as he could have told them right from the beginning, from Hour Zero – *April Fool!* – wasn't in the reproduction from one typescript to another: it was there *ab ovo*, in the first ever typing-up. On the lined Sylvine pages, for coordinate conversion, geodetic to ECEF, he'd used Newton-Raphson iteration to determine the meridian arcs that, in their turn, specified the reference ellipsoid. For the third flattening, he'd gone with Bessel-Helmert series; for the evaluation, Clenshaw summation. Typing his cipher out for distribution by the project's secretariat, he'd substituted, for convenience, Jacobi ellipsoidals – which substitution, he'd presumed, would be self-evident to everyone, all down the chain. It wasn't. He'd seen that within two minutes of the plane's disappearance, or (more correctly stated) of its failure to appear, and understood immediately what had happened. The numbers and equations that had been uploaded might, on their own terms, have been completely sound; but between the *Siren* and Septentrion, they'd lost traction – on the stations and the masts, on one another, on the territory they were traversing – and, cut loose from their fixed moorings, embarked on a frenzy of auto-conversion that had rapidly transformed the onboard navigation system into a random event space. Like a dice roll. He *had* given them a crash, after all: a pure, numeric crash, so perfect it negated any external enactment. Within two and a half minutes, he'd also understood that this sequence of causation would never, in the absence of the notebook (whose scrawled cipher was, in any case, illegible) be traced back to him.

They never found the plane. Two spotters, an RAF Poseidon and a US Navy Orion, flew around, first north, then south of the four-teenth for a week, scouring the sea for wreckage; for a week after that they extended their search westwards, to Mauritius and the Seychelles; for a third week, eastwards, towards Cocos, Christmas Island and Jakarta. Then they gave up. Amidst all the tech, the hardware, all the data acquisition tools, no one had ever thought of installing a black box. Why would they? In the 'normal' run of things, if the experiment had gone to plan, it would have been superfluous: the whole plane was a giant flight recorder. Possibly, years later, parts washed up on beaches – in Oman, or Pakistan, Australia, Holland, Norway, who knows where: a fragment of tail section or a tape machine head, an accelerometer's dial, the arm or pelvis of an instrumented dummy ... Would these scraps have found their way into a database, been locked on by and steered to the restricted section, laid to rest, in name at least, in some memorial archive? Or would they just have been prodded by child combers, like lumps of jellyfish and mermaid's purses, plastic bottles, hunks of styrofoam and all the other spawn of cargo-spillage, sea-dumping and general world-discharge, draincocks and drowned dolls, bath ducks and deformed squishies, curtain hooks, door hinges, dehumidifier grilles and baking moulds, ball valves and parts degraded beyond thresholds of their name, the host of things released from purpose-contract to meander pointlessly from zone to zone? He wouldn't have known one way or another; he was well out of the loop. He pictured the plane, though, over the months and years that followed, as having found a kind of berth, a gate slot, somewhere, in some spot for which no geodetic data point existed: an aporia, blind alley, cubby-hole or nook ... He still does now: he sees it, sometimes on the ground, at rest, and sometimes flying, still, after all these years, a white bird gliding in a parallel and empty sky, above a darkening flood.

4. *Assassiyun*

On his first morning in the dacha, Lazda takes Phocan on a trip to the Jumelans store, to help her with some shopping. It's a ten-minute drive. Old wooden houses alternate with woods for the first stretch; then, as they near the town, new-builds pop up, great mansions lurking behind walls and electronic gates.

'A Russian oligarch,' says Lazda as an icing-sugar-pink palace slides by, its cameras eyeing their little car suspiciously. 'And that one,' she continues, pointing to a mock-Arabian confection on the road's far side, 'belongs to a pop star.'

Past these two, in a giant, dilapidated compound, a five-storey structure set on stilts, with terraces and balconies and long rows of tall windows half of which are broken, wrestles with the trees that have pushed into it, or even in some case grown inside it, their roots finding sustenance and purchase in cracked concrete and exposed iron beams.

'This,' Lazda tells him, 'was a hotel for well-behaved Soviet workers. Only the good ones, party members, were allowed to holiday in Latvia. The rest had to go inland, away from the border. And this one,' she slows the car down as they pass another gutted behemoth, 'was an institute for Soviet chemists ...'

On the way back, they detour to the beach. Phocan thinks he recognises the small factory they passed en route to the house yesterday, the derelict one whose brickwork shrubs and creepers are reclaiming. He's right.

'It's the old *stikla fabrika* – the glassworks,' she says. 'It closed in the mid-eighties, before I was born. Here we are.'

They've come to the end of a narrow, overgrown track whose mud has given way to sand. Beyond it, unkempt marram grass dotted with more brick foundations, these ones crumbled right down to ground level, leads on to a beach whose sand looks large and smooth, almost transparent. The shoreline, hemmed by a long fringe of this marram grass on one side and black kelp and sea-wrack on the other, broken only by a little inlet thirty or so yards to the north of them, runs in a thin strip for several miles in each direction before jutting, to the south, the Riga Gulf side, in a point on which a lighthouse stands and, to the north, the open Baltic side, in what looks like a military installation or perhaps observatory, an array of satellite dishes and domed roofs silhouetted against the pale sky.

'A listening station,' Lazda says, seeing him peering out towards the latter. 'This area was full of them. They were all decommissioned in the nineties – now, though, they're up and running again.'

'You must have come here as a child, to swim,' says Phocan.

'I did, but not my parents or my grandparents. It was forbidden. A good swimmer could get to Sweden from here, if the water wasn't too rough. Along the entire Baltic coast, they kept the sand completely smooth, with brushes pulled by tractors, so that they could see if anyone had tried to cross it.'

Phocan squints towards the horizon, trying to make out some kind of bump or jag that might be Sweden, but can't pick out anything beyond the normal sine-wave of the sea's background frequency. When he looks back again, Lazda's vaporised, collapsed into an empty jacket, shirt and pair of jeans lying at his feet. He picks her up again ten yards away, racing in underwear towards the water. September; fuck it; why not? He strips down to his pants too, streaks along her fugitive print-trail, past kelp margin and wavelets, on into a sea no Gulf Stream current seems to have warmed up. She's a good swimmer; by the time he's caught up with her she's carved a big loop out beyond the surf line, parallel with the shore and back in again, plus run up and down the beach a few times to dry off.

'You won't,' she tells him as he crumples to the strangely vitreous ground beside their clothes, 'catch anything at that speed.'

Re-entering the car, before she starts the engine up again, she pulls a headband from her jacket pocket and slips it on, to keep her wet fringe from her eyes. Phocan, shocked by the cold and the exertion, undergoes a moment's dislocation; slunk down into the passenger seat's faux-leather, he forgets where he is, what he's doing, what year it is. He might even doze for few seconds on the way back to the house; he's not sure. Images of Lazda, her parents and her grandparents, of Lazda *as* her own mother or grandmother, head covered in a handkerchief or headband similar to the one she's wearing now, face turned away towards the sea, the whole thing greyscaled like in old home movies, telescope away once more along vague avenues of memory, or of forgetting, merge with other memories perhaps his own, or perhaps not, flicker and fade into and out of focus with the houses new and ruined, institutions, wooden shacks all flashing intermittently through a rainbow-veil of autumn foliage. By the time his circulation has restored itself, his consciousness re-found its bearings, they're gliding down the almost-intersecting tracks once more, then, passing the abandoned playground, pulling back into the garden, with the light-blue dacha looming above them to the left, aviary to the right, cubistic tree-house at the far end beyond the vegetables.

'He'll be in his study,' Lazda says as they carry the supplies into the kitchen. 'You can go there.'

Vanins is indeed in his study. It's housed in the low-lying extension to the main house. Phocan knocks, and is called in. On a worktable are laid out several box files and bound manuscripts.

'I've dug up some papers,' Vanins informs him. 'Some of my work touching on states of equilibrium. You're welcome to consult them.'

For the next two hours, Phocan does so. They're not wildly different from the ones the archivist found for him at Tehniskā Universitāte. There's an article on Hamiltonian vs. Langrangian formulations; another on fictitious forces, non-inertial reference frames, the implications of the Coriolis effect for aerodynamic engineering ... There are some lecture notes – in Latvian and Russian, but the diagrams and mathematical notation he can follow. From time to time, he looks up from them, out of the window just above the worktable. Through its panes, which have irregular consistencies, as though they'd come from different glaziers, he can see the stretch of garden lying between the vegetable patch and his misshapen treehouse. There's a well that seems to still be in use, since it has a rope-coiled winch and bucket; next to this, a tree stump with an axe lying on it; behind this, a stack of chopped-up firewood about which small birds, presumably not Vanins' but wild ones, hop and dart before retreating back into the furze of spruce trees that delineate a smudgy, incremental border between the property and the surrounding woods, which are made up of larger trees that Phocan can't identify.

'Aspens,' Vanins tells him when he asks. 'They're general around here. For paper. You'll have seen paper mills dotted around the countryside on your way out of Riga. Have you found,' he continues, 'what you're looking for?'

Phocan hesitates before answering. Vanins is looking at him fixedly. He ventures tentatively:

'There was something I saw back in Riga, in Tehniskā's archive, that I didn't quite understand ...'

'Go on,' Vanins coaxes.

'It involved,' Phocan continues, 'a small note you'd made, beneath a chart ... dynamic properties of such-and-such an aircraft ... I saw you'd drawn,' he tries to keep his breathing steady, to suppress the tremor in his voice, 'the figure *808* ...'

Another roadblock? There's no measurable pause, no slowing of the pace, but still there seems to be a kind of a glitch or stutter in the passage of the words, the information, through the air.

'Maybe I had,' says Vanins. 'What of that?'

Phocan has thought through, both in dialogue with Garnett and alone, various scenarios, ways a putative conversation on this topic might go, the kinks and switchbacks down which it might cut its path. This one hasn't been modelled, though. It seems as though Vanins is challenging him, inviting him almost: *Go on, ask me for it* ... Or is this openness a kind of judo move, a going-with-the-flow, to let his opponent's force expend itself, draw him off-balance? It's too late for Phocan to pull back; before he's even scripted the words in his head, he finds himself saying:

'You knew Lillian Gilbreth ...'

Vanins looks up, towards the window and the garden, before answering:

'We met only once, in Zürich.'

'But you corresponded.'

Vanins pauses again, then answers:

'You are not the first to have enquired about this recently. And I suspect you will not be the last. What is it in my correspondence with Mrs Gilbreth that appears so important, now, for all of you?'

Phocan steels himself, lunges in further:

'She seems to have grown excited about some of the research that you were conducting around 1969, '70 ... Something you both refer to as "the T.T. episode" ...'

Vanins lets him run on, waiting to see how far he'll go. It's as he feared; the tactic works – before he knows it he's completely lost his balance, hears himself blurting out:

'Then there's the mention of a wireframe motion model, one you made yourself after her method. I think it might even have been assigned a number in her own cataloguing system – you know: *Box 128, Box 275*, and so on ...'

Now Vanins has him trapped, arm-locked: despite his slightness, the old man seems to tower above him, to demand submission as he asks:

'And if this box existed, what would it change?'

Phocan returns the only answer he can think of:

'Everything, apparently.'

Is this capitulation, or a counter-punch? Does this all-but-straight citation of the diary entry manage to wrest some of Gilbreth's authority, to tap into it, enlist it? It's having some effect: Vanins seems to be stepping off him now. After a while he asks Phocan, more gently:

'Do you believe this?'

'Did you?' Phocan asks back.

Now Vanins really eases off, withdrawing into himself, lost in thought. Eventually he says:

'We believed a lot of things. In this respect, we Soviet scientists were like *assassiyun.*'

'Like what?' asks Phocan.

'*Assassiyun*. Assassins,' Vanins answers. 'The young men of Arabia who joined the Old Man of the Mountain's cult, after they'd been lured up to his hideout, drugged and woken in a garden where wine gushed from fountains, music spilled about the air, and maidens, nymphs, attended to their every need.'

'I don't quite follow ...' Phocan says.

'The young men,' Vanins runs on, 'thought that it was paradise, entry to which only the Old Man could guarantee; and so they joined his cult, became assassins. But it was all fake: a stage-set, levers pumping wine and sound-tubes piping music from an unseen chamber. The *assassiyun* themselves would have been operating it: last year's recruits, the year before's ...'

'The same ones,' Phocan plays along, although he still can't see where this digression's heading, 'who'd been tricked by the illusion previously?'

'Exactly,' Vanins nods. 'Why would they do this? Once they'd seen how it all worked, how *they*'d been fooled, why didn't they turn on their deceptive master and denounce the whole arrangement?'

'Maybe,' Phocan tries, 'the stage-set operators got a kind of upgrade: better perks, more wine, regular access to the nymphs ...'

'That,' concedes Vanins, 'would be an explanation – a cynical one, though. And besides, an "upgrade" is small compensation for the loss of paradise. No: I like to think that at some level, on some scale, they must have carried on believing *something*. That, even if the larger story wasn't true, they saw it as a useful fiction, that enabled something else to operate: something good and necessary – something even miraculous, perhaps ...'

He looks out at the garden again for a while before continuing:

'The Soviet era was a good one for scientists – those of my generation, at least, who weren't threatened with imprisonment. We, too, believed in something. Not the Revolution, nor the truth of Lenin's vision, nor whichever five- or ten-year plan we were engrossed in: it was something bigger and more abstract. Maybe it was the orchestration itself, its implicit promise that society, the world, could operate as one giant apparatus – that this apparatus, this intricate machinery, could transform experience and knowledge, elevate them to a higher state ...'

'... *remade as an unbound potentiality,*' Phocan quotes.

Vanins starts, surprised.

'I see you've done your homework.'

He's quiet again for a while, as though running the old article's phrases through his mind. Then, slapping its remembered pages shut, he tells Phocan:

'You're too late, though. All that was a long time ago. Whatever elevation, transformation ... whatever "miracle" we thought we might be bringing about – that has evaporated now. Like fountains when their pumps have been shut down once and for all.'

He turns his hands out, palms up, as though to come clean about their emptiness, his generation's bankruptcy, and adds:

'Everyone stopped believing, and the apparatus ran itself down. By the end the only question was what bits of the machinery the operators, or their supervisors, could steal ...'

The two men stand in silence by the desk, beneath the window. Then Vanins asks:

'What do you believe in, Dr Phocan?'

Phocan answers without hesitating:

'Geometry.'

Vanins, scrutinising him with a mixture of interest and something approaching affection, repeats:

'Geometry?'

Phocan nods.

'Same as Mrs Gilbreth.' Vanins smiles approvingly. 'You may stay tonight as well, if you wish.'

In the afternoon, while Vanins siestas, Lazda takes Phocan to the aviary. She trots on ahead of him, ducking behind bird boxes and plants, then reappearing in another spot off to the side, behind him or further ahead still, as though she knew a set of worm-hole shortcuts linking disparate parts of the space together. It becomes a kind of game, a hide-and-seek or catch-me-if-you-can, just like the morning's beach chase. This time, he catches up with her beside a sofa set into a little nook surrounded on all sides by leaves.

'Did you find what you're looking for?' she asks.

'He's reticent,' he says, thinking that she's referring to his research-note quest, or, since all pretence otherwise seems to be collapsing, directly to Box 808, the T.T. episode ... His answer makes her laugh – either because that's not what she meant or perhaps because it *was*, but not what he was meant to understand, or to acknowledge having understood, or ... The sense of disloca- tion's coming on again. This time, when he reorients himself, she's got her arms around his neck; they're kissing, sinking to the floor, the beach, the sofa, and the clothes are crumpling in a pile again, underwear this time joining them. Afterwards, they both briefly nap. The aviary's birdsong infiltrates his dozing; in his dream, the twills and chirps are voiceovers laid down by commentators, or accusatory statements made by prosecutors, at a trial, or in a newspaper report, or a similar kind of post-hoc assessment that, through some quirk of anachronism, is being applied even as the scene that it assesses is playing out. The sound of a buzzsaw wakes them: aspens being cut down, perhaps, for paper in the woods nearby, or maybe just a neighbour chopping logs. Sunlight's streaming through the windows; the birds dart around it, vanishing into their boxes, perching on the white-streaked tops and ledges to peck seeds and chirp more.

'How come,' Phocan asks her, tracing with his index finger the outline of a birthmark on her back, 'it's you taking care of him?'

'My parents,' she tells him without turning round, 'both died when I was young. He and my grandmother raised me.'

'And when did she ... ?'

'In 2001. Since then it's just me.'

This last reflection seems to snap her back into the present. She swivels to her feet and says:

'We should get dressed; he'll be up soon.'

At dinner, Vanins seems sombre. Does he know what they've been up to while he was asleep? Over small glasses of black-balsam liquor, he reminisces about Jumelans neighbours; he and Lazda speculate as to which of these were KGB-conscripted; together they decry the lot of academia in Riga, the state of its libraries and halls of residence ...

'The Tehniskā's archive building, when I visited,' says Phocan, 'seemed quite empty.'

'Everyone's left,' says Vanins. 'Or they're leaving.'

Lazda collects the plates and carries them through to the kitchen. When she's gone Vanins leans close to Phocan and murmurs:

'You could take her with you.'

'To Riga, you mean? When I go back? Are you happy for me to stay just a little ... ?'

'You won't find it,' Vanins cuts him off.

'Won't find ... ?'

'It,' Vanins repeats. 'There's nothing.'

'I don't ...'

'Equilibrium ... suspension ... stasis ... all of that. It's just bodies, in space ...'

His words trail off and he sits quite still, looking ancient, voided, shrunken, hands folded in front of him in mortuary style. Then he adds, as an afterthought:

'And geometry has its assassins too.'

Phocan's about to ask him, again, what he means; but Lazda comes back in bearing a *cidonija* pie, and Vanins leans back and looks away from Phocan, placing their last exchange under embargo. He retires to bed soon afterwards. Lazda and Phocan spend the night together in the treehouse. She speaks Latvian to him as they make love – small words and phrases here and there for which he doesn't request a translation; they seem kind and happy. They sleep for an hour or so just before dawn, then set out early on another outing to the little general store in Jumelans.

'A third dinner,' she says, 'then I'll drive you back to Riga. I go there tonight as well. You can stay with me if you like, in my flat.'

They stop by the beach again. It's colder than yesterday: the sun is gone; the autumn's pressing in. Chasing her out past the kelp- and surf-lines once more, he wonders if she'd come to London with him. Is that what Vanins meant? Maybe he'll try to press him in his study, if he's welcomed there again when they get back; or over dinner – revisit his mutterings, unpack them, see if they can be rearranged into some kind of sense. Stasis, suspension; waves and sand ... He catches Lazda sooner today; maybe she's letting him; this time they warm up one another, looking out towards a Sweden that's still un-discernible, although the water's calmer, blacker ...

There'll be no third dinner. Turning off the ditch-lined track into the garden this time, they observe, first little sign that something's out of place, two plovers and a sandpiper idling about the lawn; then, that the door to the aviary is open – not unlatched or ajar, but agape. Birds of all kinds are spilling from it freely. Lazda, whose sudden paleness he attributes, like his disorientation yesterday, to the sea's coldness, jumps from the car without turning off the engine and dashes towards the building – he presumes to seal the door and stem the birds' flow, their mass breakout. But she runs straight through it, leaving it wide open: her concern isn't the leakage but something beyond, within. A shrill squawk issues a few seconds later from the high-windowed barn's recess – a birdlike, or at least not human-sounding shriek, that Phocan thinks at first might be a peacock's, though he can't remember seeing any in there. Reaching over, turning the ignition off himself then stepping from the car unhurriedly, he ambles through, closing the door behind him slowly, as though casualness might set up its own roadblock, bar disaster from its hatching, or at least its broadcast. But it can't: after two turns he comes across her, and him. She's kneeling on the ground inside their little bower; he's floating above her like a saint or cosmonaut – or, rather, since the rope running between him and the beam, quite visible, belies the illusion of weightlessness, a Bergen acrobat, if you subtracted all the energy and motion.

Over the next few hours, lots of people come. There are ambulance crews from Riga, like their vehicles seasonally streaked in brown and yellow; more sombre blue-clad *policija* personnel; white plastic-sheathed forensics teams; pathologists and miscellaneous others. It's Lazda who deals with them. He's asked to give a statement to some kind of sergeant who speaks English, to corroborate (although there can't really be any doubt about what's just occurred) the statements being constantly solicited from her. She's surprisingly composed: organising and receiving seems to keep her going, to infuse her with purpose. Phocan, redundant, is reduced to brewing the strange black tea that they drank on his arrival and serving it out to any takers; then, when there are no more of these, to hanging about the lawn. By mid-afternoon he has recorded, mentally, a) that Latvian ambulances, like London school buses three decades ago, bear their labels, their descriptors, in unreversed form on their fronts; (b) that the treehouse in which he's sleeping is skilfully constructed, using stay rods and tension fasteners to grip its beams to the trunk, thereby avoiding any need for bolts and kingpins; and (c) that quinces, on the tree, are all but indistinguishable from pears.

How much significance does he attach to these small observations? About the same amount as the pathologist, who, mounting a ladder to undo the rope from its beam, does to the fact (visible only from this elevation) that the bird box closest to him, one of dozens dotted about the aviary, differs from the others in having only two (rather than four) walls and no roof. Inside, a kind of bird-nest shape has calcified: a central twig that rises from a brackish mass of smaller ones, droppings and seed-husks and, once risen, banks into an anticlockwise turn; then, on completing this, reverses its direction to bank back the other way, clockwise, thereby describing in the air a kind of double-helix before dropping to rejoin its starting point. Beneath this twisted mass, on the bird box's floor, three curvy white lines, lying side by side near the front edge, describe their own loops: one, the central of the three, a distended circle, or ellipse; the two bookending it more convoluted figure-eights that traverse their own paths and curl back, like the twig above them, to their own beginnings. These lines are old and faded, grey as much as white. As for their constitutive material, their 'medium': it could be paint, or it might just be bird shit.

5. The Beatitudes

Back to the grind: Goodge Street, D&G's offices, rooms full of stale sunlight and old leather, shelves that sag beneath *Halsbury's Laws of England*, every volume since 1907; beneath them, bound editions of *All England Law Reports, Scots Law Times, Session Cases* ... Dean's here mostly these days, or at Gray's Inn, or the British Library, Social Sciences (Law and Legal Studies) Section. She's working on two briefs right now, side by side. One involves straight-up infringement, of an anti-spillage mechanism for baby bottles: the copier is citing an equivalent contraption predating not only the litigant's patent application but also the institution of patent, or almost any other kind of, law *tout court* (the Ancient Egyptians used it, their defence goes). The other's a tad more complex: a music streaming service themselves under siege from a class-action test suit brought by twenty artists, suing a derivative (or just con-temporaneous) streaming service for interface-duplication. She's wading through A&M vs. Napster, MGM vs. Grokster, PMR vs. Spotify, Spotify vs. Deezer ... Buses, taxis, Clerkenwell and West End sandwich outlets seem imposing and oppressive, London accents ugly and anomalous: her mind's still in Purdue – or should that be Nantucket, Oakland, Riga, Arizona? Or somewhere *between* all these, blank spaces on a map or on a page, omissions from a catalogue, a set of letters ... She caught herself yesterday writing, in a mail to Dorley: *Since I came back from Perdue* – and let the typo stand, cementing with it her take on events, recasting the whole sojourn, those ten days, as *temps perdu* ...

In reality, of course, that time, its content, has been not lost but redacted: *that*'s the term best suited to the inexplicably aggressive reticence she first encountered in West Lafayette, and which then trailed her back to London. Peacock, D&G both went from wanting to know everything there was to know about the Gilbreth archive to not only wanting to know nothing more but, beyond that, demanding that all previously confided content, and all trails and records of their, or her, ever having carried out such research be erased – quite literally: she was to delete her copies of the dispatches, surrender working files, wipe all notes from her laptop. One Tuesday morning, two weeks after her return, a man from GCHQ turned up at the office and enquired, in friendly tones, if she could fill them in on anything she thought might turn out to be *sensitive* (his term) in any legwork she'd conducted for, say, recent clients – specially if this legwork touched on, subject-wise, the history of time-and-motion studies, or kinetics, or exchanges between East and West sides of the Iron Curtain on these subjects during the Cold War, which . . .

'Hang on there,' Dorley cut in, sending straight back out of the door an intern bearing in three teacups (she, he and the spook were the only ones participating in this meeting, which had not been scheduled). 'If it's work that Ms Dean, or any other member of this chambers, has conducted for a client, then it's – as you surely must know – confidential.'

'Yes, absolutely,' the GCHQ man replied. 'Absolutely . . .' He was about the same age as her, late twenties, and he looked as little like the avatars of MI5 that she could summon to her mind as possible: mild-mannered and light-humoured, quite informal . . . 'This is all completely off the record. We could start bouncing terms like *Investigatory Powers Act*, *UKUSA Agreement* and so forth around, but that might seem a little . . .' As though struck by a side-gust, he shifted direction, and said: 'Although, in fact, while legal advice privilege protects all communications that make up formal (as its name suggests) legal *advice*, and litigation privilege covers research conducted for the purposes of actual *litigation*, neither of these cover the fact-finding enquiries and general proddings-around of the type you've been ... the type we're interested in: strictly speaking, these aren't – as you'll know too – governed by ...'

'If you want,' Dorley was rising from his seat, 'to take this any further, you can come back with a subpoena.'

No subpoena was forthcoming. Three weeks later, though – three days ago, that is – she had a strange encounter in a restaurant. It was a small place in Southwark, a converted workshop in the narrow brick-street warren south of London Bridge where bearded, tattooed chefs bounce *bacalhau* and *camarão* in copper dishes amidst leaping flames just feet away from diners perched on stools at a zinc counter curving through the space – a tapas bar. She'd been summoned there by a friend who stood her up, breathlessly recounting down the phone an incomplete, or incompletely worked-through, story about someone's child needing to visit A&E – but not before she'd got there and sat down. Having informed the waiter-greeter-host she'd be eating alone, she found the seat beside her occupied five minutes later by a man whose accent, when he ordered, sounded vaguely Alpine – Austrian, Swiss, Tyrolean, a *Sound of Music* kind of hybrid. On sliding in, he flashed a smile her way (not straight into her eyes but slightly to the side of these, as though at something just behind her), then left her alone for the next forty or so minutes – until, plates cleared, she was scanning the *doce* section of the menu she'd been handed back, vacillating between *torta de amêndoa* and *peras bêbedas*. Then his voice, friendly, intrusive, invaded her airspace.

'Try 808.'

The stools were swivel-types. She swivelled hers round so she was facing him.

'I'm sorry?'

'808. It's the best thing they have here.'

She flipped the page forwards, to the sherries, then back again, to the *cursos principais*. The dishes were numbered, but ...

'There is no 808,' she said.

'I know,' he answered, smiling straight at her now. 'But if there were ...'

She felt a sudden heaviness, the counter and the copper and the flames all pressing in on her. Deliberately and slowly, she asked him, already half-knowing the response he'd give:

'If there were, then what?'

'It would change everything,' he completed the sequence.

'Who are you?' she asked.

He slipped a card across the zinc towards her. She glanced at it but it was turned face-down; she didn't want to pick it up.

'I'd like to pay for your meal,' he told her, smiling more aggressively.

'No thanks.'

'We'd like,' he ploughed on, switching person, 'to pay you a large fee for an hour or so's consultancy. It shouldn't present any problem, any ... conflict. Your contractual relationship with Peacock is acquitted. There is no embargo.'

She pulled her credit card out hurriedly and waved it at the waiter-host.

'Or even just your notes,' he said. 'Your old ones, that you didn't use. We'd pay you handsomely for those.'

She hadn't managed to attract her target's eye. Gathering her things – bag, phone, book, glasses case – she slid down from her seat.

'I shredded them all,' she told him, and made for the exit, paying on the way out. She kept to Bermondsey Street, which was crowded, and walked quickly north, not looking behind her until, just before the long tunnel underneath the railway line, she found a taxi. Safely installed and moving down St Thomas Street, she turned round then to see if he was following her – which he wasn't, didn't need to: if they knew about 808 and Peacock, then they'd know where she lived too. His card, she discovered after she got home, had found its way into her handbag after all: she must have swept it up in her haste to escape. Pirotti. Cassius First Motion. She burned it immediately, on her gas hob, washing the ashen remnants down the sink.

She wrestled, over the next forty-eight hours, with the question of whether or not to tell Dorley about the approach, the tap-up. Not having decided one way or the other after three sleepless nights, she reasoned that her delay in divulging, if divulging were to take place now, would itself constitute a culpable withholding. Nor would it be the first one: in her deleting, wiping and surrendering, she'd neglected, or omitted, or just not *happened*, to volunteer two files that she was never asked for – her own small act of reticence to match, or counter, Purdue's. On what had turned out to be her last day in the archive, in defiance of the reader regulations, of the signed covenant between her and Ms Richards and the Gilbreths and who knows whom else, Dean, after a quick left-right peek, had slipped out from her trouser a muted phone and snapped two pages of Lillian's jotter-book journal – the last two, the ones with all the doodles and the letter-symbols, the Italian fragments and the crayon-drawn circles and the English tag-line this Pirotti was to quote at her. She could, supposedly, have done it above board: put in a scan-request form, got her copy the next morning, but ... She'd sensed by then the change in atmosphere, a coldness issuing not *from* the archivist but *through* her, from stacks hidden and expansive and, above all, somehow sinister; sensed things closing in, a quarry bright, delicate and rare slipping away. So, furtively and with a shame-defiance cocktail burning in her gut, she'd done it: *snap, snap*, minus *snaps*. Now, back here in Goodge Street, New Kingdom anti-dribble threads and Dubset clauses she's not interested in splayed out before her, she slips the phone out, pulls the pictures up again ...

She must have stared at them a hundred times. The doodle hieroglyphics, then the strings of letters, symbols, not-quite algebra; the lines and vectors that seem to connect one fragment to another, bind them all into some kind of tapestry of reason, or at least of correspondence ... and the colours, morphing, flecks of one contained within another like faint visual echoes, a whole chromatism of epiphany whose key ... At the bottom once more, in bold letters, *Box 808 changes everything*. Floating above it to the right, tethered by connecting penstroke, the initials *T.T.* Constellated all around it, like saints, cherubs, satellites, those scrawled Italian snatches: *fattore ... farsi ... fattura ... legato con amove ... geomètra misurar lo cerchio ... l'amov che move ...* They were penned in Lillian's Phoenix rest home, The Beatitudes: shaky hand, fading eyesight. The imprint of the pencil, impregnation of the paper by the ink seem weak, washed out and faded by first time, then reproduction. In Purdue, Dean typed the sequences into her laptop, saved them to a file that she no longer has. Now, here at D&G, she strikes up a more haptic, analogue relation with them, even if it's mediated by the touchscreen of her phone: dragging her way around the pictures, finger-stretching them to zoom in on one patch of cursive penstroke, sliding them to follow its path on into another, she finds herself clutching her own pen, transcribing the shapes of words and letters out on to the back of her printed note pages ...

Fattore ... farsi ... fattura ... legato con amove ... She took Italian in school, and knows that *fattore* is author, maker or creator; *farsi* the thing that's made, and *fattura* the act of making; *legato* means tied up or bound together ... *amove*, though, doesn't mean anything. The term is half-repeated in *amov*, which doesn't mean anything either – unless it's a first go at the word popping up a little to the right and just above: *move*, moves, sets in motion. That, she's reasoned since Purdue, would make sense, its doubled presence here explained by the word's naming of Lillian's lifelong preoccupation. Now, drawing the figures out, retracing the lines as they jag and curve, doubling again their divagations in the manner of the legal scriveners of old, or the monk-scribes of even older, she comes to notice for the first time that the *v*s in *amove* and *amov* are different from the one in *move*, their right stalks more upright, curled over at the top, like the *r*s in *cerchio, misurar, geomètra ...* and *fattura, farsi, fattore* – which, in turn, leads to a realisation: they're not *v*s at all, but also *r*s. The words are actually *amore* and *amor*. *Con amore*: with love; *amor che move*, love that moves ...

Reverting to digital again, she enters this second sequence in the search bar of the desktop monitor in front of her and, 0.41

seconds later, is presented with the source of not just this but all the other fragments, too. It's Dante, *Divina Commedia* – which she should also have known: she had to study that in school as well. The final, sign-off line, the 'out': the poet or his stand-in, after passing all the way through Hell and Purgatory, through the spheres of the Inconstant, the Ambitious and the Wise, then onwards through the Contemplatives and Fixed Stars right to the *Primum Mobile*; after plotting the entire machinery of circles driving other circles, wheels within wheels, then passing even further, on into the centre, the Empyrean, *finally* gets to behold, face-to-face, *l'amor che move il sole e l'altre stelle*, the love that moves the sun and other stars …

Dean, slumped into her chair, lets forth a kind of sigh, or grunt – a sound of neither triumph nor relief, but simply of the type you let out when, too late, you've got the punchline to a joke you should have worked out several stages back. It seems so obvious: what else would it have been? Lillian's favourite book, the one she planted in the workers' common spaces and rest areas, all the waiting rooms that she designed; the one that must have seeded her mind in the first place with the notion that each action has its best way, its *diritta via* – and the one that, at the end, old eyes turned up, beatitudinous, towards the fading stars, the moon that she'd helped conquer, bobbed back like a patch of word-wrack, half-remembered jetsam to be clung at while she, too, waited to be called into whatever other room was being readied for her …

Setting the pencil down, Dean looks out of the first-floor window. It's dusk; in the street, a lamp is flickering on – and off, and on again. It's been that way for some days. D&G and several neighbouring tenants have complained, citing distraction, epilepsy-trigger risk, ratepayer shorting … Camden Council have promised to repair it later this week. The pole looks old and rusty; it might also have to be replaced. For now, though, it stands blinking intermittently, a fragile finger raising to the sky its bulbous matrimonial band.

6. The Molecularity of Glass

Phocan is leaving. Lazda might join him later, in Riga, or perhaps in London. Or she might not: he might stay in, or return to, Riga – quit Pantarey, his jostling with Sennet for ascendency, the lot ... Or they might both move somewhere else entirely: Berlin, Rotterdam, Helsinki, start afresh ... Or none of the above. Everything is possible and nothing certain. There's a kind of vertigo, exhilaration almost, that comes with moments like this, born of knowing that an old order of things has ended, that the world-as-was must be remade, or at least reconfigured. Lazda's great-grandparents, their generation, would have felt it with the People's Council's declaration, 1918: amidst all the violence, the catastrophe and death, vertiginous exhilaration of the new, of independence ... Last night, he thought she'd want to sleep, but they made love instead, repeatedly, she sobbing between each bout, clinging to him, scratching him, in passion or in anger. Did he *cause* Vanins' death – precipitate it, bridge the final gap between the deed's potentiality and its conversion into action? Maybe. If he did, though, he's a bridge for her as well, between this new time into which she's entering and the previous age in which her grandfather was still alive. And he *understands* Vanins: he's read his papers, knows what he was all about. Other bridges she seems to be burning: she decided straight away to sell the dacha; and the aviary, site of the cataclysm, the old order's end, she's going to have pulled down almost immediately, once the birds have been rehoused or just released ...

A taxi has pulled up. Phocan's getting in; it's pulling off, passing the abandoned playground, turning into the nearest of the three narrow, ditch-lined tracks. Its engine, still in low gear, makes the window of Vanins' study rattle. The taxi disappears; the window, of course, stays: it isn't going anywhere. It's a wood-framed window with four panes. The panes, as Phocan noticed two days ago, seem imperfectly matched to one another. And with reason: they're not just of different ages but of different constitutions too. Three of them (from garden side: bottom left, top left, top right) are made of float glass – soda-lime-silica-constituted, batch-mixed, tin-bath-poured, roller-lifted, lehr-cooled and strainlessly annealed, machine-cut rectangles displaying a regularity, indeed a sharpness, of light propagation with refraction kept right down at <1.5 per cent and scattering, reflection and such manner of distortions similarly minimised. The fourth, though (bottom right), has been cut from different quartz-cloth: cylinder-blown sheet glass, trench-swung, stand-cooled, heat-scored, flattened and hand-measured – tailored, as it were, to order, to the frame's dimensions. Where the other three panes are replacements (occasioned by, in chronological progression: one frost-crack wrought by an exceptionally cold February; one quince, thrown by a young Lazda at a darting cousin whom it – obviously – missed; and one tawny pipit lured, *assassiyun*-like, by the artificial flowers and sky and general depth-illusion laid across its surface by the guileful Old Man of ray optics), the fourth is original: an 1896 piece, putty-set into fresh aspen timber by Vanins' father when he built this dacha.

He, Kārlis, the father, obtained this pane from the glassworks beside Jumelans – no longer, as Phocan saw, operational, nor even really present, its batch-house, furnaces and packaging huts discernible now only as brickwork footprints in the unkempt marram grass through which summer bathers traipse on their way down to a beach whose sand they might still notice is laced to an unusually high degree, a point of saturation almost, with glass fragments, smoothed and coarsened edges posing no risk to their unshod feet. There is a circularity to the beach's mineral constitution: for decades it was its own sand that, shovelled, winched and chuted, fed the glassworks' doghouse, where it mixed with sodium and calcium and magnesium and barium landed by the sack-load from the vessels that once plied the inlet – and, contrafluvially, the blown cylinders' off-cut fragments, the crushed alkali or cullet, that was spat back out to lie around the beach until it was scooped up and thrown back down the batch-feed's gullet once again: sand turning into glass, glass into sand, an endless loop. Or so it seemed, until the glassworks closed in 1985. This one veteran pane, though, still bears witness, through the variant, and varying, texture of its vitreous mass, its imperfect transparency, to the old Jumelans *stikla fabrika* character. How? Unlike the newer ones, it contains bubbles, waves, inclusions, reams and pleats. Looked through from study side, it introduces to the garden little folds, occlusions, doublings – each one near-imperceptible alone, but in amalgam overlaying the flow of branches, well and wood stump with a set of tiny visual hiccups, backwashes or eddies that's at once bewildering and quite hypnotic. All windows around here (since they all came from the *fabrika*) used to produce this effect – which is to say that, viewed from the inside of houses, churches, offices and schools, the entire region, all its scenes and people, used to hic and eddy like this, pause and run and gloop to these same quirky Jumelans rhythms ...

There's been debate in recent years, in the more speculative fora of the world of academia, nebulous zones where physics, palaeontology, even musicology start unravelling across one another, about whether or not certain objects and materials could – in theory, at least – be viewed as ready-made or 'inadvertent' recording devices. In 1968, the normally placid proceedings of the International Congress of Classical Archaeology, co-hosted by the Deutsches Archäologisches Institut and the Berlin Ethnologisches Museum (Abteilung Materielle Ethnologie), were ruffled by the presentation of one o. Prof. Friedrich Kelpler, who'd dropped in from Karlsruhe – or, to the ears of his fellow delegates, another planet – where he held the Chair for Ästhetik und Theorie der Medien. What caused all the kerfuffle (picture scowls, snorts and disruptive muttering, even – unprecedented – walk-outs) was o.

Prof. Kelpler's claim that potters' ribs, needles and fluting tools would etch into the wet, receptive surface of thrown clay as, spinning, it was coaxed into the form of bowl or amphora a set of furrows very similar to the grooves carved into lacquer by the heated stylus of a gramophone recorder; furrows that, just like the stylus's, would impregnate the clay with sonic vibrations of the atmosphere surrounding them – which vibrations, clay once hardened, would become immortalised, at least for as long as the ceramic object lasted. Thus, in effect, or retrospect (this was the o. Prof.'s central thesis), an Attic potter's workshop served as a two-thousand-year *avant-la-lettre* recording studio. To yelps of incredulity, Kelpler ran a reel-to-reel of sounds (crackles and scratches set against a whistling background) that he claimed to have picked up by 'playing' an Apulian krater using a hand-held crystal cartridge.

Two years later, after Kelpler's 'findings' had, against the wishes of most of its editorial board, been published in *The Journal of Archaeological Science*, a second article appeared, in *Ethnos*, this time co-authored by Yale anthropologist Kent Foster and Lund acoustician Åke Engström, both well respected in their fields. They claimed to have verified Kelpler's hypothesis, or at least its mechanical possibility, by recording, by means of a vane whose impedance at attachment point into wet clay was $ZM(12/11)2$ (groove modulation velocity thereby being set at $vg = 2 pS/(ZM(12/11ss)))$, their own voices singing '*Ja, må han leva*' (it was Engström's birthday), and then subsequently reviving these voices with a custom-made tone arm and off-the-shelf Euphonics U15P pick-up.

This second article opened the floodgates: from '75 onwards, archaeoacoustics research labs sprung up in universities around the world; Mycenaean kantharoi, Corinthian alabastrons, Thracian mortaria, pithoi and pelikai and pyxides from Syria to Hibernia were off-mastered, pressed and distributed. Words, phrases, whole stretches of dialogue in Aeolic, Doric, Latins Classical and Vulgar were detected, intercut with barks of Roman dogs, cries of Athenian street-merchants; one archaeoacoustician, in Chicago, even claimed to have eavesdropped on Homer trying out his *Rhododáktylos Ēós* line while stopping by to watch a kylix being spun … The craze came to an abrupt end when no-nonsense Columbia emeritus Wade Gudron Jnr detailed, in the spring 1982 issue of *Hesperia*, the counter-experiments in which he'd reproduced the playback element of Foster and Engström's (and most subsequent archaeoacousticians') sessions but – devastatingly – not their recorded-content one: in place of ceramic objects, he'd run arm and pick-up over bricks, sandpaper, a table top, a pair of jeans and even, with the level cranked to max, thin air. When he demonstrated, both in sound and sine-wave visuals, near-identical 'voices', 'barks', 'cries' 'phrases', etc. (not to be outdone, he rendered audible not just one but three lines from *The Odyssey*), produced quite evidently from no more than a combination of random static and the listener's imagination, the game was up.

Or rather mothballed: funding streams may have atrophied, but a life-line, a clutching-straw of sorts was thrown out in the form of a postscript- or addendum-article, placed in *Phoenix* (1984, fall issue), by Cameron Blaine Ph.D., Reader in Linguistics at Laurentian, Ontario. Blaine argued, quite correctly, that, while archaeoacousticians' putative ability to separate the signal of antiquity from the noise of contemporary hardware and enthused projection had been thoroughly discredited, nonetheless the *existence*, and indeed the buried *presence*, of the signal in the object had, by Engström, Foster et al., and even by Gudron Jnr, been adequately established. The melodies might be, for now at least, unheard; and, until the requisite hardware (one, admittedly, with needle<haystack signal-magnification ratio) came along, they would remain inaudible; but they, and their immortal words, were *there* – 'if,' as Blaine signed off, channelling George Herbert, 'we could spell …'

And glass? Is it not, as much as clay, a 'plastic' artefact? In the absence of oscillation-inscribing ribs and needles, the gramophone-analogy may not, in this case, hold – but here the science, if anything, is stronger. While a stylus merely translates into spiral grooves the sound-waves captured in its feeding diaphragm, blown glass is formed by – *as* – the direct imprint of the human diaphragm itself: *Atem*, πνεῦμα, breath of life. And after setting, flattening, cutting, even installation, its 'solidity' is no more than apparent, an illusion that takes in the short-term contemplator only. To the *longue-durée* gaze it is perpetually fluid, molecules migrating over decades, even centuries, about a three-dimensional plane: top to bottom, side to corner, outer to inner surface, all about the swirling Equatorials and Gulf Streams of its oceanic body. This process is reactive: glass is super-sensitive. In 2009 MIT engineering professor Dave Able and his team, in partnership with Microsoft and Caul Research, using equipment that made cartridges and pick-ups look as ancient as the potter's studio that Homer did or (most likely) didn't visit, filmed, without any audio input, an empty tumbler standing on a drinks-table beside which one of Able's graduate students was declaiming 'Mary had a Little Lamb'. While to their naked eyes the tumbler was quite still, when replayed at a speed of 4,300 fps, motions, caused by sound-waves hitting its surface, of one tenth of a micrometer, or five thousandths of a pixel (inferable through boundary fluctuation, or just changes in the pixel's colouration as one region encroached on another), were rendered visible and, through Caul's algorithm, translated back to sound, until *And everywhere that Mary went her lamb was sure to go* warbled back out of a speaker half an hour after its first, natural iteration. Although, in this instance, it was the real-time disturbance in the glass's form that furnished such a level of retrievability, the glass, as Able's team knew all too well, would have continued its displacements far into the future at levels lower and more micrometric still – in terms both of its edges, their vacillation through the air about them, *and* of the internal scurry of its sound-shocked particles within the confines of their gathering-containing cylinder, up and down the sides, along the rim, the convex pools extruding from its base-plane: so many pinballs ricocheting endlessly off solenoid-filled bumpers, kickers, slingshots, off each other – and then, even after that, the bumpers' *memory* of being hit, replaying in quivering aftershock, detectable on no seismograph perhaps but solidly, materially, at nano-scale, the scale of atoms, *happening* ...

And if sound, why not light? Do photons, too, not bounce and multi-ball around? *Light*, the fifteen-year-old Phocan was made to recite mantra-like in GCSE Physics class, *travels in straight lines until A Level*. Even *air* can bend and warp it, send it arabesqueing into mirages, *fata morganas*, floating castles. So windows ... windows are to light what mazes are to rats, or pots to lobsters: looming edifices full of switchbacks and blind alleys, forks and three-way junctions, secret passages that magic travellers to far parts of the labyrinth, or even duplicate or triplicate them till they occupy two or more stretches at the same time – but, like all enchanted palaces or funhouses, exact their toll, a levy measured in the photons that are doomed to traipse about their corridors for ever. *Absorption* (as Phocan's teacher informed him when he turned sixteen, popping with one thrust his optics-cherry) is the term for this entrapment: not, strictly speaking, *loss* of light, but rather its snaring, and eventual conversion into heat – which, just like sound, wreaks havoc with those flows and currents, spreading its own interference waves, disturbance patterns that in turn spark new disturbance patterns, chain reactions, on and on. Viewed from this perspective, isn't every window a light-capturing machine? An event recorder, like the murder victims' eyeballs said to retain imprints of the acts they've witnessed? Even ones with low refractive indexes, like Vanins' study's three newish, float-glass panes, claim as many as fifteen of every thousand photons seeking safe passage through them. And the fourth: the kinky, stuttering, gaze-tripping Jumelans *stikla fabrika* pane? This one's voracious, swallowing *seventeen* and up, a Scylla and Charybdis furnace-fused into one giant, vitreous monster whose very flesh retains the heat-conversion traces of innumerable devourees.

If we could spell ... What would this pane divulge? The light residues of which histories does it store up? No murders, certainly – just visits to the well; the stumping of the birch that once stood next to it, then the stump's service as a platform for the chopping into firewood of smaller birch and aspen logs; proliferation of the spruce branches, their annual pruning; springtime growth of grass, its summer scything; rain, snow, more rain, sunlight, moonlight, starlight, the accumulated meteor-streaks of a hundred and twenty-two Augusts and Septembers; ditto those of (averaging out to account for species variation) forty-three generations of birds darting, pausing, swooping, in one tawny pipit's case for the last time; mainly, nothing more than tiny oscillations in grass blades and twigs ... And somewhere, lodged in the still-shifting contours heat-marked by those billions of levied photons, broken, scattered and kaleidoscoped to a degree no high-speed camera or algorithm yet devised could reverse-engineer, one scene, from 1969: of Jesēnija – Raivis's wife, Lazda's grandmother – standing in the garden, moving and not moving simultaneously.

She would be planted, feet apart, between stump and well, playing a novelty game better known in the last few decades by the proprietary title 'Swingball' but in those days referred to as 'tether tennis' – playing on her own, with (or against) herself. The set, purchased by Vanins on a recent trip to Zürich, consisted of a pole whose whittled base was sunk into the earth and to the upmost portion of whose mast a coil or spiral was affixed; to the coil, in turn, a ring clip had been fastened – fastened, that is (being looped around rather than welded on), to the coil's overall helix although not to any one spot of this, thus enjoying (if that's the word) free reign to corkscrew its way up and down the spiral's length. To the clip a string was tied; the far end of the string, a metre away, fused into a tennis ball. Jesēnija Vanins (née Lazdiňš) was hitting this ball with a racquet: first with one side, forehand, then, as it swung on its leash round the pole back to her, with the other, backhand. It was April; in the Atlantic Ocean, the Apollo 9 had splashed down some days earlier; in the sea of Japan, a US EC-121 reconnaissance plane had splashed too, downed by a North Korean MiG-21; in Britain, the first vertical take-off jet had just been trialled; in Riga, at the Universitāte, the entire administrative board had resigned under student pressure, replaced by new and more permissive blood. A handover, or changing of the guard, winter to spring, seemed to hang in the texture of the garden's air as well: a finer and more grainy quality of light, a dotting of the visual field with midges, dragonflies and bees, whose buzzing laid an intermittent base note underneath the *thwock, thwock* tenor of the racquet's strikes ...

It was the mechanism that had made Vanins buy the set: this curved metal bar along whose length the ring clip glided had instantly reminded him, when he'd first caught sight of it in the *Sportwarengeschäft*'s display window, of Lillian's models; of hands tracing their turns and loopbacks, again and again, the repetition copying the same paths over to the tracers' bodies, consigning them to memory of limbs and muscles. On this spring morning (mid-morning, that long stretch of unconcern that sets in an hour or so after breakfast), it seemed to Vanins, watching from his study (he was writing a paper for the *Soviet Physics Journal*, on the reasons for the N1 programme's failure), that Jesēnija was playing the tracer's, the path-learner's, role, performing movements programmed into and dictated by the core form of the coil, as though she and not the ball were its final extension, gliding in locked orbit. With each of the ball's anticlockwise loops her shoulders would reach with the arm and racquet to greet its return – and with these, in their wake, the segments of her back would take off, one after the other, like so many cohorts of an army obeying orders to decamp, to strike out on a march, each unit moving separately and yet in conjunction with the larger troop formation; and, as though chasing these, her hips, too, would rise, hoisted on thighs that in turn were driven by soft knee-hydraulics, by articulated calf-and-ankle mechanisms further down; all in the space of half a second. Then, the ball being met and dispatched on its clockwise counter-loop, her arm, in each second's remaining half, would sail back, wrist bending the other way to reset hand and racquet angle, a boat smoothly changing tack, easing its way through calm, compliant water to the spot (unmarked on any chart yet implicitly, through seamanship so ancestral it's become almost genetic, *known*) at which it would once more bump up against the yellow buoy or, more accurately, fellow (if counter-directional) voyager, *sputnik*, this small sphere that on contact always found itself, if not in the exact same location, then at least in the same place relative to its circumnavigation's compass ...

The window was, of course, integral to this scene, to these effects. As Vanins watched her through it – that is, through three old Jumelans panes (the frost-cracked one had already been replaced), the main part of the action framed, as circumstance of height and desk-placement dictated, within the pane that now survives – its glass not only stretched Jesēnija's movements; in its glucose thickenings and accretions, it seemed to expand the duration of these movements too, doubling each moment and replaying the doubled passage in a kind of simultaneous slow-motion. Jesēnija, twenty-six, was already expanding on her own, waist and bust widening as she laid in fat in preparation for Dagnija's, Lazda's mother's, birth (the pregnancy, having one week earlier cleared the three-month hurdle, was no longer secret). Her body, as she swivelled one way then the other, seemed to store up and replay for him a wider set of movements and positions, their associated scenes, from early courtship onwards: a gesture made when greeted in the street on one chance meeting; the way she'd once set a cup down in a cafe in Alberta iela; how she'd reached for her coat afterwards, flung a scarf round her neck; or flung the neck itself back, laughing, when he'd told her a joke one day on the bridge in Bastejkalna Park; had done the same each time he kissed her in a certain spot, under the chin ... These and scores of other moments, transposed and repeated, merging with his own partial reflection in the glass, sparked in him a sudden awareness of synchronicity, of processes all happening at once – or rather, being re-melted, blown into and held within some new formation, an arrangement relegating the time of their actual happening to insignificance. Nor was he observing this from outside: he was held by the formation too, gathered and absorbed in its consistency: watching, remembering and anticipating fused together, rhythm and suspension merging, *thwock, thwock*, with his pulse-beat …

How long did he watch for? Hard to say, in light of these reflections. It would be wrong to call the episode 'timeless'; that is, to try (rhetorically at least) to place it out of time. It was packed full of time, and times – so saturated with them, though, as to defy all measure. Vanins was, it's true, entranced – but even in that trance, amidst its swirl and billow, he maintained a sharpness, a keen perspicacity. As the parts of the kinetic symphony presented by Jesēnija and the tether-tennis set seemed to detach themselves, to wander from their posts while still somehow ensuring that each post continued functioning, he started seeing racquet, ball and figure (torso, elbow, thigh, etc.) not as what they *were* but rather as objects in a long celestial dance, all acting on each other: racquet attracts ball, which attracts figure, which carves rhomboids, sinusoids and gyres into the air, which in turn draw racquet – all of this drawing and holding his attention, which in its own turn (was Jesēnija aware that he was watching?), fuelled and sustained the dance, sent all its parts careening round their orbits and meridians once more: another cycle, and another … Vanins thought – how could he not? – about his work: of states of equilibrium, sines and cosines, vector sums and net force. But, rather than being harnessed as correlative for these, a prompt for new practical applications, the tether-tennis symphony seemed to take hold of them and send them into orbit too. Everything – work, the world, politics, even physics – seemed suspended, flipped into a mode of operation in which operation itself has been stood down and, in that very passiveness, that *uselessness*, been opened up to every possible new use. At one point it occurred to him that he was watching nothing less than life, in its pure, concentrated form, unhidden by the camouflage of purpose – but he put that thought on hold, since to name, to give a label to the phenomenon he was engaged in contemplating would have gone against its nature, nature of which his abandoned contemplation, contemplation for its own sake, was a merging, doubling and careening part …

He did, though, even in abandonment, experience a sense of urgency, of mission. Over the next weeks, and months, this urgency, this mission, would act on him like a coiled helix, dictating his activities. Right now, though (now, then, whenever – ask the windowpane), its first motion took the form of his right hand reaching – slowly, cautious not to frighten off a thought so delicate it might take flight, or just evaporate, at any second – down to ruffle the pages of his essay draft in search of a clean sheet. Failing to find one, he turned over the most recently composed page, covered on one side only, and, on its virgin verso, wrote in English, beneath the heading *T.T.*:

Dear Lillian,

I think I've made a discovery …

7. The Wrangler

Under the mews's cobblestones, below buildings that, prior to their conversion into advertising, architecture, investment-portfolio management and film-production company offices, slept and fed and watered Fitzrovia's draught and livery horses; off the courtyard, past an iron door whose perfunctory chain lock persistent junkies are continually unpicking; down a stone staircase on which both light and oxygen levels noticeably decrease every two or three steps; beyond another, state-of-the-art double door that neither addict nor anyone else not armed with trifecta of swipe card, RFID tag and daily-generated pin code has yet managed to outsmart; in an expansive if compacted basement whose humidity and temperature are recalibrated every five and a half minutes lies Degree Zero's render farm. There, behind glass dust covers, eighty-two motherboards denuded of their casing and arrayed either upright in long lines, like after-dinner mints, or horizontal, one above the other, like shelves built to store nothing but shelf, flicker and blink in restless computation. Between these and across floor, walls and ceiling snake two hundred and eight yards of cabling. Tower fans, also shelf-sized, rotate sentinel among them. Their modulating roar, the motherboards' relentless hum, the general tremble of electric overcharge all rise through earth and bricks above; below, they shake plasma and membranes of all plastic, metal, glass and wood and, not least, the lone human who's on duty here tonight.

Do we know him? We do: it's Soren, he of the velveteen hairs. He has, as hoped, 'progressed'. No longer a mere runner, he has been promoted to the post – still entry-level, but a salaried one nonetheless – of render wrangler. His job: to monitor, from dusk to dawn, the passage of the endless gigabytes that make up each of *Incarnation*'s images, through the SVN-filters into the server; to assign to each frame's cluster a processing pen fenced off from all the others yet at the same time, inasmuch as they all feed off and into the same source and output channels, conjoined; to see to it that these pens don't become overcrowded, blocked, stampeded; to ensure the welfare and, indeed, to verify the basic genetic purity of each one's charges, checking for scripting errors, unforeseen corruptions and all manner of infirmity that, if not picked up and isolated at this stage, will mutate and multiply through the next, and the one after that – contagion that, worst-case scenario, will eventually erupt across the skin of the released film in an outbreak of glitches and anomalies that would cost DZ their reputation and (needless to say) Soren his job. More specifically: this job entails watching, on his desktop, logged into the server through VNC client, the revision numbers roll past and refresh themselves; checking how much memory each processor, or 'proc', is using, and reallocating a portion of its labour to another when the figures go too high; updating the SVNs; running system admin … Sometimes Soren moves methodically, from one proc to the next; sometimes he darts between them randomly, spot-checking, keeping them all on their toes with the element of surprise. From time to time he pulls up all the procs' vital statistics simultaneously, lays them out side by side in multi-screen, columns of numbers and figures all jiggling together: a muster-parade roll-call, to ascertain whether there's been any slacking off. If he spots sloppiness or snags, he brings offending stragglers back into the fold by issuing an shh command. He does this manually, types into the Blender script the letters *shh* – as though he were some kind of whisperer, lulling and soothing not a single restless animal but hundreds all at once. This render farm has more processing power than most countries. It's managing calculations that would take a human a whole lifetime – to work out the position of a hair, the passage

317

and rotation of a piece of dust, the luminescence of a fork's tine, frame by frame by frame ...

Incarnation's render has been scheduled as a twelve-week task. 44,928 frames, to be rendered at an average speed of sixty-one minutes and fifty-six seconds per frame, with twenty-three being concurrently processed at each given moment, equals 2,016 hours. It's running round the clock, every day of the week, no breaks for public holidays. Soren is one of four wranglers – the most junior, which is why he's got the graveyard shift. So here he is, tonight: corralling, *shh*shing, verifying, updating, cross-checking, plucking sample lines of code out of the millions that shuttle past like (if you want old-school, analogue comparators) newspapers on the conveyor of an offset press, or reels of cross-weave rolling off the loom of some giant fabric plant – the difference being that each of Soren's interventions, rather than carrying the process forwards, helping to fire the morning edition off to waiting stands, newsboys and breakfast tables, or to bring the tapestry closer to completion, sets it back: it's an unpicking, registered by a small back-tick on the aggregated progress bar that has its own dedicated screen both here on the farm's wall and on the remote desktops of the many supervisors and coordinators, editors, compositors, accountants and so forth who track it like impatient suitors to whom an answer, yay or nay, *some* kind of resolution, is long overdue.

To unpick or back-tick ourselves: *Incarnation*'s render *had* been scheduled as a twelve-week task. That figure's been revised to fourteen. It will go up further: no one doubts that. We're in Week Eleven. Right now, most of the frames working their way through the procs are drawn from the film's final, seven-minute sequence, which depicts the KFS *Sidereal*'s break-up as it drives manically, suicidally, towards Fidelus. As the ship powers its way past the star's outer heliopause, into its heliosheath and on towards the boundary of its termination shock, the plasma-discharge sloughing off the sun's upper atmosphere, racing at supersonic speed from its corona, proves too much for the vessel's constitution. Screws and rivets bend and elongate and shoot off like so many poppers on a baby's one-piece; panels of sheet-metal sheer away and tumble down-hull, gouging into heat shield, wing and skirt new gashes where their jagged sides make contact; stabilisers, banks and a whole storage bay detach themselves and, rather than simply hurtling away, hover, vortex-held, expanding and imploding simultaneously, their forms, dimensions and properties, the very laws by which they're bound, gone haywire. The bow wave has indeed, as Briar proposed, brought on a general fucking with all terms and values. Basic oppositions – up/down, attraction/repulsion, togetherness/separation, even inside/outside (of an object, of the ship, of people's bodies) – seem to be collapsing. A rapier (maybe Tszvetan's, lethal implement that stove Merhalt's skull, that led to the seduction and thus, indirectly, to the present pass, or maybe just a random rapier whose history we can only guess at – either way, denuded now of all pasts, which slough off particulate as well), moving of its own volition, lunging and patinandoing in mid-air down an auxiliary corridor, is shattering into ten thousand shards but still managing to sear through the jugular of a stoker whose own vital frame, though similarly crystallising and disintegrating, writhes in affliction, as though each of its newly minted fragments retained the memory of the whole of which they until recently formed molecules; the stoker's blood, spilling, mingles with distant stars, *becomes* the stars that are now fully visible through the *Sidereal*'s hull although the hull, somehow, is still there, both contained by and containing the external space that it was built to keep at bay. Things proximate – grid-panels, ring-latches, attenuators – seem to stand at infinite distances; things far or forgotten – distant nebulae, *brinquedotecques* and *gzhiardini*, relics of Argeral childhoods – seem to be close at hand: it's a catastrophe happening here, sure – an annihilation, an extinction – but there's also, ultra-paradoxically, a counter-movement of formation, of *emergence*, going on as well, a sense of something edging its way, through all the chaos, to the threshold of the visible, the comprehensible . . .

Tszvetan and Tild, like salmon fighting their way upstream to the pools from which they spawned, have pulled and scraped and lunged themselves back to the place where it all started: the Observatory. They've writhed and threshed their way through hatches, slid along conjoining tunnel walls to which gravity has at first pinned them down, then, suddenly reversing its direction, thrust them onwards, as though willing them towards their goal. From time to time they've had to push aside a stoker's body, or observe a dying one being vacuum-sucked into the interstellar void. The stokers' faces, both alive and dead, all have the same expression carved across them: never terrified or anguished, but satisfied, contented, *happy* even, proud of having seen through to its endgame and beyond a fierce devotion from whose pledge they drew their strength and purpose, drew their very essence as retainers. Death, conjunction with the stars, cements this essence, renders it eternal. Even amidst the carnage, Tszvetan and Tild register these attestations of a faith oblivion can't snuff out; vindicated and spurred on by them, they plough on through disintegrating airlocks and equipment bays, battery modules, water-storage tanks, up past what used to be the *Sidereal*'s starboard trusses; tumble up, down and along the geometry-defying, now semi-fluid double-helix of the uncoiling spiral staircase; and, finally, find themselves spat, internally vomited, into the viewing platform's spherical and cyst-like chamber.

The sapphire-glass dome – perhaps because it was so thin and provisional in the first place, scarcely more solid than a bubble – has held up to now, although it's only a matter of time before it, too, disintegrates. The instruments, the spectrohelioscopes, astrolabes, dioptras and torquetums, are flying through the air, colliding with each other and the central console, with the globe-within-globe reader whose controls are running all amok, casting out names, coordinates and legends, defunct cartographies dredged up from unravelling memory, on to a territory also unravelling, buckling, shredding. The radium-coloured zigzags in Tild's hair are tangling and unravelling too, transversals warping and distending with the globe's schizoid projections. The G-force is playing tricks with her and Tszvetan's facial muscles, tautening and stretching mandibles and orbitals and infraorbitals, setting them in arrangements that are manic and yet also strangely calm – like the stokers' expressions, acquiescent, *happy*, utterly committed to a process that's been willed and dared, and that's now daring them. Tszvetan, wrenching at Tild's shoulder, turning both their bodies round so that they're facing outward, bulging eyes pressed right against the sclera of the dome's own bulging eyeball, says to Tild:

'It's waiting for us.'

Despite all the roar, the splintering and smashing, he doesn't have to shout. The magnetospheric overhaul, the atmospheric stripping brought on by the solar wind, has imposed intimate acoustics in which the sound-waves carrying his voice convey it to her as directly as if he'd spoken straight into her skull, or in the dome, the whispering gallery, of a silent cathedral. At the same time, propagating without amplifying it any more, they carry it all over: along each of the *Sidereal*'s tunnels, corridors and bays, up and down its sump-tanks, masts and vent lines, skirts and cones and baffles – and beyond, over Fidelus's termination shock, throughout its heliosheath. The intimacy's general. It encompasses way-distant clusters, all the hypergiants and subgiants, binaries, deltas and cepheid variables, the furtive aggregates of dusty clouds, the welcoming abyss into which, willing the dome to shatter, he and Tild are preparing to leap. Is that what Tszvetan meant by 'it'? Is that what's waiting for them? The abyss? Or did he mean the leap itself: the doing of it, the enactment of its moment, the split second at which time makes contact with eternity? His words, replaying now like a universal echo, vest all power of decision in the *it*, not in the lovers: it's the *it* that's clasping them within its holding pattern, offering them their only course of action, the choice of doing what they have no choice but to do: to yield, to surrender to this omnipresent and elusive place, this instant whose happening can take place only as a pause, a waiting ...

Motherboards hum. Tower fans' roars modulate as they rotate. Soren checks the time: 3:21 a.m. He does this on his desktop, since he's not allowed to have a phone down here, nor any other interface with what's beyond the door. The upper world could end without him knowing it; could *have*, somewhere between frames 37,204 and 37,275, between the last SVN update and the one before, between a dust fleck's impetus towards a new rotation and the putting of this into motion, the conception of a shadow cast out by a fork tine and the shadow's generation, ended. Soren often finds himself entertaining – running, updating, revising – fantasies of emerging, blinking, into the next day's light to find that London has been nuked, zombie apocalypsed or fire-and-brimstoned from existence. He was raised Methodist, taught to believe in the end of time, in rent and rapture. *Render*: the word, now, still carries echoes of his first encounter with it, Mark 12: 17 – *Render therefore unto Caesar the things that are Caesar's, and unto God the things that are God's.* And of his second, also in the church in which he sang each Sunday, surpliced and cassocked choirboy, number 103 in the Welsh Hymnal: *All laud we would render: O help us to see ...* He hears, from time to time, more frequently the tireder he gets, the hymn's words, the tune, its cadence, slinking through the farm's background, foreground and surround sound, replaying in his head, an ear-worm:

> Immortal, invisible, God only wise,
> In light inaccessible hid from our eyes ...

... then *Something, blessèd, glorious, Ancient of Days*, then more light: *unresting, un-something and silent as light ... pure Father of light; Thine angels adore thee, all veiling their sight ...* and *clouds which are fountains ... something ...* and then back to light again: *'Tis only the splendour of light hideth thee ...* It's not just him remembering, half-remembering, them: the lines are being sung to him actively, it seems, by voices not quite human – maybe super-, of a higher order, angels, dancing in the circuitry, light inaccessible, wisdom pronounced in muffled tones, in shh code; or maybe sub-, the half-formed tongues of entities themselves only half-formed, half-thought, held within some limbo of not-quiteness: foetus-beings, unbaptised, unsaved, their fallenness surrounding them like artefacts, RGB-separated halos of imperfection. In the last fully rendered sequence, committed to SVN as avi file 7,021, light from Fidelus, its corona's plasma-stream, is washing the *Sidereal*'s command antenna, pouring into and through it, liquefying it while, reciprocally, the antenna, its assembly mount and the surrounding fuselage are pouring out too, shedding their forms to flow, proton, electron, alpha particle, into the sunlight, like gold melting. Rendering, as Soren knows full well because it's what his mother thought his job involved when he first told her about it, can mean smelting iron, lead or brass; also reprocessing (this is what his *grand*mother understood his new métier to be) the overspill of slaughterhouses, the already-butchered carcasses of cows or chickens: grinding, steaming, crushing them still further to extract the fat or tallow, to squeeze out a tiny bit more profit, one last ounce of mulch ...

On his desktop, through the VNC window, Soren watches frame 37,289 go through its one hundred and sixty-fourth render pass. The physics, the material properties, the specular qualities and a dozen other factors have been overlaid, grafted on one another, and the finished image is now looming into view. It's a close-up of Tszvetan's skin: his bulging forehead pressed right up against the now almost impossibly overpressured sapphire glass. Skin is translucent; it's notoriously hard to get the balance of fleshiness and luminescence just right in a normal setting (sitting in a bedroom, walking down a street or even riding a horse or spaceship into battle in a stable light environment), let alone when you've got multiple reflections and a general collapse of the physical field in which both light and skin reside. And then the porousness, the hairs ... One integer, one digit off the mark, and suddenly you'll have great clumps of thick-weave pushing through the membrane like diseased rabbit fungus. In those instances he has to pull the frames out, send them back into production, and the progress bar back-ticking too. Those are the easy calls: the harder ones come when it's just one or two pixels, one fragment of flesh or hair or shadow in the wrong place for a fraction of a second, miniature sub-error no one's going to notice – until someone does, not necessarily his line manager, nor even Herzberg, Dressel, *Incarnation*'s ten or twenty million viewers; it's that twenty million and first, that nerd who spots it on his fifteenth streaming, pulls it out, posts it on badrender.com, and the shame wends its way slowly but surely back to Soren, settles on him like a rash. Even harder: if the *image* is fine but he can see an error in the code behind it, inactive for now, but ... Does he wave it through since no one else is going to know; or will this error, like a bullet in an unused chamber, work its way round eventually, a few roulette turns on, and splatter brains, his or someone else's maybe but his *fault*, forensically retraceable to him, to this decision or avoidance of, this moment of deferral ... ?

Tszvetan's temple, although bulging and stretching to the limits of epidermal tolerance, is intact. Its underlying code is sound. Tild's skin, too, tautening in manic yet calm determination, retains its integrity; her hair's geometry may be going wildly wrong, but it's going wrong in a way consistent with the render code, the *right* way. Stokers, too, and grilles, airlocks and panels are flying apart *correctly*, each of their parts following trajectories consistent with those of each of the other parts, the collisions between, the currents and back-swells acting on them generated by the previous currents and collisions, the trajectories and back-swells plotted by the software. As each frame completes its final pass, it's posted on the same screen as the progress bar, remaining there until the next completed frame replaces it. The order of succession follows that not of the film itself, its narrative, but rather of the sequence in which each of the twenty-three frames being worked over in each batch is spat out of its rendering pen, assigned an avi number and held up for scrutiny both here and in DZ's linked spaces, like (to go old-school once more) a newly developed photographic print being pegged up dripping on a darkroom clothesline. The last one out, the one drying on the progress-bar screen right now, shows, in close-up, a pressure-gauge dial mid-eruption, glass face cracking like sheet caramel, the needle detaching, propelled outwards on its spring like an ejector seat. The next, replacing it now, shows, in wide-shot, a long jet of light that was correction engine similarly leaping from the ship – initially as a coherent streak, then fraying as its wavelengths fluctuate and part, then finally, at the shot's far edge, being reamalgamated as the colour-threads are gathered and subsumed, like candyfloss strands, by the larger clumps of light spinning and amassing in Fidelus's heliosheath. Here's that Livnära fork again, free-floating trimaran cast loose from the *Sidereal*, ploughing its way hungrily towards Fidelus as though to devour it, to *be* devoured. This is an orgy of consumption, cosmic autophagia, space eating itself, chucking itself up, swallowing itself again, viscera and linings involuting to ingest whatever's just ingested them: plasma-wave, loading bay, dome, termination shock, temple, abyss ...

Tszvetan and Tild are through the Observatory's pane now – through it *and* within, both *here* and *there*, as though they'd broken through the boundary not just of the sapphire glass but also of their bodies, of their senses, at once dispossessed and occupying the other side of them, looking at both themselves and space, all space, from any and all points, possessing each of them convulsively. Seeing is touching; light is vision; *laud we would render*; *71 per cent complete* ... And, most miraculous of all, amidst the deformation and the involution, there are forms: there is consistency; faces and landscapes – eyes, smiles, zigzags, outlines of Kernwinal Hills and Marais wildlands – still, flying in the face of possibility, persisting ...

The sequence-file Soren's got open on his desktop, playing and replaying through the speakers, is the one containing Tszvetan's line: *It's waiting for us*. As it loops, it, too, breaks down: *swaitingf ... swaitingf ... swaitingf* ... It's 4.17. The splendour of light hideth. The adoring angels are speaking in tongues now, echolalia. The room, like the *Sidereal*, like termination shock and heliosheath, is melting and reforming. In the choir, they kept their vestments in the sacristy off to the side, on hooks, beside the albs and stoles and cinctures of the clergy. Reverend Edwards always liked to watch the boys change, their white flesh. Shh. Soren's dozing. Photons shoot off the corona. In The Beatitudes, Lillian's eyes are blighted, cataract-occluded, lenses glazed and clouded. Faded colours, halos, rays of that deep light which in itself is true, *nel suo profondo vidi che s'interna*, saw gathered together, *legato con amore*, bound by love into a single volume, leaves that lie scattered through the universe, *squaderna*, shh, substance and accidents and their relations, I saw as though they fused in such a way, that what I say is but a beam of light.

Out past the double door, on the stone staircase, halfway up or maybe halfway down, two junkies are, like Soren, on the nod. Do they have names? Of course – but these will only show up near the end of some long credit roll nobody ever bothers watching, least of all them. The farm's noise carries to them, but out here it's less aggressive, its roar muffled, almost lulling. It's still physical, though, a buzz and tremor rolling out in waves, washing their crumpled bodies, holding them in place. As each new wave crosses the unmanned border of their consciousness it ripples slightly, bending and diffracting; then it, too, starts to disintegrate as it heads further in, towards the lower reaches, to a blackness neither rays nor traces penetrate.

Acknowledgements

The Making of Incarnation's composition benefited from start to finish from the willingness of various technical experts to submit their wind tunnels, water tanks, mo-cap workshops, gait labs and post-production studios to my scrutiny — an act all the more generous given the often sensitive or redacted nature of the work carried out therein. To Mark Quinn, Marvin Jentzsch and Christian Navid Nayeri, Adam Shortland and Caspar Lumley, Andy Ray and Richard Graham I'm very grateful. Also, for extramural tutorials on CGI, physics and copyright law, to David James, Martin Warnke, Donn Zaretsky and Alison Macdonald; for Greek guidance, to Penny McCarthy and Daviona Watt; and to David Isaacs, for research and assistance throughout. I would also like to acknowledge the financial support and hospitality of the DAAD Artists-in-Berlin Program, who gave me a year-long fellowship.

In wider-lens view, the novel's contexts and trajectories both arose and found their shape, as always, in dialogue with a host of other artists, thinkers and friends. Ruth Maclennan first directed me towards the Institute for Industrial Psychology's archive. Melissa McCarthy opened my eyes to the significance of Queequeg's tattoo-copying antics. Mark Aerial Waller pulled the world of archaeoacoustics onto my radar. Omer Fast shared his drone-pilot interview notes with me. Ieva Epnere and Kristaps Epners snuck me into restricted faculty buildings and storage bunkers all over Riga. Florian Dombois directed smoke and lasers around me in his exquisite contraption on the roof of Zürich's Hochschule der Künste. The St George's Walk episode of 'Ground Truth' grew out of a workshop with five pupils — Rosa Brennan, Carina Clewley, Milla Kahl-el Gabry, Annie Stables and Leah Swarbrick — at Prior Weston Primary School in London; Webster's speculations in 'The Girl With Kaleidoscope Eyes' out of a live-writing session in Berlin's K Gallery for 'The Death of the Artist', No. 7 in *Cabinet* magazine's '24-Hour Book' series. To these, and many other collaborators, I'm indebted – as I am to my excellent editors on both sides of the Atlantic, Dan Frank and Michal Shavit, and their colleague Ana Fletcher; to my magnificent cover designers Peter Mendelsund and Suzanne Dean; to my tireless agents Melanie Jackson, Jonathan Pegg and Marc Koralnik; and to the even more tireless Eva Stenram.